THE LiFE
DAiSY DEVLiN
DESiGNED

Sharon Black

POOLBEG

Published 2024 by Poolbeg Press Ltd.

123 Grange Hill, Baldoyle, Dublin 13, Ireland

Email: poolbeg@poolbeg.com

Sharon Black © 2024

© Poolbeg Press Ltd. 2024, copyright for editing, typesetting, layout, design, ebook and cover.

The moral right of the author has been asserted.

A catalogue record for this book is available from the British Library.

ISBN 978-1-78199-673-7

www.poolbeg.com

Printed by L&C Printing Group, Poland.

ABOUT THE AUTHOR

A recovered journalist, Sharon Black is a member of Writing.ie, has published short stories in women's magazines and has placed in various short story competitions. She is both a Writers Ink and Curtis Brown Creative alumna, and her debut was long-listed for the 2023 Retreat West 'Opening Lines'.

When she's not writing, she reads, walks, sees friends and drinks a lot of coffee. She's in a local, long-running book club with five amazing women, where books and wine are consumed in roughly equal amounts. She loves theatre, old Hollywood films, every romantic comedy ever made and edgy stand-up.

In recent years, she has developed an unnaturally close relationship with Google Maps, thanks to her appalling sense of direction. She is highly allergic to shopping. Except for bag shopping.

She blogs at 'This Funny Irish Life', and can also be found on Facebook, Instagram and TikTok as sharonblackwriter and on X as sblackwriter.

Sharon lives in Dublin with her husband and family.

The Life Daisy Devlin Designed is her second book.

ACKNOWLEDGEMENTS

If writing a first book is difficult, then writing the second is definitely harder. I'd like to thank Paula Campbell at Poolbeg Publishing for believing that I could do it.

I'd also like to thank my incredibly talented editor, Gaye Shortland, who always understands what I'm trying to do, and what I need to do to make it better.

Thanks, also, to designer David Prendergast and to Paula Campbell for my gorgeous cover. It's perfect!

My thanks to Ken Jordan who gave me answers to some technical questions about helicopters and light aircraft – any mistakes are my own! And a shout-out to my son, who named a fictional river when I couldn't think of a good one!

Thank you to my two daughters who read various drafts of this. I'm also incredibly grateful to fellow author, Anne Hamilton, who very generously read the whole book in a weekend before I submitted it.

A big virtual hug to all my family and friends, including those in the writing community. I'm very lucky to have you all.

Finally, my sincere thanks to you, dear reader. And a small request to consider leaving a short review – it helps more than you know. Over to you – I hope you love it.

Sharon xx

DEDICATION

For Gary, with all my love

CHAPTER 1

"Right, we have to win this year." Daisy Devlin marched into the office of Discerning Designs shortly after 8 o'clock, and put a cardboard tray with three takeout coffees on her desk. She turned to the other two. "You do know what day this is?"

Laura unfolded herself from behind her desk and crossed the room, her heels echoing lightly on the wooden floor in the high-ceilinged, open space, and picked up the two Americanos.

"It's Monday, babes." She perched herself neatly on the edge of Fionn's desk, and handed one of the coffees to him. "You probably should have taken the day off to recover, Daisy. Weren't you down in Galway minding your sister's twenty kids at the weekend?" She gave a dramatic shudder.

Daisy picked up her flat white. "Four kids, Laura. And my parents were the ones minding them." Although Rosie had rung at least twice a day to check up on them. Her sister was a total control freak.

"*Hmm.*" Laura rolled her eyes. "All I'm saying is you'll be at least partly to blame if Rosie's family is bigger in nine months' time."

That didn't bear thinking about. Daisy sat down at her desk and turned to their intern. "What day is it? Get the answer right, and I'll do your coffee round tomorrow."

Fionn grinned. "First, can I say you are *killing* that whole fifties look? But I'm going to be cheeky and say stop playing it safe with navy pumps. Go for killer heels in bright orange – they'll pick up those flecks in your outfit."

Daisy examined the tiny flowers in the full skirt of her vintage navy dress.

"Orange shoes, Fionn?" Laura shook her head. "How do we even let you answer the phone?"

Daisy and Fionn ignored her.

"Secondly," Fionn continued, "I know the answer because it's on my calendar. Submissions to the Interior Architect of the Year Awards open today."

"Exactly." Daisy took a gulp of coffee, wincing as it burned her throat. She looked at Laura. "So?"

Laura flicked a thread from her immaculate cream trouser suit. "So, I don't think any of my projects this year would be suitable." She pulled a face. "I finished those two commercial ones and then that awful one for Mr and Mrs Three-bed Semi."

Daisy took a floral scrunchie out of her skirt pocket and pulled her thick, red hair into a high ponytail. "Stop being such a snob! I'd kill to live in a three-bed semi."

"Yes, but you wouldn't insist on having Grecian columns in your kitchen extension." Laura tutted. "There should be a law that says if you've no taste, you shouldn't be allowed to make a fool of yourself."

Daisy and Fionn exchanged a grin.

"Anyway," Laura was brisk now, "I've nothing I can enter. So unless some amazing project lands in my lap this week, and I manage by some miracle to get it finished in three months' time, I'll have to wait until next year."

"You can submit once you can guarantee it'll be finished by the judging date." Fionn finished his coffee and dropped the cup in the bin beside his desk.

"Still not holding my breath!" Laura sighed and turned to Daisy. "What about you?"

Daisy switched on her laptop and monitor. "My best bet is Freya's place. It'll be a stunning family home when it's finished."

Laura wrinkled her nose. "I thought she and her husband said they didn't want the house featured."

"It's a privacy thing, and they're worried about security." Daisy looked thoughtful. "But I've managed to persuade clients to change their minds before ..."

Fionn cleared his throat. "Will we tell her the news, Laura?"

"Ah, yes." Laura ran a hand over her smooth, pale hair, which was secured in a messy low-knot. "Granary House has been sold."

"*What?*" Daisy sat bolt upright. "Are you sure?"

"Yes, it's all here." Fionn gestured towards his monitor.

"Read what it says."

"It's all stuff you know already, I think." Fionn clicked his pen on and off, stopping when Laura glared at him. "'*One of the oldest houses in County Wicklow to come to the market in recent years ... sits on four acres of land ... includes a walled kitchen garden and orchard ... was run until two years ago as a guest house ...*' Doesn't say who bought it."

"I can't believe it's finally been sold!" Daisy finished her coffee, half wishing she'd bought a pastry but, as Laura was a health nut, who did Pilates three times a week and the Clontarf park run every Saturday morning, and Fionn seemed to live on air, she always felt a bit uncomfortable eating sugary foods around them. "It needs a lot of work, but structurally it's perfect, and the Georgian proportions are amazing."

Laura arched an eyebrow. "The new owners might sit on it for a while. And, even if they decide to start work immediately, they mightn't bother using an interior architect's firm at all."

"Or they might go with another firm." Daisy was thinking. "Another firm who will probably canvass for the job. Let's send out a brochure."

Fionn sat up a bit straighter. "I'm on it."

Daisy shot him a grateful look. "How are the assignments going?"

"I'm on track with my final projects." He swept a carefully arranged side fringe out of his eyes. "I know I've said it before, but I'd love to work here when I qualify."

Daisy and Laura exchanged a glance.

"We'd love that too, Fionn, but ..." Daisy knew there was no need to say anything else. As a small agency, they'd stretched themselves to give Fionn a part-time internship during his college final year, but they'd never had more work than two interior architects could handle.

Laura's mobile rang and she swiped a long, manicured finger across the screen.

"If the cat got sick again this morning, it's your turn to take him to the vet," she said to whoever was on the phone. She flicked Fionn a sly look. "Actually, it might be cheaper to get him put down. Or just run him over."

Fionn's eyes widened. "Tell me she's taking the piss."

Daisy grinned. "We have to hope."

"*Fuck* me!" Laura's voice rose.

Daisy tried not to laugh. When she'd first come up to Dublin from Galway twelve years before, and met Laura Nealon in college, the south Dublin girl had at first struck her as far too refined to swear. The fact that Laura could actually make grown men blush had endeared her quickly to Daisy.

"You're absolutely sure? Fine, fine, I'll see you later." As Laura hung up, she swore under her breath. "That was Brian," she said slowly.

"I guessed." God, she could do with a second coffee before having to hear about Laura's bloody husband.

Fionn put his hand up. "Am I too young and innocent to hear this?"

Laura ignored him. "Brace yourself, babes. Matt Deveraux is back from the States."

Daisy felt a bit lightheaded. "He's back?" Her voice seemed to be coming from far away. "You mean for a visit?"

"According to Brian, he's back for good."

Laura was watching her closely.

"*Um*, who's Matt Deveraux?" Fionn asked.

Laura didn't take her eyes off Daisy. "He's Daisy's ex. Shut up, Fionn."

"So, he's back." Daisy shrugged a little shakily. "I probably won't ever run into him."

"Right." Laura sighed and folded her arms. "I guess that depends."

"On what?" Daisy managed.

Laura pursed her lips. "He's the new owner of Granary House."

It took Daisy a few moments to recover. "So, when did Matt get in touch?" His name tasted strange in her mouth.

Laura shrugged. "I'm not sure. Probably today, if Brian's only telling me now."

A look passed between the two women, and Daisy knew Laura was remembering exactly the same thing as she was. The four of them had once been so close, wiling away endless hours in the rundown house Matt and Brian had shared in college and in their early twenties – until Matt had gone abroad. Matt Deveraux: smart, a bit shy, slightly geeky, and her boyfriend of five years.

Daisy folded her arms and aimed for a professional tone. "He's definitely bought Granary House?"

Laura gave her a hard look. "Here it comes."

Daisy sat forward in her chair. "What do you mean by 'Here it comes'?"

"I mean you shouldn't get involved but no doubt you will."

"How would I be getting involved?" Daisy's voice had risen and she took a deep breath. "Transforming Granary House would be a dream job, Laura, you know that. And it would be the ideal project to submit to the contest!"

"I also know it'd be a terrible idea to work with him." Laura's voice softened. "Why would you risk it?"

"I'll just leave you two to … *uh* …" Fionn stood and slipped quickly out of the room.

After he left, Daisy got up, walked over to one of the sash windows that overlooked the street below, and peered out.

Discerning Designs occupied a divided first-floor room of a converted Georgian house, a stone's throw from Dublin's fashionable St Stephen's Green. The two women had spent the last five years steadily growing it, but it had suffered a setback during the Covid pandemic and, after an initial upsurge when they reopened, things had quietened down. They couldn't afford to ignore any potential business.

She turned to Laura. "I wouldn't be risking anything. Matt and I haven't seen each other in five years. We've both moved on. But this is a sign! This was meant to happen! If I don't pitch for this job, I'll always regret it."

Laura looked like she was trying to choose the right words. "What if it's a sign to run in the opposite direction? Have you forgotten what happened, Daisy? The guy just left. Five years together and he –"

"I remember what happened." Daisy's tone was sharp. "And, yes, I admit I was very hurt at the time."

"You were devastated," Laura said quietly.

Daisy shivered slightly and wrapped her arms more tightly around herself. "And then I met James and I moved on."

Laura nodded. "I know, babes."

Daisy blinked hard and turned back to stare out the window. "It might actually be good to see him. I could get ... closure."

"You *could* get closure," Laura said. "Or you could just not go there. You could really mess things up with James. And what about you? This is a potential head-wrecker."

"That wouldn't happen." Daisy huffed. "We're grown-ups. And this is exactly the business opportunity I've been wanting for so long."

Fionn came back into the room. "Too soon?" He looked at Daisy, who waved a hand in his direction.

"Sit down. I've decided. I'll contact Matt and, with a bit of luck, we'll get the chance to redesign Granary House."

Fionn flicked Laura a quick look. Her lips were tightly pursed.

The silence stretched until Fionn broke it. "Sound."

A flicker of worry passed across Laura's face. Then she gave a one-shoulder shrug. "I wouldn't touch him with a ten-foot barge pole, but it's your choice."

Daisy smiled to cover her annoyance. She was long used to Laura's scepticism, but it stung that she had so little faith in her. It didn't matter that the thought of seeing Matt again terrified and confused her in equal measure. Running her own business, pitching to clients and working with crews to deadlines, meant constantly pushing herself out of her comfort zone.

Except this is completely different, Daisy, this is personal. She pushed aside the fluttery feelings in her tummy and the annoying voice in her head. If Matt agreed to her proposal, their working relationship would be just that. And if it brought her closure, so much the better.

If she *did* land the redesign, she wouldn't bother mentioning it to James. There'd be no need – he didn't share all the details of his work with her. These days, he hardly shared anything with her. Anyway, this would be just like any other job.

CHAPTER 2

Daisy's phone was ringing just as she got home that evening. "Rosie? Just got home. I'm at the front door. Let me just get in ..." She was hit by a blast of music from the kitchen as she shouldered open the door. Hanging up her coat, she allowed herself a quick glance in the mirrored panels that fitted flush with the wall in the narrow hallway.

"*Okay, I'm in.*" She had to raise her voice so she could hear herself. "So did you and Séan enjoy the weekend? I'll bet you didn't even get out of bed, *haha.*"

Rosie tutted. "Stop being so childish, Daisy."

Stop being so annoying, Rosie. Her sister was the most uptight thirty-five-year-old on the planet. Their mother was more chilled-out than her! Actually, their mother was more chilled-out than anyone. Maybe she could just hang up? Except Rosie would probably accuse her of being childish again.

"Just messing with you, Rosie."

Something smelt good, she realised. Maybe James had got home early and was making his Chicken Korma. She couldn't remember the last time he'd made it.

"Daisy, are you still listening?"

"*Er*, you were thanking me for helping to mind the kids at the weekend."

"No, I wasn't." Rosie sounded indignant. "Penny told me you spent the whole weekend in town seeing your friends, and the only time you saw them was at meals or to sneak them chocolate."

The child was being groomed in her mother's image, Daisy thought. In fairness to her parents, they hadn't been remotely bothered that she hadn't hung around while Rosie and Séan had been off celebrating their tenth wedding anniversary. They'd always been relaxed, but becoming grandparents had elevated them to a whole new level of Zen.

"Rosie, have you rung just to lecture me? Because you could have saved it up for your usual Friday phone call."

Rosie huffed a sigh. "I'm phoning about the twins' birthday next Saturday. I put a reminder in the family group."

Crap, she'd muted the family WhatsApp group because it had been full of messages from Rosie instructing their parents about her kids, while she and Séan skived off for their dirty weekend. Daisy couldn't understand why Rosie didn't just message their mother privately about food intolerances, GAA practice and bedtimes, but her sister was a law onto herself. Now, she'd completely forgotten about the twins' birthday. She'd never have gone down for the weekend, if she'd known she had to hightail it back down so soon.

"It's in my diary. And I'm, *er*, Penny's godmother."

"Annie's," Rosie sighed.

"Right. And they'll be four."

"Five."

Daisy stepped out of her heels and, with her free hand, tucked them in beside James' shoes on the shoe rack under the coat rail.

"There's a lot of noise in your house, Daisy."

"*Um*, yeah, it's Kayley Lynch, you know, that American country singer?" Alma, the Swedish post-grad student who'd been renting their spare bedroom for the past two years, liked her.

Daisy really hoped James just happened to have her playing – they could do with a night to themselves.

"So, what do you think?" Rosie was saying.

About the noise? The party. Daisy stifled a sigh. "Yeah, we'll be there, don't worry."

"I'm not worried," Rosie said. "I just wondered whether you'll be staying over with Mum and Dad, or with us. We've plenty of room."

"I know, yeah."

Rosie and Séan lived in a six-bedroom bungalow, and Rosie was forever going on about road frontage and picture windows, and the fact that their kitchen was bigger than Daisy's whole house. Daisy knew her sister was horrified by the fact that she and James shared their meagre fifty-five square metres with a complete stranger, just to help with their mortgage. Still, the thought of being under the same roof as Rosie and all her kids for even a night was too much. "It's grand, we'll stay with Mum and Dad. It'll be nice for them to see James."

"*Hmm*, they were saying that you came down on your own on Friday night."

"Yeah, well, James was working, and I wanted to catch up with friends. Sure, he'd feel like a spare tool hanging around." That was definitely enough about her and James. "What would the twins like for their birthday?"

"Well, Penny likes books and Annie likes art, but keep it small, Daisy. You know Séan and I don't like anything over-the-top."

"There goes the Knuttel I'd planned to give Annie, so."

"You're hilarious." Rosie's tone was dry. "The party starts at two, but why don't you scoot down a bit early, and help us get ready? We're having a bouncy castle and face-painting on the day, and the boys are allowed to invite whoever they like – so fingers crossed for a decent bit of weather."

Should she tell her that there was another storm forecast for this week, Daisy wondered. Nah, her brilliant sister could figure that one out for herself.

"Listen, Daisy, I have to go, it's mad here. See you then, bye."

Rosie hung up and Daisy rolled her eyes. Her older sister always pretended Daisy was the one trying to keep her from her vastly busy life. Although, to be fair to her, if *she* had four children under the age of eight, she'd be busy too. Or probably just dead from exhaustion.

Daisy slung her phone back into her skirt pocket and went into the kitchen, to see her boyfriend of five years twirling Alma out from his long, lean frame and back in again, like they were on some sort of country music dance show.

James caught her eye and they stuttered to a stop. "It's Kayley Lynch." He grinned sheepishly, pushing a hand back through untidy brown hair.

"I know, yeah." Daisy tried her best to smile, but she strongly suspected it looked more like a grimace.

"Good evening, Daisy," Alma said.

She was always excessively polite around her. She saved that Swedish warmth for James. Now Alma was giving her that penetrating stare she had, like she was judging how she looked. She wondered what the petite twenty-three-year-old with her pixie haircut and gender-neutral clothes in equally neutral shades, thought of her colourful, vintage wardrobe. Although she was pretty sure her clothes weren't the only thing Alma was judging. Daisy sucked in her stomach, which at that moment gave a very unladylike gurgle.

"Nice smell." Daisy folded her arms. "Is that what I think it is?"

"Chicken Korma!" James came over and dropped a quick kiss on her lips. "I've been teaching Alma how to make it."

"I love experimenting with food," Alma said.

Daisy didn't believe that for a moment. The only thing Alma seemed to cook was spaghetti with Swedish meatballs. And soup. Which was fine by her, because they'd all agreed early on that Alma could use the kitchen to make her own meals.

"Alma decided she'd eat with us this evening," James said.

There wasn't a trace of apology in his voice, Daisy noticed. She'd bloody kill him! Still, it was just dinner. And Alma would probably go up to her room to work for the rest of the evening. She was a final-year postgrad in nuclear physics or something equally intimidating, and seemed to be able to study and party with equal intensity. Despite the fact that there were only seven years between them, Daisy always felt ancient around her.

As Alma checked on the rice, James set the table, and Daisy debated leaving them to it while she grabbed a shower. She wondered if they'd have to keep renting out the room after Alma finished in the autumn. James was always telling her that they couldn't afford the mortgage, all their bills and have some savings, without the extra income.

"So, how was your day?" James handed her a bottle of beer.

"Grand, you know yourself. You?" Even after all this time, she felt like she was playing house in front of Alma, when all she wanted was to pile some curry into a bowl and eat in front of the telly.

He pulled a face. "Same as it's been all year."

Daisy flashed him a sympathetic smile. She'd met James when she was twenty-four, less than a year after Matt had simply walked out of her life. James had been twenty-seven, and had just started a small software company. Ironically, it had been exactly the same thing Matt had hoped to do.

At the time, Laura had warned her about being on the rebound. Although James had taken his time before asking her out, Daisy sometimes wondered if she *had* been on the rebound. How long did it take to get over someone, anyway?

Even now, she wondered had she simply not wanted to be on her own after Matt had left. It would have been hard, she knew, but everyone said that being single for a while made you more independent, more discerning.

Immediately, she felt guilty for thinking she mightn't have ended up with James, if she'd been more discerning. James was such a good guy. Even if he *was* pretty distracted these days. She watched as he added some seasoning to the korma, beaming at Alma as she stirred it in. Definitely distracted!

"Oh, I nearly forgot." James reached into his pocket.

For a brief moment Daisy allowed herself to imagine that he'd got her something. Before they'd bought their house two years before, they'd regularly surprised each other with little fun gifts. She suppressed a sigh as James handed Alma a small, unwrapped box.

"For your collection!"

Alma's face lit up as she opened it and pulled out a plastic figurine with an oversized head. "A Funko Pop!" She flushed. "Thank you so much!

For a moment, Daisy thought she was going to launch herself into his arms. Instead, she grinned stupidly at him for another long moment.

Daisy forced another smile. Ever since Alma had told James that her big brother used to buy her Stranger Things Funko Pops – little figures with tiny bodies and giant heads – and how much she missed him since coming to study in Ireland, James had surprised her a few times by buying them for her instead. Alma had tried to pay him, but he'd always refused.

Daisy tried to ignore the niggling feeling that it was downright weird to buy gifts for someone who rented a room from them.

As James ladled out the curry into some mismatched bowls that Daisy had picked up from their local Oxfam shop, she mentally skimmed over the events of the morning.

After some persuasion, Laura had asked Brian for Matt's new number, and Daisy had agonised for ages over what to message him. In the end, she'd simply texted: **Hi Matt, I heard you were back. Congrats on buying Granary House. I'd love to pitch for its redesign, and would be delighted to give you a very competitive quote. Best, Daisy.**

She'd checked her phone during the day, but he hadn't replied. It had taken her until the afternoon to pluck up the courage to ask Laura to check the number with Brian. Laura had shot her a worried look, but she'd double-checked the number.

Daisy tried to rationalise Matt's lack of response. Clearly, he'd never expected to hear from her. He might have even thought her pitch was an excuse to see him. Embarrassment curled through her. The last thing she wanted was Matt to think she was still pining for him. She didn't want his pity. In fact, she wanted him to know that she was fine. Better than fine! She wanted to prove to him that she'd made a success of her life. In every single way that mattered.

Plus, she reasoned, working for Matt could spell total disaster! Or they might find that they were still madly attracted to each other, and they'd both managed to suppress it for the last five years. Which would be ... a total disaster, obviously.

At the same time, it was definitely a sign that Matt had bought a house she'd wanted to redesign for so long. Daisy was a firm believer in signs – she just hadn't always read them properly. Once, she'd thought she and Matt had the perfect relationship. She'd envisioned a future where they might even marry and have a family. And look how that had turned out! Even now, she wondered how she'd missed those signs – the foreshadowing of a bombshell.

What if Laura had been right, and she'd made a huge mistake by contacting him?

But if Matt decided to ignore her text, it was probably for the best. Things hadn't been great between her and James for a while, and having Matt back in her life might ... what? Make things worse? How would that be possible? Her stomach squeezed. In the past year or more, James had been subtly pulling back from their relationship. She couldn't remember the last time they'd even had a proper conversation.

Daisy had tried to pinpoint exactly why, but the only thing she could think was that he regretted making the commitment to buy a house together. Even more worrying was that as he'd pulled away from her, he'd *gravitated* towards Alma. Daisy didn't actually believe that James was cheating on her, but she'd definitely been sidelined. Because while James and Alma had connected over their Nintendo Switches, Daisy, whose own hobbies ran to knitting cute sweaters and upcycling vintage clothes, found herself completely excluded.

Which made her more determined than ever not to let her private life affect her career. She wouldn't apologise for wanting a real chance at an award she'd gone for every year since landing her first job in the industry.

The reality was, she needed a win. And that had nothing to do with Matt.

CHAPTER 3

"They've delivered the wrong fucking island unit, love." Kenny, the foreman for Freya Maguire's Victorian house, rubbed the back of his stubble-head and looked around the half–finished room.

Daisy stayed calm. "I'm sure they haven't, Kenny. I designed this kitchen myself, so it's been made to that spec."

Kenny sucked his breath in through his teeth. "No offence, love, but maybe you got some measurements wrong." He pointed to the huge slab of marble on the floor in the middle of the room. "That's the top of their island unit, and it's supposed to be just two and a half metres. If we were still doing this in old money, love, you'd be short a couple of feet!"

He handed Daisy the hard copy of the drawings she'd given him.

She took a professional measure from her pocket and, ignoring Kenny's pointed sighs, checked the slab and the unit it was supposed to fit. "Shit." She straightened up. "You're right."

The foreman huffed. "So what do you want me to do?"

Daisy looked around the large basement where the kitchen was being installed. "Take a break. I need to see if I can sort it."

Kenny turned to the two other men on his team, who were running piping along a back wall. "Tea break, lads. Somebody find the biscuits – and they'd better be the good ones."

Daisy left them to it, sliding open one of the big glass doors to the newly laid sandstone patio, warmed by some welcome March sun. Sitting down on the bench beside the garden's side wall, she blotted out the delighted shrieks of Freya's youngest child, who was being chased by her minder, and checked over her original drawings, before calling the suppliers.

Several frustrating minutes later, she hung up. This was worse than she'd thought. It wasn't a simple delivery mix-up – they'd made the wrong size.

And they'd be ten days waiting for the right size. She couldn't afford a delay like that. She sent Freya a quick text, asking if she could call her. Freya worked as a solicitor for a busy firm, and Daisy just hoped that she'd get a minute to check her messages.

A moment later, Freya rang. "I'm on a break – how's it going?"

Daisy filled her in.

"*Bollocks!*" Freya said.

"I don't want to delay the kitchen."

Freya sighed. "Me neither. What do you suggest?"

Daisy took a breath. "Actually, I have an idea."

A couple of minutes later, she ended the call and came back into the kitchen, where the three men eyed her over their mugs of tea.

"We sorted then, love?" Kenny helped himself to another biscuit.

"All sorted, Kenny." Daisy beamed. "But I will need to call on your excellent carpentry skills."

She waited politely as Kenny made a show of thinking about it. She'd known Kenny since she and Laura had set up their business, and she trusted his judgement completely. And, since his wife's death just four months before, he'd thrown himself completely into his work. After a few moments, he sighed and put his cup on the counter.

"Tell me what you have in mind."

There was an unmistakable gleam of interest in his eyes.

⁘

Freya arrived home just as Daisy was getting ready to leave.

"Hiya, didn't expect to see you still here." She gave Daisy an expectant look as she hung up her jacket.

"Well, there was a lot going on! And a few fires to put out, but nothing to worry about."

Freya smiled distractedly. "I hope Holly didn't get in your way? What time did Saoirse get back from school with her?"

"Oh, mid-morning. They're in the garden having a picnic now, I think." Daisy had wondered why she'd been home so early, but it was none of her business.

"Good. I just hope this one is made of stronger stuff than the last." When Daisy frowned slightly, she added, "The childminder. She's our second this year. We're paying her very well, so fingers crossed."

Daisy gave a polite smile. Freya rarely shared anything personal – Daisy had found her to be one of the most closed-off clients she'd had in a long while. During their first meeting, she'd attempted to break the ice by chatting a bit about her own family and had mentioned Rosie and her own young children. Freya had nodded politely before very firmly changing the subject. After that, Daisy had stuck to house matters.

"Come down and see the kitchen. Kenny's also made a start on Holly's bedroom."

Daisy had been a bit taken aback when Freya had asked her to turn the master bedroom's walk-in wardrobe into a small bedroom for their youngest, whom Daisy figured was the same age as her own twin nieces. In her experience, most women wanted more wardrobe space, not less. She'd gently suggested there was ample space in the older girls' room which ran right across the back of the house. But Freya had been adamant.

"You're doing an excellent job, Daisy," she said now. "I can't believe how fast it's all coming together." She unbuttoned the cuffs of her blouse and rolled up her sleeves. "Now, talk me through the kitchen issue, or I'll have to suffer Kenny mansplaining it."

Daisy followed Freya back down to the basement, smiling at the idea of Kenny mansplaining anything. Most of the time, she had to drag any information at all out of him. He tended to work on a need-to-know basis.

Freya and her husband Neil had moved into the Victorian redbrick after Freya had inherited it, and had got in touch with Discerning Designs to completely redesign and modernise it.

Structurally, it was in good condition, but Daisy had known it would need an overhaul of the electrics and plumbing. After consulting with the couple, she'd also organised underfloor heating, solar panels and a smart pump-system that continually cleaned the air.

"We want a functional but beautiful home," Freya had said. "Remember, there's seven of us. And get rid of all that old furniture. No offence to my grandmother, but all that dark wood depresses me."

A quick look at the original furniture had confirmed Daisy's initial thoughts. Most of it was well made – solid and beautifully crafted. Just not to Freya's taste. As an experiment, Daisy had taken away an old chest of drawers and had it upcycled, stripping away all the layers of dark lacquer, before painting it a pale grey with navy trim, and replacing all the dark round handles with modern horizontal drawer-pulls.

"If you don't like it, I'll bear the expense myself and take it away," Daisy had said.

"Are you joking?" Freya had looked amazed. "I love it!"

Thrilled that most of the old furniture could be reused, Daisy had hired a couple of experts to work on site for some of the bigger pieces, including wardrobes. Once the exteriors were finished, she'd got Kenny to overhaul the interiors – fitting smart, functional double rails, and modern shelving and drawers that maximised the space.

Now Freya looked at the top of the island unit, which Kenny had laid carefully on the floor. "I see what you mean – it's far too short, isn't it?"

Daisy nodded. "Kenny's ordered a large piece of white oak, to match the cupboard doors. He'll carve it into a semicircle and attach it to the end of the unit, to make a feature of it." She found herself holding her breath. Even though she'd agreed the plan with Freya on the phone, experience had taught her that clients often changed their minds hours later.

But Freya's focus seemed to have switched to the garden. "That's all fine. So, when will everything be done?"

"If everything goes to plan, about five weeks – including the finishing touches."

"Good." Freya shot her a brief smile. "If that's everything, I want to spend a bit of time with Holly."

Daisy took the hint. "I'll let myself out."

She went back upstairs to the hall, retrieved her jacket, zipped her laptop back into her rucksack, and grabbed her bike helmet.

Halfway down the front steps, she realised she'd forgotten to ask if Freya had reconsidered letting her enter her home for the prestigious industry award. The sticking point for the couple was that if the house was shortlisted, it would feature on TV5's *Home Design of the Year* programme, and Freya was adamant that none of them wanted to be on TV.

Daisy unlocked her bike, wheeled it to the road and clipped on her helmet. As she cycled off, her thoughts returned to their little company. Business had slowed for them in the last year, with people gravitating towards the bigger interior architect firms, especially those boasting awards. Even to shortlist for this award would be huge. Daisy picked up the pace and released a breath. This would be their year: she would make it happen.

CHAPTER 4

Fionn pulled out his air pods, clicked out of something on screen and pushed his tongue into the corner of his cheek.

Daisy looked over at him. "Say it. You'll feel better."

"I'm not sure you want to hear it."

Daisy frowned. "I always want to hear your thoughts."

He hesitated. "Yeah, it's not really a work thing, though."

"Is it an astrology thing?"

"Yeah."

Daisy had learned that apart from interior architecture Fionn's passion was astrology. After listening to him explain the ruling moons and planets for Taurus, she'd downloaded the 'MyStarScope' app on her phone. It offered daily, bite-sized forecasts for every sign and, even though she didn't take it seriously, she liked that all the predictions were so positive.

"I wouldn't mention anything except that at the moment there's a seismic shift happening for you," Fionn said seriously.

"Just for me?" Daisy was glad Laura wasn't in yet – she had no time for astrology. "Or is this for all Taureans?"

"Of course not!" Fionn swept his fringe across his forehead. "I used the time and date of your birth and studied the recent movement of your ruling planet Venus to see if –"

"You've lost me, Fionn!" Daisy hid a smile. MyStarScope that morning had simply read that with the moon in Capricorn it was a good day to take chances. She just hoped it didn't mean that she should try out a new coffee shop.

Fionn looked a bit unsure. "Should I shut up?"

She felt a stab of guilt. Fionn was the first intern they'd taken on. Daisy had taken him out on site a few times, and given him some projects to do, but a lot of the time he just doubled as their secretary and looked after their website and social media. She wondered if he was a bit bored.

"No! Please go on."

"Well, as you know it's not an exact science." Fionn chewed on his lip.

Daisy nodded. "Obviously."

"But it looks like someone from your past is going to come back into your life, and will completely change everything."

"I see."

Clearly, this was Fionn's attempt at keeping her spirits up. He knew how badly she wanted the chance to work on Granary House. But, as Matt hadn't bothered to reply, she knew what an unlikely possibility that was.

"What about your crystal collection?" she asked. "Is it still down in Cork at your parents' place?"

"Yeah. Well, except for a couple of amethysts."

"Amethysts?"

"They're good for anxiety."

Daisy's heart squeezed for him.

"I had to persuade my mam not to use all my moonstones for decorating her pot plants around the front door." He flicked his fringe out of the way. "I really have no room for them in Dublin. Plus, Crona, one of my housemates, is in a prayer group and she gave me a Bible for my last birthday." He widened his eyes. "Some things aren't worth the hassle."

Daisy managed to keep a straight face.

"Though sometimes," he went on, "about important issues, it's better to be honest – especially with family. Like, it was a bit of a struggle for Mam and Dad to accept who I am, but they're cool now."

"It must be difficult to come out," Daisy said carefully.

Fionn looked confused. "Oh, they knew I was gay. I meant me being a pagan. I still have to keep that a secret from my gran."

"Sorry I'm late!" Laura burst through the door. "Did someone get coffee?" She glanced over at Fionn's desk.

"You're not that late." Daisy checked the time. "It's not even half past nine. Are you okay?"

"Me? Fine. I had a thing – it ran over."

"I'll get you a coffee." Fionn stood and popped his Air Pods back in.

"You don't have to." Laura sighed. "Actually, yeah, decaf?" She gestured to the Air Pods. "What are you listening to?"

"Shania Twain."

"Oh." Laura looked surprised. "I didn't think you'd be into her stuff."

"I've eclectic taste," Fionn said solemnly.

Daisy cleared her throat. "Have you heard of Kayley Lynch?"

"Of course!" Fionn nodded. "She had that big hit 'From My Heart'."

"A modern classic," Laura deadpanned.

Fionn beamed. "So you've heard her stuff?"

"No." She turned to Daisy. "Are you a fan?"

"No, but Alma is always playing her."

"She's massively popular – or she was," said Fionn. "You know, she's just out of rehab. Someone leaked a video of her ranting at a member of her band and it went viral, and her American record sales crashed. Then she had to cancel all her US concerts because she was getting sober. I'd say it's the only reason she decided to tour Europe right now." He flicked his fringe out of the way. "She'll be in Ireland at the start of June. I've tickets to see her in the 3 Arena." He seemed to remember what he'd been about to do. "Daisy, another coffee?"

"*Uh*, no thanks."

"One decaf Americano, so." He paused. "They do those little wrapped Italian chocolates?" Laura glared at him and he added hurriedly, "Right, no chocolate, back in a few."

Daisy looked over at Laura after he left. "You sure you're okay?"

"I'm fine." Laura rooted through her bag and pulled out a small folder, shaking out a lipstick and another small wrapped item that had become trapped inside it. Hurriedly, she dropped the latter back into her bag, but not before she caught Daisy's eye.

"You're probably wondering," Laura began.

Daisy felt herself colour. "Hey, it's none of my business."

"It's a disposable needle." Laura sighed. "Self-injection contraceptive. I had to pick it up from the clinic on my way in, and they needed to check something. That was the delay."

"Oh." Daisy couldn't imagine having to inject herself. "Would it not be easier to take the pill?"

Laura smoothed a hand over her hair. "It doesn't suit everyone."

"I suppose." It struck Daisy that, despite their closeness, Laura had gradually stopped sharing personal stuff after she'd married Brian. She wondered if it was some sort of married-people-loyalty thing.

"It didn't suit me, anyway." Laura sat down. "I was a complete bitch on it. I mean, worse than I normally am."

Had Brian told her that, Daisy wondered. "Sounds like the kind of thing a man would say," she said lightly.

"James?" Laura looked at her closely. "Or are you talking about Matt?"

God, she couldn't tell her she meant Brian. And she couldn't say Matt. The last thing she wanted was to get Laura started on him.

"*Uh*, James, yeah, but not as bluntly as that – I mean, he wouldn't call me a bitch."

It was ironic about Laura and Matt! Daisy had met him through the college film society, and it had been Matt who'd introduced Laura to Brian. Now, Laura hated Matt with a passion that Daisy couldn't seem to manage. She wondered sometimes whether it'd be better if she *could* hate him, and worried that she was stuck in some sort of holding pattern. It was exhausting just thinking about it.

"So, I'm heading back down to Galway this weekend. Rosie's twins are having their fifth birthday party. I'm hoping there'll be wine."

Laura arched an eyebrow. "I'm pretty sure it's illegal to serve it to five-year-olds."

Daisy grinned as her mobile phone started to ring. "Crap, where did I leave it?"

"Try your bag." Laura reached over and handed it to her.

"Thanks." Daisy groped around for a moment – it needed a major declutter. Her hand closed around the phone and she pulled it out to check the caller ID.

Oh God, it was Matt.

CHAPTER 5

She wasn't ready. Four days of radio silence and now he called? He was deliberately messing with her head.

"Are you going to answer that?" Laura asked.

Daisy met Laura's eyes. "It's Matt. I'm not sure if I'm ready, Laura."

"What did you expect? You messaged him!"

"I know." Daisy's mouth dried. She reached out to grab her bottle of water, accidentally hitting it off the table and sending it rolling across the room.

Laura went and picked it up and unscrewed the top before handing it to her.

"Thanks." Daisy gulped some down.

"He's persistent," said Laura. "Still ringing."

"Okay, what do I say to him?"

"You could try hello." Laura shot her a quick, sympathetic look. "Or maybe 'Hello, fucker'?"

Daisy was too nervous to laugh. This had been such a bad idea.

The phone stopped ringing.

Fine. She could just ring him back. She'd phone him back when she could breathe properly again. But if she left it too long he'd think she was doing that because he'd left it for ages to phone her.

"*Shit.*"

Laura sighed. "Are you going to call him back?"

"I can't! Not now! Or maybe I should, should I?"

Laura sighed. "Fuck it, it's like first year in college!"

Daisy's phone started to ring again, and she dropped it onto her desk, where it moved towards her, buzzing like a small, angry animal.

"It's Matt again."

"Are you not going to answer again?"

"You're not helping, Laura."

Daisy took two deep breaths and swiped.

"Hi, Matt." She sounded breathy and tried to quietly clear her throat.

"Hi, Daisy."

His voice sounded too intimate so close to her ear. "Hang on. I'll just, *um*, put you on speaker. I can actually hear you better like that. And I hate having a phone clamped to my ear, don't you? I'm in the office. Laura is here." Shit, she was babbling! And Laura was glaring at her.

"Oh, right. Hi, Laura, how are things?" Matt's disembodied voice filled the room.

Daisy batted her hand frantically at Laura, who simply shook her head.

"Sorry, Matt, she's just *uh*, had to step out for a minute."

Laura made a rude gesture at the phone, and Daisy turned her chair towards the window to help her focus. She took a deep breath.

"Thanks for getting back. And welcome home." She dug the nails of her right hand into the fleshy part of her left hand in an attempt to steady her voice.

"It's good to be home. And to hear your voice. How have you been?"

"Me? Great, yeah, the business is doing well. *Um*, how about you?"

"I'm fine." Matt paused. "Look, I'm really sorry it's taken me four days to get back to you, but I've been really busy."

She heard Laura walk out of the office and turned to check that she was alone.

"Daisy? You still there?"

She swallowed hard. "I'm here." He sounded genuinely sorry. Maybe he hadn't been playing with her. Maybe he had a good reason for waiting until today to phone. *Why did you message him, Daisy?* "So, Granary House? Congratulations!"

"Thank you. Look, I'd like to talk to you about your ideas, maybe get a look at some of the other work you've done? I could meet you for lunch."

Matt sounded brisk, and Daisy brought herself up sharply. He might have no intention of renewing a friendship with her – but he mightn't even want to hire her either. Which meant she probably had one shot to persuade him to let her redesign the house.

"Actually, I got to look at the place when it first went up for sale, and I made a couple of sketches." She hurried on. "It's such an amazing house, I couldn't resist it. They might give you some ideas."

Matt chuckled deeply, and Daisy's stomach clenched hard.

"In that case, maybe we could meet today? I'm coming up to town anyway. We could meet somewhere close to your office?"

Daisy hesitated. He'd ignored her message for four days, and now he expected her to drop everything for him. But she *had* said she had some drawings to show him. And if Matt wanted to get straight to business, she didn't want to play games. She turned her chair slightly as Laura came back in.

She knew how Laura felt about her pitching for this job and she wouldn't change her mind – but this was what *she* had been hoping for and she wasn't about to change hers either.

"Why don't you choose somewhere really good?" Matt was saying.

"Somewhere really good?"

"For lunch." There was a trace of amusement in Matt's voice. "It's on me."

Potential clients never paid for lunch. Then, again, she rarely took a client to lunch. It wasn't how she did business. But Matt was more than a potential client.

As if he'd read her mind, he added, "I'd really like to see you again."

A nervous excitement shivered through her. "Would one o'clock suit? I'll text you the name and address."

"That's perfect. See you then, Daisy."

She hung up and took another long drink of water, as she tried to calm her breathing. She didn't look in Laura's direction.

This was good, she told herself firmly. This was the sign she needed.

CHAPTER 6

Matt was waiting when Daisy arrived at The White Goose. She'd deliberately chosen the gastropub around the corner from the office, as they'd never been there together. Now, as she walked towards the table, he got to his feet, smiling.

Daisy managed a shaky smile in return, and wondered how it was possible for a man to be better-looking after five years.

He'd always been tall – at six foot three inches, he was taller than James – but he was broader now, filling out the dark blazer and white shirt he wore over blue jeans. It suited him, she thought. His dark curls were a little shorter, and his features seemed stronger and more defined.

But those dark-blue eyes and full lips were exactly the same. She remembered how it had felt when Matt had looked at her like she was the most important person in the world. She remembered exactly how he kissed. And how he made love. A surge of panic shot through her, and she had to resist the temptation to turn and walk out. Was she completely mad? Here she was, inviting Matt back into her life when she'd spent the last five years trying to forget him.

"Hello, Daisy."

She swallowed. "Hi, Matt." Now what? Should she offer to shake his hand?

Matt saved her by stepping around the table and pulling her into a brief hug.

Breathing in, Daisy got a whiff of soap and the merest hint of an unfamiliar aftershave. Just as quickly, he released her and stepped back around the table.

"Good to see you."

"Yeah, and you." This was pathetic. She wasn't that twenty-year-old student who'd first fallen for Matt Deveraux, or the twenty-four-year-old woman left devastated when he'd gone to America for a summer, and had decided to stay. This was a business lunch and it was up to her to set the right tone. She sat down and waited for Matt to fold himself back into the chair, before offering a professional smile.

"Congrats again on buying Granary House. Although I was a bit surprised when I heard."

"That I've bought an old house in the Wicklow countryside, miles from the nearest town?"

Matt grinned, and Daisy took a deep breath to steady herself. Matt's family were from Kilkenny city and, like her, he'd rented in Dublin during college. The first time they'd met, she'd told him she was from Oranmore in Galway, and he'd laughed and said he'd forgive her for being a culchie because he loved her red hair.

"Surprised that you're back in Ireland, too," Daisy said. "Are you home for good?"

"That depends on a few things." He glanced up as the waiter appeared to ask for their drinks order. Matt looked at Daisy. "I guess it mightn't be appropriate to order rum and Cokes?"

Their drink of choice at the end of a night all those years ago. They'd slowly sip one each, stretching out the evening. Where was her self-control? This was *not* where she wanted her brain to go right now.

"Sparkling water for me," Daisy said.

Matt nodded. "I'll have the same, thanks." After the waiter left, he said, "Your text was quite a surprise."

Daisy's forced a laugh. "Is that why you took four days to reply?"

"No." Matt smoothed down the curls at the back of his neck in a gesture Daisy remembered. "I hadn't considered redesigning the place. I'm still not sure if I want to. But I needed a few days to consider, so I wouldn't be completely wasting your time. And I was being truthful when I said I've been busy."

Daisy got the feeling that there was something else he wanted to say, but she wouldn't push him. Their drinks arrived, and Matt picked up his glass. "Cheers!"

Daisy clinked her glass against his. James always refused to toast with water, she thought. *Business lunch, Daisy: focus.*

Matt gave a small smile. "You haven't changed a bit, Daisy."

"You have, sort of," she blurted out, heat flashing to her cheeks as Matt gave her an amused look.

He laughed. "I probably don't look quite as underfed as I did when I was twenty-five."

As you did when you left. There were so many questions she wanted to ask, but she couldn't ask them now, or she'd send him running straight back to the States.

"So, how have you been? Brian mentioned that you and James bought a house."

So he'd asked Brian about her! Unless Brian had volunteered the information, which was unlikely. Brian's favourite topic of conversation was himself. Matt, on the other hand, had always wanted to know everything about her. What she did, who she saw, where she went.

While a part of her wanted Matt to know how successfully she'd moved on without him, another part wanted to draw a very firm line under her private life. Matt had lost the right to know anything when he'd walked away. Still, client or no client, she couldn't be rude.

"Yeah, a couple of years ago." She tried to read his expression, but it was impossible.

"It's a tiny two-bed with no garden, but it's in Dublin, and it's all ours." She took a deep breath. "How about you? Anyone special in your life?"

Matt shrugged. "A few girlfriends down the years. Nothing serious." He held her eyes for a moment.

So he'd bought Granary House by himself! She cleared her throat. "How's Charlie?' She'd only met his older brother a few times when she and Matt had been together. At the time he'd been the quieter of the two, but Daisy had always got the impression that he was very straightforward.

Matt's expression closed again. "I haven't seen him in a while. Last I heard, he's fine."

Daisy drank some water as she cast around for another topic of conversation. "*Um*, so what have you been doing in the States?"

"Working in IT for one of the big airlines." He gave her a slightly odd look. "I thought you'd have heard."

How would I hear, she wanted to snap. If Matt and Brian had kept in touch all these years – which seemed likely – then Brian hadn't bothered to fill Laura in on the highs and lows of Matt's life abroad. Although it was equally likely that Laura had decided never to mention Matt's name again.

"I hadn't heard, but that sounds pretty cool," she managed.

"Yeah?"

There was a definite edge to his voice. It felt like they were stepping awkwardly around each other. He was probably as nervous as she was.

"So, what prompted you to buy Granary House?" she asked. "Hang on, did you get back to view it before you made an offer?"

Matt seemed to relax a bit. "Would you believe, no? I viewed it online and then chatted to the estate agent. I made an offer after the structural engineer's report."

Daisy knew exactly what the house had sold for, and she had a pretty good idea how much would be needed for its upgrade. Clearly, his career was going well.

She hauled her bag onto her lap and took out her tablet, quickly powering it on and finding the file on Granary House, with the 3D models for the redesign of the kitchen, reception rooms and master bedroom.

Obviously you don't have to go with any of them – it'll just give you an idea."

"I really like the kitchen."

"Modern rustic." She was used to hearing praise for her work, but she felt giddy hearing Matt compliment her.

He nodded. "Looks like you had more than just a professional interest in it." He glanced up. "Would you live there yourself?"

He'd always been able to read her, she remembered. Which didn't mean she should let him slip right back into her life. She tried to bat away the question.

"Wouldn't everyone?" Not James, she knew. Still, if money were no object, and she could convince her suburban-loving boyfriend to move to the country, Granary House would be her dream home.

"Some of us anyway." Matt smiled. "And I just fell in love with this place on first sight. So, can I see some of your other designs?"

"Oh, sure." She clicked onto the finished designs of Freya's house, and Matt moved his chair around the table so he was sitting beside her.

Daisy forced herself to concentrate, which was difficult given his proximity. "It's partly about the type of house it is, but also about what the client wants."

He looked impressed. "If I were to get the place redesigned, I'd like to get the main house done first, and then the guest wing."

Daisy frowned in thought. "As far as I remember, the guest wing is accessed from the hall in the main house."

"Yep, dead handy. And it's small, and a lot cheaper to heat. It really just needs some new kitchen appliances and a lick of paint."

Their food arrived.

Daisy tucked her tablet into her bag as Matt moved his chair back around the table.

"So, what about your job?" She speared some pasta on her fork. "Will you work remotely?"

"The company I was working for did a merger a few months ago, and I took a decent payoff. But I'm consulting for them now." Matt shrugged. "It means I can work from anywhere."

Still, an old house in the middle of the Irish countryside was an unusual choice.

"You know Granary House used to be a bed and breakfast, don't you?" she said.

He laughed. "Yep, but I've no plans to reopen it as a B&B. I'm only thirty, Daisy. We're practically the same age, remember? Now seemed like the right time to come home and settle down, maybe have a family. I never really saw myself doing those things in the States."

Daisy stared at him for a moment. He'd come home to settle down? It didn't matter. She produced a small notepad and pen from her bag.

"Why don't you give me a broad idea of what you'd like for the house?"

"Sounds good." He sat up a bit straighter. "Where do we begin?"

———※———

"I'm slightly surprised you don't want to start knocking walls down," Daisy joked a while later. "Or have you really been paying attention while I've been going on about the house's proportions?"

"You know I always appreciated good proportions," Matt said with a cheeky grin.

Daisy felt heat rise to her face.

He seemed to take pity on her. "This is where I want to live. It's important to me that it feels right. And we're on the same wavelength."

They were, she thought. And they'd always complemented each other's differences. She'd been more outgoing, and had made friends easier during college. Matt had been quiet, his only real friend back then had been Brian. And later, her and Laura. But he'd been happier when it had just been the two of them.

At the time, she'd been a bit disappointed that he wouldn't come to Galway for weekends with her family and friends, but she'd accepted that he was shy. And maybe a bit self-centred, in the way a lot of people in their early twenties were. Still, his leaving had been a shock. There'd been no clues, not a single suggestion that he was unhappy. He'd never even hinted about staying in the States.

After they'd all graduated from college, she, Laura and Brian had gone straight into jobs. She and Laura had worked for other design firms to gain experience and build their savings. While they were working, Matt had opted to do a postgrad, and when he'd finished he'd headed to New York the summer Daisy and Laura had set up their company.

He'd told Daisy it would be a four-month internship. When he'd decided to stay, it had shaken her to her core, and left her wondering if she'd ever really known him.

Or how much she knew anyone.

He pushed his plate away now. "So, decision time."

Daisy found herself holding her breath. Matt had already paid a lot for Granary House. She'd hardly blame him if he didn't want to spend more money so soon.

He gave a lopsided smile. "You have the job, Daisy."

"Brilliant!" She beamed, resisting the temptation to hug him. That would definitely send out the wrong message. "I'm glad we're on the same page."

"Why wouldn't we be?" Matt's tone was light. "You get the chance to work on your dream house and I get the best interior architect in Dublin."

"Right." Daisy deliberately ignored the niggle of doubt. She couldn't get cold feet now. She'd contacted him, she'd pitched for the job – now he was giving it to her. It didn't matter that they had a history. "Once I see the house, and find out exactly what you want, I'll be able to draw up plans and give you a quote."

Matt rubbed a hand across the back of his neck. "Hey, it's just money, right?"

Daisy tried to gauge whether he was boasting, but he sounded more philosophical than anything. She opened her phone diary. "I could call out Tuesday, around eleven?"

"I bought a good coffee machine. Do you still drink lattes?"

"Oh, good memory. Flat white now, but latte is near enough." She caught the waiter's eye and motioned for the bill. "I'd better get back."

"I'm glad you reached out," Matt said with a grin.

"Reached out?" Daisy laughed when Matt gave a sheepish look.

"Is the house the only reason you got in touch?" he asked.

God, she wasn't ready for *that* conversation yet!

"*Um*, actually, there's an annual competition for the industry. I'd like to enter Granary House."

He nodded. "What would I have to do?"

Daisy chose her words carefully. "TV5 showcases the shortlisted houses for their *Home Design of the Year* programme, so if we make it onto the shortlist, we'd be interviewed. And I always prioritise the award projects, because they have to be finished on time."

She held her breath as he seemed to think.

"I don't see any problems," he said finally.

Was that a yes! It sounded like a yes! She was going to redesign Granary House *and* enter it for the award! *Play it cool, Daisy.*

"Good, we'll work towards that, then."

The waiter came over with the bill and, as Daisy reached for it, Matt's hand closed over hers. She managed to slide the bill towards her, her pulse racing as she pretended to study it.

"Daisy?"

She looked up.

"I'd like to get the bill," he said.

"Ah, listen, I'll just stick it on expenses."

Matt looked amused. "Yeah, but you work for yourself."

"And you'll have enough expenses once the work starts." Daisy put the company's credit card on the table and flashed Matt a brief smile. "I insist."

He sighed. "I could never argue with you."

Was that why they'd never really argued during their five years together?

She'd always assumed it was because they'd always agreed on things. Now she wondered what else they remembered differently. Not that it mattered. She was getting to design Granary House, and Matt had agreed to let her use it for her awards entry. It was a sign.

Her smile widened. "You won't regret this, I promise."

He held her gaze longer than necessary. "Having my ex-girlfriend redesign my house? Yeah, probably not."

CHAPTER 7

Daisy tried to calm her nerves as she drove slowly along the winding back roads of Wicklow towards Granary House the following Tuesday. After the initial excitement of landing the prestigious project, the reality of what she was taking on was starting to hit home.

She was going to be working for Matt. Redesigning what was clearly his dream home. And hers, if she could ever afford a place like that. She just hoped she could do it justice.

Now she had the job, she'd briefly considered telling James. It would normalise it, she thought, remind her that she wasn't doing anything wrong. This was just work.

James had been on the phone, pacing up and down the sitting room, when she'd got home the previous evening. Judging by the scowl on his face when she'd looked in, she'd assumed it was a business call and had left him to it.

Eventually he'd come into the kitchen.

"Mum and Dad said hello." He'd taken a beer out of the fridge. "Nothing new with them. Daniel and Fiona are marching steadily towards world domination, so the pressure is completely off me."

Daisy had known better than to argue. She had tried, unsuccessfully, to reassure James that he was as successful as his older siblings, both of whom had moved to England before she'd met him. Daniel was a doctor in London, and his sister lectured at one of the colleges in Oxford. Privately, Daisy wondered if James actually felt more overshadowed by his dad, who ran a huge property firm. Either way, it hadn't felt like the right time to mention that she was going to be working for her ex-boyfriend.

Now she indicated left onto a small road, flanked on one side by the River Hevren. Shortly after she swung right through the large iron gates, and up the short driveway to the house.

Its grand, stone facade was covered with ivy, but Daisy knew it had undergone a lot of structural work under its previous owner. It included a sizeable kitchen extension and conservatory to the rear, which overlooked an easterly facing kitchen garden and, behind that, a half-acre of orchard and three acres of unused land.

The ground became gravel beneath the car wheels as Daisy pulled in beside Matt's Jeep. Quickly, she exchanged her runners for pumps, and got out, her Mary-Jane heels sinking a little into the stones. She smoothed down the fitted forties-style skirt that clung a little too uncomfortably to her curves. Determined to make a good impression, she'd paired it with a cropped, hand-knit red sweater that she'd designed and made herself.

As she collected her bag and locked the car, Matt opened the front door.

"Hi." Daisy could feel a pulse beat in her neck, as she managed what she hoped was a warm, professional smile. How did you smile at your ex, anyway?

"Hey." Matt tipped his head. "It's so quiet out here, I heard your car from the back of the house. Come in, coffee's nearly ready."

He turned and walked back into the house, leaving Daisy to follow. She released a breath, not sure whether to be relieved or disappointed that he hadn't attempted a kiss or hug at the door. But maybe he'd decided to keep things business-like between them.

She followed Matt down to the generous kitchen, where a rich smell of coffee filled the air. The sun slanted in through the windows, warming the flagstone floor and outdated units that ran along the opposite wall. In the centre of the room was a long, pine table.

"I inherited it all with the house," Matt said cheerfully. "But I brought the coffee machine and a few other things from the States. It makes me feel like I'm on holidays, using European adaptors. So, do you still drink dairy? I have oat and soy …"

The notions! Daisy smothered a nervous laugh. When she and Matt had been together, she could hardly remember him having any sort of milk in the fridge. But back then he'd shared a house with Brian and a couple of others, so a well-stocked kitchen had been low on the agenda.

"Dairy is fine, thanks."

"Give me a minute." He frothed up a jug of milk and poured her coffee into a mug.

He handed it to her and she took a careful sip. "Not bad."

He grinned. "Don't give up the day job just yet, so?"

They stood in the quiet warmth of the room together, drinking their coffee.

Matt placed his mug on the counter. "It's a bit weird, isn't it?" He looked at her. "Us, together again like this, after all these years."

She clearly remembered their last time together, just before he'd left for New York. She'd replayed it over and over after he had told her he wasn't coming back, wondering what she'd said or done wrong. She'd tried to recall if Matt had said anything that night, given her some sign that he wasn't planning on coming home again.

But he was probably just making small talk. She shouldn't read too much into it. And she wasn't ready to delve too deeply either – not yet. Even though the question she'd been asking herself for the past five years burned her mouth like the first hot gulp of coffee.

She took a breath. "Why don't you give me the grand tour? I'll measure the rooms and take notes and photos. Then we can sit down and go through everything in detail."

Matt inclined his head. "Bring your coffee and we can get started."

Daisy was acutely aware of Matt's closeness as she followed him around Granary House. Even though she'd seen it before – its high-ceilinged hallway and reception rooms that stretched the width of the house, the five ensuite bedrooms upstairs – being here with Matt made it feel like her first time.

He lingered in the largest bedroom at the front of the house. "I think this would be the master bedroom."

"Right. Brilliant." Her heartbeat picked up as her gaze tracked across the worn floorboards. She walked over towards the window, stopping as she noticed the expanse of floor that looked newer and brighter.

"I reckon the bed was there," he said.

He met her eyes, and she nodded.

"Fair bet. We can always put it somewhere else, of course."

He shook his head. "I like to sleep near a window."

I remember. She stared at him, wondering if he could read her mind. Total head-wreck! What was she doing here? *He's a client, Daisy, remember? You're here to redesign his house, not think about his bed.* Although that last bit would be part of it. From a design point of view, obviously! She smiled brightly.

"Let's see what sort of shape the bathroom is in."

⚜

"So, what's your honest opinion?" Matt said half an hour later, as they sat down at the kitchen table.

"Honestly?" Daisy crossed her legs, swinging her foot absently. "I think it was worth every cent you paid for it. And I agree about the guest wing – it's in far better shape than the rest of the house."

"Excellent." He waited.

"So, structurally, it's in good repair. You've five spacious en-suite bedrooms, which we can completely update." She grinned at Matt's comical expression. "Consider the floral wallpaper and matching curtains banished. The two big bedrooms would also be perfect for walk-in wardrobes."

"Fine."

"Good." She glanced around. "Are you particularly attached to that conservatory?"

He shrugged. "Why, do you think I should get rid of it?"

She shook her head. "If we put in a support beam, we could give you a bigger kitchen with a gorgeous dining area. And you'd have all the extra light coming in."

"Sounds good."

"We could also turn one of the reception rooms into a great home office."

Matt chuckled and Daisy shifted a bit self-consciously. "What?"

"You." He shook his head. "Sorry, it's just so cool to see you like this after all this time. I hadn't thought of you like this."

So he'd thought of her. She'd thought of him. Too much. It was something she'd never admitted to anyone, not even Laura.

When she said nothing, he added hurriedly, "You were always creative but, here you are, running your own company. I'm just really glad for you."

Daisy had learned that people tended to assume that creative people weren't smart at business. Back in their early twenties, Matt had always referred to her as the creative half. And she had always thought of him as the smart one. It had been part of his appeal.

"A home office sounds like a great idea," he said. "What about you? Do you ever work from home?"

She shook her head. "Not really." James did. But she didn't want to talk about James.

"Tell me more about this award."

She beamed. "It's like the Oscars for the industry. Laura and I try to enter every year with our best projects."

"Do you compete against each other?"

"No." She laughed. "Either of us being shortlisted would be a win. I've been longlisted a couple of times, though."

"So, what happens now?"

She took out her tablet and an A4 pad and placed them on the table. "I want to get some more ideas from you first. Then I'll go away and draw up plans."

"I'd like to keep a few bits." Matt looked around the kitchen. "This table, for example.'

Daisy's pen stilled on the page and she glanced up.

He shook his head. "What? You're going to tell me now it's full of dry rot, aren't you?"

She blinked. "No, not at all. I was actually thinking the same thing about the table. Most clients just want me to get rid of old furniture they've inherited. I usually end up stripping everything out, unless I can convince them it's worth up-cycling."

"Is this?"

Daisy took a closer look. "Yes, I think so."

"Good." Matt looked pleased. "Apart from that, I'd probably describe my style as pretty minimalist. No clutter."

Which was not something she'd ever have associated with him.

"I've changed a lot since college," he said.

Daisy's heart thumped a bit louder as she stared at him. When had he started reading her mind again? It had always been his superpower.

"We can streamline the whole house, make it inviting, but easy to keep. I'd like to introduce some maximalist notes ..." She stopped, noticing Matt's puzzled expression. "I have some examples on screen that I can show you. Don't worry, we'll keep its character, what makes it special. The sooner I can have you approve all the plans, the sooner we can make a start."

He smiled. "I'm glad we're doing this, though."

Daisy met his eyes. He wasn't just talking about the house.

In an overly bright tone, she said, "It'll be worth it when we're finished."

Matt said nothing, and Daisy knew he'd guessed that she'd deliberately misunderstood him.

CHAPTER 8

"Why don't you just say what's on your mind, Laura?" Daisy saved her changes on the 3D model of the interior of Granary House.

Laura frowned and leaned back in her chair. "Nothing. Okay – these dimensions are wrong. They have to be. I've inputted everything, and there should be room for a double sink!" She waved a hand at the screen. "I'm pitching to a potential client in Wexford."

Fionn cleared his throat delicately. "Mind if I take a look?"

"Do you think I'm not capable of drawing up a kitchen plan?"

"You'd be helping me," he said mildly. "I've got my final assignments coming up, remember? They could throw everything, including the double kitchen sink, at us."

Laura fixed Fionn with a hard stare. "I'll send the model to you now, but if I catch you gloating I'll bloody kill you."

"You're the reason I love interning here," Fionn said brightly.

Daisy snorted in amusement. She gave Laura a moment to send the model, then turned to her. "Forget the kitchen design for a moment. You haven't asked about Matt. Why not?"

"The visit on Tuesday?" Laura shrugged. "Fine – how did it go?"

"Great, no issues at all! We got a lot done, and I think he'll be easy to work with."

Laura arched an eyebrow, before turning back to her screen, and Daisy shifted uncomfortably as she caught Fionn's eye.

"What shape is the house in, Daisy?" he asked.

She flashed him a grateful smile. "Great, to be honest. A bit shabby after lying empty for two years, but there's no huge structural work needed. We seem to agree on the broad strokes, so once he signs off on the designs, we can get stuck in. And the crew I've working on Freya's house have had a cancellation, so they said they can start next week."

Laura pushed her glasses onto her head. "What did James say?"

"About what?" Daisy frowned. "About the new job?"

"Yes, babes." Laura's tone was crisp. "About the fact that your ex-boyfriend is your new client."

"I haven't mentioned it," Daisy said casually. "I mean, I don't talk about the tiny details of my job, Laura. James wouldn't be interested."

"Matt is hardly a tiny detail." Laura smirked. "Or maybe he is. He was your boyfriend, not mine."

Daisy wished she could laugh but she found it difficult to joke about Matt. Especially now he was back. And she couldn't risk Laura and Fionn knowing just how much ... her breath caught painfully for a moment and she had to force herself to relax.

"James and I don't talk about work, that's all," she said more firmly.

"Hmm." Laura tapped her fingernails on the desk. "Fine! Changing the subject – do you fancy a spa weekend for your thirtieth?"

"Spas aren't really my thing, Laura – you know that." Daisy flashed her a look of apology. "Thanks, anyway."

Fionn cleared his throat and Laura glared at him.

"You haven't figured that double sink out already surely!"

"Um, no, actually."

Laura looked mollified. "What is it then?"

"I've been studying your horoscope."

"Telling you my birthday was a big mistake."

Fionn tugged on his shirt collar. "If I have a problem I work out a horoscope. It rewires my brain so I can sort out the problem later. Like this double sink!"

Laura folded her arms. "I'll indulge you for one minute."

"So, I did a reading for you," Fionn said, "and you're approaching a crossroads in your life where you'll have a big decision to make."

Laura rolled her eyes. "As if that doesn't sound like every **single** horoscope I've read in my life." When Fionn didn't reply, she added, "Why do you believe this stuff?"

He shrugged. "Why do people go to church? They believe in God though they can't actually see God. But we can see the stars! We know when our ruling planets align for us. It's all there if you know what you're looking for. And it's way more tangible than anything else I've come across."

"I suppose it doesn't say what this major decision is, does it?"

"That's not how it works."

"Of course it's not." Laura looked pointedly at her watch. "Time's up. Back to work: the bills won't pay themselves."

Daisy's phone buzzed. It was a message from Matt.

Hey, I have to drive up to Dublin this afternoon to pick up a few things. Fancy meeting for a quick coffee? You can show me some early plans if you have any. And I've something to tell you.

She studied the message. 'Something to tell you?' That couldn't be about the house, not when they'd already met and discussed everything. He obviously wanted to talk about them. Or maybe he wanted to tell her something else? Something that had nothing to do with them. Maybe he was about to get married. He could have a child! No, she'd have heard, wouldn't she? Although she hadn't heard anything at all. Still, it was way more likely that he wanted to talk about the two of them. Oh my God, this was happening! This was what she wanted, right? To find out why he had stayed in the States. To find closure. She could do this! She had to do this! She took a deep breath and texted: Meet you at Grey's Tea House at the end of Merrion Square, say 3.30pm?

A moment later Matt sent a thumbs-up.

She put her phone away and tried to calm the nervous fluttering in the pit of her stomach. She wouldn't say anything to Laura. Laura had made her feelings very clear, and she didn't want any more angst between them. She just hoped Laura didn't think she was being rude about her birthday offer. The truth was, she'd gone up two dress sizes in the past few years, and she'd prefer to have freezing cold showers every day for a year than lie half-naked on a bench while somebody kneaded her cellulite. Sometimes she wished she was more like Rosie, who had fit back into her jeans within weeks of having her babies, even the twins.

God, she really hoped James would agree to come down with her to the birthday party this weekend! Although he'd probably hate it. He liked her family, and he'd always been good with Rosie's kids, but knowing Rosie, half of Galway would be there, including most of the gang they'd both gone to school with. Why couldn't she have a small family party? Her nieces were only in their first year of primary school!

"I figured out your double sink," Fionn said.

Laura shot him a look of disbelief. "Already?"

"I'm sending it back to you now."

Laura said nothing as she peered at her screen. Finally, she nodded. "Well done."

He shrugged modestly. "It was just a small miscalculation."

"Maybe I should take up astrology," Laura grumbled.

Daisy caught Fionn's eye and sent him a tiny wink.

CHAPTER 9

"It's really good to see you again so soon. I haven't met up with too many people since I've been back."

Matt was sitting across from Daisy later that afternoon, stirring half a spoon of sugar into his coffee.

She could actually feel her heart thumping in the back of her throat as she waited, but managed to school her features. "Well, I can stay half an hour, but then I'll have to get back to work."

He gave a cheeky smile. "Why, will your boss fire you? Listen, I have some news. I've been approached by a music promoter who wants to use Granary House's grounds for some gigs this summer. Some other outdoor venue fell through, which is why it's so last-minute."

Daisy stared at him for a moment. That was it? That was what he'd wanted to tell her? She struggled not to let her disappointment show.

"*Um*, how did the guy even get hold of your number?"

Matt laughed. "He didn't. He saw that the place had been sold and just turned up on my doorstep. Anyway, the money's good, and I couldn't really afford to say no, not with all the expenses I'll have."

He had a point, she thought. She tried to visualise what the grounds looked like beyond the kitchen garden.

"I can get landscapers in for you," she said. "They usually start after I've finished, but we'll work around them. Okay, I've some ideas to show you." She opened the gallery on her phone and handed it to Matt. "Swipe right. The first is a 3D design for your study, then early sketches for the kitchen and dining area, then a mood board: colours, ideas for textures and so on."

He grinned. "This is since yesterday? Impressive!"

"The mood board was easy enough. I had a pretty clear idea of the look you wanted by the time I left."

"Sounds like you've fallen in love too," Matt said.

"Sorry?"

His eyes glinted. "With the house."

"Right." She laughed, trying to ignore the thought that had just flashed to mind. If she and Matt had never broken up, would they now be the proud, joint owners of Granary House?

"So is James still running that company of his? TakeOff, right?"

Daisy pulled herself out of her fantasy. "*Um*, yeah, he's working hard." *And pretty much all the time!* She hurried on. "But Dublin's a pretty small pond, Matt – you made it in the States."

"Maybe I should have stayed here."

He wasn't joking, she realised. She took a deep breath. "Why didn't you?"

He shot her an odd look. "I didn't exactly have a choice."

Because there'd been bigger, brighter opportunities abroad? Or because he'd had enough of the two of them? Either way, the result had been the same.

She remembered the exact message she'd left on his voice mail: **Hi Matt, I don't get why you left without even talking to me, or trying to see if we could work long distance. I guess you've decided we can't.**

His only response had been a short text: **Hope you get the life you deserve, Daisy. Matt.**

At the time, she'd thought her message was ultra-cool. Now she realised it had revealed the depths of her hurt.

When Matt had texted back, she and Laura had analysed those nine little words to death, and pestered Brian with questions he couldn't or wouldn't answer.

Daisy also knew that beneath Laura's sharp, sarcastic exterior, she was fiercely loyal to her friends. If Brian had told Laura Matt's real reason for breaking up, Laura's instinct would have been to protect Daisy even if that meant keeping things from her.

She checked the time. "I have to go. Look, I'll have all my plans ready for you in a few more days. Phone or email if you've any questions or further ideas."

"Can I walk you back to your office?"

"It's only around the corner, but sure."

The air felt heavy and humid as they stepped outside.

"Apparently there's a storm on the way." Matt pushed his hands into his pockets. "I'm just hoping there won't be any powerlines down near the house. The broadband is a bit of a joke as it is. What about you? Are you still afraid of thunder?"

"What?" Daisy tried to laugh it off. "I was never afraid of thunder."

He raised an eyebrow. "Lightning, then."

Daisy said nothing. When they'd been together, it had been the perfect excuse to stay overnight with him. But now it felt too intimate – not to mention ridiculous – to admit that she was still afraid.

"There's a lot of storms forecast for the next few months." She tried for a deliberately casual tone. "Blame climate change!"

"Let's hope it won't interfere with the landscaping."

Which could be a problem! There was a reason she advised her clients to leave outside work until the weather was better. Not that good weather could ever be guaranteed in Ireland.

Still, most people weren't trying to turn three-and-a-half acres of overgrown land into an outdoor concert venue!

"This is me." She stopped outside the nineteenth-century Dublin townhouse.

Matt looked up at the building and laughed. "Of course it is!"

Daisy smiled. "Hey, we just have a small, first-floor room. But I love it."

"Thanks for meeting me, Daisy."

Before she realised what he was about to do, Matt leaned in and gave her a soft, fleeting kiss on the cheek.

"No problem. I'll be in touch." She turned, fumbling as she keyed in the code for the heavy door. When it clicked open, she pushed it in, glancing briefly back over her shoulder at Matt.

He gave a small wave before she let the door shut, and leaned against it, waiting for her face to cool down. *Get a grip, Daisy – it was a kiss on the cheek.*

She couldn't overthink her and Matt. Only what if she was right? What if Matt still cared for her? And what if that was the real reason he'd come home?

CHAPTER 10

"The problem is, the twins have had too much sugar." Rosie poured herself a second glass of white wine and propped her hip against the huge island unit in her Galway kitchen that Saturday afternoon.

Daisy drank some more of her own wine as she stared out through the wall of glass that wrapped around Rosie's sprawling house, and overlooked her equally sprawling garden – most of which was currently covered by two enormous bouncy castles.

As usual, Rosie had not only invited every single child in the twins' class, along with their parents, but their neighbours, friends and casual acquaintances and all of their kids. Daisy had a hard time trying to find her own parents when she'd arrived.

"I think all kids eat too much sugar at a birthday party, Rosie. It's kind of the point."

Rosie gave a little sniff. "I've told Séan he can take our gang to the park later to run off that energy." She folded her arms. "So, how's work going?"

Daisy brightened. "Great, actually. I'm coming to the end of one big project, and I'm just starting another one."

Rosie clicked her tongue. "I can never understand how people don't know how to decorate their own houses. It's basic: don't mix patterns and remember the Rule of Three."

Daisy made herself count to five. She wouldn't rise to the bait. Rosie knew well that she wasn't an interior designer. Even if she were, there was a lot more to it than that.

"Well, you must be finding yourself stuck in the office a lot these days." Rosie placed a hand on Daisy's arm. "You don't look like you're getting much time for you."

Daisy finished her wine. "How do you mean?"

Rosie pulled back her shoulder-length hair, a paler version of Daisy's, and secured it with a small, brown bobbin.

"Well, no, nothing. Only, are you getting any exercise?"

"I cycle to work a lot." Daisy stared at her.

"Oh, class." Rosie frowned.

Was her sister body-shaming her? It was a pity she'd finished her wine – she could have thrown the rest of it over her! Except she wouldn't. She and Rosie didn't actually fight. Not since Rosie had hit her teenage years, learned the art of passive-aggression, and had spent the whole of her adult life perfecting it. The easiest thing was to listen and nod along, never disagree. There was no point: Rosie was always right.

Penny burst in from the garden. "Mummy, when can we have the birthday cakes? Everybody wants to see me blowing out my candles, Mummy. Annie wants her birthday cake too. Please, Mummy?"

Rosie's face gentled. "In a few minutes, loveen, I promise. Did you say hello to Daisy and thank her for your present?"

Penny turned to her. "Hello, Daisy, thank you for my present."

"Hope you like it, Penny."

Penny looked solemn. "I don't know what it is." Before either adult could say anything else, she turned and ran back outside.

Rosie met Daisy's eyes. "Sorry, you know what they're like. I'll help her sort through her stuff later."

"Ah, no worries." Daisy shrugged.

Rosie's tone softened a bit. "Look, about what I was saying before. You and I have different metabolisms, so I know it's hard for you to shift the weight, but –"

"James likes me exactly the way I am." Which was probably an absolute lie. These days, James was more interested in spending time with their waif-like lodger than with her. But she couldn't admit that to Rosie. She didn't want her to feel sorry for her or launch into another lecture about how to keep her man!

"Well, don't take him for granted, Daisy. You want to hang on to James."

"Jesus, Rosie, what do you – ?"

Before Daisy could finish, Séan came in from the garden. "You girls having a go at each other?" He winked at Daisy, who grinned back.

"Rosie thinks I'm taking James for granted because I'm getting too fat."

Séan rolled his eyes. "Fuck sake, Ro!" He turned to Daisy. "You're gorgeous – I still fancy the knickers off you."

"*Séan!*" Rosie flushed hotly.

Daisy felt a bit sorry for her. She had a habit of walking herself into situations. Rosie and Séan were so different – Daisy still couldn't understand how they'd ever got together. But Séan was good for her sister. He stood up to her, and he kept her grounded.

"We brought some beer. I put it in the fridge," Daisy said.

He flung open the large fridge freezer. "That's why you're my favourite sister-in-law." Taking out a can of Heineken, he snapped it open and took a long drink, before putting it on the counter. "The kids are having a great time altogether, although Ben threw up into one of the rosemary bushes."

Rosie gave a gasp, and Séan pulled a face.

"Ah, don't be stressing, I hosed it all down, and sure it'll be good fertiliser. Anyway, have you seen that sky? There's a storm coming."

"It might hold off a bit," Daisy said quickly as she spotted Rosie's expression.

"Why didn't you tell me Ben was sick?" Rosie demanded.

Séan took another slug of beer and wiped the back of his hand across his mouth. "I just did!"

"You're supposed to be *watching* the kids, Séan! I told you I wanted a glass of wine and a quick chat with Daisy."

Séan shook his head. "Aren't they all alive and having a great time?" He picked up his beer again. "Have you seen James?"

Daisy peered out into the garden. "He's not outside?"

"He disappeared a while ago. I thought he came in here."

"Maybe he did." Daisy sighed. "I might go look for him."

"Don't be long," warned Rosie. "We're nearly ready for the cake."

Daisy left Rosie and Séan in the kitchen and slipped out to the hall. Eventually, she found James, hunched over his laptop in a corner of the big living room at the front of the house.

"James?" She came in and closed the door behind her. "What are you doing?"

He looked up. "Getting some work done. Nobody will miss me for a few minutes."

Daisy stared at him. "I'm missing you, and so was Séan. But that's not even the point. You're missing this! I can't believe you brought your laptop to a kids' birthday!"

"I'm sorry!" He sighed heavily. "And I wish this stuff would wait! To be honest, I really should have stayed at home."

And after he'd finished, Alma could have cooked for him, before they snuggled up together with their Nintendo Switches. Her brain froze at the thought. Was that what had happened last weekend when she'd been down to visit her parents? She dug her nails into her hand and took a deep breath.

She tried to see things from his point of view. Her family wasn't James' family. And after five years together, James still referred to her as his girlfriend, rather than his partner. He wasn't that close to his family either, although his parents only lived in Howth. They were both lovely people, Daisy thought, but James had a stupid chip on his shoulder and couldn't seem to get past the notion that he wasn't living up to their expectations. He also seemed uncomfortable with the fact that his parents were wealthy, and had offered them help on more than one occasion.

All the more reason why he should embrace her family, Daisy thought. None of them were well-off. And, with the exception of Rosie, none of them were the least bit judgey.

"Just come and hang out with us for a while. Everyone needs time off!"

He shot her an apologetic look. "Just give me another minute?"

"Fine!" Daisy slipped out of the room.

Maybe she was asking too much of him. He'd told her he'd have to work this weekend, but she'd told him he needed a break and pretty much insisted he come with her. Maybe she'd become one of those needy, demanding girlfriends. And if she'd been the same with Matt, that could be the reason he'd left! Feeling a bit dizzy, she leaned back against the pale, cool wall, closing her eyes to breathe deeply.

As she walked back into the kitchen, she noticed it had started to rain.

CHAPTER 11

Daisy sat down at her parents' big kitchen table that Sunday, and tried to ignore the fact that for the second weekend she was on her own.

James had taken the car and left shortly after the twins' party the day before, but had suggested Daisy stay and catch up with her family.

Yesterday she'd been furious. She hadn't said anything to James but the last thing she wanted was to be with someone who didn't want to be with her. She'd found herself thinking again about Matt. One of her many theories about why he'd left was that after five years together Matt had felt stifled. His summer in New York had given him a taste of freedom, and he'd decided to embrace it. Now, she and James had been together the same length of time she'd been with Matt!

Daisy passed a bowl of peas to Annie. She'd be heading back up on the train to Dublin later on with all the college students. At this moment, sitting here with her parents, her older sister and brother-in-law and their four children, she felt exactly like the student she'd once been, coming home to visit at the weekend.

Not that she'd made a habit of it, she thought, a bit guiltily. In fact, she probably saw her family a lot more now than she had as a student. Or to be more precise, while she'd been with Matt.

"Isn't this a real treat having you all here?" Daisy's mother, Miriam, beamed around the table. "All the flowers in my garden." She winked at Penny who carefully spooned some peas and gravy into her mouth.

"You only have two flowers, Nana: Mummy and Daisy. The rest of us have real names," Penny said.

Daisy hid a grin. Their parents had been hippies in the seventies and had simply decided there was no reason to ever change.

As a result, Rosie and Daisy had enjoyed a laidback childhood which, Daisy guessed, was probably why Rosie had rebelled by becoming what their mother deemed 'mainstream'.

She also knew that she was more like her mother than Rosie was. Whereas her older sister lived in a uniform of starchy shirts and well-designed, utterly boring trousers, Daisy had inherited Miriam's love of colourful, vintage clothes.

Miriam chuckled at Penny's remark, before turning to her eldest daughter.

"Have you decided what you're going to do in September, Rosie?"

Rosie seemed to stiffen. "Not yet, Mum."

Daisy shot them a confused look, and Miriam sighed. "Rosie's five-year career break will be up then. She could go back to work as a physiotherapist."

"Occupational therapist," Rosie corrected, and Miriam gave a knowing smile.

"Exactly. You're doing a wonderful job at home, loveen, but you don't want to waste all those years of study. Not when you could be doing so much to help. Sure, isn't there a fierce shortage of people qualified in your field?"

Daisy always found it strange that their own mother had stayed at home to paint but had strongly encouraged that both of them pursue 'proper' careers. Although Miriam always insisted that she was creative, and her painting was more than a hobby. In fairness to her mum, she *had* sold a few of her paintings down the years, mainly to some of the local businesses, who liked to be seen to support one of their own.

Daisy just hoped she didn't try to sell her latest project: a life-sized, nude self-portrait.

"I really haven't decided anything yet." Rosie looked over at Ben. "Ben, don't eat so fast." She turned back to her mother. "I've four children, I'm on two parent associations, *and* I'm chairperson of the Tidy Towns committee. I'm busy enough."

"Maybe for now," Miriam said. "All I'm saying is be careful before you completely throw away a career. It might suit you at the moment to be at home, but you've a great brain and it won't be too easy if you want to get back in another few years. For a start, your age might go against you."

"Maybe you could go back part-time," Daisy said. "You know, two days a week, or something."

Judging by Rosie's expression, Daisy imagined she'd be less horrified if she'd suggested that Rosie run naked through Eyre Square.

"Can we change the subject?" Rosie said tightly.

Séan cleared his throat and turned to his father-in-law. "How are the chickens, Eric?"

The older man ran a hand over his spotlessly clean, grey beard. "Ten of the happiest girls around," he said. "Clever, too. Do you know they can sense changes in the weather? We don't need anyone to tell us when there's a storm coming." He looked around at his grandchildren. "They do the chicken dance when it's going to rain." He batted his arms and made some loud clucking noises, causing the children to dissolve into giggles. Grinning, he turned back to Séan. "I've just finished extending their run, so they're safe as houses."

"Are we eating one of your chickens today, Granddad?" Rosie's younger son, Sam, asked, apparently more curious than anything.

The twins shrieked and dropped their forks.

"Relax, kids!" Eric waved a hand at the table. "I bought these birds in the local butcher's yesterday. Our hens are specially bred for egg-laying, and they'll live long, happy lives and die peacefully of old age."

There was a tense pause, when Daisy wondered if half of Rosie's children would suddenly declare themselves vegetarian, but they seemed to decide it was all right to eat chickens they'd never actually met.

"Oh now, we've a bit of news, haven't we, Mim?" Eric nodded at his wife, who beamed at him. "Of course." She clapped her hands. "To celebrate our fortieth wedding anniversary in June, we're going to throw a big party."

"Will it be like ours?" The twins bounced up and down.

"A bit." Miriam winked at them.

"*With a unicorn bouncy castle?*" Annie shrieked.

"No, loveen, but we're going to have a huge big tent in our front garden and have lots and lots of people."

"What?" Rosie looked horrified. "Seriously, Mum?"

Daisy guessed Rosie was worried that her parents would simply throw open their home to the whole town. And that she'd get stuck with helping to plan the logistics of it all. Privately, she wondered if her parents could really afford to hire a marquee and cater for the numbers she knew her generous mother would insist on inviting. Her dad's salary as an English and history teacher was modest, and she was pretty sure that whatever her mother made just about kept her in canvasses and paintbrushes.

"Of course I'm serious." Miriam tucked her long hair, heavily streaked with pinks and purples, behind her ears. "It'll be fun."

"I fancy a good DJ," Eric said, tapping Sam on the hand. "We'll get them to play the Chicken Song."

"All the local DJs are useless," Rosie said dismissively. "You'll need a halfway decent band. At least it'd lend some atmosphere."

It was astonishing, Daisy thought. She could almost see the cogs in Rosie's brain starting to whirr into motion.

"As long as they can play some Garth Brooks stuff," Eric said, helping himself to some more potatoes. "Oh, and a few Kayley Lynch songs, too. I like that one – 'One More Like You'."

Daisy grinned. "That's not very rock and roll of you, Dad!"

"Just mixing it up a bit, Daisy flower." He winked at her.

"You know she's coming to Ireland this June?" Daisy drank some of her mother's home-made elderberry wine. "She's doing a night here in Galway. You and Mum could go and see her."

Miriam glanced at Eric. "Well, if you're stuck for something to get us, I suppose you could buy tickets. But, to be honest, your dad is the real fan." She patted Daisy's arm. "The party will be very relaxed, loveen. You can invite James' parents. Oh, and Laura, too. How's she keeping, anyway? And that husband of hers – although you don't like him, do you?"

Daisy stifled a sigh. Her mother could be very blunt.

"Laura is great, Mum. Brian's just a bit of a ..." She stopped as she noticed Rosie's warning look.

"Twat?" Miriam said.

"*Mum!*" Rosie tutted loudly.

"They're married a few years now, aren't they?" Miriam said, completely ignoring Rosie.

Daisy shifted uncomfortably at the table. Laura and Brian had married at just twenty-four, the same year her relationship with Matt had ended.

The timing had been terrible, and Laura had even offered to delay the wedding, but Daisy had known how unrealistic that was. The hardest thing she'd had to do was to be there as Laura's bridesmaid, without Matt. But she'd done it. And, somehow, she'd moved on.

Miriam poured herself a second glass of wine, took a large gulp and swirled it around her mouth before swallowing.

"Do you think they'll have their own chicks?" she said.

"Ah, Mum, I don't know," said Daisy. "Maybe not." Laura had never hinted that she and Brian were trying, nor had she shown the slightest interest in children.

Miriam gave a thoughtful nod. "Well, if I were her, I'd be getting my eggs checked."

"Jesus, Mum," Rosie muttered.

"And what about you and James? Miriam continued. "Pity he couldn't stay, by the way. Anyway, no harm in getting yours checked too, Daisy flower."

"Checked?" Daisy echoed.

"Maybe get some frozen. I went into menopause at thirty-seven, remember? I was always fierce sorry not to have any more chicks."

Miriam gave her husband a wistful smile, as Séan went bright red, and all four children gave her confused looks.

Finally, Penny spoke up. "Does your friend keep chickens too, Daisy?"

Daisy smiled brightly at her. "She does, Penny. Lots of them."

***

"So, what's really going on?" Rosie asked, as she drove Daisy to the train station later that afternoon.

Daisy glanced across. "How do you mean?"

"With you, Daisy. You were pretty quiet at the table. You don't seem yourself. You and Mum are usually giggling away about something when you come down." When Daisy said nothing, she added more gently, "Is it James?"

Daisy felt her chest tighten. After the hurtful remarks Rosie had made the day before about her weight, the last thing Daisy wanted was to admit she was upset with James. She wished he'd stayed the night. They could have gone out for dinner in Galway city and had a few cocktails – maybe even caught a session in one of the pubs – before getting a late taxi back to her parents' house. They were young, and they'd no kids to tie them down, but in the last year – two if she were being honest – the passion and the romance had almost completely disappeared. She was pretty sure that wasn't normal after five years together. But they seemed stuck.

She'd always thought it was only married couples who found themselves stuck. People who'd been married for years, maybe. Or couples with kids, who were so stressed by parenting and holding everything together at home, as well as hanging onto their jobs, that they hardly had time for each other. But Rosie and Séan seemed happy, even if Rosie was a bit of a dose sometimes.

She'd thought she and James were happy too.

Buying the house together had felt like a real commitment. The only downside had been having to rent out the spare room, and they'd assured each other it would only be short term. But Alma had been living with them for what felt like forever, and their little home – that she'd so carefully designed and decorated – felt more like a student house share. One where she felt she didn't belong.

"It just feels weird being down two weekends in a row." Daisy took refuge behind the half-truth, and tried not to think about James driving back home to Alma.

Who *really* knew what anyone would do, she wondered. James seemed … stressed. Which was probably why he was taking refuge in computer games all the time. Or maybe he was just bored.

Had Matt become bored with her too? And if Matt could leave, why not James? She couldn't risk missing the signs again!

"Daisy?"

"*Hmm?*"

"Are you sure that's all it is?"

Rosie looked so concerned that Daisy found herself caving. She might as well tell Rosie the truth now – she had a habit of extracting information one way or another.

"Matt's home."

The car swerved slightly, as Rosie took a moment to right the wheel. "Your Matt?"

"He's not *my* Matt! He hasn't been my Matt in a long time." Daisy looked over at Rosie. "Don't tell Mum and Dad. They claim to be pacifists, but I wouldn't put it past Dad to hire a hitman."

There was a short silence. Then Rosie spoke slowly.

"Row back, now. How do you know he's home? Did he get in touch?"

"*Er*, well, no."

"Oh Jesus, please don't tell me *you* got in touch."

"He bought Granary House and I pitched to redesign it."

When Rosie gave her a blank look, Daisy said, "It's a historic house in Wicklow I've wanted to redesign for years."

"*That's* your excuse? Who do you think you're talking to, Daisy?"

Rosie pulled up at the train station, and Daisy got out and grabbed her overnight bag from the back seat.

"Thanks for the lift."

"Daisy, be honest, was that the only reason you got in touch?"

"It felt like a sign, Rosie!"

"God almighty, Daisy, you're as flaky as Mum. What's that supposed to mean?"

Her sister knew nothing about her life, Daisy thought – and she understood even less! When she didn't reply, Rosie just shook her head.

"Promise me you won't do anything stupid."

Daisy silently counted to five. "I promise, okay? This is strictly business. And maybe closure." She flashed her what she hoped was a reassuring smile but, judging by her sister's expression, she didn't believe her.

As Daisy walked towards her platform, it struck her that she didn't believe it either.

CHAPTER 12

Daisy was still feeling on edge when she got to the office on Monday. She'd arrived home late Sunday evening, to find James and Alma gaming on the sofa. Neither of them had appeared to notice her as she'd hovered in the door.

"Hi, Alma." She'd adopted her brightest tone. "How was your weekend?"

Alma had given her a startled look. "Good, thank you, Daisy. *Yes, got you!*"

Daisy had stared at her for a moment, before realising the last bit had been meant for James. "Great." She'd pasted on a smile. "James, could I speak to you for a minute?"

"Sure." He'd flashed her a quick look. "Can it wait a minute? We're in the middle of this!"

Daisy had tried to read Alma and James' body language to decide whether they'd spent the whole weekend having frantic sex, but it didn't seem any different than usual. She'd closed the door loudly, made herself a mug of green tea and gone to bed.

Laura arrived in. "Fuck, it's like a sauna in this place." She walked over to the window and undid the latch to push up the bottom pane. "So, you survived another weekend with your sister's four hundred kids!" She sat down behind her desk.

Daisy looked over. "They're kind of fun."

"If you say so. Did you and James get a break?"

"*Um*, not really." Daisy tried to sound positive. "He had to go home early – things are pretty tough in work right now."

"He's the boss, babes. If the company's struggling, he'll just do what he has to."

"He still has to answer to a board, Laura. And what do you think he'll be able to do?" Daisy frowned. "Because if he knew, I'd say he'd be doing it already."

Laura shrugged. "If it comes down to it, other employees will be given the push."

Daisy shifted uncomfortably in her chair. Was she implying that James would fire people so he could hang on to his job? Laura rarely mentioned James but, sometimes, she noticed, she could be quite dismissive of him. It was strange, she thought. Laura didn't know James that well, and he'd certainly never done anything to hurt her. Better to change the subject.

"Mum was asking after you at lunch yesterday."

Laura visibly brightened. "How is she? I love your mum!"

"Yeah, she's great." Daisy sighed. "Until that second glass of homemade wine, when she'll start lecturing you about the perils of early menopause and the wisdom of freezing your eggs."

Laura shot her a slightly odd look, and Daisy wondered if she'd overshared. Probably! It was one of the downsides of having parents who overshared – sometimes it was a bit hard to establish boundaries. She cleared her throat, and added hurriedly, "They're planning this massive anniversary party in early June for their fortieth wedding anniversary. Rosie has already started planning it. The woman loves a project!"

"Good for them," Laura said vaguely, peering towards the door.

"What about you? How was your weekend?"

Laura sighed. "I saw my own mum. She asked if I wanted to go out for lunch with her on Sunday."

"*Um*, just you, or ...?" Daisy had always got the feeling that Laura's mother wasn't Brian's biggest fan, but what mother invited her daughter to lunch on Sunday without inviting her son-in-law? Although even Laura had a tricky relationship with her, Daisy knew.

"Just the two of us," Laura said. "It was her birthday, so we went out to her favourite French restaurant." She glanced towards the door again. "Where's Fionn? I was going to ask him to get me a decaf."

"He's at the dentist. I'll get the coffees."

Daisy stood. Laura yawned.

"Are you sure you wouldn't be better off with the real thing?" Daisy said.

Laura shook her head. "I've started to train for the marathon. So I'm changing my diet a bit, and cutting out caffeine."

Daisy stared at her. "You're running a marathon? Like, the big one? That's twenty-six miles!"

"I know how long it is." Laura smoothed back her hair. "Brian's been training since last year, and he asked me to do it with him. Anyway, I've been doing the park run for ages. I'll be ready."

"Okay." Daisy frowned. "I'd no idea."

Laura shrugged. "Sorry I didn't mention it."

"No, no – I'm just a bit surprised." That was definitely the sort of thing you mentioned to a friend, Daisy thought, trying not to feel annoyed.

She was coming back with the coffees when she bumped into Fionn.

"Hey, Fionn, I can get you one of these if you like."

He put a hand over one side of his mouth and shook his head.

Daisy grinned. "Okay, maybe let the anaesthetic wear off first."

They walked up the double flight of stairs to the office, just as Laura was coming out of the bathroom, her eyes noticeably puffy.

Daisy said nothing as she placed the decaf on Laura's desk.

"So, a bit of news," Laura said, sitting back down. "I've been asked to do a job for a friend of mine – Stephanie."

Daisy looked up. "Have I met her?"

"Nope. She used to do the park run – it's how we met. Unfortunately, she's now expecting triplets, so her life is about to come to an end. And I've got to pull off some miracle on their teensy budget. To be honest, I don't know why they're even hiring me."

"Why are they?" Daisy noticed Laura's expression. "No, I get it that you guys are friends but, if they're that stuck for money, why aren't they saving it for baby stuff?"

"Because her parents are giving her the money, with the promise that she uses it on the house." Laura raised an eyebrow. "They also seem to think that we work for the love of it and don't actually need to be paid properly.'

"They've probably already had so much expense," Daisy mused.

Laura stabbed at her keyboard and glared at something on the screen. "Who? Her parents?"

"No, your friends. Having triplets is usually down to IVF."

"*Hmm.*" Laura swore quietly at the screen. "*Bloody thing!*"

Daisy bit her lip. Laura was frustrated by the projects she'd worked on in the last while. None of them had given her the sort of scope she'd had with Freya's place, and now with Granary House.

"You do the Clontarf park run, don't you, Laura?" Fionn asked.

Laura tutted. "How are we still talking about this?"

Fionn looked confused. "*Uh*, were we?"

"Never mind." Laura sighed. "Yes, I do. Why?"

"My auntie and cousin do it – Mam said they started about a month ago. You probably know them."

"Fionn, have you any idea how many people turn up for the park runs?" Laura spoke with exaggerated patience. "Hundreds! How would I know them?"

"They both have shaved heads, so they're pretty easy to spot."

"Why are their heads shaved?" Laura looked a bit bewildered.

Fionn shrugged. "My auntie's going through chemo, and my cousin shaved her head in solidarity."

"Oh, sorry." Laura nodded. "Nice gesture. But I don't know them." She turned to Daisy. "Speaking of which, how's Kenny doing? You know, since his wife …"

Daisy suppressed a sigh at the mention of Kenny's wife, whom he'd lost to cancer. She glanced at Fionn who had dropped his gaze. Laura could be a bit thoughtless sometimes.

"I forgot you haven't been working with him in a while," she said. "He's grand. I think he just likes keeping busy. *Em*, Fionn, you know that Kayley Lynch is kicking off her Irish tour at Granary House on the first of June? If you like, I can ask if you can meet her."

He brightened. "This is why I love working here!"

"Hey, does anyone feel like drinks on Friday after work?" Laura said. "Fionn?"

"Sorry. One of my housemates is throwing a welcome party for the new people, and I have to go."

"That sounds brutal," Laura said. "Daisy?"

"*Uh*, can't do this Friday." She spent a few minutes searching for her pencil, before remembering she'd stuck it through her hair above her ponytail.

"What about the following one?" Laura said. "Fionn, that suit you?"

"*Arrgh*, I can't." Fionn pulled a face. "I'm going to a twenty-first back home in Cork."

"Don't worry about it." Laura turned to Daisy. "If it's just the two of us, we could probably invite the lads."

"You mean James and Brian?" God, James barely wanted to visit her family. She couldn't imagine him wanting to go drinking with Laura and Brian.

"Come on, Daisy," Laura said. "It's been ages since we've all been out together!"

For excellent reasons, Daisy thought. Still, Laura seemed so enthusiastic, and they hardly ever socialised outside the office anymore. "Sure, yeah." Now all she had to do was to persuade James.

Laura flashed her a smile. "It'll be like old times."

CHAPTER 13

MyStarScope Taurus: Life is like a buffet right now. Dive in.

Daisy arrived at Matt's house shortly after nine and took a few moments to compose herself. She wasn't sure what was making her more nervous right now: beginning a huge project like Granary House, or the thought of being around Matt again.

She'd taken extra care with her outfit, and had got an early hair appointment, so that her normally wild tresses now lay in soft waves around her face.

Matt answered the door in jeans and a T-shirt. "Come in." He smiled. "You're right on time. I was just about to have breakfast. I made pancakes."

They'd been his party piece – her favourite had been the wafer-thin ones with Nutella.

"I've made a stack of them. And I've sugar and lemon, or Nutella, if you prefer."

So he'd remembered! *So what, Daisy? It's chocolate spread – loads of people like the stuff!* She hoped this wasn't the buffet her horoscope had predicted.

"Actually, I'll just have a coffee."

"They'll go to waste if you don't help – " Matt stopped as the doorbell rang. "That might be your workmen."

"Probably."

He left to answer the door.

Daisy sighed. The last thing she needed were constant reminders of what she and Matt used to love to do, or the food they loved to eat together. She owed it to herself to remember *exactly* how it had been with Matt – not just the good stuff. Because, obviously, there had been bad stuff too. She couldn't think of any right now apart from how things had ended, but it was bound to come back to her.

Daisy heard Kenny's familiar gravelly voice in the hall. She was helping herself to a coffee as they came into the kitchen.

"I'll have one of those too, if it's going." Kenny pulled his small, black beanie down over his head, and scratched at his chin.

Daisy poured another cup. "Splash of milk and two sugars, right?"

"Yup. I've two lads coming this morning, but I can make a start. I've had a look at your plans." He took the mug from her and turned to Matt. "Are you thinking of reopening this place as a B&B?"

"God, no!" Matt laughed.

"Well, you can always change your mind. Now, I've ordered a big support beam so we can knock through this wall into the conservatory. Are we keeping the glass roof?"

Daisy nodded.

"We'll mind it, so." Kenny looked around. "We can start stripping out the old units. I'll leave everything outside until the skip arrives."

Matt ran a hand across the back of his neck. "I'll take some breakfast into the guest wing, Daisy. Call me if you need me."

"What's his story?" Kenny said, after Matt left.

Daisy spoke carefully, conscious of not wanting to give away anything personal. "He was living in the States, and he came back and bought this place."

"Has he a partner or family joining him?"

"*Er*, no."

Kenny scratched his head. "Beats me why he'd want to buy this huge old place and live here by himself, but I'm happy to take his money. How are your mam and dad doing? You been home to see them recently?"

"Yeah, last weekend. And the one before." Daisy smiled. Kenny's wife had known her parents' nearest neighbours in Oranmore, which was how he'd been recommended to her. "Dad's just built a new coop for their chickens, and Mum –" she stopped, remembering the nude self-portrait, "is, *er*, still painting."

"Oh, I found these, wait till I show you now." Kenny took out his phone, and turned the screen so she could scroll through a dozen black-and-white landscape photos. "I transferred them to my phone – they were the last ones herself took."

"They're beautiful, Kenny." He rarely spoke about his late wife, so on the rare occasion he shared something Daisy gave him her full attention.

"They are." Kenny nodded vigorously, but looked relieved when the doorbell rang again.

"That's probably the fellah who'll be stripping all this out with me this morning."

He left to answer the door, and returned with a solidly built man in his mid-twenties, who sported a man-bun and a tattoo that curved up around his neck.

The newcomer looked Daisy up and down, and gave a broad grin. "Heyya, love. Nice place!"

Kenny shot him a glare. "Alec, this is Daisy Devlin, the interior architect for this job."

Alec seemed even more amused. "Interior architect? Fair fucks." He turned to Kenny. "Where do I start?"

"We're starting with those old kitchen cabinets. Don't touch the Aga or the table."

From the hall came the sound of a woman's voice, and then Matt's laughter.

Kenny tugged on his beanie. "Sounds like the new electrician's here. She'll be looking over the place, although we probably won't need her just yet."

Matt came back into the kitchen with a young woman with dyed-black, curly hair. She sported a variety of piercings, black eye make-up and black lipstick, which lent her a distinctly gothic look. She looked about seventeen, Daisy thought, a bit nervously.

"Hey, Kenny!" The young woman nodded to the others.

"Niamh, this is Daisy Devlin, the interior architect," Kenny said.

Daisy smiled warmly at her.

Niamh returned her smile and flicked an interested look at Alec. "Who are you?"

"Alec is one of my carpenters," Kenny said.

Alec gave a snort of laughter. "I suddenly feel very old."

Niamh gave him a hard stare, before turning back to Kenny. "I'm gonna see how much basic work I'll have to do, but I'm guessing you've got plans, yeah?"

He gave a brief nod. "Go ahead."

"I can show you around," Matt offered.

Niamh beamed up at him. "Lead the way."

"Will you be around for a while, Daisy?" Kenny said after they'd left, and Alec had started stripping out the kitchen units.

She nodded. "I've measurements to take, and I want to get some orders in. Listen, there's been a bit of a complication – Matt's signed a deal with a music promoter to put on a series of summer concerts in the grounds. They'll kick off at the start of June, so I've landscapers starting their work in a few days. It shouldn't interfere with your work, though."

Kenny ran a hand across his stubble beard. "You hoping we all get finished by then?"

"Do you think you can?" Daisy raised an eyebrow.

He looked around. "Nothing like a challenge."

"I thought I'd take refuge up here for a while – there's a lot going on downstairs." Matt appeared at the door of the master bedroom as Daisy was taking measurements down the centre of the room.

"Oh, hi. All good?" She straightened up.

Matt pulled a face. "Niamh and Alec seem to be having some sort of disagreement about something, so I thought I'd stay out of the way."

"What?" She rolled her eyes. "Kenny's around, he'll sort them if he needs to. Alec is new to the crew. Sometimes guys have a hard time working with women."

He nodded and walked over to the window.

She let her gaze wander to the single photo in the room, displayed on the marble mantelpiece above the large Georgian fireplace.

It was of Matt with a young woman in ski jackets and goggles, posing in front of a snow-covered mountain. The woman was smiling, her hand up as if to pull back the long blonde hair that was being blown across her face, partially obscuring it from the camera.

"I noticed that photo earlier." Daisy folded her arms. "She's pretty."

"An ex-girlfriend." Matt smiled and ran a hand across the back of his neck. "I know what you're thinking: it's weird that I have photos of my ex on display. But I like that picture, and it would be weirder to cut her out. Anyway, I've found if you try to shove the past away, it has a habit of catching up with you."

He looked at her longer than necessary, and Daisy slid a hand self-consciously over the pulse at her neck.

"Right. *Uh*, so ..." She looked around the room. "Yes, I'd like to put a statement half-wall right here, with a walk-in wardrobe behind it." She paused as a loud crash reverberated through the house. "Sounds like the last of your kitchen."

"No going back now." He grinned. "Although I'm finding it hard to visualise the end result."

She laughed. "You mean you didn't do 'modern rustic' or the pared-back 'Georgian elegance with maximalist accent module' when you were in college?"

He grinned. "It was clearly a failing of my IT course."

"I finished a house last year," she said, thinking. "It's quirky, all different-height ceilings and hidden rooms. But I used a lot of maximalist accents in the redesign, and I'm pretty sure the owners wouldn't mind giving you a tour."

"And you'd come with me?"

"Of course."

This would be no different to anything she'd done for previous clients. "I'll arrange for us to see it. *Um*, before I forget, do you know what time of the day you were born?" She opened the notes file on her phone.

"What?" He looked amused. "Why?"

"It's a feng-shui thing." She hoped she sounded convincing.

"I've no idea. All I know is that I was eight days late. Mam never let me forget."

"That'll help." She put it in her phone.

"Is that stuff actually useful?" He was smiling at her.

She beamed. "Invaluable."

CHAPTER 14

"You know, I feel like we haven't been out on our own in ages." Daisy took James' hand across the table in their local Indian restaurant that Friday evening.

At eight o'clock, the place was buzzing, and pungent aromas wafted around the small room.

James pushed his other hand back through his hair. It could do with a cut, she thought. Not that she'd tell him that. She wasn't his mother. Or Rosie!

"Well, we were just down in Galway together." He looked a bit puzzled.

Which definitely didn't count, she thought, suppressing a sigh. They fell silent for a few minutes as they studied the menu. Daisy took a deep, slow breath. Maybe she could still get them back on track – it felt so long since they'd really been *together* together.

And, if things went well, she could casually mention that she was working for Matt. It was only a big deal because she was hiding it. Plus, maybe telling James that Matt was back would ... what? Give them something to talk about? Bring them closer together? It could start a row!

"Daisy?" James was looking closely at her. "Are you okay, love?"

"*Hmm?* Fine, yeah." She smiled brightly.

"Have you decided what you want?"

"*Um ...*" She made a quick decision. "Vegetarian Saag."

He nodded, casting one last quick glance at the menu. "I'll get extra rice and naan bread. And we should order more beers while we can. The service tends to be a bit slow here."

Daisy made a mental note not to eat too much. If this was the buffet mentioned in her horoscope, the predictions had become disappointingly pedantic!

After they ordered, Daisy picked up her beer. "Cheers!"

James clinked his glass against hers.

"So." She sat up straighter. "We're celebrating."

"A work thing?"

"I wish!" She shook her head. "*Our* two-year anniversary of us getting the keys of our house."

"Wow, is it?" He smiled. "Look, I know you'd have liked something bigger, Daisy, but Rathmines is close to everything. You can't compare it with the huge houses your parents or mine live in – they're out in the middle of nowhere."

James' parents lived in Howth! Which was hardly the middle of nowhere, but she wouldn't point that out. "James, I completely agree!" She could never understand why he always got so defensive about their home. The only possible explanation was that he privately regretted turning down his parents' offers of help. Either way, she couldn't mention that Matt was now the proud owner of a five-bedroom historical home in Wicklow. "So, *um*, how *are* your mum and dad?"

James shrugged. "Fine. Mum says they've painters in again. It's like they don't know what to do with their money."

She'd better say nothing.

James moved the cutlery slightly on the table. "How's everyone in the office?"

Daisy relaxed slightly. "Laura's training for the marathon!"

"Laura?" He looked surprised. "She never struck me as the type."

She laughed. "You hardly know her, James!"

It was true! By the time she and James had got together, Laura and Brian were already married. The four of them had gone out together a few times, but James and Laura had always seemed careful around each other. Daisy knew that James had been trying to make a good impression, but that Laura had thought they wouldn't last. To add to the pressure, James had quickly made it clear to Daisy that he didn't like Brian.

She smoothed her dress over her stomach. "Maybe I should take up running. I don't think the cycling is enough."

She waited for James to tell her she was getting plenty of exercise, but he just nodded vaguely. Great, he obviously agreed with Rosie that she was overweight! Maybe that was why sex had been a bit … robotic between them recently. She'd been chalking it up to stress on James' part but, if she were being completely honest, it had felt like they were both simply going through the motions. There *had* been a couple of times he hadn't even been able to … Daisy took a deep breath. She wouldn't think about that tonight.

Their food arrived, and they spent a while piling their plates with sauces and extra rice.

"This looks great." James forked some curry into his mouth. "You should try some!"

Was sauce-covered curry more fattening than Vegetarian Saag, Daisy wondered vaguely. She dutifully scooped a small amount off the edge of his plate.

"So, how are Mike and Ciara?" she asked. They'd both been in college with James, and had helped set up TakeOff.

James drank some beer. "Both working as hard as I am."

Daisy waited.

"I'm not sure what you want me to say," James added. "They don't have the same responsibilities I have." He rolled his shoulders. "Can we talk about something else?"

He turned his attention back to his food, and Daisy sighed. She'd lay bets there were secret agents who talked more about their work.

She watched James eat for a few moments. He was good-looking, she mused – tall and slim, but with decent shoulders, even though the nearest he came to exercise was when his video game persona was being chased. She was pretty sure she was still attracted to him. She just wasn't sure there was an *actual spark* anymore.

Which had to mean he wasn't attracted to her, because she was pretty sure it took two people to spark. But if she were honest, she felt invisible around him sometimes.

Matt, on the other hand, seemed acutely aware of her. The truth was, he *wasn't* like any other client. No other client knew how she took her coffee, or what her favourite food was. No other client looked at her the way Matt did. At times, it felt a bit like she'd found her way back to the path she'd stepped off five years ago.

Which was confusing, and completely unfair to James, who ... Daisy blinked ... who was now frowning at his phone.

"What's wrong?"

James shook his head. "Mike's messaging about something."

"At this hour?"

"Yeah, well, there's a lot going on right now."

"Do you want to talk about it?"

He shook his head. "I'm sorry, I can't."

He should just change his last name to Bond, she thought. "So, are we going to go to Daniel's fortieth birthday party in July?"

James sighed. "I'm not thinking about that, it's ages away."

"It'll be a bit of craic, James. And, like, he's your brother – it'd be wrong not to go."

"We're not like your family, Daisy. We're just not that close." James tore off some naan bread and started to chew.

"So think of it as a fun weekend in London. We can plan some stuff, see a show. We haven't been away in forever and we can definitely afford –"

"Daisy, please!" James said. "Sorry, look, can we talk about it nearer the time?"

"Absolutely. No worries." She tried not to look disappointed. Why had she even bothered? It would be exactly the same then. She wished he'd make more of an effort with his family – he couldn't be happy with the way things were.

Or maybe she was completely self-deluded, and James was simply unhappy with *her*.

"James, we're okay, aren't we?" She looked at him.

"Yeah, we're okay." When Daisy said nothing, he sighed. "I just can't play happy families at the moment. I'm sorry, I don't expect it to make sense.

Daisy felt a familiar twinge of panic. Was he talking about his own family – or the two of them? Now she thought about it, he had never hinted that he wanted more from their relationship. She had always been reluctant to talk about their future, terrified that they might discover they wanted totally separate things. It didn't matter that they'd been together for five years, or that they owned a house – they'd never sat down to discuss what they actually wanted. Instead, they'd sort of drifted along, and she'd just assumed they'd wanted the same thing. She'd heard of people who'd been together for twice as long as them, but as soon as one person had The Talk, the other person broke it off. What if James wasn't in this for the long haul?

And what if *not* asking meant she was about to miss another sign, experience another sliding-door moment in her life?

Or was she overthinking everything? Here they were, enjoying an evening out. Tonight wasn't about deep, philosophical questions or puzzling over signs and sliding-door moments. It was about the two of them being together and having fun.

She tried to think. Sex: it would be the perfect end to the night. Because when it was good between them, it was actually pretty good. Surreptitiously, she checked there were no bits of spinach stuck between her teeth before flashing James what she hoped was a seductive smile. "I think I have a fairly good idea what you'd like to do when we get home!"

James looked at her gratefully. "Really?" He ran a hand through his hair. "Is it okay if we leave now?"

"Totally okay." She felt a little zing of happiness, as he motioned for the bill.

As they left the restaurant, she said: "Is it bad to hope Alma is out for the night?"

James laughed. "I don't know why you're worried about Alma being there. It won't matter. I never even *hear* her when I'm in the office – she's actually pretty thoughtful."

"In your office?"

"Yeah, in my office. Where I work." He looked at her. "Are you sure you're okay, Daisy? Because you're acting a bit … off."

"Yeah, no, all good." Daisy cleared her throat. He was going home to *work*? *That's* what he'd assumed she was talking about? He flashed her a quick smile, but she thought she heard him suppress a sigh.

CHAPTER 15

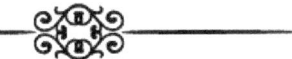

MyStarScope Taurus: You are going through a transitionary period, but today is a good day to find the balance between the life you lead alone and your partnership with someone close.

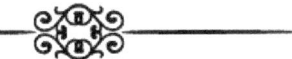

"So, you get why I wanted you to see Claire's house?"

Daisy and Matt were sitting at a small table in a café in Sutton the following week, after Daisy's former client had given them both a tour of her redesigned late-nineteenth-century home.

Claire had hugged Daisy tight as they'd taken their leave.

"I know that award is a big deal in your business, Daisy, and I'm not dismissing it. But look at the bigger picture: you give people the homes of their dreams. What's more important?"

Now Daisy dunked a small almond biscuit into her coffee and waited to hear what Matt thought.

"It was good to see it," he said. "There isn't a single straight wall in that place!"

Daisy laughed. "Yeah, it's always an extra challenge. But it lends character."

Matt leaned back in his chair. "I have to admit, it feels different now I have skin in the game. Not that I didn't enjoy seeing all those showhouses you used to drag me to on a Saturday morning."

"You must have hated it." Daisy felt herself blush.

"No, it was fun pretending to be interested buyers." He raised an eyebrow.

Daisy glanced away and concentrated on blowing needlessly across her coffee. How could she forget? Every time she allowed herself to think about those five years of her life, she'd remember how she'd imagined their future unfolding.

"I'll bet your own house is stunning," Matt said.

Daisy latched on to the change of subject. "I like it, but it's bijou, which is such a great word for tiny, right? I mean, I'd love more space. Who wouldn't?" She stopped, shrugging away the rest of her thoughts. She and James had saved so hard to buy their home – it felt like a betrayal to talk about it with Matt.

She just wished she wasn't so annoyed with James right now. After they'd got home the previous night, he'd gone straight to his office. She had gone to bed just after ten, but had woken around midnight to hear James and Alma talking quietly outside the bedroom door. She hadn't been able to make out what they'd been talking about but, after James had slipped quietly into bed, it had been easier to pretend to be asleep.

"You always had a thing for old houses," Matt said. "You even liked that dilapidated old redbrick I lived in during college."

A sudden memory of a big, unmade bed pulled into the middle of a high-ceilinged bedroom flashed into her mind. If she closed her eyes, she could still see those draughty, single-glazed windows, stained, uneven floorboards and boarded-up fireplaces.

God, it was way too warm in here! Maybe she could ask them to leave the door open for a while.

"So, what happens after the house is finished?" she asked. "Have you made any other plans?"

"Not really." Matt gave a lazy smile, and Daisy's eyes followed his fingers as they snagged in the curls at his neck. "More hopes, I suppose."

Was she really sitting here after five years listening to Matt Deveraux discuss his dreams for the future? It was completely surreal.

"I want to meet someone, Daisy. I want to have a family, fill that big house if I can."

As he held her eyes, she felt her skin prickle with warmth.

Had she been right? Had he come back home to see her?

"So, *um*, apart from me and Brian, have you seen anyone else since you got back?"

She half-expected him to deflect the question.

"I went down to see the folks." Matt leaned back in his chair. "They still live in Kilkenny, although Dad's semi-retired. I saw Charlie too."

Daisy tried not to look surprised at the mention of Charlie, given how reluctant he'd been to discuss him before.

"He's running the family pub now."

"Really?" Daisy tried to remember. "Wasn't he working for one of the big stockbrokers? You two had planned to go into business together."

Matt's lips thinned. "That was the plan."

Except Matt had gone to the States. So he'd let his brother down too: maybe that was why they'd fallen out. Matt had never admitted to it, but Daisy had the feeling that was what had happened. She took a breath. "Do you ever regret going to the States? Deciding to stay there?"

He gave her a long look. "I did what I thought was best. What about you, Daisy? If we could go back, would you do things differently?"

"Why do you ask?" Was this it, she wondered. Was this his roundabout way of telling her he regretted what he'd done, how he'd treated her? She braced herself for a confession, an explanation, but he simply shrugged.

"No reason. You got everything you wanted, right?"

Daisy bit back a snappy retort. It was partly her fault – she didn't have the courage to ask him straight out why he'd left. She wondered how long they'd continue to dance around each other.

"I've been very lucky with the business." *Nothing like glossing things over.*

In the silence that followed, Daisy could feel the atmosphere sour slightly. She couldn't leave things like this.

"So how *is* Charlie?"

Matt gave a harsh laugh. "Married, three kids, bought himself a nice little place on the outskirts of Kilkenny city. Charlie always landed on his feet."

The idea that his brother had decided on a complete career change because Matt had decided to stay in the States didn't add up. She had a strong feeling that Matt was holding something back. But now wasn't the time.

And, if she were being honest with herself, she felt rattled by the thought that Matt had recognised some sliding-doors moment in their past too.

She was the first to break eye contact. "I'd better get to the office."

"Yeah, I need to get some work done too. Thanks for this morning, though, I enjoyed it."

"My pleasure." Daisy slid back into professional mode. "I'm glad you got to see a finished project." She was pretty sure Matt wasn't referring to Claire's house. But she was equally sure that neither of them was ready for a deep-dive discussion.

It should be so simple: Matt was her past, James was her present.

But since Matt's reappearance, her past and present felt like they were on some sort of collision course. And for the first time in five years, she'd no idea what her future looked like.

CHAPTER 16

Daisy got home early the following evening to get ready for drinks with Laura and Brian in Pink Gin, the new cocktail bar at Grand Canal Dock that Laura had suggested. Although it would have made more sense to go straight from work, she was half-afraid that James would either forget, or just not bother to show, if she'd arranged to meet him there.

Slipping out of her shoes, she ignored the sounds of the TV from the sitting room, and headed to the kitchen to make tea and toast. With a mug of tea in her hands, she went into the sitting room, and stopped to stare at the little scene in front of her.

Alma was sitting cross legged on the sofa, singing in Swedish, while James was sitting beside her, picking out the guitar chords like they were practising for bloody Eurovision!

Daisy felt a bit sick. James used to play guitar all the time. They'd first met at a party, where he'd been making his way through his full repertoire of Ed Sheeran songs, including her favourite, 'Lego House', and she'd sung along, not caring that she was a terrible singer.

Now, she couldn't remember the last time he'd even taken the guitar out of its case! But here he was, accompanying their bloody lodger. Who, admittedly, had a very sweet voice. Except that wasn't the point.

"James?"

The two of them stopped and looked around.

"Oh, hey, love, I didn't hear you come in." James ran a hand through his hair. "Are you home long?"

"Just in." Daisy's gaze slid to Alma. Was it her imagination or did she actually seem annoyed at the interruption? She found her hard to read sometimes.

"What are you guys up to?" She tried to smile, but her face was hurting.

Alma gave her a puzzled look, and Daisy suddenly wished the toaster would explode, so she'd have an excuse to leave quickly.

James cleared his throat. "Alma asked if I still played." He shot the other woman a sheepish smile. "I'm completely out of practice, but Alma's got an unbelievable voice, right?"

Daisy reminded herself quickly that she'd caught them in a duet – not in a tangle of naked bodies. "Yeah, I agree, unbelievable. So, *uh*, do you want some tea and toast before we go out?"

"We're going out?" James frowned.

Daisy took such a deep breath she felt momentarily lightheaded.

"For drinks with Laura and Brian? I thought that was why you were home early too."

There was a brief silence. If James tried to wriggle out of this, she was going to stab him with a butter knife.

He sighed and stood his guitar against the wall. "Sorry, it slipped my mind." He shrugged apologetically at Alma, who actually seemed to be sulking now. "I'll go change."

He was buttoning up a clean shirt when Daisy came into the bedroom shortly after.

"How come you agreed to go out with them?" He caught her eye in the mirror. "Brian does my head in."

Daisy stepped up behind him, leaning into his back and wrapping her arms briefly around his waist. She felt him sigh, and then he closed his hands around hers.

"Me too," she said. "But Laura asked us. It'll be good for us to get out with friends. I mean, you don't actually want to spend the whole evening hanging out with Alma, do you?"

The moment the words were out of her mouth, she wished she could take them back. She sounded like a total bitch! A paranoid bitch! Except what if she was right? What if it was a sign?

James turned, his face flushed. "Hanging out with Alma?" He shook his head. "Will you listen to yourself? She lives here too. Would you prefer if I just ignored her?"

Shit, this wasn't the right start to the evening!

"Of course I don't want you to ignore her! Look, tonight should be a bit of craic." Daisy smiled brightly. "I'll be ready in five minutes."

James gave a small shake of his head. "I'll wait for you downstairs."

After he left, Daisy plopped down on the bed. Things would get better, she thought. Maybe after Alma finally went back home. And when James figured out things at work. Meanwhile, tonight was exactly what they needed.

＊＊＊＊＊

She should never have agreed to drinks this evening, Daisy decided a while later. The bar was too busy, and every single person in the place was too loud and happy. And, for the first time *ever*, she felt wrong in her favourite 1950s-style red-and-white polka-dot dress. She also decided that her feelings had nothing to do with her clothes and everything to do with Alma!

"So, how's life with Jimmy and Daisy-flower?" Brian winked at Daisy.

She pinned on a smile and slowly counted to ten. She wished Laura had never told Brian about her parents' pet names for her and Rosie. Her mother was right. The guy was a twat.

James muttered something and got up from the table.

Laura frowned as she watched him leave. "Is he okay?"

"Sure. Gone to the loos, I guess."

Daisy kept her voice light, hoping he hadn't just decided to leave. Not that she'd blame him – although she might have to kill him. "So, how did you two come across this place?"

"Came here with some of the work gang a few weeks' ago." Brian picked up his Jack and Coke. "Jesus, the craic we had that night!"

So it was Brian's recommendation, not Laura's. Brilliant! Daisy let her attention wander around, hoping to spot James, but stopped as another familiar face hove into view. *Was that Matt?* It looked like him. He seemed to be with a group, some of whom she vaguely recognised from their college days. What were the chances that he was here in the same place, on the same night, as her and James?

Her eyes slid sharply back to Brian. Had he somehow engineered this? Matt might have mentioned he was meeting up with friends – maybe he'd even asked Brian to join them. It couldn't be a coincidence! She jumped a bit guiltily as James came back and sat down.

"What?" He frowned at Daisy.

"*Hmm?* What?" Daisy smiled and did her best not to let her gaze slide back over to Matt.

"So." Brian pointed his finger at James. "I hear you're still sharing your place with that student, Allie or Millie, or something. Didn't I see you guys hanging out the other day in town?"

"I doubt it," James said tightly.

"Yeah, it was definitely you." Brian flicked Daisy a look. "Short, blonde hair, right? The two of you were in Bewleys."

Daisy found herself digging her nails into the fleshy part of her hand, her smile frozen in place as James seemed to think.

"Oh, right, yeah, I bumped into her in town. She was coming from college, and we had a coffee together."

He threw back some of his drink, and Daisy got the feeling that he was deliberately avoiding looking at her.

"Why didn't you come over and say hello?" he said to Brian.

Brian shrugged. "I had a meeting, so I didn't really have time. Anyway, didn't want to interrupt."

"God, Brian!" Laura gave an embarrassed laugh.

James' jaw tightened. "Why would you be interrupting?"

"No reason." Brian grinned. "Can't imagine what it's like having someone live with you like that. I mean, your place is so small. Does she bring back friends? Boyfriends?"

"She prefers to go out to socialise." James' tone was even. "Daisy and I both respect her private life."

In the silence that followed, Daisy pointed to her empty glass. "I'm going to get another one of these. Laura, what are you having?"

"I'll come with you." Laura slipped off her chair. "Same for you, lads?"

Daisy caught James' expression as they turned to head to the bar, but for once she didn't care. She was furious with him for not telling her that he'd had coffee with Alma in town, especially as she'd been caught off-guard in front of Laura and Brian. And she completely dismissed the little voice in her head reminding her that she was being a total hypocrite.

Instead, she turned her feelings of anger towards Brian. It was bad enough that he'd brought up Alma, but it was unbelievable that he'd made that stupid remark about the size of their house, given the fact that he and Laura were renting!

"Hey, watch where you're going!" A woman with an armful of drinks glared at her.

Daisy muttered her apologies, before slightly changing her route to the bar. She wished she hadn't told Laura that James had refused his parents' offer to help them buy a bigger place. It was clear that Laura had mentioned it to Brian – who seemed to love making James doubt himself. Which was strange, she thought, remembering what a risk-taker James had been when she'd first met him, how confident he'd been about everything.

At the bar, Laura turned to her. "Let me get these."

"Okay, thanks." Daisy glanced surreptitiously around the room again, but there was no sign of Matt. Somebody elbowed her in the ribs as they jostled for a space at the bar, and she tapped Laura's shoulder. "Back in a few."

Without waiting for a reply, she weaved her way back through the bar and took sanctuary for a few minutes in the ladies', washing her hands and touching up her make-up. As she came back out, her head smacked into the chest of a man going into the adjacent loos.

"Sorry!" She got her balance, and found herself looking up into very familiar, dark-blue eyes. "Matt!"

"If this was a film, that'd be our cute meet," he said, smiling, and Daisy found herself laughing.

"Who are you here with?" she asked.

"Ah, you know, some of the old college gang. You?"

"*Um*, James and Laura and Brian."

He nodded and looked around. "Bit different to the sort of places we used to go to, isn't it?"

"You mean those scruffy, student pubs?"

He looked at her. "I kind of miss them."

There was that little spark again. Suddenly, she wished that everything could be like it used to be, and they could just leave and catch a late film somewhere.

"Excuse us." Two women passed them on their way to the bathrooms. Both of them eyed up Matt, Daisy noticed.

"I'd better get back," she said. As she went to step away, she spotted James heading in their direction. "*Oh, shit!*"

"What?"

"James is coming over."

Matt lifted an eyebrow. "What's the problem?"

Daisy tried not to panic. She wasn't sure if James would even recognise Matt – they hadn't been in the same year in college – but she couldn't chance it.

"He doesn't know I'm working for you," she said quickly. Did she have time to dive back into the loos? No, there was a bit of a queue now, and she couldn't skip it. Any moment now, James would look up and see them.

Before she realised what he was doing, Matt pulled her around the corner out of James' line of sight and stepped in close, effectively blocking her from the others at the far end of the bar.

He bent towards her ear. "Just don't move for a few seconds."

Daisy could feel her heart thumping against Matt's chest as he was pressed closer to her. A door banged shut, and then Matt was stepping back and saying something.

"What?" She blinked up at him.

"I said he didn't see you. Or me."

"Right." She wet her lips, aware that her heart was racing. "You could have just walked away, Matt! That was pretty risky!"

"Was it?" He looked a bit sheepish. "Sorry, I didn't mean to make you uncomfortable. It was just the first thing that came to mind."

Daisy released a slow breath. Maybe she was overreacting. She'd panicked when she'd spotted James, and Matt had simply tried to help. For the sake of their professional relationship now, she'd let it go.

"I'd better get back."

"Yeah, me too." He rubbed a hand over the back of his neck. "See you soon?"

For a second she wasn't sure what he meant. "At the house!" She managed a nod. "Yes, right." Flashing him a tight smile, she stepped past him, and headed back across to their table.

Laura had already returned with the drinks – she must have done two trips, Daisy thought guiltily – and was sitting chatting quietly with Brian, their heads tipped intimately close. Daisy studied them for a few moments. From here, they seemed happy, in sync. Maybe she and James appeared that way too.

Laura spotted her, and sat up straighter.

"You okay, babes?" She frowned. "You look kind of flushed."

"Just a bit warm." Daisy sat back down, and took a sip of her drink, silently willing Laura not to draw any more attention to her. Why had she agreed to tonight? She loved Laura, but she *had* to know how much

Brian seemed to dislike her and James. Maybe she and James could just leave after this round? She imagined them walking home, breathing in the night air while they held hands and chatted.

Except what would they talk about? She couldn't bring up the subject of Alma again, or James would completely shut her down. The truth was, she was afraid if she pushed him too hard, she'd hear something she didn't want to. Saying nothing was just ... easier for now.

She noticed Brian looking at something behind her and she froze, wondering if he'd spotted Matt. But then James sat down beside her.

"Thanks for the drink." He picked up his beer and Daisy raised her glass.

"Cheers!"

"All right, James?" Brian said.

Daisy noticed that he gave Laura a tiny nudge and felt herself flash hot and cold. Had Brian and Laura spotted her and Matt together? Is that what they'd been talking about?

James smiled blandly at Brian, before turning to Laura. "So, are you entering that industry award this year?" he asked.

Laura pulled a face. "Probably not, I've nothing suitable."

"Laura's just starting a new project for a friend of hers who's about to have triplets," Daisy said, relieved that the conversation had moved on to something safe.

"Stephanie who used to live one floor down?" Brian said. "Aren't they pretty much broke?"

"That was how we met," Laura said quickly, "and we started doing the park run together. Anyway, their new place won't have the wow factor, not on their budget. But Daisy's job might."

Automatically, Daisy glanced over to where Matt had been, but he and his friends seemed to have moved on. She widened her eyes slightly at Laura, before realising that Brian probably already knew that she was working on Matt's house. Which meant he could out her at any moment.

Brian flicked her a sly look. "So what's this job with the *wow* factor?"

Daisy felt herself grow hot and cold, as she wondered how far he'd push it. "I've nearly finished a house in Ranelagh but I'm still trying to persuade the owners to let me use it."

He seemed to lose interest, and Daisy met Laura's eyes in a question across the table.

In answer, Laura gave an almost imperceptible shake of her head.

Daisy glanced away. Laura mustn't have told Brian. If he knew, she was certain he'd have brought it up. For the millionth time, she wondered what Laura saw in him. He hadn't always been like this, had he? He'd seemed all right when she'd been with Matt. Although maybe he'd made the effort with her for Matt's sake. Then again, who knew anything about someone else's relationship? She'd thought she'd had the perfect relationship with Matt. And until recently she'd thought she and James were pretty secure. The reality was that she didn't know anything anymore.

As she tried to tune in to something Laura had started chatting about, something else struck her. Matt was clearly in touch with Brian, which meant Matt hadn't mentioned her either. But it wasn't like they were doing anything wrong.

She sneaked a glance at James. If she wasn't doing anything wrong, why was she keeping it from him? She'd convinced herself of the reasons why, but explaining it might be a lot more difficult.

CHAPTER 17

MyStarScope Taurus: An old flame rekindles warm feelings – be careful you don't get burnt.

"Sorry I'm late." Daisy hurried into the office the following morning, and sat down at her desk to pull off her runners and slip on her pumps.

"Did you cycle in?" Laura wrinkled her nose as she glanced towards the window. "It's raining."

"No, I just couldn't find parking, so I had to walk for a couple of blocks." Daisy pulled her hair into a ponytail. "Alma's sick so I offered to do a few things for her this morning. I had to get her an appointment with our GP."

"What's wrong with her?" Fionn said.

Daisy sighed. "Bad sore throat. Probably all the bloody singing she does."

He looked thoughtful. "What star sign is she?"

"No idea. I don't think her birthday's until later in the year, though."

"*Hmm.*" Fionn chewed on his lip. "Throat infections are more of a Taurus thing."

"Which is me," Daisy muttered.

Laura shook her head. "You know, if your career as interior architect doesn't take off, Fionn, you could set yourself up as an alternative medical consultant. Diagnose people by their star signs!"

"Still, it could be strep," Fionn said, ignoring Laura. He swept his fringe across his forehead, and Daisy noticed his fingernails had been painted a deep blue, with tiny stars and moons stencilled on them.

"Fabulous nails," she said.

Fionn smiled. "Thank you. I remember my sister got strep during her Leaving Cert and spent the whole summer recovering." He seemed to notice Daisy's expression, because he added hurriedly, "But I'd say it was because she was stressing over exams, when she should have been resting."

Daisy took a breath. "God, I just hope it isn't that with Alma. I'd have to look after her."

"If you don't, James will have to," Laura murmured.

Daisy could feel her chest tightening, and she wondered if Laura had noticed James' weird reaction when Brian had mentioned Alma.

In spite of James' obvious early efforts to win Laura around, it seemed that even after five years Laura was still wary of him. What if Laura had been right? What if she was destined to go through life choosing the wrong men? What if –

"Laura, did you say anything to Brian about me working on Granary House?" Daisy tried to sound casual.

"No." Laura flicked her a sharp look. "That doesn't mean he doesn't know, or hasn't guessed, but he hasn't mentioned anything to me. Why?"

So he couldn't know. He'd definitely have said something! It was nuts! There was a time she'd quite liked Brian. Then again, there was a time when Laura had liked Matt. She'd told Daisy that she and Matt were a perfect match! But what did anyone know at that age? Daisy had thought the four of them would be friends forever. Then, after Matt had dumped her, Brian had turned on her too. It made her furious to think of it.

"You know that Brian and I don't spend all our time talking about you and Matt," Laura said.

Colour flashed to Daisy's face. "There is no me and Matt. Forget I said anything."

Laura folded her arms and leaned back in her chair. "You know the weirder thing, babes? That Matt hasn't mentioned you to Brian."

Which was exactly what she'd been thinking last night. "How do you know he hasn't?"

Laura looked closely at her. "I think Matt likes to have his secrets. He always did."

Laura was right. Matt was still keeping the biggest secret from her – the one she hadn't been able to stop thinking about all these years.

"Is he in touch with his brother?" Laura sounded thoughtful.

"Yeah, he's running the family bar in Kilkenny."

"Charlie? Wasn't he some hot shot accountant or broker, or something? He was certainly a lot smarter than Matt."

Daisy bristled. "Maybe Charlie just fancied a change in career. We don't really talk about personal stuff."

"Oh-kay." Laura arched an eyebrow, and Daisy glanced away.

She shouldn't have even mentioned Matt! Especially after running into him like that. Now that he knew she was keeping him a secret from James, she was nervous at the prospect of seeing him again. Which was crazy, because nothing had actually changed. At the same time, it felt like something significant had shifted.

Alma phoned her halfway through the morning. "The doctor says I have strep throat." Her voice was barely a whisper on the other end of the phone.

"Shit." Daisy sighed. "Did she give you an antibiotic?"

"Yes, but I have to take some time off college, so I'll eat in my room. It's quite contagious."

Daisy's phone extension rang and she motioned for Fionn to answer. "*Er*, thanks, Alma. Sorry, must go." She hung up and looked at Fionn. "It's strep. Looks like James and I will be doing room service."

He shot her a look of sympathy. "I've Matt Deveraux on the line for you."

Deep breath, Daisy. She nodded to Fionn and picked up the call, swivelling her chair towards the window.

"Hi, Matt." She cleared her throat, pressing the back of her hand against her warm cheek.

"Hi, Daisy." Matt sounded agitated. "Look, Kenny's run into a problem with the bathrooms. He's talking about completely rebuilding walls. Could you come and take a look?"

Daisy tried to sound reassuring. "You can't foresee everything that happens on a job, Matt. What's the problem?"

"When they took down the plasterboard, they found the wall had been filled with old underwear and socks!"

"You're joking!" Daisy started to laugh.

"Nope. Your guy has wedged some wood in instead. Look, I don't want to play hardball, but there's a bigger picture here and Kenny just isn't getting it. I told you Kayley Lynch is performing on the first of June? She and her film crew are coming two weeks before that to start filming her in Ireland. And they'll be using Granary House."

"I thought it was just the grounds, Matt."

"Her people want to use the house and gardens to film her composing and rehearsing. They want footage to show on screens during her Irish concerts, or future concerts or something."

"Matt, there's no way the place will be ready in two weeks."

"But the heavy work could, couldn't it?" Matt said. "Kayley's people will pay extra to make it happen."

Daisy hoped that was an understatement.

"We can give it a go." She opened her phone diary, scrolling through her plans for the day.

Most of it was phone calls or online orders. "I'll get out to you around lunch and have a chat with Kenny."

"I promise to feed you," Matt said.

Daisy could tell he was smiling. Even though she felt a bit manipulated, she found herself smiling in return.

"I'll see you then." She hung up and caught Laura's expression. "What?"

"Just wondering how high you can jump in those shoes."

Daisy told herself it was no different from anything she'd do for any other client. "Very cute."

CHAPTER 18

"It's my Knight in Shiny Buttons!" Matt flung open the front door and stepped back to let Daisy into the hall.

She beamed at him, wondering if she should mention that she'd knit the cropped green cardigan with tiny pearl buttons herself, but Matt was already striding away towards the kitchen.

There were two vans parked in the driveway, but the house was quiet.

"Where is everyone?" she asked, hurrying to catch up.

"The crew are on lunch break in the garden."

"Right. Listen, Matt, Kenny knows what he's doing." She hoped Kenny didn't think Matt was being a bit highhanded. Although in fairness to him, he tended to let most criticism roll off him. "It's not like the house would have fallen down."

He sighed. "I know, I'm sorry. To be honest, I'm half-regretting agreeing to let out the grounds. And now all this! What was I thinking?"

Idly, Daisy wondered when Matt found time to work – though being in a different time zone probably meant working odd hours. Which had to be tricky, even if nothing else was getting in the way.

"It's hard to say no to such a good deal." She folded her arms so she wouldn't be tempted to reach out and touch his arm like she used to when he'd been worried. Instead, she excused herself and stepped outside, closing the sliding door behind her.

Kenny, Alec and two other men were sitting at the patio table eating lunch rolls and drinking mugs of tea. She nodded as she met Alec's eye, and he nodded back, looking at her with interest over the rim of his mug.

"Howaya, Daisy." Kenny scraped back his chair, and stood, offering it to her. "Sit yourself down, I'll get another one."

Daisy sat, and waited until Kenny came back with a rather battered chair for himself, while the others shuffled around to make room for the extra chair.

Kenny gave Daisy a level look. "Yer man filled me in on this nonsense with the singer and the camera crew. Fucked if it makes any sense to me. One minute he's renting out the grounds for a load of summer gigs; the next some singer and her hangers-on are taking over the whole place to make a documentary. Sure, who agrees to that while they've got builders and decorators in? They'll be in our way."

"I hear you, Kenny. But I don't think Matt could turn down what they were offering. So given that he's our client, would it be possible to get all the heavy work done in the next two weeks?"

Kenny looked around at the others, who simply shrugged. They were all waiting for Kenny's decision. He rubbed his nose and sighed heavily.

"I reckon all those bathrooms were put in around the mid-1930s when this place became a guest house," he said finally.

Daisy nodded. "I agree."

"Which means a lot of the internal walls were just sand and rubble."

"Or in this case, underwear."

"None of them are load-bearing walls. But they *will* have to be rebuilt – they're coming apart."

Daisy nodded again.

"I told yer man that, but what would I know? I'm only the bloody foreman."

God, the last thing she needed was tension between Matt and Kenny. Especially with this new deadline.

"Don't take it personally, Kenny. Matt's always been a bit of a control freak."

Kenny's eyes narrowed, and Daisy realised her slip.

"*Um*, we went to college together." She caught Alec's eyes, and glanced quickly away, focussing on Kenny. "So, what do you think?"

Kenny folded his arms. "I'll have to hire more men."

Daisy nodded. "How many?"

"Three, probably."

"Do what you have to, Kenny. I'll make sure the budget allows it."

"He seems to think the budget is a piece of elastic," Kenny grumbled. When Daisy gave him a blank look, he sighed.

"He's gone and changed his mind about the bathrooms. Wants those smart toilets instead. You know, heated seats and built-in bidets. Makes no sense unless he's turning it back into a posh B&B, in my view. What's wrong with bog-standard loos?"

Daisy hid a grin, privately wondering exactly how deep Matt's pockets were. "What the customer wants, Kenny."

"Don't I know!" He got to his feet. "Right lads, you heard the woman: tea break over."

They trooped inside, past Matt, who Daisy could see had cooked and served up rashers and pancakes.

When they'd left, she sat down at the kitchen table and cut into a pancake with the side of her fork.

"Kenny will have to hire three more men to get all the heavy work done before Kayley Lynch arrives. Which means I'll have to charge you more, Matt. It won't be a stupid amount. I just need to know you're on board."

"Absolutely, thanks for sorting this."

He reached out, and rubbed his thumb lightly across the back of her hand.

Daisy swallowed hard on the pancake, as his touch sent tiny pleasure signals to the rest of her body, then jerked her hand away as the kitchen door opened and Kenny came back in.

"So, just to be clear: we're stripping away the tiles in all five bathrooms. And we'll rebuild whatever we need to."

Daisy nodded. "Go ahead, Kenny."

Kenny gave Matt a pointed look, and left again.

Daisy folded her arms. "I want to have a look at the bathrooms too but, honestly, it's nothing to worry about. I can check a few more things while I'm here, but after that I need to get back to the office."

"Sorry for dragging you out." Matt ran a hand through his hair.

"Don't apologise." *Not for that.*

"Listen, Daisy, I know things were ... complicated between us, but maybe we could have a fresh start?"

Did he mean as friends? She still wasn't sure what *she* wanted.

The doorbell rang, and Matt left to answer it.

Moments later, Daisy heard Niamh's voice in the hall, before the two of them came into the kitchen.

"Hi, Daisy." Niamh smiled at her as she dumped her work bag on the floor and shrugged out of a black leather jacket.

"Hey, great band." Matt pointed to Niamh's 'My Chemical Romance' T-shirt. "You have to help us eat some of this food, by the way – I've made way too much."

Niamh made a show of inspecting the table. "A coffee with one of those pancakes?" She flicked her dark curls back off her shoulders.

"Coming right up. Daisy, do you want a coffee?"

"*Um*, no thanks." Daisy couldn't help feeling relieved at the interruption. A part of her knew she was playing a dangerous game – but it was one she was willing to play.

CHAPTER 19

By eleven o'clock on Monday, Daisy had got an email from the landscapers to confirm they'd be ready to start on the Granary House grounds later that week.

James had spent the whole weekend working, emerging from his office to eat, before disappearing again for hours at a time. Daisy had even tried, unsuccessfully, to persuade him to come to the local food market on Sunday for a while.

It struck Daisy that apart from Laura she still didn't have many friends in Dublin. Part of the reason was because she'd met Matt so young, and they'd quickly formed a tight unit with Laura and Brian in college. The other reason was that her college class had been small – thirty students in all – and many of them had emigrated after graduation.

If Alma had been feeling better, Daisy would have gone down to Galway. Instead, she spent Saturday morning in town, picking up storage for Freya's house, and got home to find Alma dozing on the couch. After Alma woke up, she'd asked for chicken soup before taking herself off to bed, where Daisy had kept her fed and watered for the rest of the weekend.

Now, Daisy found herself struggling to focus on the day ahead. She looked over the long checklist she'd made for Freya's house. All the heavy work had been done, and its transformation from a dark, stuffy, old-fashioned house to a bright, practical family home, full of warmth and character, was almost complete. She knew she should be pleased, but she couldn't get past the uncomfortable feeling that she kept missing chances to fix her actual life.

She leaned back in her chair and met Fionn's eyes as he glanced up and flicked his fringe across his forehead.

"I've finished those 3D models. I'm sending them to you now," he said.

"Thanks, Fionn."

He hesitated. "Is there anything else I can do? You kinda look like you've something on your mind."

Either she had a ridiculously readable face, or Fionn was a mind-reader too.

"Actually, there is something." Could she really ask their student intern to do this? "If I give you somebody's details, could you do a horoscope?"

"Is this Matt Deveraux?"

A mind-reader definitely. He was on to her. "Eh, yes." Blushing, she scribbled down Matt's birth details. "It's a feng-shui thing."

"Absolutely. I'm on it," he said, straight-faced.

"Right, thanks. *Em*, one more thing, Fionn? Don't mention it to Laura."

"My lips are sealed."

"Speaking of Laura, did she call?"

"*Uh*, no. Maybe she's on site somewhere?"

Daisy tried to think. Laura *had* mentioned she was being consulted on a new build, but she was pretty sure she hadn't planned to view the house for another week. She suppressed a sigh. Deep down, she knew she wasn't frustrated with Laura, Freya or even Alma! It was James. And Matt. Not to mention that work on Granary House was now being rushed.

Laura eventually arrived in, dumping a Louis Vuitton satchel and a bottle of Evian water on her desk.

"Right, what earth-shattering events did I miss?" She eased herself gingerly into her chair.

Daisy wondered if she was overdoing things. She hadn't been training as long as Brian and, knowing Laura, she was trying to catch up.

"A guy called Ted Fields rang and left a message about a fountain," Fionn said. "The one for the courtyard. He said you'd know."

"Go on." Laura unscrewed the lid of her water and took a careful sip. When Fionn hesitated, she added, "Out with it, Fionn! I'm not going to bite your head off."

"He said it was delivered this morning and he wants you to arrange to have it taken back because it's not big enough."

Laura closed her eyes for a minute, and Fionn exchanged a quick look with Daisy.

"Screw him. If he calls again, Fionn, tell him I'm out on site and can't be reached. I went over this a dozen times with him, but he doesn't understand that bigger isn't always better. Or tasteful. But why would he listen to the person he's paying to make the right decisions for his house? Stupid man."

Daisy frowned. "Are you feeling okay?"

Laura glared at her. "Why? Because I'm giving out about a client? Or because I'm giving out about a man!"

After the weekend she'd had, Daisy hadn't the energy to pursue it.

"We're having to push things hard on Granary House to get everything finished on time," she said, changing the subject. "Kayley Lynch will be here in a couple of weeks. Matt says she's planning to use the place for rehearsals and stuff."

Fionn looked like he might faint from excitement.

"Kayley Lynch is gonna be here in two weeks? Just like, hanging around?"

"I'm not exactly sure how much hanging around she'll be doing." Daisy pulled a few loose threads off her skirt. "I'm sure she'll have a pretty tight schedule. Is her tour going well?"

Fionn beamed. "Totally! Although she's still getting a hard time in the press. But she could make a ton of money if one of the big streamers picks up her documentary."

Laura looked bemused. "Maybe she could fall off the wagon again. That'd make things interesting."

Daisy shook her head. "Dark, Laura, even for you."

Laura grinned, then her expression changed and she hurried out of the office. Daisy and Fionn exchanged a worried look. When she reappeared a few minutes later, she looked pale.

"Were you out last night?" Daisy asked carefully.

"Of course not. I'm training for this marathon, remember?" Laura huffed. "It's this training diet Brian has me on. I know it's necessary, but I'm not used to all the carbs!"

Since when had Brian become a nutrition expert? And Laura was worse, agreeing to something like that just to keep the guy happy! But maybe that was the secret of a successful relationship? Maybe if she and James had a shared project, they'd feel less like housemates and more like soulmates. Although she was pretty sure it would take a lot more than a shared project to make things better between them.

Laura looked at her and Daisy had the uncomfortable feeling that she knew exactly what she was thinking about Brian. She rolled her shoulders, trying to ease out the tension. Running the company together used to be fun, a natural extension of their friendship. Even when she'd been with Matt, it had felt like her and Laura against the world.

Lately, it felt like there was a distance growing between her and everyone important in her life.

"So, what are you planning for your birthday?" Laura asked after a while.

"Are you going to have a party?" Fionn's eyes lit up.

"With cocktail sausages and Rice Krispie cakes?" Laura's tone was teasing, and Daisy laughed.

"James is taking me out for dinner." She caught Laura's expression. "I know you went to Malaga for your thirtieth, but ..." She shrugged. She and James hadn't taken a holiday since they'd bought the house, even though the idea of renting out the room was so they'd have money for a few luxuries.

"How's Alma?" Fionn asked quickly.

"*Hmm?* Oh, yeah, a bit better." She decided not to mention that James had gone out the previous evening and bought Lemsips, Vitamin C and a hot-water bottle with a fluffy pink cover. Daisy figured she'd have to be on her deathbed before James bought her a hot-water bottle.

"I wonder will Matt remember your birthday." There was a slight edge to Laura's voice.

Daisy tried to look disinterested. "If he does, he'll just wish me a happy birthday. It's not a big deal."

"*Riiight ...*"

Fionn muttered some excuse and left the room.

Daisy sighed. "Listen, Laura, there's nothing at all between Matt and me. This is about the house."

"Bit of advice, Daisy? Leave it at that! Don't look for anything else, or you'll end up getting hurt again."

Daisy said nothing. A few weeks ago closure had seemed pretty straightforward. Now, she couldn't ignore all the signs pointing to change. And that meant taking a leap into the unknown.

CHAPTER 20

"Surprise!" An explosion of party whistles, cheering and clapping greeted Daisy as she and James walked into the upstairs area of Bar 55, where James had suggested they go for a drink before dinner.

She stared, momentarily overwhelmed, as friends and family threw streamers and popped bottles of sparkling wine. The room was filled with balloons and fairy lights, and a huge *Happy 30th Birthday* banner hung over the bar.

She blinked, and looked at James, who was grinning widely. "You did this?" How was it even possible? How had she ever doubted him?

"Me and Alma. Laura helped."

Daisy cupped her hands over her face. Maybe that was why James and Alma had been spending so much time together lately? They'd probably been planning this for her!

"I don't know what to say. Thank you!"

He kissed her. "Just enjoy it."

She felt his hand on her back as he guided her into the room, where she tried to register everyone buzzing around her.

"Happy birthday, Daisy flower!"

She spun to see her dad in a floral shirt, denim jeans, and a faded, well-washed corduroy jacket. He opened his arms and she stepped into them, hugging his tall, slender frame.

"Thanks for coming, Dad."

"I wouldn't miss my baby girl's big birthday." Eric pulled back, smiling at her. "Anyway, James tells me it's a good place for craft beer. I'm well up for that."

"Is Mum – ?"

"Over there." He nodded to the far side of the room. "She's at the buffet with your sister. Rosie's probably positioned herself there so she could identify the most boring food for those poor kids." He winked. "But I love her too. Now, I'll see you later, have fun!"

He disappeared into the throng, leaving family and friends to grab their turn with her. A drinks waiter passed and James took two glasses of sparkling wine from his tray, handing one to Daisy. "To you!"

He clinked her glass and Daisy smiled shyly.

"Now what?"

He gestured around the room. "Everyone's here for you, Daisy. Go do what you do best."

"Dance with me later?" She smiled at him, and he gave her another quick kiss.

"You bet."

⁓

She joined Laura quite a while later at the bar.

"You sure you had no idea, babes?" Laura slanted Daisy a look. "A Dirty Martini for the Birthday Girl and a Virgin Margarita for her best friend," she told the barman.

Daisy giggled. "I can't remember the last time I drank this much, Laura. Maybe I should have one of those virgin things too."

"It's your birthday, Daisy! And the only reason I'm not drinking is because I'm on antibiotics for a stupid UTI."

Daisy felt a pang of sympathy for her. "Do you think you're pushing yourself too much to be ready for this year's marathon?" she said. "You could do next year's instead."

Laura rolled her eyes. "Chill, Daisy. It's your birthday – you're supposed to be having a good time, not worrying about other people. Now, drink up and stay in bed tomorrow with James!"

The barman placed their drinks in front of them, and Laura took a sip. "Tell Alma to piss off for the day."

Daisy giggled again. "God, I feel so bad. I thought James and Alma were ..." She caught Laura's expression. "I mean, I thought they were leaving me out of something." She tucked her hair behind her ears to reveal delicate, emerald-drop and diamond earrings. "What do you think? They're vintage – James' birthday present to me."

Laura lifted one earring to examine it. "Nice!" She glanced over at James. "He's obviously doing well for himself."

Daisy beamed. "Yeah, but I only get to be thirty once!" She couldn't admit that she'd thought the tiny green velvet box had contained an engagement ring. Although she didn't know how she'd have felt. Would she have panicked and said no? Or worse ... yes?

Laura laughed dryly. "I'm not just talking about the earrings, I'm talking about all this! Renting out this place, all the catering – it wasn't cheap."

Laura was right, and James had done it all for her – she'd just been misreading the signs! Daisy felt a rush of happiness.

"Laura, before I get too drunk, I want to say –"

"Stop!" Laura held up a hand. "Are you about to get mushy on me?"

"A bit."

Laura sighed. "Say it. Quickly."

"Thank you for being part of this. You're my best friend, and I love you."

CHAPTER 21

"Fancy running into you here!"

Daisy spun around at the sound of the familiar voice. "Matt!" She narrowed her eyes. "Did you remember, or … ?"

Matt grinned. "Of course I remembered." He kissed her lightly on the cheek, and she breathed in the scent of his subtle aftershave. "For you." He handed her a small, beautifully wrapped gift, the size of a ring box.

Daisy blinked. "Thank you."

"I hope you don't mind me turning up?" He sounded unsure. "Brian invited me."

"Of course not. I'd no idea they were organising this."

"Not a clue?" He looked at her.

She shook her head. "Honestly, James just said he was taking me out for my birthday." Automatically, she found herself anxiously scanning the room for James, guiltily relieved when she couldn't see him anywhere. When she turned back to Matt, she thought she saw a flash of annoyance on his face, and wished she hadn't mentioned James. Then he smiled, and she told herself she'd imagined it.

"Open it?"

"Sure." Daisy felt her face warm as she fumbled with the intricately tied ribbon. "You shouldn't have got me anything, Matt." *It's a tiny box, small enough for jewellery. Oh God, he'd bought her jewellery – exactly like James.*

"I didn't."

"You didn't?" She looked down at the wrapped box and then back up at him, trying not to appear too confused. Carefully, she tore open the wrapping and opened a small, black-velvet box to reveal a key. "*Haha!* If you've bought me a car, I'll have to say no."

Matt grinned. "It's a spare key to the house. I thought if I wasn't there, or if I was busy, you could just let yourself in."

Why hadn't she thought of that? It made perfect sense. It was a practical gesture, not a gift at all. She decided not to make any comment about its odd presentation, and smiled brightly at him instead.

"Thank you, it's such a good idea!"

Scooping it out of the box, she noticed it was attached to a key ring: a tiny photo moulded in hard plastic. "Wow, I'd almost forgotten about this picture!" It was of her and Matt one New Year's Eve in Trinity College front square. She'd gone home for Christmas, she remembered, but had come up to Dublin that morning, to bring in the new year with Laura, Brian and Matt – her first New Year's Eve with him.

In the photo she and Matt wore puffa jackets and woolly bobble hats. Their arms were wrapped tightly around each other, their breath almost visible in the ice-cold, night air, their excitement palpable, as they smiled for the camera. It reminded her of the other photo in Matt's bedroom, and she felt a sudden surge of jealousy that the only photo he had on display in his house, was of him with some other woman. Clearly, she was losing her mind.

"*Um*, did you get it especially made?" Was it weird that he'd given her such an intimate photo on a keyring? It was like he was making a point.

Matt looked surprised. "No, I've had it a while. I discovered it in the move and I thought you'd like to have it."

She studied him for a moment, unsure whether he was playing with her. They'd had one each. Hers was just a small framed photo in a box in her parents' house. The keyring was a nice touch, she supposed. And maybe he viewed it the same way as the photo of him and his ex-girlfriend at some ski resort.

"I saw your folks when I came in," Matt said. "I'm not sure if they remembered me, though."

There wasn't a chance that they hadn't recognised him; it had only been a few years, and her parents never forgot a face. Still, if her dad *had* seen him and had decided to ignore him, that was definitely the best-case scenario. Once they didn't mention anything to James.

Matt frowned at something over Daisy's shoulder and she spun nervously, dizzy with relief when she saw Laura approaching.

"Hello, Matt." Laura's smile seemed frozen to her face.

"Hi, Laura. Good to see you."

Laura's expression didn't change. "I didn't expect to see you here."

Matt gave an easy shrug. "Brian invited me. You haven't changed a bit."

"Neither have you, I'll bet." Laura flicked her attention to Daisy. "Your mum's looking for you."

Daisy peered around the room. "Is she okay?"

"I think one of Rosie's kids ate too much and got sick, and your mum's with them."

"Probably Ben." Daisy grinned. "I don't think he's got an off-button. I'd better go see if she wants any help." She turned to Matt. "Excuse me."

He waved her gently away. "Catch you later."

Laura's smile turned into a grimace, as she tucked her arm firmly through Daisy's, and marched her across the room towards the bathrooms. "Not if I see you first," she muttered.

Daisy waved and mouthed a few hellos to people they passed. "Laura, what are you doing?"

"You know what I'm doing!"

Daisy sighed. "You can't be rude to Matt like that, you know."

"Give me one good reason why not." Laura pushed open the door to the ladies', where Sam and the twins were running up and down, and Daisy's mother was spritzing some of her homemade lavender perfume and looking perfectly relaxed.

"Daisy!" The twins ran over and threw their arms around her, before racing off again.

Daisy's mother smiled. "Did you go looking for back-up, Laura?" She laughed. "We would have managed. Still, I didn't get a proper chance to talk to my birthday girl earlier. Doesn't she look wonderful this evening? Where did you get your dress, Daisy?"

Daisy smoothed down her flared, poppy-red dress. "It's from my favourite second-hand place, New Lease. I just put some pockets in."

Miriam stuck her hands into the pockets of the sparkly blue, kaftan top that she'd teamed with darker, equally sparkly Capri pants. "I put pockets in this too." She looked closely at Laura's elegant, knee-skimming dress. "Is that silk? Almost impossible to have pockets in that." She scrunched up her nose.

"And it would ruin the very sexy line." Laura winked and Miriam chuckled.

Rosie emerged from the cubicle with Ben. "Here, wash your hands, now."

Ben turned on the water and caught Daisy's eye in the mirror. "Mummy says you're thirty. That's pretty old."

"Ben!" Rosie shot him a frazzled look.

Daisy just grinned. "It is, yeah, but I've decided not to get any older after this."

Rosie turned to her mother. "I've got this, Mum. Why don't you all go back to the party?"

Laura looked relieved, and excused herself immediately.

"Dad's at the bar with Séan, I see," Daisy said, when she and Miriam went back outside. "I think they're comparing craft beers."

"Your dad'll be singing in another hour." Miriam sounded unbothered. "Are James' parents coming, do you know?"

"I don't think so. Probably not their kind of thing."

"I thought they were very pleasant any time I met them. Obviously they couldn't make it."

Or James didn't bother inviting them, Daisy thought. Was it bad that all her family and friends were here, but not James' parents?

"How's Matt?" Miriam asked.

Daisy tried to read her mother's expression. "You saw him?"

"As soon as he came in."

"He mentioned you." Daisy wrapped her arms around herself. "He didn't think you and Dad would remember him."

"Does he think we're senile?" Miriam tutted. "Listen, Daisy, you're a grown woman and I know you'll always do what you think is right for you. But just remember what Matt did! You don't want to mess with you and James."

Guilt gnawed at her. She was pleased that James had organised this evening, but it didn't fix everything between them.

"It's not like that, Mum, honestly."

"Does James know that he's here?"

Her mother and Laura were in league with each other!

"Not exactly. The thing is, Matt moved home and asked me to redesign his house. Actually, he just gave me this."

She handed the key to Miriam, who turned the keyring over in her hand.

"I have this photo in a box of your old things at home. It was taken on New Year's Eve, wasn't it?"

Daisy nodded. Looking at the tiny photo, she could almost taste the cold air and feel the warmth of Matt's arms around her.

"I remember that Christmas, Daisy," Miriam said, slowly. "You invited Matt down to stay over the New Year, because he'd no plans to go home, and you wanted to go out with your old school gang. When he wouldn't come down, you changed your plans and went back to Dublin."

New Year's Eve in Galway had always been special, Daisy thought, as she managed a smile. "I wouldn't hold that against him, Mum, he was very shy back then."

"Hmm." Her mother gave her an appraising look. "Is he on his own?"

"Yes, but I'm just redesigning his house! And it just so happens that I never discuss any of my clients with James, so why would I make Matt an exception?"

"You're not a doctor, Daisy! I don't think you'd be breaking client privilege. If he finds out that you've been working on your ex-boyfriend's house and you never mentioned it, he'll wonder what else you've been keeping from him."

"No, he won't! Anyway, we trust each other." She trusted James, didn't she? She wasn't completely sure she trusted him around Alma. She flashed her best no-need-to-worry smile.

The bathroom door opened and Rosie and her gang came out.

"Rosie, why don't you get Ben a fizzy drink?" Miriam suggested. "That should settle his stomach."

"This fellah won't be having anything more," Rosie muttered, as she took Ben's hand and headed back across the room.

After they left, Miriam swept a hand back through her thick, brightly coloured hair.

"I love this band – they're playing all the best seventies stuff. I'm going to see if your dad wants to dance." She gave Daisy a hug. "See you later."

CHAPTER 22

James appeared at Daisy's elbow, just as she was starting on her fourth margarita.

"Hey, you having a good time?"

Daisy raised her glass. "The best!" Tonight would probably be a turning point in their relationship. They'd spend the next few hours having the best fun – it'd be like old times. And then they'd go home and have amazing sex. And James would realise how much he'd been neglecting her, and he'd stop playing video games with Alma and accompanying her on the guitar while she …

"Hey, we haven't danced yet!" She slipped her hand into his, pulling him towards the dance area. "Come on, the party's only starting. Rosie and Séan have gone back to their hotel because the kids were tired! And my cousin Niamh had to leave with her two boys as well. Although I'm glad they got to blow out my birthday candles – they'll remember that."

"I'd say everyone will." A corner of his mouth lifted in a smile. "Nobody's had any of the cake."

Daisy giggled, aware that she was slightly tipsy. "It's chocolate biscuit cake, so I've decided to ignore the spit."

"Yeah."

James seemed a bit distracted, Daisy thought. As if he was looking for someone.

"Did you invite your parents tonight?" she asked.

"No, I didn't think it'd be their kind of thing." He frowned. "Why?"

"*Uh*, no reason." What was she supposed to say? That he should have invited them even if he thought they wouldn't come? That it was a bit weird not to invite them?

"Listen, I feel bad about this, but I have to go back to the house for an hour." James pushed a hand back through his hair. "One of our American clients is having a problem, but I won't be long, I promise."

Daisy stared at him. "You're *leaving*?"

He seemed to tense. "Daisy, it's just for an hour. Alma's a bit wrecked too, so I'm taking her home. She's probably not over that strep."

"So she's going home with you?" Daisy was starting to feel a bit lightheaded. Maybe she'd get something to eat before she had another margarita.

"We're sharing a taxi, yes," James said patiently. "I'll see you soon, okay? Go have fun." Giving her a quick kiss, he turned and walked towards the door, where Alma was standing, waiting. She gave Daisy a cutesy wave.

As Daisy forced herself to wave back, she wondered if anyone else had noticed her boyfriend had just left her birthday party with their Swedish lodger. There was a joke in there somewhere, she thought. She just needed to find it.

She eyed up the bar. To hell with James. And Alma. This was her party and she was bloody well going to enjoy it!

"It's Britney! Come on, Daisy, dance with me." Fionn took Daisy by the hands and pulled her back onto the dance floor.

Daisy burst into fresh giggles. "*Oh! My! God!* Is there any song that you *don't* like, Fionn?"

"I love all this retro stuff," Fionn shouted over the music. "And the DJ is pretty hot too!"

Daisy danced, her arms above her head, as she found herself scanning the room, pretending to herself that she wasn't searching for Matt. A few of her older relations had left, but there were still plenty of people drinking and dancing.

Her gaze trailed slowly back across the room, her stomach clenching hard when she spotted Matt near the bar. He seemed to be deep in conversation with Brian.

As she watched them, she had a sudden, clear memory of her joint twenty-first with Laura. They'd been in final year when Laura had suggested the party.

"I know the manager of Trojan Dock on the quays," she'd said. "We can hire out the whole place, and invite everyone we know. It'll be awesome!"

Daisy, Laura and their friends had all loved it, as had Miriam and Eric. Daisy hadn't been so sure about Laura's parents. They'd arrived separately, and didn't dance together all night. Daisy remembered one of the guys making a pass at Laura's mother, before throwing up all over her shoes.

As if he could feel her gaze, Matt looked over and, as his eyes locked with hers, he raised a glass in her direction. Daisy gave a small, self-conscious wave in return. After a few moments she saw him cross the room and sit down at a table near the edge of the dance floor. She motioned to Fionn that she was taking a break, then went over and slipped into the spare chair beside Matt.

Matt smirked at her. "Why did you sit down? I came over here to look at you dancing."

"What?" She felt her face heat.

"Yeah, I mean, Brian's great, but I thought I could do with some comic relief." His face was poker-like, until Daisy shoved him hard, and he burst out laughing. "To be honest, I don't know anyone else here, except you and Brian."

"You know Laura."

"I don't think Laura is thrilled to see me."

He had to know why!

"I was talking to my mum earlier." She shot him a look. "She remembered you."

He smiled, but said nothing.

He'd changed, she thought. He'd got cooler, less geeky. She supposed confidence did that to a person. "So, do you think you've changed a lot since you left?"

Matt seemed to think. "I'm a better dancer than I was. Definitely better than I was at your twenty-first!"

The look he was giving her could probably set something on fire. She knew exactly what he was talking about, and it wasn't dancing. They'd been dating for six months by the time she'd turned twenty-one. That night had been the first time they'd had sex.

He leaned towards her, dropping his voice conspiratorially. "Actually, I haven't danced yet this evening."

Daisy giggled, her breath catching. "Great, I'll just sit here and watch. I could do with some comic relief."

Without breaking eye contact, Matt got to his feet and carefully pushed in his chair. Very deliberately, he held out his hand.

Daisy shook her head, feeling her pulse pick up.

"I've been dancing for ages." She sounded squeaky. *Very cool, Daisy.*

"One dance? It's not as much fun dancing by myself."

The band started to play 'Sweet Dreams' by the Eurythmics, and Matt tipped his head to one side. "Remember this?"

"This, and all the other eighties stuff you made me listen to!" Daisy shook her head.

"I'm pretty sure I subjected you to my favourite music from *every* decade," he said.

"The Eurythmics were your favourite, not mine." How could she resist him? She got to her feet, stumbling a little as she made her way to the floor.

"Relax, come here." Matt pulled her towards him, placing her left hand on his shoulder, and twining his fingers through her right hand.

"What are you doing?" Daisy glanced quickly around, thankful there was still no sign of James.

"Do you know how to tango?" His eyes glinted.

"No, and neither do you."

"There's a lot you don't know about me, Daisy."

"You can't tango to Eurythmics, Matt."

"You can tango to this song, Daisy. I have. So, the question is: can you follow me?"

Oh God, once she'd have followed him anywhere if he'd asked. Briefly, she wondered what everyone would think, before deciding she didn't care. It was her party, and nobody here except Laura, Brian and her parents actually knew Matt. And James? She'd worry about James later.

"I'll do my best," she promised.

They started to move, and after Daisy's first, fumbling steps, she found herself inching infinitesimally closer to Matt, focusing on him as he led her through the next few moves.

She looked up. "I'm doing the tango! We're doing the tango!"

"Who'd have thought?" He smiled.

"I know, right?" She felt a flush spread up to her neck.

"I was just thinking of the first time we danced together."

"It was nothing like this, Matt!"

Matt shook his head. "This is so much better. But we're missing something – I should have a rose between my teeth." He flashed her an over-the-top smile, and Daisy giggled again.

As the final strains of the song drifted across the floor, Matt put his mouth to her ear.

"Do you want me to dip you?"

Daisy shivered deliciously. That she was dancing with Matt rather than James tonight had to be a sign. She and Matt had spent the night together at her last big birthday – now, here they were again. Maybe in years to come, she'd understand why it had happened this way. She nodded, gasping as she felt the ground slide away from her feet, her head and upper body thrown suddenly backwards.

Matt held her tightly and moments later she found herself upright again.

As she and Matt pulled apart, people around them began to clap. Daisy gave a tiny, self-conscious bow but, as she started to leave the dance floor, the first strains of Bruno Mars' 'Just the Way You Are' began to play over the sound system.

She looked at Matt. "You didn't ..."

Matt's eyes glinted. "It was our favourite song, remember?"

An invisible string was pulling every nerve-ending into the pit of her stomach, as she allowed Matt to lead her back into the middle of the floor. Around her, friends and family were dancing, their arms wrapped around each other. Beside her, her aunt and uncle were managing to do an old-fashioned waltz.

"*Happy birthday, sweetheart!*" her aunt called out as they danced by.

Daisy gave them a little wave, her pulse picking up as Matt clasped his hands behind her back. Tentatively she put her hands on his shoulders, relaxing as he maintained a small gap between them. If she closed her eyes, it could just be the two of them. It could be her twenty-first again, when she and Matt were young, invincible and deeply in love. It was nine years ago. It was yesterday.

"I can't remember if they even played this at my twenty-first," she said.

"You still look twenty-one."

She gave a wobbly smile, clutching on tighter to Matt as she lost her balance.

"I think I've had too much to drink."

Matt grinned. "Never."

The song came to an end, and reluctantly Daisy dropped her hands to her sides. Her phone buzzed in her pocket, and she noticed James' name flash up on the screen.

"Excuse me, I have to –" She swiped to answer the call, leaving the dance area, and ducking quickly out the door, shivering as the cool air hit her bare skin. "James?"

"Daisy, I'm sorry, this is a bigger problem than I thought it'd be, so I'm not going to make it back to the party."

Daisy took a breath. "Do you not have software engineers who can sort it?"

"It's not that simple, Daisy."

It never was, she thought. Did he think that because she was surrounded by people she knew, it didn't matter that he wasn't coming back? That it didn't matter if he couldn't put her first for one night?

James sighed. "I feel really bad, honestly. Look, can you get a taxi home later?"

Daisy blinked rapidly, determined not to ruin her make-up. "Yeah, grand."

"You're sure?"

She forced a brightness into her tone. "I'm sure. Listen, Laura is calling me back in. Gotta go. Catch you later." She hung up, almost dropping her phone as she shoved it back into her pocket.

She stood for a moment, digging her nails into the soft flesh around her thumb, as she took deep breaths. Vaguely, she was aware that somebody else had come outside too.

"Are you okay?" She heard Matt behind her, but she couldn't trust herself to turn around in case she broke down. Instead she nodded.

"Grand, yeah, I'll be back in in a minute."

"Mind if I stay out here with you?"

"I don't mind." Had he guessed about James? She wished she didn't feel so stupid. Matt had come tonight to be with her. She turned to him. "I'm glad you're here."

Instinctively, she stepped closer and gave him a hug, and realised she didn't want to pull away.

It was Matt who gently pulled back first. "I'll bet I'm gladder than you."

She gave a small smile, knowing he was doing his best to make her feel better. She wouldn't think about tomorrow.

"Best birthday ever," she whispered, half to herself.

Gently, he tipped back her chin. "Birthday kiss?"

Don't overthink it, Daisy. "Birthday kiss." A pulse beat wildly in her neck as Matt pressed his mouth to hers. Then she closed her eyes, and kissed him back.

CHAPTER 23

**MyStarScope Taurus: With Mars in ascension this week,
somebody may threaten a close relationship.**

"Mrs Jones, the best thing you can do is to make a wish list for your kids: careers, marriage, how many grandchildren you'd like." Laura paused. "Of course I'm not joking – feng shui is a serious business. Now, make the list and we'll see what we can fit in the budget." She put down the phone and looked over at Daisy. "Mrs Feng Shui. She's on a tight budget, so one child might have to choose between kids and a career."

Daisy grinned, her day-and-a-half old hangover rapidly vanishing. "You really can't take the piss, it's not professional."

"I'm just embracing the madness of my client." Laura gave Daisy a long look. "You don't look great."

"Yeah." Daisy sighed. "Is it possible that I could still be hungover?"

"Doubtful, babes." Laura turned her attention to the screen.

Daisy slipped in behind her own desk. Clearly, the churning sensation in the pit of her stomach was something else, she thought. Guilt, probably, over the small matter of having kissed her ex, at a party organised by her current boyfriend. She'd blame everything on drink. God, she was delusional. She couldn't just blame it on drink! The truth was, the last time she'd had a big birthday bash, there'd been no awards to win, or mortgage to pay, or a live-in boyfriend who spent way too much time with the twenty-three-year-old who rented their spare room. And who'd skipped out on her before they'd hardly spent a single moment together on her big night! In fact, she'd spent half the evening fending concerned queries about his disappearance. In the end, she'd told everyone he'd gone home with a migraine. "I didn't realise James suffered with migraines" – her mother had sounded sceptical.

Daisy looked over at Laura. "So, wasn't Saturday amazing?" she demanded. "Did you have a good time? I had a great time."

Laura flicked some imaginary specks of dirt off her slim-fitting skirt. "I'm glad."

Daisy wondered if Laura somehow knew about the making-out incident. She could have seen them. Or maybe somebody else had seen them and word had got around, and now everyone was wondering if James knew. God, what had she done? Nothing, she'd done nothing! It was a birthday kiss! Okay, maybe a bit more. She'd replayed it over and over in her head, recalling how they'd closed every last tiny space between them, fitting together like a perfect memory during those impeccable few moments.

"Did you send me all the photos you took?" Daisy said casually. She'd barely lifted her head from social media all day Sunday, as she'd searched through countless Instagram stories from the previous night, checking for incriminating pictures of her and Matt together. Thankfully, there'd been nothing.

She struggled to organize her thoughts for Laura. "James told me you helped organise it."

"*Hmm.*" Laura shrugged. "You can thank me for the choice of venue. James wanted to rent out some bar in your local hotel."

Daisy tried to think of something witty to say but failed. So he hadn't picked the actual venue. It didn't matter now.

James had been asleep when she'd got home and, by the time she'd got up, he'd barricaded himself into his office, and she'd told herself she was too hungover to face him. The truth was, all she could think about was how James and Alma had left the party together, hours before anyone else. Worse, she couldn't seem to find the words to tackle him about it. Anything she said would just cause a row.

When he'd finally surfaced again, she'd asked if he'd managed to sort his work problems. James had mumbled something about more complications, and asked her if she'd had fun at the party, but Daisy had stopped listening. She couldn't believe that he'd gone to so much trouble to organise a surprise party – and then almost ruin it by refusing to put her first for a single night.It had been Matt who'd rescued the evening for her. She'd forgotten what a good dancer he was, how much fun he could be, how he kissed and what his body felt like when –

"Did he get over his migraine?" Laura flicked her a sharp look.

"What? Oh, James, yeah, he's fine."

"*Hmm.*" Laura smoothed a hand back over her hair. "Didn't Alma leave around the same time?"

"Yeah, I think so." Daisy did her best to sound off-hand. "She didn't really know anyone there, so she just came along for a while to be polite. I mean, James *had* to invite her." Although she could have made an excuse not to come – she didn't have to say yes! She stabbed the power button on her laptop. "Where's Fionn? Did he come in?"

"I sent him for coffees."

Daisy sighed and searched around for another topic. "How's Stephanie?"

"Completely hormonal and absolutely huge. That's what happens when you decide to birth a litter. She'll probably never return to normal again." Laura frowned at something on screen, as she tapped away on the keyboard. "She's decided on minimalist, child-friendly and open-plan. I could probably plan it in my sleep."

Fionn came in, holding a cardboard tray with three coffees. Laura tapped the desk beside her. "Finally. Decaf, yes?"

"*Er*, yes."

Daisy suppressed a sigh. At a guess, Laura was probably still upset because Matt had turned up. And it was typical of Brian to have invited him, and not mention it to Laura. He'd clearly been betting on maximum embarrassment, which definitely would have happened if James hadn't left. But it wasn't like she and Matt had spent the whole night together. Although she felt a bit bad that she hadn't spent more time with her parents. They'd danced together most of the evening, and Daisy had envied their comfortable chemistry.

"Isn't James a pure dote for doing this?" Miriam had said, as she'd hugged Daisy goodnight.

Daisy had pasted on a bright smile, and agreed that he was. Her mother hadn't mentioned Matt again, but Daisy had been able to read between the lines.

"You know, I was a bit surprised to see Matt there," Daisy said carefully.

"I didn't invite him." Laura was sharp.

"He told me Brian did."

Laura shrugged. "Maybe Matt remembered your birthday, and said something to Brian. Or Brian told him about the party and Matt invited himself. Who cares? Most of the time stuff gets lost in translation, anyway."

What did that mean? Daisy briefly caught Fionn's eye, but he hastily glanced away.

She felt a bit sorry for him – watching your employers squabble must be a bit like watching your parents fight, she thought.

Laura announced she was going to the shop, and Daisy expelled a slow breath.

"Sorry about that, Fionn," she said after Laura had left.

"Don't sweat it."

"Laura isn't exactly Matt's biggest fan," Daisy added.

"I know, yeah." He chewed his lip. "Speaking of which, remember you asked me to do that horoscope for him?" He leaned over and handed her a typed page. "It explains what planets were in ascension during the date and place of his birth."

Daisy looked it over. "Great. *Um*, does this reveal anything about him now? Like, anything in particular?"

"A few things." Fionn looked thoughtful. "He's quite a secretive person, who's prepared to wait for what he wants. He also finds it difficult to trust."

Had that been the problem in their relationship? But she couldn't remember any time when Matt had mistrusted her. She'd certainly never given him any reason to.

"By the way, you and Matt are two of the most compatible signs in the Zodiac: Taurus and Scorpio!"

Maybe that was why he was back in her life. And after what had happened at her party, he definitely seemed to want more.

She just had to wait and see what that meant – for both of them.

CHAPTER 24

@Celebwatch88 pretty wild that @KayleyLynch is gonna be spending three weeks in Ireland finishing her European tour and meeting Irish relations. Like has anyone told her that everyone in Ireland just hangs out in the pub? Sounds like a pretty bad combo for an addict IMO.

Daisy recognised Kayley Lynch as soon as she arrived at Granary House on Wednesday morning. The country singer, Matt and two men she assumed were with Kayley, were having breakfast on the patio.

Daisy tried not to stare. According to the singer's Wikipedia page, she was twenty-eight. With her frayed denim jeans, pink T-shirt, long, sun-bleached hair and tanned skin, she looked more like an American student on Spring Break.

A brief look of confusion crossed Matt's face when he saw Daisy but, as he got to his feet, his expression relaxed into a smile.

"You used your key! So, introductions! Daisy, this is Kayley Lynch and her team. Guys, this is Daisy Devlin, my interior architect."

Daisy smiled brightly. "Lovely to meet you all. I wasn't expecting you so soon."

"Hey, there!"

Kayley stood and Daisy ran a self-conscious hand over her skirt, as Kayley treated her to a brief, assessing look. She shook Daisy's hand, her mouth stretching into a cool smile.

She should say something, Daisy thought. But right now she couldn't even remember one of her songs! "You're always on in my house!" she said instead. Which was true, even if she wasn't the one who liked her stuff! "So, how long will you be in Ireland?"

"A few weeks. It's the last part of my tour, so we have some time to play around." Kayley gave a one-shouldered shrug and sat again. "I wanna meet up with some family, work on some new stuff." She touched the large white stone that hung around her neck on a fine silver chain.

One of the men cleared his throat. "Todd Onati." He stood, tall and solid, his thick, silver hair a contrast to his deeply tanned skin, and shook Daisy's hand. "I'm Kayley's manager." His accent was similar to Kayley's. "Matt's been telling us how you're organising for everything to be finished for us. We all appreciate that."

"Well, we're on schedule." It had been heart-breaking to see the half-acre of orchard completely demolished before a giant rotavator could make it ready for roll-out grass, but it had been necessary.

"Awesome coffee, Matty, thanks," said Kayley.

Matty? Daisy flicked a look at Matt, but his smile hadn't wavered.

The other man stepped forward and shook Daisy's hand. "Tim Meaney. I'm the publicist."

Daisy blinked as she looked at the younger, fairer man. Late thirties, she'd guess.

"You're Irish?"

"Cork city, never lost the accent!" He cleared his throat. "We'll get out of your way. I'm sure you guys have a lot to talk about, and we want to explore the grounds."

After they left, Daisy smiled a bit awkwardly. "I'm sorry if I crashed in – I didn't know they'd be here. But it's kind of exciting to have someone like Kayley Lynch here, isn't it? I only discovered that my dad's a bit of a fan!"

"Yeah, they got in last night." Matt scrubbed a hand over his face. "I made bacon and eggs, but Kayley's raw vegan, and the other two ate at the hotel. Fancy some breakfast?"

Daisy's stomach growled.

Matt looked at her expectantly. "You can show me what you're planning to do today while we eat, if it makes you feel any better."

"It does." Daisy sat down and closed her eyes for a moment, enjoying the sun on her face, as she listened to Matt in the kitchen. She wondered if she should try to talk about the kiss. Maybe she could work up to it.

Matt came back some time later with a plate of scrambled eggs and bacon and two mugs of coffee. "The bacon was hot in the oven, but the eggs are fresh."

"Thanks." She picked up her knife and fork. "So, Kayley seems to make herself at home pretty fast. She's already calling you Matty!"

He laughed. "I noticed. But I'd say settling in fast comes with the territory when you're touring. Anyway, I've more important things on my mind this morning."

He gave her an appraising look, and Daisy glanced away, her stomach clenching hard.

He wrapped his hands around his mug of coffee. "You know, I wasn't sure whether I'd be welcome at your birthday, but I'm glad I went."

She glanced back up. "Me too. Probably drank a bit too much, though." *Perfect cop-out, Daisy.*

Ironically, she was pretty sure it was only her and Brian who'd enjoyed having Matt there.

"Brian told me Laura organised it." He gave a lopsided smile. "I think she'd have preferred if I hadn't shown up." Before Daisy could say anything, he added, "I didn't see James."

"He was around." Probably better they didn't talk about James. And anyway, why had Brian said Laura organised it? The guy couldn't bear to give James the tiniest bit of credit!

She drank her coffee, and wondered for the hundredth time if she'd seriously misjudged Matt. She'd always blamed him for what he'd done. Now she wondered if there'd been something she'd missed. She wished she could ask him straight out. Before her party, she'd tried to tell herself that she couldn't afford to overstep that boundary. But now …

"So, what are we doing today?" Matt said.

She blinked. Maybe he wasn't going to mention the kiss, then. Maybe he'd already dismissed it as a birthday kiss – he might even regret it.

"Daisy?"

She smiled brightly. "Right, sorry. Colour schemes and final touches."

He looked amused. "Did I not already agree to all that?"

"Those were the broad strokes." She hoped Matt wouldn't realise she'd deliberately drawn out the process. "Today, you're looking at paper and paint choices in every room. There's less than a month to Kayley's concert, so it's better to be prepared in case there's a long wait for something. I've material samples, photos and testers to put up around the house, so you can visualise how it'll look."

"I already told you I trust you to make the right decisions."

"But this is the part that most people find fun!"

Matt rubbed the back of his neck. "You have me for the morning, but I have to meet a potential client after lunch."

He smiled, holding her gaze for longer than necessary, and Daisy tried to ignore the chaotic flutters in her stomach.

Who needed to actually *talk* about a kiss, when the guy in question was looking at her like that?

She took a deep breath. "We should get started."

She wished Granary House wasn't being fast-tracked.

Once it was over, she'd have no excuse to see him. And no reason to torture herself anymore either. Only she didn't want a return to the status quo. It was the only thing she was sure about.

❦

The house was empty when Daisy got home that evening. She poured herself a glass of wine and sat down at the kitchen table, letting her mind wander back over the day.

Even though Matt hadn't mentioned her birthday party again, Daisy had got the impression that they were edging closer to the discussion she knew they'd have to have.

Kayley had made a point of thanking Matt again before she'd left with the two men.

"The place is super-cute, Matty," she'd said. "The band will totally vibe with it."

Matt had seemed glad when they'd gone, and Daisy wondered if he was starting to get cold feet about letting out his house. He was probably dreading the further disruption, and the strong possibility that he might find the press camping outside.

Now, she heard the front door open, and braced herself for Alma's return. But it was James.

"Hey, you're home early. I'm knackered."

He threw his keys onto the countertop, opened the fridge and took out a can of Heineken. Tearing back the tab, he collapsed into a chair.

"How was your day? Is Alma around?"

Daisy stared at him. "No, why?"

"No reason." He drank some more beer, and winced. "I'm going to chill for a while, I feel like shite."

"If you're feeling that bad, maybe don't drink?" Daisy flicked on the kettle. "You should have a Lemsip or something."

"Yeah, maybe." He took his beer and wandered out of room.

Daisy heard the sitting-room door close, and a moment later the sound of the TV rumbled through the house. She sighed, wondering if she should cycle up to the local takeaway for fish and chips.

She brought the Lemsip into the sitting room, and put it on the coffee table beside his beer. James looked up. "You're a star."

"I was thinking of getting fish and chips."

"I can't eat anything."

"Oh." Daisy sat down. "Is your stomach okay?"

"Yeah, it's fine." James turned back to the TV. It seemed to be some dark, Scandinavian drama set on a remote island. He was probably planning on discussing it with Alma.

She sat down beside him. "Do you have a headache?"

"No." He let his head flop back against the sofa. "Why did you go around telling everyone I had a migraine on your thirtieth, by the way?"

"I didn't tell everyone." She felt herself flush. "Mum asked where you were and I –"

"Why didn't you just tell her the truth?" He sounded bewildered.

"Because ... who leaves their girlfriend's thirtieth birthday party to go work, James? You're not a bloody fireman!"

"Maybe you'd prefer me if I was." James closed his eyes.

Daisy stared at him. What did that mean? She didn't even have a thing for firemen! Well, not especially. "Of course I wouldn't!"

"*Ummh*." He turned his head towards her and opened one eye. "You sure?"

What was he on about? "Are you talking about sex?"

"You think I want to dress up as a fireman?" James' voice was dry. "Why, do you want me to?"

"*Um*, well, it's not that I *don't* want you to." James was looking quite interested, she thought. Or puzzled ... no, definitely more puzzled than anything. "I mean ..."

Daisy lapsed into silence. When had they last had sex? It had been weeks ago, maybe even a month! They were always tired or stressed. Or James was bloody working! Plus, the walls were so thin that Daisy spent most of her time wondering if Alma could hear them, which made it difficult to relax.

Anyway, it shouldn't be about quantity. It should be about love and commitment, and seeing your girlfriend's family and staying for her thirtieth bloody birthday party!

Maybe they should talk. Although she felt a bit talked-out after earlier! No, James was her boyfriend – she had to try.

She moved to the only other seat in the room: an antique armchair she'd fallen in love with, but that looked a lot more comfortable than it was.

"James, what's going on?"

He sighed and swiped the hot drink off the table, grimacing as he took a sip. "I bumped into Brian today."

Crap!

"He said you were dancing with some guy for ages at the party. He said you did the tango! And then I saw some photos of you and some guy on Rosie's Insta."

Frantically, Daisy tried to remember what Rosie had put up on Instagram. Nothing stood out, except for a few blurry pictures of her dancing with Fionn.

"You know what Brian's like." Good, she sounded normal. "Where did you see him?"

"He was in the deli in Sandyford, where I was getting my lunch."

"Right." God, she was going to sneak into Laura and Brian's in the middle of the night and smother Brian with a pillow. Only then she'd end up in jail and James would turn to Alma for comfort. Laura probably wouldn't be too happy either. She took a breath and held it for as long as she could, trying to slow down her pulse.

"So, did Brian say anything else?" She did her best to sound casual. "Did he enjoy the party?"

James rolled his eyes. "I don't know." He pinched the bridge of his nose. "*Did* you tango?"

"Yeah! The guy I was dancing with knew how, so I sort of followed him."

James gave her a strange look. "Who was it?"

"Some friend of Brian's. I forget his name." Daisy turned and pretended to be interested in the TV.

"What the fuck were his friends doing at your party? I didn't invite them."

"Laura probably did." Daisy felt herself go hot and cold.

"You'd think she'd have mentioned it."

"She probably forgot, James. Anyway, it's hardly a big deal." She remembered something Laura had said. "It wasn't too expensive, was it?"

"What?"

"You know, everything: the venue hire, the food, the whole lot."

"No." His expression was shuttered as he turned back to the TV.

Daisy heard the front door open. "Are you sure I can't get you anything while I'm out?"

James sighed. "I don't know – a bottle of 7UP?"

"Grand." She looked at him closely: he seemed to be a bit flushed. "I wonder if you're coming down with something."

"Great, that's all I fucking need." He buried his nose in his honey-and-lemon drink.

Out in the hallway, Alma was putting her things away.

Daisy grabbed her helmet. "Hi, Alma, I'm going out to get some fish and chips. Do you want some?"

Alma smiled politely and shook her head.

"Good. I mean, fine." Daisy flashed her a slightly manic smile. "*Uh*, James is in the sitting room, but he's not feeling too well, so it's probably best if you leave him alone."

Alma frowned. "Is it strep throat?"

"I don't know."

Alma looked solemn. "It's highly possible, Daisy."

Daisy took a breath. "Well, you're unlikely to get it again. So there's no need to worry about James."

Before Alma had a chance to reply, Daisy left.

As she cycled up the road, she wondered if Alma could be right. Didn't you get strep through close contact with someone who had it? James and Alma were bloody close!

James couldn't be happy with the way things were, could he? She tried to imagine how she'd feel if James left. But even if they did split up, did she really want to take a chance again with Matt? Matt, who'd shown up for her on her birthday. Who'd shown her every day since his return just how much he'd changed.

She'd never before felt so utterly confused.

CHAPTER 25

American country singer Kayley Lynch flew from Dublin to Cork this morning to meet third cousins John and Noelle Lynch, who run 'Lynch's', Bantry's popular gastropub. A spokesman for Kayley said that she wouldn't be drinking, or sampling the pub's signature 'Surf 'n' Turf', as she is just out of rehab and is also raw vegan. The singer – whose hits include 'From My Heart' – arrived in Ireland two days ago for her three-week visit, and is staying in Dublin's five-star Shelbourne Hotel. Her first Irish performance will be on June 1 at Wicklow's Granary House, followed by Dublin's 3 Arena on June 3, before continuing her tour in Galway, Cork and Limerick.

Kayley's publicist added that 'Kayley is excited to be here and able to connect with her father's Irish family'. Her great-great-grandparents emigrated from Cork to New York before eventually settling in Colorado, where she was born and raised.

The singer has been surrounded by controversy since a video of her appearing to verbally abuse former employees went viral. Since then, her US record sales have plummeted, and she's been forced to cancel her US concerts.

Ireland will be the last stop in her European tour which included Holland, Germany, France, Italy, Spain and the UK. The singer is accompanied by a camera crew who are making a documentary of the tour highlights.

Kenny and his crew were busy by the time Daisy arrived at Matt's place the following day. It had been a relief to leave for work, although she was a bit worried about James, who'd woken with a sore throat and high temperature, and announced he was working from home.

Meanwhile, the family WhatsApp group was buzzing with daily messages from Rosie. The previous evening she'd posted links to different companies in Galway offering marquee hire, so that their parents could decide on the size they wanted, and compare prices. This morning, she'd posted another link to her spreadsheet, with a list of people who could do catering and music. If Rosie didn't go back to her old job, Daisy figured somebody should just make her Mayor of Galway.

"Morning, Daisy," Kenny said gruffly as she walked into the kitchen. "Watch the circular saw, love."

"Thanks." Daisy stepped neatly over it, and looked around the room. Everything had been stripped out, the wall between the original kitchen and the old conservatory was gone, and the middle of the room was full of scaffolding so that Kenny's crew could replaster the ceiling. Daisy knew that once the replastering was finished, the new kitchen could go in in a day. But right now, it was a building site.

"Here's the boss!" From the other side of the room, Alec, clad in tighter jeans than Daisy had ever seen on a building site, gave a mock-salute.

She gave a polite smile. "Hello, Alec."

"Have you nothing to do?" Kenny said.

Alec cocked one dark eyebrow. "Just being sociable."

Kenny glared at him for a moment longer, before turning back to Daisy. "There's something I need to show you in the living room."

Daisy walked ahead of him, stepping awkwardly around a huge green-and-gold harp in the middle of the room.

"I'm assuming this is Kayley's?" she said.

Kenny rolled his eyes. "It was in our way so we moved it here. Yer man said it's a prop, and they need it later." He closed the door over. "Listen, Daisy, there's something I should have mentioned about Alec before I brought him on the job."

"Okay?"

Kenny huffed a sigh. "I took the guy on as part of a prisoner release scheme. It's his first job since he got out."

"*What?*" Daisy glanced nervously at the door. No wonder the guy was muscled and tattooed: he'd probably been involved in one of those Dublin gangs, and had spent years in prison with nothing to do except push-ups in his cell. Maybe the tattoos represented members of his gang family, or the hits he'd made, or –

"He got a year for stealing cars, with six months suspended," Kenny said, interrupting her thoughts.

"Stealing cars?" Daisy echoed, relaxing slightly. "Ah, that's not so bad." When Kenny shot her an odd look, she added hurriedly, "I mean, he's not a murderer." She gave a weak laugh.

Kenny looked a bit offended. "Lookit, Daisy, I wasn't sure about taking him on, but he'd no priors, and everyone deserves a second chance. But I thought you should know. And I'll be keeping a careful eye on him. Especially around Niamh, with her being the only woman on the crew."

Daisy nodded, trying to process this. "*Um,* thanks for letting me know, Kenny. I'm sure it'll be grand. Anything else?"

Kenny looked relieved. "Well, Niamh's busy. She doesn't like the original job done on the electrics and, sure, with all the extra stuff going on, it's easier to start from scratch."

"You mean, completely rewiring the whole place?" Daisy folded her arms. "That seems a bit drastic."

"I have to trust her." Kenny scratched his head. "I can't start second-guessing skilled tradespeople, so if she says she needs to redo the electrics –"

"No, I get that." Daisy nodded. "It's just that you've never worked with her before, have you? And she's quite young."

"You were quite young when I started working with you." Kenny pursed his lips. "You still are, compared with an old fart like me! And I've never questioned you."

God, she'd managed to upset him! "You're right, sorry, Kenny. So what's Niamh doing right now?"

Kenny pointed a thumb towards the ceiling. "She's upstairs talking to yer man. According to himself, the whole place is too dark. So I told him he could have Blackpool Lights once he cleared it with her."

Daisy suppressed a sigh. That was the first she'd heard that Matt felt the house hadn't enough light. He'd already agreed to keeping the original windows, which had been retrofitted by the previous owners.

"Excuse me." She headed upstairs, following the murmur of voices coming from the master bedroom. From inside, she heard Matt's deep chuckle but, when she went in, the room was empty.

"*Hello?*" Daisy called out.

"Daisy?" Matt appeared from behind the half-wall that faced the door.

"Hi." For some reason she couldn't put her finger on, Daisy felt wrong-footed. "Kenny said you and Niamh were –"

Matt turned as Niamh came out from behind the wall.

"Oh, hi, Daisy." Niamh tucked her hands into the front pockets of her jeans. "I love the walk-in wardrobe, but I was just telling Matt it could do with more lighting." She flicked Matt a smile.

Daisy tried to imagine how a walk-in wardrobe with sensor lights on every door and slide-out drawer could do with more lighting, but she nodded encouragingly.

"Great. *Um*, just run everything by me too, yeah?" A movement behind her made her turn.

Alec was at the door. "Niamh? Kenny's looking for you downstairs. He wants you to finish something before lunch."

"Tell him I'll be there in a few," Niamh said.

Alec smirked. "Tell him yourself, kiddo." He sauntered off.

There was an awkward silence after he left, and Daisy was acutely aware that Niamh seemed annoyed and embarrassed.

"I'll catch up with you later, Matt." Niamh's smile seemed a bit forced. "I guess I'd better see what Kenny wants."

"Sorry if I went over your head, Daisy," Matt said, after Niamh went back downstairs. "I guess she made me realise how dark the house might be in winter."

Not to mention lonely, Daisy thought, looking around.

"No problem. Just remember there'll be lots of occasional lighting, and dimmer switches on your wall and ceiling lights. Anything new should be in keeping with the overall design."

A slow smile spread across Matt's face, and Daisy felt her own face warm. "What?"

He shook his head. "I was just thinking – there's nothing more attractive than a woman who knows her stuff, explaining to a man who doesn't."

Daisy rolled her eyes, but found herself grinning. "You know that's inherently a sexist remark, don't you?"

"Sorry." His smile widened. "Should have known you'd never let me get away with it."

Daisy's face grew warmer. "I need to go talk properly to Niamh." She looked around. "Maybe you could work up here – it might be quieter."

"Don't worry about me." He smoothed down the curls at his neck. "I can work in the guest wing. Kenny said the kitchen gets worse before it gets better. And don't forget that Kayley and her crew will be here next Monday."

Daisy raised an eyebrow. "Yeah, I'll stay out of her way as much as I can. Anyway, she has a reputation for being a bit difficult. Or a lot difficult!"

Matt shrugged. "Everyone deserves a second chance," he said.

There was that phrase again. Daisy had the impression that he wasn't just thinking about Kayley. Was he thinking about himself? Or, the two of them? Was he afraid to say anything straight out, perhaps hoping she'd let him know how she felt first? But, for that to happen, she needed to find out what had happened five years ago.

She gave a hesitant smile. "Catch you later."

CHAPTER 26

Daisy was on edge when she got home that evening. She'd left Granary House around lunchtime, and had arrived back to the office to find Laura had gone.

"Did she say where she was going?" she'd asked Fionn.

He'd chewed his lip for a moment. "No, just that she was taking the rest of the day off."

Which meant if she'd had to stay on in Matt's, Fionn would have been in the office by himself.

Laura definitely didn't seem as invested in Discerning Designs as she once had been, and Daisy had the uneasy feeling that she was pulling away. Running their own company together had always been their dream, but now she wondered if Laura might be starting to feel claustrophobic.

Her phone buzzed and she checked to see a message from James. **Gone to doc, don't worry about dinner for me**. She messaged a quick thumbs-up and put her phone away. Hopefully it was just a bad cold.

She flung open the fridge door, wondering what Alma would make for dinner. Alma didn't bother to hide the fact that she wasn't a fan of Daisy's cooking, even when she made an effort. She was also pretty sure that Alma had only ever learned to cook for one, and she always made exactly the right amount. Clearly, James' lessons hadn't extended as far as the wonderful Irish tradition of making far too much food and having leftovers.

Daisy rooted around in the freezer and found a single sausage – how was there a single sausage, she wondered – and two potato waffles slightly iced over in the bottom of a box.

With a sigh, she threw them all on the grill and poured herself a large glass of wine, drinking a third of it straight away.

When Rosie phoned, Daisy stuck her on speaker.

"Hi, Rosie, how's it going?"

"Busy out, you know yourself."

Daisy had a good idea what Rosie's day looked like: her sister had told her often enough. But for a moment, she wondered what it felt like. Rosie was in control of her own little dominion – and Daisy had no doubt that it all ran like clockwork. By comparison, Daisy rarely felt in control of any aspect of her life, even when a job seemed to be going well. There were so many moving parts, she couldn't take anything for granted.

"What about you? You sound a bit off," Rosie said.

Daisy took a deep breath. "Ah yeah, it's been a long couple of days."

"How's it going at Matt's?"

"*Um*, good, hectic."

Dutifully, Daisy filled her in on the upcoming concert and filming at Granary House.

"Look at you, rubbing shoulders with the rich and shameless," Rosie said, when Daisy had finished. "Or at least Matt is. You never know what might happen there!"

"She's not his type." Daisy tried to shake off her annoyance.

"Because they're practically the same age, and she's beautiful, talented, and rolling in money?" Rosie's voice was dry. "I can see how that would be such a turn-off for Matt!"

While Daisy counted to ten, she reminded herself that Rosie didn't even *know* Matt.

"Thanks for coming to my birthday party."

"It was great. Pity James had to leave, though. How are the two of you?"

There was no way she was going to tell her perfect sister with her perfect marriage that things between her and James were crap.

"Grand. He wasn't feeling great last night, so he's gone to the doctor."

"I was talking to Alma at the party, and she told me she'd had strep recently. Does James have it?"

"I'm not sure," Daisy said. "But it's very contagious. I mean, you only have to breathe on someone."

"Right," Rosie said, after a pause. "So, what were you and Matt chatting about that night? And please don't tell me it was work. It's just, Mum is a bit worried."

Daisy felt a surge of irritation. She was thirty years old, but the rest of her family still treated her like she was sixteen. She did her best to sound offhand. "I can't remember, just stuff."

Rosie sighed. "Be careful around him, Daisy, please. I don't trust him at all, and neither should you."

"Rosie, you probably met Matt about three times in your whole life!"

"So has he explained why he ran off to the States?" Rosie said, ignoring Daisy's outburst.

"Not exactly," Daisy conceded.

"Imagine that."

Daisy took a deep breath. "Can we not do this, please?"

"Okay, not another word." Rosie's tone softened. "But I'm always here for you, if you want to talk."

In the background, Daisy could hear her nieces and nephews. It sounded like they were all killing each other.

"And don't shut Mum and Dad out either, okay?" Rosie continued. "Look, they didn't want you to know, but they coughed up half for your birthday party."

"*What?*" It came out as a squeak. "What exactly did they pay for?"

"I just told you! Stop freaking out, Daisy – it would have been a lot for James. Listen, I'd better go, it's getting a bit wild here." She hung up.

Daisy was still staring at the phone when James arrived home carrying a small pharmacy bag.

"What did the doctor say?"

James dropped the bag on the table and scrubbed a hand across his face. "It's strep. I told the doctor I couldn't afford to take a week off work. I got an antibiotic."

Wonderful, she'd probably get it now too. She opened the grill: the sausage and the potato waffles were burnt on one side. *Crap.*

***

Daisy was in a half-state between waking and sleeping, when the other side of the bed sagged gently. She rolled over to see James slipping under the covers.

"Hi," she mumbled.

"Sorry, I didn't mean to wake you. Go back to sleep."

"Weren't you in bed earlier?"

"Yeah, I couldn't sleep so I went downstairs to get some work done."

She rolled over properly to face him. "You can't work in the middle of the night when you're sick."

"In a perfect world, no." He sounded exhausted.

She felt herself tense. "James, what's going on?"

"With what?"

"With everything." She hesitated. "With us."

"You want to talk about us? *Now?*" James sounded a bit incredulous.

Her heart pounded. Did she? Maybe now wasn't the best time, not when he was sick.

He turned onto his back, and stared up at the ceiling. "Maybe you're right. I guess we never really get to talk, do we? Tell me about your day."

This was it, she thought. She'd just tell him she was working with Matt and it was no big deal, that he was just another client, and that she was finally getting a chance to enter the award with an amazing house. Except it would be a lie.

"Rosie rang," she said. "She told me about my folks helping out with my birthday party. I don't think she meant to, it just sort of slipped out."

"Jesus!" James sighed. "Look, the truth is, I wanted to take you out to dinner for your thirtieth, and then your mum offered to have a party down in Galway, but I knew it'd be easier to have it in Dublin."

Daisy couldn't speak for a moment. So the party hadn't even been James' *idea*!

"I want to thank them for helping anyway. I mean, I wouldn't have known ..." *Shit, shut up, Daisy, or you'll sound like you're accusing him of taking all the credit.* Except he *had* taken all the credit on the night. Not that it mattered, he'd still done loads. And he'd bought her those beautiful earrings! She reached out and ran a hand over his chest. "How are things at work?"

"Honestly, you don't want to hear about it."

"Yes, I do!" This was exactly what was wrong, Daisy thought – keeping stuff from each other wasn't healthy!

James didn't speak for a few moments. "Things are shit in work. In fact, we're having to let people go. And I took a pretty big pay cut recently."

"What?" Daisy could feel the hairs on her arms prickle. "I didn't realise, you never said. Could the company go under?"

"Not if I can help it." His voice was tight. "We're trying our best to scout out new clients at the moment."

"Right." Daisy lay tensely in the bed. If things got bad enough, could the board simply push him out? It wasn't impossible, she supposed. But if it did, they'd survive on her salary. Just about. Still, there was absolutely no way she was going to tell him about Matt.

She tried to think of something comforting to say, but nothing came to mind. TakeOff was the company he'd helped to start – and it meant as much to him as Discerning Designs meant to her.

James turned on his side to face away from her. "G'night, Daisy."

"Goodnight," she whispered.

CHAPTER 27

@Celebwatch88 idk but it seems @kayleylynch has piled on the weight since coming out of rehab – looks like she's swapped vodka martinis for big macs

Granary House looked like a cross between a rehearsal studio and a film set by the time Daisy arrived on Monday. She slipped past a group of people taking cameras, microphones, sound booms and lighting equipment out of the back of a van, and carrying it into the long reception room, where Kayley seemed to be directing everyone.

James had been asleep when she'd got up, and she'd figured he'd work from home again, so she hadn't woken him.

She stuck her head into the kitchen, glad to see the replastering of the old ceiling had started. As she came back up the three steps into the hall, she spotted Kayley's manager standing outside the sitting-room door.

"They're getting ready to record an interview," Todd said quietly. "Matt's in there too."

"He's watching it?" *What happened to staying out of the way?*

"He's in it! Kayley thought it'd be cool to make him part of it: he's got some patter about the history of the place. And Kayley's talking about why she's loving it here in Ireland. Listen, Daisy . . ."

Todd moved towards the front door, and Daisy followed him.

"Your guy with the man bun?" he said. "Talk to me!"

Daisy blinked. "That's Alec, one of Kenny's men." Where was this going?

Todd gave a curt nod. "Kayley's used to fans, you know? But she doesn't have the same ones always hanging around, and we keep the crazies away. Man Bun's comin' on a bit strong so I need for you to talk with Kenny and tell his guy to back off."

God, how had she suddenly got sucked into the world of a celebrity singer? Still, she had a job to do, and she'd do whatever she had to, to get it done.

"I'll mention it to Kenny, I'm sure there won't be a problem."

She excused herself, and headed back through the kitchen and stepped out onto the patio, shivering slightly as she closed the door behind her. In the last half hour, the wind had picked up and huge clouds scudded darkly above – a clear sign that the latest storm of the year was on its way. She walked down through the walled garden, grateful that the half-acre of vegetable beds and walkways would be left undisturbed. At the end of the garden, she turned and looked back towards the house, assessing it critically. It looked well; it would look even better when they integrated the old conservatory into the new kitchen.

She spotted Niamh striding towards her, her dark curls pulled back from her face, a vape in her hand.

"Hey." Daisy gave a friendly smile. "How are the electrics coming along? Any problems?"

Niamh shook her head. "I've got it. I just wish certain people would let me do my job!"

Daisy frowned. "How do you mean?"

Niamh took a puff of her vape. "Kayley Lynch! Absolute weapon! She's here about three seconds and she thinks she owns the place. This morning when I was talking to Matt, she appears from nowhere and has the cheek to send me off on some lame job. And, like, Matt's way too polite to say anything to her."

Daisy nodded sympathetically. Matt was in a difficult position, but there was no point trying to explain to Niamh that he had to keep Kayley happy.

"Look, all I know is that they're recording some interview this morning, and they wanted Matt to be part of it because he owns the house. And they've probably a schedule to keep."

"Right, because the rest of us have nothing to do." Niamh kicked at the ground.

Daisy thought for a moment. "Whatever Kayley wants you to do, just run it by me or Kenny."

Niamh rolled her eyes. "It's not like she's even an A-lister. Anyway, whatever." She tucked the vape into a pocket in her work trousers, and stalked back towards the house.

Daisy sighed, then turned slowly around. From here, she could just make out the nearest neighbouring house. It was at least a half a mile from Granary House, and on higher ground. By comparison, Granary House was in a valley. Hopefully that would mean any concertgoers would get a decent amount of shelter if the weather were to turn bad.

As the first heavy drops of rain started to fall, Daisy went back inside to start her work.

***

Matt and Niamh were laughing together in the kitchen when Daisy came in to grab some lunch, and Daisy was relieved that Niamh seemed to have forgotten about her earlier annoyance. A job was only as good as every member of the team and, given the deadline they had to meet, she couldn't afford to have Kayley make things difficult.

She caught Matt's eye as she put on the kettle, which was now on a tray on the stone floor in a corner of the room.

"That's pretty heavy rain out there," he said.

"Yup." Daisy straightened, flashing Niamh a quick smile. "We're due another storm."

"Are you afraid of thunder and lightning, Niamh?" Matt flicked Daisy a sly glance, and she flushed hotly.

"Like, when I was five!" Niamh sounded indignant.

Matt arched an eyebrow. "I'll bet you were a cute kid."

Niamh burst into giggles, and Daisy suppressed a grin. She'd almost forgotten what a tease he could be.

Her phone rang and she wandered into Matt's study to answer it, closing the door behind her. "Hi, Mum."

"Hi, Daisy." Miriam paused. "Tell me if it's a bad time, loveen?"

"No, I'm grand, Mum."

Miriam sighed. "That's what I'm wondering, now."

It was the party, Daisy thought. Her mother probably knew that she and Matt had spent time together at her birthday party – a long time.

"Your cousin Izzy has that tango up on her Instagram story, Daisy."

Daisy felt a bit sick. "Can you see his face, Mum?"

"Ah, Daisy, will you listen to yourself? If you weren't doing anything wrong, you wouldn't be asking that. James doesn't even know Matt was there, does he?"

"No, Mum, and he doesn't have to!" Daisy lowered her voice. "James isn't friends with anyone I'm friends with on social – apart from Rosie and Séan."

"That's not really the point."

Miriam's voice was gentle, but Daisy felt a flare of annoyance.

"We were catching up, having fun. It was my birthday – I was allowed to have fun!" Great, now she sounded like her teenage self. She took a deep breath. "Try not to worry, Mum. We weren't doing anything wrong." *Not much.*

"I know, loveen. I don't mean to throw cold water on it for you." There was a brief pause. "While I think of it, I was hoping you could do me a small favour."

"Anything, Mum."

"Could you get Kayley Lynch's new album, and ask her to sign it? As an anniversary present for your dad from me. Rosie told me that she's using Matt's house for rehearsals, or something."

"Consider it done." Daisy heard a noise outside the door. "*Uh*, I'd better go, Mum, I'll stay in touch."

"Be careful. I love you."

"Love you too, Mum." Daisy hung up, and slipped her phone back in her pocket. Her mother hadn't warned her to be careful since she'd first come to Dublin for college!

The door opened and Matt came in.

"Sorry," Daisy said. "I'll get out of your way."

Matt smiled. "No rush."

Daisy folded her arms. "So, fair warning: a lot of the carpentry is going to have to be done indoors today."

"I'll use headphones." Matt walked further into the room. "I think Kayley and her team were hoping to get some shooting done in Powerscourt today, but I reckon they just ended up going back to the hotel. That weather is shite."

Daisy grinned. "There you are."

"There I am what?" Matt looked amused.

"That just sounds a bit more like you, that's all. Like you used to sound."

"Like I never left?" Matt's expression closed, and Daisy wished she hadn't said anything.

Upstairs, Kenny and his team had started work on the three smaller bedrooms.

"*Be careful, boss!*" Alec's voice stopped her at the door of one of the rooms, and he pointed to the floor.

"Circular saw, right! Thanks, Alec."

He grinned, and shot her a cheeky wink.

Her mother's warning wasn't necessary, Daisy thought. She just had to go with her gut.

159

✣✣✣✣✣ ✣✣✣✣✣

"We're off, Daisy." Kenny eyed her carefully. "You'd be as well heading home yourself. That rain is bucketing down, you don't want to get stuck on any of these roads."

Matt laughed. "It always looks a bit worse out here in the country. It'll be fine. Anyway, thanks for everything today, lads, I really appreciate it."

Kenny gave Matt a brief, hard look, before nodding curtly at Daisy. "Will I see you tomorrow, then?"

"*Um.*" Daisy thought for a moment. "No, probably not. Phone if you need me."

Kenny nodded. "Mind yourself, now."

Matt smiled widely as he held the door open, shutting it as soon as Kenny and the others left. He turned to Daisy, who was leaning against the wall. "Why do I get the feeling that Kenny doesn't like me?"

"Are you buying him the good biscuits?"

"Chocolate Mikados."

"I wouldn't worry, then. Kenny can be a bit grumpy until you get to know him, but he's actually great." She wondered if Kenny was still annoyed by what Todd had said about Alec.

"Alec hasn't done anything inappropriate," he'd told Daisy. "He's probably just a bit starstruck, that's all."

Daisy couldn't imagine Alec being starstruck, but she'd simply said that she'd leave things with him.

"I'll take your word for it," Matt said now, as he walked down the hall to her. Daisy caught a hint of his aftershave: woodsy and subtle. "Hey." He gave her a long look.

"Hey, yourself." She tried to wet her lips.

"We could stand here, I guess."

"*Um.*" A slow flush crept along her neck. "Kenny's right, I should probably head off."

"Stay for a coffee? I always have one around this time."

Daisy shook her head. "How do you ever sleep?" The moment the words slipped out, she remembered he'd always been a restless sleeper, waking frequently during the night, sometimes getting up to smoke a joint. She wondered if he was still the same. And if he'd guessed what she was thinking.

"I can make decaf, or tea, if you prefer." Matt's voice was light.

She should definitely go. But things had felt a bit off earlier, and she told herself it was important for the job to make sure they maintained a good relationship. "Yeah, okay. A coffee."

He smiled. "Come on, we'll go next door."

Daisy took her time to look around the small, open-plan guest wing, as Matt made coffee. Had it been a good idea to stay? Now that she was off the clock, being alone with Matt threatened to stir up too many old feelings. One coffee, she told herself, then she'd leave.

"How did your movie debut go earlier?"

He laughed, and handed her a mug. "It was interesting."

"Interesting good?"

He shrugged. "I wasn't expecting to be involved in her documentary."

Daisy nodded. "By the way, I think Niamh felt Kayley was ordering her around today."

Matt looked thoughtful. "Niamh's a sweet kid, but she's probably a bit insecure. And I get the impression this is her first really big job, because she asks my opinion about *Every – Single – Thing*."

He opened his eyes wide, and Daisy grinned.

"Probably. Still, I told her that if Kayley asks her to do anything, she should run it by me or Kenny first."

"That's hardly necessary, Daisy."

Daisy wondered how Matt had just managed to undermine her, and dismiss Niamh so easily. Before she could say anything, lightning streaked through the sky, and moments later thunder rumbled loudly.

Daisy shivered as she peered out the window. "It's a good thing Kayley and her crew got away at lunch."

"Yeah, the road's probably flooded." Matt was matter of fact. "You might have to stay."

Daisy took a shaky breath. "I thought you'd be desperate for some peace and quiet."

Matt smiled. "This *is* peace and quiet."

Don't read anything into that, Daisy. She cradled the mug in her hands, and distracted herself by watching as rivulets of water ran along the deep stone sills outside.

"That's pretty bad rain." She frowned. "I presume you were able to get insurance for this place?"

"It cost a bit more than I'd have liked, but yes."

Why were they talking about weather and house insurance? Maybe they'd never talk about what happened. Maybe that's what Matt wanted. It was easier to ignore, she supposed.

"I'd better go." She was dreading the journey home in a thunderstorm, but she had no choice.

She shrugged quickly into her jacket and grabbed her bag.

"Talk to you tomorrow," she said. "Kenny and the decorators will be back in the morning."

In the hall, she opened the door, pointed her key fob at the car and dashed out, trying to avoid the puddles.

As she closed the driver's door, the windows steamed up, and she switched on the engine, yanking up the heater and setting the highest wiper speed. She glanced up to see if Matt was still there, but he'd closed the door.

As the windows cleared, she turned the car and started down the driveway, trying to remember where the potholes were. The second she drove through the gate and turned left onto the small road that led to the main road, she realised the river had burst its banks.

"*Shit.*' Daisy slowed to a stop and assessed the road. Maybe she could drive really slowly.

"*Daisy!*"

She jumped. Matt was standing at the passenger side of her car, knocking at the window. He'd dragged on a raincoat, but his hair was soaking wet, and rain streamed down his face.

She whizzed down the window a couple of inches.

"What are you doing?"

"Trying to stop you getting completely stuck. I've just seen this road from upstairs, and you won't get through tonight. I'm really sorry."

"Matt, I have to!"

He slicked his hair off his face. "Come back to the house and see for yourself. If you try to go on, you'll need a boat to rescue you."

"Okay." Daisy exhaled. "Get in."

Matt slid in beside her. Daisy reversed carefully back through the gate, and then drove back to the house.

❦

Back in the guest wing, she peeled off her coat as Matt turned up the thermostat.

"Maybe I could call a taxi to come to the main road, and I could walk up to meet it there," she said, shivering.

"Daisy, we're a mile from the motorway! You'd basically be wading through a mile of river – it's too dangerous."

"*Shit!* I should have left with Kenny. He obviously got out in time."

Matt sighed. "I'll report it now, although I'm not sure what good it'll do. The river should subside naturally – enough to drive through. Let me get you some dry clothes."

As Matt went upstairs, Daisy messaged James. **Working at client's house in Wicklow, road badly flooded so staying over. Back tomorrow xx**

She was putting her phone away just as Matt reappeared.

"I've left some towels and dry clothes in the bedroom for you, and I'll throw some frozen dinners in the oven."

163

He flashed her an apologetic look, and Daisy managed a nervous smile.

It wasn't his fault that the river had burst its banks, or that she was stuck here for the night. And at least she didn't have to go out into that storm. The universe seemed to be throwing them together: she just had to follow the signs.

CHAPTER 28

"You look kind of good in that, you know." Matt grinned cheekily as Daisy came back downstairs wearing an oversized grey tracksuit.

Daisy was pretty sure she looked like a pregnant donkey, but she'd been soaked through to her underwear, and all her clothes were now hanging over the backs of a couple of chairs upstairs.

"You lit a fire." She crossed the room to the log stove and held out her hands to warm up.

"I thought we could do with one."

Matt checked on the food cooking in the oven, and Daisy's stomach rumbled as the smell wafted through the room.

She eyed the sofa. It wasn't very big but she'd manage for one night. Upstairs there was a king-size bed with a roll-top end, but there were no other beds yet in the main house. Her eyes slid to Matt.

"You're taking the bed tonight," he said, reading her mind. "I have a blow-up mattress I can bring down."

"I can take the ma– "

"Don't argue. Just make yourself comfortable. I want to take out the dinner."

With a sigh, Daisy sat at one end of the sofa, and checked her phone, hoping James might have let her know how things were going: nothing. She hadn't heard from him all day. Matt returned with plates of steaming food and a bottle of wine.

"It's Shepherd's Pie." He looked a bit apologetic. "Not very summery, but turns out it's just what the doctor ordered with this weather."

Daisy put a plate on her lap and started to eat. "Wow, this does not taste like a frozen dinner!"

"They're from a deli in Avoca." Matt poured the wine. "They'll do until I get myself organised enough to cook."

"Do you still enjoy cooking?" There'd been a lot of pancakes, spaghetti bolognese and fajitas when they'd been together, she remembered.

"I prefer it when I have someone to cook for." Matt grinned. "Although with my new kitchen, I'll have no excuse."

"So, did you have someone to cook for in the States?" Daisy swirled the wine gently in her glass.

He looked at her. "Sometimes. I never lived with anyone there, if that's what you're asking."

What was she asking? It felt like they were dancing around each other. "That woman in the photo upstairs – was it recent?"

"Recent enough." He sighed. "It's complicated."

Daisy wondered if it was behind his decision to come home. "All of this." She gestured vaguely around the room. "It was a pretty dramatic move, Matt."

"I know, yeah." He shrugged. "Maybe I'll get a dog. I could buy some farmers' boots and go for long country walks."

Daisy started to laugh. "Come on, it's not really you, is it? The big house in the country, the isolation.'

"People are full of surprises."

She stopped laughing as she met his eyes. It wasn't the first time he'd said that. And this time she wasn't imagining an edge to his voice.

"Tell me more about New York?" she said.

Matt seemed to be choosing his words. "It was great for a few years. I had an apartment in one of the villages. You know those old brownstones you see in films?" He raised an eyebrow. "There was even an artisan bakery on the corner where I got my bread and organic coffee."

"God, the notions!" she teased.

"I *did* have a favourite hotdog stand."

"Better!"

Matt got up to throw another log into the stove, and Daisy watched the flames flicker up around it. She stretched, wriggling her feet in the dark, wool socks she'd borrowed.

She felt cocooned here, with the rain beating down outside. When had she and James last spent the night on the sofa together, just snuggling?

Matt sat back down beside her. Oh, brilliant, now she was thinking about snuggling!

"Do you know what I've just remembered?" Matt said.

Snuggling? "Um, you've ice cream in the freezer?"

"Sorry." He grinned. "I was thinking of that time we spent a couple of days away in that little hotel in Donegal. The one with the shepherd huts?"

"They'd double-booked us with that elderly couple, so they offered to put us up in one of their huts for free!" Daisy buried her face in her hands. "I still have nightmares about being woken by that spider."

"To think that your screams were the last thing it heard before I had to kill it."

"Hey, only one of us was getting to spend the rest of the night in that hut!" She shook her head. "I'm pretty sure they heard me screaming in the hotel!"

"We *did* get a few funny looks the following morning at breakfast." Matt was deadpan. "Although I figure they assumed we'd been having really great sex."

It was pointless trying to pretend to be cool when your face matched your hair colour! All these memories that she'd managed to bury, or at least blur, were suddenly sharper than ever.

"Are you getting too warm?" Matt was looking closely at her. "We can move the sofa a bit away from the fire."

"No, I'm fine, thanks." She pressed a cool hand against her warm cheek.

He got to his feet. "I'm going to leave some clean sheets for you in the bedroom. Have some more wine, I won't be long."

CHAPTER 29

Daisy got up and wandered over to the window, aware of a slight draught along the ledge. She took out her phone to check if there was anything from James: nothing. She rang him again, relieved when the call was picked up.

"James?"

"Hello, Daisy? It's Alma."

Her skin prickled. "What's wrong?"

"Nothing. James just went to bed. I told him I would answer his phone if you rang. He was very tired."

For a moment, Daisy was speechless. How had James agreed to leave his phone with Alma? He didn't even like *her* answering his phone! She swallowed hard.

"Good, yeah, glad he's sleeping. *Um*, did he get my message earlier about me being stuck in Wicklow?"

"Of course." Alma paused. "Please don't worry, Daisy. I will keep an eye on him."

"Look, no need to do anything, Alma. Thanks for answering my call, but if it rings again, James' voicemail will pick it up."

"Sure." Alma sounded unfazed. "Will you be home tomorrow?"

"I could be home at any time," Daisy said with forced cheerfulness. "I have to go now. Bye." She hung up. What was *wrong* with Alma? What was wrong with *James*? She jumped when her phone rang again, before she realised that it was Matt's.

"Matt?" Should she take it upstairs to him? She picked it up, surprised to see Kayley's name on the screen. Why was Kayley Lynch calling him?

She put it down and let it ring out; Matt would see the missed call. Feeling a bit awkward, she walked over to fill the kettle, scrolling through her Instagram feed as she waited.

Matt came back downstairs. "I'm glad you're making yourself at home."

"Oh yeah, I was wondering if you had any infusions."

"Should do." He'd picked up his phone before putting it on the counter to search one of the cupboards. "I've blackcurrant and lemon, raspberry, and green tea."

"*Um*, I think your phone rang."

"It's work." He rubbed a hand across the back of his neck. "I'll ring them tomorrow."

Work? She supposed Kayley fell loosely into that category. Not that it was any of her business. She was about to close Instagram, when something caught her eye.

"Matt, isn't that the front of the house?" She looked closer. "It's on Deuxmoi."

He moved closer to look. "Yeah, what the hell?"

She scrolled to the second picture on the post. "It's just photos of Kayley's crew arriving," she said.

Matt frowned. "I didn't notice any photographers hanging around."

She tried to remember. "No, but they could have been anywhere."

"Yeah, but it's a bit isolated out here." He shook his head. "Like, where the fuck were they hiding?"

She swiped to the last picture. It was one of Kayley and Matt in the driveway.

She looked a bit closer. Almost out of the frame was Alec, standing near the door, his gaze seemingly trained on Kayley. She sighed. Kayley was a pretty big star and she was fairly sure Alec's attentions were normal. But she'd mention it again to Kenny. If Todd was even half right about

Alec, she couldn't ignore it. But there was no point saying anything now. Instead, she put her phone away.

"Listen, Matt, if you need to work tonight, I can go upstairs."

"No, there's nothing I need to do." He dropped the infusions into a couple of mugs. "We can just talk if you want."

It felt like an invitation, she thought, as she watched him pour the water into the mugs.

"I know you're wondering why I came back," he said, finally.

Daisy found herself holding her breath.

"The thing is, I thought I had everything I wanted, but lately I've been wondering if I should have stayed and fought a bit harder."

"To give your career a chance here?" Daisy's voice was husky.

"Partly. And I think I should have fought for you."

For a few moments, Daisy couldn't breathe. Instead, she stared at Matt, until she realised he was probably waiting for her to say something. *Stick to the truth, Daisy.*

"Why would there have been a fight, Matt? You went to the States that summer and you decided to stay. Period!"

Matt sighed. "I didn't think you'd want to do this."

"I do." Daisy swallowed. "I've never understood why you just left. You didn't even break up with me properly. It hurt." It still hurt, but she wasn't sure if she wanted to admit it.

He stared at her and she held his gaze.

"I heard about the party," he said, folding his arms across his chest. "Brian told me."

"What party?"

"The one in your boyfriend's house that summer I did my internship in New York."

Daisy frowned, trying to think. She hadn't even known James at the time. "What are you talking about?"

"Come on, Daisy. Brian told me he was supposed to go that night, but he was sick, so Laura took you along instead." He sounded resigned.

Memories floated back. A warm, dry night in a student house off the Drumcondra road, so packed with people that most of them had ended up in the garden, drinking and smoking weed. It had been a small miracle that nobody had called the Guards, but nearly all the neighbouring houses had been rented by students.

She'd never tried weed before that night. Or since. Even now, she squirmed, remembering how she'd thrown up in a bush, before messaging Laura that she was going home, and she'd see her the next day. At the time, she hadn't even known it was James' house – there'd been a gang of people living there.

"Yes, I remember. But I don't understand ..."

"Brian told me he heard you'd stayed over with James."

"*What?*"

"You slept with him, Daisy. So I just made things easier for you."

CHAPTER 30

Matt's eyes narrowed. "Shit, are you going to faint?"

"No." Relief shivered through her at the concern in his voice. "I just can't believe that's what you thought! Like, all this time, that's what you were thinking about me? I never cheated on you, Matt."

"Daisy, please don't!"

"No! I don't get why you thought I'd cheat on you! On us!"

Matt rubbed the back of his neck. "I don't know what to believe, anymore. I thought you'd hooked up with James that night, so I decided I was better off staying in New York after the internship. The next thing I heard, you were with him, so ..."

She wished for one moment that she hadn't pushed him for the truth, that he hadn't suddenly, horrifically ripped the bandage off the wound.

"I met James a few months after you left, Matt." She managed to keep her voice even. "And, after that, it was ages before we started dating."

Matt's face seemed to drain of colour.

Helplessly, Daisy looked down at her tea, wishing it was a glass of wine. *Ah yes, Daisy, alcohol: the short-term solution to all your problems.*

"Matt, why didn't you just ask me straight out? Because some stupid rumours about a party was a pretty flimsy excuse to end a five-year relationship."

His eyes slid away. "It wasn't just that. There were a few things going on at the time. To be honest, I was in a pretty bad place."

For a moment, she wished she'd just left on time. That she'd been happy to leave the pain of that text – of that whole time – buried deeply. That she'd never wanted to find out the truth.

"You broke up by *text*, Matt! You could have talked to me!" Furiously, she blinked back tears. "None of this makes any sense. We were together five years, and you thought I'd sleep with someone else because you went away for one summer? You believed some stupid rumour – " She wanted to yell that he'd never deserved her for believing that.

"I'm really sorry, Daisy." Matt scrubbed his hands over his face. "If I could go back …"

For a while, they sat in silence, as Daisy tried to process everything.

"You know what I thought when you agreed to hire me?" she said finally. "That this was your way of saying sorry, of looking for closure."

"I *did* want closure. I missed you, Daisy. I've thought about you a lot since I left."

Something still seemed off. Or maybe Rosie was right, and she was looking for signs that just weren't there.

"I missed you too, Matt."

This was such a mess. She was with James. Even if they'd grown apart. But being alone like this with Matt was dangerous, especially now they both knew the truth. Knowing he'd left because of a misunderstanding was a head wreck. She should have tried harder at the time to find out what was wrong. It had been as much her fault as his: she'd just let him go. Panic surged through her, and she pushed herself shakily to her feet.

"I should go to bed." It all felt like too much – all she wanted right now was to be on her own.

"I'm sorry, this is a shitshow." Matt glanced away. "I think I handled it badly." When Daisy didn't reply, he added, "Maybe we both need some space to think?"

Daisy nodded.

"I left some other stuff out for you, but if you need anything else …" Matt smoothed his hand nervously over the back of his neck.

A memory of their first night together flashed to mind. She'd borrowed his toothbrush and spent the whole next day wondering if he'd really wanted her to stay.

"I'll see you in the morning, Matt."

"I have a spare toothbrush."

He spoke so quietly, she wasn't sure if she'd imagined it. For a moment they stood, looking at each other. Daisy wasn't sure which of them made the first move, but in the next moment she found herself standing so close to him she could hear their joint breathing and the thumping of her own heart. If she turned her face slightly to the side, Matt would kiss her cheek. He might even hug her. But she couldn't move.

He stepped infinitesimally closer, and for a brief moment Daisy felt a bit faint. *Breathe, Daisy.* She hoped there weren't any wine stains on her teeth. This was such a bad idea.

Except ... he was looking at her the way he used to. She watched, hypnotised, as he reached out and brushed her hair away from her face. As Daisy's breathing shallowed, she felt ... *shit*, was she about to faint? *Don't faint, Daisy.* She gasped for air, hoping Matt hadn't noticed. There was still time: she'd just say goodnight.

"You haven't changed a bit." Matt's voice was husky.

Haha, just two sizes bigger. And the war against feminism rages on, one self-deprecating thought at a time. Focus, Daisy!

Matt still wanted her. Which was astonishing, given that until about five minutes ago, he'd thought she'd slept with James while they'd still been together. *James, your current boyfriend, remember?*

Briefly, she closed her eyes and tried to concentrate on James. But Matt seemed to interpret it as an invitation, because before she knew it she was being pulled into his arms, and he was kissing her, and her arms were winding around his neck, obeying a five-year-old muscle memory.

Oh! God! She leaned in, excitement shooting through her as Matt angled her head to deepen the kiss. He felt so good. Had he always felt this good? He'd definitely got better!

"Jesus, Daisy." His lips left hers to trail down her neck, and Daisy heard herself moan as his hands slid under the top of her tracksuit.

She froze. No, not her tracksuit: his. The one she'd had to borrow because her own clothes were still wet. Because she'd left it too late to get home. Which was the only reason she was here right now! She opened her eyes and gulped in some air.

"*Stop!*"

Slowly, Matt straightened. "Are you – ?" He frowned. "Did I hurt you or something?"

Daisy shook her head, wondering if she'd detected a hint of annoyance. He was probably just confused. Which was understandable, given that her own levels of confusion were currently off the charts.

"I shouldn't ... I don't think this is a good idea."

Crapitty-cap, how had she let that happen? No, the how was pretty clear: she still really wanted him. Here they were, under the one roof – with one bed. If her life was a romantic comedy, it'd definitely be happening! James would never have to know – nobody would get hurt!

Reluctantly, she pulled away. "I'm sorry, Matt."

He said nothing, and Daisy wished that she could go back in time and talk to the Matt she'd known that summer he'd left for New York. *Please say something, Matt.*

"It's fine." He gave a tight smile. "I'll see you in the morning."

"See you in the morning." *Smile, Daisy, it'll be okay. Let him know it'll be okay.*

Upstairs, she quietly shut the bedroom door behind her, and sat down on the bed, her thoughts unravelling, her heart cracked wide open.

The last five years of her life boiled down to a stupid sliding-doors moment. If Matt had never gone away that summer ... if she'd never gone to that party ... if that rumour had never started. If he'd just asked her the truth!

She lay back and stared up at the ceiling, with its original coving and beautiful, ornate centrepiece. The first tears slid down her face, soaking the crisp, white linen pillow.

CHAPTER 31

MyStarScope Taurus: A relationship may deepen through dialogue, but if both of you feel ready to commit further, make sure you're on the same page.

For her first waking moments, Daisy couldn't remember anything that had happened the previous night. Then, the memory of her kissing Matt flooded back, making her almost sick with guilt.

What had she been thinking? She'd only had one glass of wine, so she couldn't even blame drink! She lay, staring at the ceiling, wondering how she was going to face him. But she had no choice: she had to pull herself together and figure out what she was going to do now.

Although, had anything *actually* happened? Like, was a kiss even cheating? She tried to imagine how she'd feel if James snogged somebody else. Alma, maybe. She couldn't even go there right now – it was way too stressy.

She swung her legs out of the bed, hoping her clothes were dry. There'd be no time to drive all the way home, and turning up at the office in one of Matt's tracksuits wasn't a good look. Only her clothes were downstairs. They'd still been damp when she'd gone up to bed, so she'd waited until she'd heard Matt going into the bathroom, before slipping down to leave them to dry near the fire.

Pulling the tracksuit on, she opened the bedroom door and stuck her head around to listen. The place seemed quiet: maybe Matt had gone into the main part of the house. She hurried downstairs.

"Hey, good morning." Matt was at the small electric stove, pouring oil onto a frying pan. "I was about to make some breakfast. Will I count you in?"

Daisy shook her head. "I should really get on the road." She pointed to her clothes, draped over the backs of two kitchen chairs.

"About that." He pulled a face. "The road's still badly flooded."

"*Shit.*"

"The local council says they're sending people out around lunchtime with suction hoses to clear the worst of the water off the road."

She was going to be stuck here until lunchtime?

As if he'd read her mind, Matt added, "I'll leave you alone if you want to work from here this morning. I'm sorry, it's not ideal."

Daisy reminded herself again that none of it was his fault; she just had to be professional. Which was a bit tricky after what had happened.

"It's grand, I'll manage." She grabbed her clothes from the chairs, relieved that everything seemed dry. "Back in a few."

Upstairs, Daisy showered and dressed, feeling a bit better once she was properly dressed. She phoned James, but after three rings it went to voicemail.

"Hi, just checking in." She did her best to sound casual. "We're still waiting for the road to be cleared, so I'll go straight to work and I'll see you this evening." She was about to add that she loved him, but stopped herself. After what had happened between her and Matt, it felt wrong. Without another word, she hung up.

In the bathroom, she pulled her hair into a low knot, and reapplied her make-up, grateful that she always carried some for touch-ups. That was the thing about her job: people expected her to be stylish and 'finished' looking. It inspired confidence.

As she headed downstairs, she wondered if they could just *pretend* the kiss had never happened.

"Perfect timing," Matt said, putting breakfast on the table.

"Great. I usually just grab some toast in the morning, or a pastry on my way into work. Although I always get a coffee. Two, sometimes." And now she was babbling. Nervous babbling! He'd never guess.

"Why don't you just stay another night and I'll really spoil you."

He shot her a sly smile, and a mix of desire and panic spiralled through her. She'd spent one night at Granary House and look what had nearly happened! But clearly, they couldn't ignore it. "Matt, about that kiss – "

"About last night," Matt began at the same time.

Shit, he regretted it, she thought.

"It was late," he said. "We both got a bit carried away."

"Exactly." She nodded vigorously. Good. This was what she wanted. Or at least, it should be.

"It doesn't mean I'm not still attracted to you," Matt said slowly. "I'll be honest. I wondered how I'd feel when we met again. Like, would there still be a spark?"

"And you thought you'd still feel something even though you thought I'd cheated on you?" Only why was that so strange? Every day for the last five years she'd thought about him.

His jaw tightened. "I'm sorry I never asked. It wouldn't have made everything right, but it would have helped." He rested his elbows on the table and met her eyes.

Why wouldn't it have made everything right? He'd said there'd been other things going on at the time. But surely she deserved an explanation now? Especially as it was pretty clear after last night that they were still attracted to each other! Last night ... God, she had to stop thinking about last night. It had definitely complicated things a bit. More than a bit.

What if it was a sign, though? If she ignored it, she could end up experiencing another sliding-doors moment.

Matt pushed his plate away. "I meant what I said about wanting closure. Or that's what I wanted when I got back."

"Right." Daisy stared at the congealing eggs on her plate. "What about now?"

"I'm not sure if that's enough anymore."

She looked up, unsure how to respond. She knew he was just out of a complicated relationship. But it was the only thing she knew about these last five years. Despite how familiar Matt felt, he wasn't the same person. She wasn't either. She got up and took her half-finished food and coffee to the sink.

"You don't have to do that." Matt came over, and put his hand briefly over hers.

"Thanks for breakfast." She smiled brightly as she met his eyes. "I'll work in the main house until the road is cleared."

He gave a brief nod. "I'll let you know."

Upstairs, Daisy leaned for a moment against the bedroom door, her mind racing. Matt had finally admitted what she'd suspected. But he'd hurt her badly before, and she'd no guarantees that he wouldn't do it again.

The truth was that nothing was guaranteed. Not Matt, not James, not even her friendship with Laura. And, more importantly, she knew now that she'd done nothing wrong. It had all been a misunderstanding. The only problem now was that she'd no idea what was supposed to happen next.

CHAPTER 32

@Deuxmoi: **Kayley Lynch and her band in high spirits as they leave Dublin's fashionable Bitter Honey Club in the early hours of the morning.**

By the time Daisy got to the office that afternoon, she was convinced Laura would take one look at her, and know exactly what had happened. Or what had *almost* happened, she reminded herself.

Now she knew why Matt had left, it was painful to imagine how different their lives could have been if he'd just asked her the truth about that stupid party.

She also knew she wasn't ready to tell anyone about it. Laura already hated Matt enough, and Daisy guessed that if she told her why Matt had left, she'd judge him even more harshly than before. She couldn't understand why Brian would have told Matt something like that. Even now, she suspected it had just been an awful mistake. And she wasn't ready to accuse Brian and risk alienating Laura.

She needed time to sort through everything for herself. Which meant she had to pretend that everything was normal.

"Anything new this morning?" she asked brightly.

Laura narrowed her gaze. "Why are you talking like that?"

"Like what?" Daisy wrapped her hair into a knot and stuck a pencil through it to hold it in place.

"Have it your way." Laura shook her head. "The latest from Mrs Feng Shui is that my design won't 'allow her middle daughter to find love'!' Other than that, nothing to report."

She flashed a huge fake smile and Daisy laughed, shaking out some tension.

"Is she reading *Feng Shui for Idiots* or something?"

"If that book exists, I should read it. At least we'd be on the same page. I mean, why employ someone like me if you're going to spend your whole time telling me I'm wrong?"

"Tell her to put some moonstone under her mattress," Fionn said, looking up from his laptop. "Or her daughter could wear it as jewellery."

Laura held up a hand. "Stop! The poor girl's only a teenager! Her mother's just batshit crazy."

No wonder Laura was frustrated. Daisy knew from previous experience how difficult clients could be. By contrast, she'd been very lucky in her last few jobs.

Both Freya and Matt had agreed with Daisy's broad vision for their houses, and she had an amazing house to enter for the award. Her mind wandered back to what Fionn had said.

"Fionn, is moonstone white?"

"Yup." He typed something quickly on the keyboard, and turned the screen so Daisy could see. "That's moonstone. It attracts love, and it's Gemini's alternative birthstone."

It was the same stone Kayley had been wearing around her neck the first time Daisy had met her, she realised.

Laura looked amused. "Do you know everyone's birthstone, Fionn?"

He swept his fringe out of the way. "There's only twelve traditional, and twelve alternative ones to remember. Plus, I'm a Gemini!"

Daisy's phone rang and Matt's name flashed up on the screen.

"Hi." She glanced over at Laura.

"Hi." Matt's voice was warm. "I just wanted to check that you got to work."

"*Um*, yep, there's a bit of damage along the riverbank, but the road was okay." Daisy walked over to the window and looked out. She could see a tour bus pulling up across the street. "I'm sorry I had to intrude for so long – thanks for putting up with me."

"You'd never intrude."

He sounded so sincere. She half-turned, aware that Laura and Fionn were probably listening to every word.

"I messaged Kenny earlier about the flooding, so I'll make sure he knows the road's okay now. And you know where I am if you need me."

"Yes. Thanks."

Daisy hung up and messaged Kenny with the update. Then she sat back at her desk, carefully avoiding making eye contact with the others.

She'd woken frequently during the night, conscious that Matt was on a mattress downstairs. Each time she'd woken, she'd wondered guiltily about James. Had he missed her? Or had he been too sick to notice? She should be grateful to Alma, she supposed.

Fionn scraped his chair away from his desk. "Coffee? Usual, everyone?"

"Not for me," Laura said. "I got one on my way."

"Daisy?"

"Yeah, thanks, Fionn."

After he left, Laura whipped around to glare at Daisy. "Why didn't you say that you spent the night at Matt's place?"

God, she wasn't ready. "I was there late yesterday evening and the river burst its banks, and flooded the road. I'd no choice, Laura, and nothing happened."

"The fact that you even stayed over!" Laura looked at her carefully. "So, did you talk about anything?"

If she admitted that they had, she could let something slip. Daisy shook her head.

"You're better off not dredging up all that history, babes," Laura said firmly. "You owe it to yourself not to get hurt again, so just be careful. In fact, don't talk about anything!"

"Laura, 'careful' is my middle name! Honestly, you have nothing to worry about!"

We just kissed and nearly ended up having sex.

"Good, yeah." Laura crossed her legs.

Daisy studied her for a moment. "Is everything okay?"

"All good." Laura's smile seemed a bit strained.

Maybe Laura guessed that she wasn't telling her the truth about Matt. But it was more than that. Laura had changed. Daisy wondered if everything was okay between her and Brian. If they weren't, why would she stay with him?

For the same reason you're staying with James? It wasn't that things were awful with James, she thought. It was just that they didn't seem to be going anywhere anymore. Was this what happened? Did people just stay together out of habit? She supposed it was normal enough.

And how could she imagine that she had some magical insight into someone else's relationship, when she couldn't even figure out her own.

With a sigh, she opened her drawings of Granary House and went through a checklist. The last bits of work were going well, thanks to Kenny and his team. And at the rate they were going, the painters and decorators would be finished most of the house in another week. Her mobile rang again, and she braced herself for another call from Matt. But it was Kenny.

"Hi, Kenny, I was just about to call you. The road was cleared earlier, so you should have no problems."

"Yeah, I'm on my way. Just wanted to check that we're doing all the new floor-to-ceiling units in the second reception room today?"

"Yes. The painters will do the wall that won't have shelving." She was pretty sure they'd gone through those details before.

He grunted. "Did you get away last night okay?"

So that was why he was calling her! "*Eh*, no, there was mad flash flooding and it was too dangerous, so I ended up staying over."

There was a muffled noise that sounded a bit like swearing, followed by a moment's silence.

"Right." Kenny cleared his throat loudly. "Look, Daisy, I know I'm probably a bit out of line, but we've known each other a long time, and sure I'm old enough to be your dad."

Daisy glanced over at Laura, but she seemed to be busy. "*Uh huh?*"

"Right. Now." Kenny cleared his throat again, and Daisy pulled the phone away from her ear for a moment. "I know you know this fellah, or you used to. So I hope you don't mind me telling you to be a bit careful. I don't trust him. I don't know why, but that's it now."

Daisy scrambled for an answer that wouldn't sound like she was being defensive.

"I'm sorry now if I've overstepped," Kenny added.

Daisy suspected he was more embarrassed than sorry. She was also starting to wonder if he was in the Keep Daisy Safe Club with her mother and Laura.

"Not at all, Kenny." She forced a smile, knowing he'd hear it in her voice. "I appreciate that but you don't have to worry."

"Right," Kenny said. "I'll see you soon, so. Bye, now."

He hung up, and Daisy put her phone away, avoiding Laura's eyes as she turned on her laptop. She wondered what Matt had done to make Kenny dislike him. He barely knew Matt. Then again, she'd known Matt intimately for over five years and he'd still managed to shock her!

"Babes?" Laura looked over. "Does James know where you stayed last night?"

Daisy folded her arms. "No, he doesn't know I'm working for Matt! I just told him I had to stay over at a client's house in Wicklow because the road was flooded."

"Oh-kay. So what happens if Granary House is shortlisted? James will know it's in Wicklow, and he'll know who owns the house. It won't take him long to put two and two together."

"*Um*, I'll cross that bridge if I come to it. I mean, it would only happen if Granary House actually placed. And it mightn't, right?"

Laura gave her a hard look. "No, it mightn't," she said slowly. "But what's the point in entering it if you don't want it to place? And I know you, Daisy, you want to win. So what if you suddenly get everything you want, and James finds out you've been lying to him? He'll know that you've been seeing your ex-boyfriend and you spent the night at his house! Just the two of you!"

"James trusts me, Laura. And nothing happened at Matt's." *Just that kiss.* Daisy clenched and unclenched her fists.

"Look at it from his point of view, babes," Laura said. "When he finds out you've been keeping the whole Matt-being-a-client-thing from him, he's going to wonder why."

Of course he would. Only now she'd spent the night in Matt's house! Daisy suddenly felt queasy. How had she not thought of that?

CHAPTER 33

There was no sign of James or Alma when Daisy got home that evening. As she went upstairs to change, she wondered if James had been feeling well enough to go into the office for a while. She had her blouse unbuttoned as she opened their bedroom door but stopped short at the little scene that greeted her. James was in bed, and sitting beside him, on the art-deco chair Daisy had inherited from her aunt, was Alma.

"What the – ?" She scrambled to button up her blouse again.

"Oh, sorry!" Alma stood, looking a bit confused as she realised Daisy had been undressing.

"No bother." Daisy looked directly at James. "What's going on?"

"James has a high temperature," Alma said before he could reply. She pointed to the thermometer on the bedside locker, and Daisy picked it up.

"It's 39.2. Did you take Paracetamol?"

He nodded. "I feel like shit. Alma made me some real chicken soup."

He smiled at Alma, and Daisy forced herself to smile at her too.

"Brilliant, thanks, Alma. Listen, you can get back to whatever you're doing."

"I'm going out with a friend who's visiting from Sweden. James was recommending a good place to eat."

She gave James a look that Daisy couldn't read. It was like some secret language they had, Daisy thought, feeling a stab of pain behind her eyes.

Alma opened the door. "There's more soup in the pot if you want it."

She left and Daisy sat down on the bed.

"That was good of her to make the soup," she said carefully.

"Yeah, she's great." He leaned back against the headrest. "How was last night? Must have been a bit weird having to stay with those people in Wicklow."

"Ah no, it was grand." Heat flashed to her face. "They had a spare room so I had an early night, and the road was cleared this morning."

"Was there bad flooding?"

"Bad enough." Better not to be too specific.

James grimaced. "The storm wasn't even that severe. Imagine living there!"

Daisy gave a vague nod. It wouldn't put her off moving back to the country, but James had grown up in Dublin and she knew he found it difficult to imagine anything other than city life. It was Matt who'd surprised her the most. When they'd been a couple, he'd probably come down to Oranmore a handful of times, because he'd claimed it had been miles from anywhere interesting. Daisy figured that living in a busy, noisy city had made him appreciate the upsides of rural life.

"So, what were you and Alma chatting about?" she said.

He shrugged. "Just what she was telling you, really."

A coldness settled in her stomach. She'd never doubted James until this last year. Deep down, she knew he was hiding something from her. Unless he wasn't bothering to hide anything! What if all the signs were there, right in front of her, and she'd been ignoring them? What if James was just waiting for the right moment to end things, or worse, hoping she'd make the first move?

He slid back down under the covers. "I'm wrecked, I'm just going to get some sleep."

"Right." Daisy was relieved to get away. "Let me know if I can get you anything."

As she slipped out of the room, James had already closed his eyes.

Alma was in the hall when she came downstairs.

"Have a good night." Daisy forced herself to smile again.

"Thank you." Alma paused. "I was looking at videos of the flooding in Wicklow."

"Yes – it was very bad."

"I read that Kayley Lynch is going to be gigging in Wicklow. At an old house?"

Daisy did her best to sound disinterested. "Yeah, I've heard that too." Before Alma could say anything else, she excused herself and walked into the kitchen, closing the door firmly behind her. Oh God! Did Alma guess that she was working there? Was it some sort of game that she was playing?

Leaning her hip against the wall, she stared out at their tiny patio. It wasn't the only game Alma was playing. There was definitely something up with her and James.

But it was really just a feeling. She had no actual *evidence* that there was anything going on. For now, the best course of action was to do nothing.

CHAPTER 34

American country singer Kayley Lynch is embroiled in a new scandal, after a second leaked video has gone viral. It appears to show Kayley verbally attacking former band member, Newry Stone, after Newry accused Kayley of racist remarks. Kayley has denied the remarks were racist, and claims that she was simply defending herself. The video comes just three months after another video, where Kayley appeared to verbally abuse a member of her band, who'd threatened to sue the singer for not being properly paid.

Kayley Lynch is currently in Ireland for the last leg of her European tour. She is staying at Dublin's five-star Shelbourne Hotel.

Daisy was glad to be working at Freya's house the following day. Since Matt's revelation the night of the storm, her emotions felt ridiculously close to the surface, and she'd found herself second-guessing all her choices since he'd left. She hoped that a bit of time apart would put things in perspective.

Freya seemed distracted when she answered the door.

"Hi, Freya, all okay?" Daisy stepped into the hall, and shrugged out of her coat.

Freya gave a brief smile. "I'm just working from home. Holly's off school sick."

Daisy nodded, making sure her expression didn't change. She'd noticed that Holly seemed to take a lot of time off school, although Daisy had never seen her sick. Freya always seemed more watchful around her too. It reminded Daisy of the way Rosie kept an extra eye on Ben.

She took out her iPad. "Mind if I start upstairs?"

"Sure. Oh, quick question just before you –"

"Yep, let me open up your file."

"No, it's not that. I was wondering if your sister knows a good occupational therapist in Dublin." Freya folded her arms. "There's a private wait list of three to four months – that's too long. And it's not therapy that's needed, just a diagnosis."

Daisy remembered that she'd briefly mentioned what her sister did, during her first meeting with Freya. Clearly, the woman had a knack of mentally filing stuff away.

"*Um*, sure, I can ask her for you." Was Freya worried about an elderly parent? Daisy wondered if either of her own parents would need an occupational therapist someday. They were so young, it seemed pointless to worry. But for the first time, she felt grateful that Rosie lived so close to them.

"Thanks, Daisy. So, the painters are finishing the girls' bedroom, I think, and Niamh is finishing some electrics in the kitchen." Freya turned and went into her study, closing the door firmly behind her.

Daisy went upstairs, hoping Freya was wrong about the decorators. When she'd checked the previous day, they'd finished the big bedroom at the back of the house. But she found Evan repainting the lower half of the walls a dusty rose.

"Howya, Daisy, come to check up on us?"

She shook her head. "Snag list. I thought you finished this yesterday?"

"We did." He gave her a pointed look. "But this morning we found the whole lower part of the wall covered in navy-blue."

"You're kidding."

"*Ha*, I wish!" Evan shrugged. "Freya said one of the younger kids decided to get creative yesterday evening." He scrubbed a hand over his face. "Once Freya doesn't start complaining about a late finish. We have to give her daily updates!"

"If there's any problems, Evan, just let me know." Daisy's phone buzzed, and her stomach flipped when she saw Matt's name flash up on the screen. "Excuse me." She swiped to answer as she went back downstairs. "Hi, Matt."

"Daisy? Any chance you could get Niamh out to the house ASAP? Our electricity is gone, and Kenny's dug his heels in, says she's on another job that he can't pull her from. I've told him he has to, or I get another electrician." He sounded furious.

"Hang on, Matt, when did your power go?"

"About half an hour ago. And, before you ask, it's not a local outage. It's just our house."

Daisy tried to think. "You know, you could be on a different power line to your neighbours, so even if –"

"It's not that, Daisy! Look, I don't know what's happened, but somebody's screwed up and your foreman doesn't want to take any responsibility."

Daisy started to defend Kenny, when she heard him shouting in the background.

Matt cursed, and for the next few minutes Daisy was forced to listen to what sounded like a muffled argument between the two men.

Finally, Matt came back on the phone. "Look, here's the thing, Daisy: Kayley's moved into the guest wing. She wanted to get away from the paparazzi, and she's got all her rehearsals and filming happening. And your workmen have downed tools, so if we don't get the electricity back, that's a day lost."

Briefly, Daisy shut her eyes. "Let me see what I can do." She hung up before Matt could say anything else.

Almost immediately, Kenny rang, and she took a couple of breaths before answering the call. "Kenny, what's happening?"

"*Jesus Christ, Daisy!*" Kenny practically snarled down the phone. "Yer man's bad enough on a good day, but the moment something tiny goes wrong, he shows his true colours. He's been bad-mouthing my crew."

A little voice in Daisy's head told her that Matt was acting like an entitled gobshite. But she reminded herself that he was probably under a lot of strain.

She spoke carefully. "Look, Kenny, I think Matt's under pressure with Kayley and her band and crew around the place. Any idea what the problem might be?"

Kenny huffed a sigh. "Nothing I can see, but I'll talk to Niamh."

"She's here with me in Freya's house at the moment."

"I'll phone her," Kenny said. "She might be able to tell me what to do over the phone."

Niamh was still working in Freya's kitchen a short while later.

"Did Kenny get you earlier?" Daisy asked.

Niamh shot her a brief look. "Yeah, he did. He told me not to bother going out to Matt's place to fix the problem. And I told him there was nothing I could do over the phone."

"Right." Daisy tried to be diplomatic. "I guess he didn't want to pull you off another job. And I'm sure another electrician –"

"Nobody knows the electrics at Matt's place like I do." Niamh grabbed a screwdriver from her bag.

Daisy thought quickly. "True. But you've done such a great job another electrician should be able to figure out what's wrong."

Niamh muttered something that sounded vaguely rude.

Daisy sighed. It was going to be one of those days.

CHAPTER 35

Daisy was still thinking about Freya's request when she got to the office after lunch. Her initial impression of Freya was of someone who didn't let anything get to her, and who knew exactly what she wanted. That hadn't exactly changed, but Daisy was starting to see a hint of vulnerability.

She wasn't sure what had been wrong with Holly but, whatever it was, she seemed to have made a speedy recovery. Still, Rosie claimed that kids got sick quickly and got better just as fast. Daisy wished the same rule applied to adults.

Now she sank gratefully into her chair and took a deep breath.

"*Um*, did someone light a scented candle?"

"Do you like it?" Fionn beamed.

Laura rolled her eyes. "Wait for it."

Daisy tried to identify the smell. "It's different, what is it?"

"An air diffuser with frankincense oil. It's for creativity and focus."

"And handy if we stumble upon any Wise Men," Laura muttered.

"I've never smelt frankincense before." Daisy got up and walked over to the small side table where Fionn had placed the diffuser in the middle of a small white plate, with three colourful crystals.

"Never?" Laura looked at her in mock-horror. "How is that even possible?"

Daisy grinned. "I'm assuming the crystals are meaningful, Fionn. They're kind of giving off Irish-flag vibes."

He sat up straighter. "So, there's a moonstone for me, a citrine for Laura, because she's a Scorpio – that's the gold one – and an emerald for you."

"Emerald?" Daisy wrinkled her nose. "That's pretty traditional."

Fionn shrugged. "There's really only one birthstone for Taurus. They're kind of an awkward sign."

"*Wow*, thanks. Any messages, by the way?"

"*Uh*, nope."

Hopefully, Kenny had got things sorted. And once Freya's job was finished, she'd be able to focus completely on finishing Granary House. Ideally, she'd love to have one or two extra projects lined up, but after an initial upsurge of business after the pandemic, things had slowed considerably in the last couple of years.

"How are things with you, Fionn?"

He swept his fringe carefully out of his eyes. "Work-wise, it's all cool. I'm able to stay late in college, which is a total save, because I can't get anything done at my house."

"Things still that bad?"

He sighed. "The two people who were supposed to stay a couple of days? They bought themselves a double airbed! I don't think they're ever going to leave."

"What if the landlord finds out?"

"Who's going to tell him? Anyway, they've nowhere else to go." He shrugged. "How's James?"

Daisy opened Freya's long snag list on her iPad. "Oh, still sick." She looked back up. "I keep thinking I'm going to get strep as well, but it hasn't happened. Which is great, obviously, but a bit, you know … strange."

"Well, yeah." Fionn looked thoughtful. "Although I didn't get it when my sister did. Nobody in our house did. She got it from her boyfriend. Mam was ready to kill her."

"Her boyfriend?" Daisy echoed.

Fionn's eyes widened, as he seemed to realise what Daisy was thinking. "But, like, there's probably loads of ways you can catch it. It doesn't just have to be through –"

"Oh God, yeah, I know." Daisy laughed weakly. If James *had* snogged Alma, it would be karma. Would things be clearer if she knew for sure? It'd definitely be a sign. Although there was so much else going on, it was easier not to know. She put her head in her hands. *Daisy Devlin: self-confessed ostrich.*

⁂

Daisy rang Rosie as soon as she got home.

"What's wrong?" Rosie asked immediately.

Why did her sister always think the worst? Daisy counted to five. When that didn't work, she counted to ten.

"Daisy, are you still there?"

"Sorry, the line dropped for a moment. *Er*, nothing's wrong. I just wanted to ask if you know any occupational therapists here in Dublin? Or even near Dublin?"

There was a silence. "Why?" Rosie said, finally.

"A friend of mine asked me to ask you," Daisy said. "Well, not a friend, she's actually a client. She wants to go private and doesn't want to have to wait – well, actually, I think she's enquiring for someone else but I don't know who. She's very – eh – private."

"Whoever it is needs a referral from a doctor." Rosie sounded brisk. "Would it be for an older person, do you think?"

"No idea. But normally it would be, right?"

"Not necessarily. It could be a young person who's been in an accident, although in that case they'd be assessed in hospital." Rosie paused. "But it could be a child. Lots of kids are referred to OTs for diagnoses."

"Diagnoses?"

"A good OT can diagnose everything from developmental delays to dyslexia to autism."

It was Holly, Daisy thought, with a flash of insight. It was probably why Freya always seemed so worried about her, why she seemed to miss so much school.

And why Freya wanted her in her own room, close to her and Neil. She'd bet it was why the couple had been through so many childminders.

"Yeah, it might be a child," she said.

"Then she'd need a paediatric OT."

Like Rosie, Daisy thought. Except Rosie lived on the far side of the country, and was currently on career leave.

"How's work going on Granary House?"

Daisy was a bit surprised. Rosie never remembered specific details about her work. Although her sister was probably less interested in the house than its owner.

"*Um*, fine. We're having to do the house and gardens pretty quickly because the grounds are going to be used all summer."

"What's it like having Kayley Lynch around?" Rosie said. "Don't get me wrong, I wouldn't be mad about her music, but you'd feel a bit sorry for her. Nothing would pay you for the abuse she's getting online."

"I suppose so." Daisy was about to add that Kayley was a pain in the arse, but stopped herself in time. Rosie was right: nobody deserved it.

"Anyway, I'm glad you're nearly finished," Rosie was saying. "The longer you hang around Matt, the more danger you're putting yourself in."

Technically, that boat hadn't set sail, Daisy mused. But it was definitely pulling out of the harbour. "How are plans coming along for Mum and Dad's anniversary party?" she asked.

"Oh, class. I listened to three bands, and I've picked the best one. They'll play all the stuff Mum and Dad like."

Daisy half-listened as Rosie went into detail about her music choices.

"Cáit Furey's younger brother is the lead guitarist," she said. "So they gave us a good rate."

Daisy was trying to remember who Cáit Furey was, when Rosie asked about James.

"He's sick at the moment." Daisy wondered how much detail to give, but then decided to be honest. As a mother of four, Rosie fancied herself a font of all knowledge about illnesses, and Daisy figured she might have a few tips. "It's strep – he just got an antibiotic for it."

"Strep?" Rosie sounded a bit surprised. "Have you had it too? You'd better be careful not to catch it, Daisy, it's really contagious."

"Yeah, I know."

"So, how did he get it?" Rosie sounded thoughtful. "Who was I talking to recently, who said they had it?"

God, she shouldn't have said a word. "No idea. How are the kids?"

"Happy out." Rosie paused. "Although I might just ask the doctor about Ben when we're there next. He *does* seem to throw up a lot. I think he might be allergic to something."

Food, Daisy thought. The boy was allergic to food: too much of it. But if her sister didn't hear it from an expert, or better still, figure it out for herself, she'd dismiss the idea immediately.

"By the way, Mum's been trying to sell that painting of hers." Rosie sounded grim.

Daisy thought for a moment. "The nude? Can you not persuade her to hang it in her bedroom, or something?"

"You think I haven't tried?" Rosie huffed. "The worst thing is that Dad's told her it's the best painting she's ever done."

"*Shit!* I mean, I suppose it probably is. Like, objectively."

"Daisy!"

"Sorry! Where's she trying to sell it?"

"The open-air market in Galway, you know the one. She took a stall!"

"You don't think they're a bit short of money, do you?" Daisy said. "Maybe they're starting to realise how much this party is going to cost, and this is Mum's way of helping out."

"If it's true, it's her own fault." Rosie sniffed. "Séan has offered to do her accounts so many times, and Mum keeps turning him down and telling him she's quite capable of doing a few tax returns."

"Maybe I could have a word?" Daisy offered.

"That's a great idea," Rosie said, quickly. "She might actually listen to you. And I've enough going on without having to deal with this! Listen, I've got to go. Don't forget to ask whether it's a paediatric OT your friend is looking for."

"Thanks, Rosie."

"Yeah, don't mention it, just talk to Mum. I'm going now. Bye." Rosie hung up.

Daisy tried to imagine her mother at the weekend markets in Church Lane, trying to sell her life-sized, nude self-portrait. She supposed she should be grateful she was living in Dublin.

CHAPTER 36

MyStarScope Taurus: With Neptune in your Orbit, you should view challenges as opportunities to grow.

"Oh crap, Matt, what happened?" Daisy stood in the kitchen at Granary House the following Monday, and stared at the huge hole in the conservatory roof directly above the scaffolding and the shattered glass all over the floor.

Matt folded his arms tightly across his chest. "I'd have thought that was pretty obvious. Kenny didn't secure this properly."

Daisy's stomach clenched nervously. "Matt, hang on. I've worked with Kenny for years. There's no way he'd mess up scaffolding. And it doesn't explain the hole in the ceiling." She peered closer. "Wait, isn't that where the ceiling fan was?"

Matt's lips thinned. "It fell down."

Daisy walked carefully across the room, trying not to step on any glass. "It's here – it's broken too." She squinted up at the ceiling. "You're lucky the way this roof was constructed. You've only lost a couple of panels, the rest of them seem to be intact. But we *will* have to get the whole thing checked."

"*Fuck!* This is going to delay everything, isn't it?"

"A bit," Daisy admitted.

Matt rubbed the back of his neck. "How much is a bit? I need this job done, Daisy, and I can't afford any more delays."

Daisy pushed away her annoyance. "Look, we probably shouldn't be disturbing anything. I'm assuming your insurance will take care of this. Have you called them yet?"

"*Er*, no." Matt cleared his throat.

"Okay, well, let's wait to see what Kenny has to say. He might have an idea what –"

"*Christ on a bike, what the fuck happened?*"

They both turned at the sound of Kenny's voice. He seemed to be assessing the scene. "Out of there now, Daisy. It's not safe." He glared at Matt as Daisy picked her way carefully back across the room.

"I've had a quick look, Kenny," she said, once she was back at the door. "There's only a couple of panes of glass gone, and the rest seem fine. We're just not sure what happened."

"I'm going next door to make some coffee." Matt left abruptly.

"If the house was on fire, yer man would make sure he had his bloody coffee," Kenny grumbled.

Daisy sighed. "He has to call his insurance company too."

Kenny grunted, swapping his beanie for a hard hat from his tool bag, before walking into the room. He studied the ceiling for a moment, before turning his attention to the scaffolding.

"The scaffolding doesn't seem damaged." Kenny gave her a level look. "This floor is all sticky. Beer, I think, judging by the smell. But I'll want a serious word with yer man. Someone was messing around!"

"Kenny, let's not jump to any conclusions," Daisy said as she heard Matt coming back into the hall.

"I never jump to anything, Daisy." Kenny took off his hard hat, and ran a hand across his stubbled head. "I'm just calling it as I see it."

Matt came back into the kitchen carrying a tray with three cups of coffee.

"It's all right." He handed a coffee to Daisy, and offered the second one to Kenny. "I saw Kayley when I went next door. Her band all crashed there last night, after a late session. I think things might have got a bit out of hand."

"Here? In a room full of scaffolding?" Daisy flicked Kenny a nervous look.

"No." Matt looked uncomfortable. "By the looks of it, they were in the living room for most of the night. But the bass guitarist, Greg, came in here and climbed to the top of the scaffolding. Kayley said he spilt beer all over the planking and slipped, so he grabbed on to the ceiling fan to steady himself." He shrugged. "I think we can guess the rest."

"*Fucking gobshite!*" Kenny said.

For one tense moment, Daisy thought Kenny might be talking about Matt, but Matt seemed to assume he was referring to Greg.

"So, is this fellah paying for the damage he's done? Because either way, we'll just have to keep going and add this onto your bill." Kenny drank some coffee and wiped his mouth with the back of his hand.

"Keep going, please," Matt said tightly. "I'll speak to Kayley's manager. But you might want to ask that workman of yours what he was up to the other day when I saw him messing around with this."

Kenny stared hard at him. "What are you on about?"

"Alec! He had a screwdriver – he said he was checking the structure to make sure everything was okay."

A pulse throbbed in Kenny's neck. "If that's what Alec said he was doing, that's what he was doing!"

Matt jutted out his chin. "Fine, well, we can't prove anything –"

"There's nothing to prove," Kenny ground out. "We know for a fact that your house guests were messing around with my scaffolding!" Kenny gesticulated towards the structure, causing some coffee to spill.

"By climbing on it?" Matt gave an angry laugh. "Sorry for thinking that that's what it's for!"

"It's not a fucking toy!"

"Guys, stop!" Daisy said, quickly. "I'm sure Matt will talk to Kayley's manager to make sure this won't happen again and *um*, Kenny, you can recheck the planking to make sure it'll be safe for your crew to use."

There was silence for a moment.

Then Matt shrugged. "Okay by me."

Kenny still looked annoyed. "We'll inspect the ceiling, and see what needs to be done." He glared at Matt. "Tell your guests to stay out of here. In fact, tell them to keep out of our way altogether. Otherwise, I can't guarantee your house will be finished on time."

Matt rolled his eyes. "Pretty sure this won't be a big deal, Kenny. Now, if you'll both excuse me, I've got stuff to do." He turned to go.

"There's just one thing I don't understand," Kenny said.

"What?" Matt uttered the word with exaggerated patience.

"How come you didn't know this was going on?"

A muscle flickered in Matt's jaw. "I was out."

Kenny gave him a disbelieving look. "And you didn't notice any of this when you came back?"

"I went straight to bed," Matt said dismissively. "Daisy, I'll be in my office if you need me."

Daisy managed a smile. "Sure."

"*Gobshite*," Kenny muttered after Matt left.

There was no mistaking who Kenny was talking about that time, Daisy thought, hoping Matt hadn't heard. Trying to shake out some tension, she wandered into the main living room. There were empty cans, bottles and cigarette butts everywhere, and the old wood floor was visibly stained with spilt drink. She felt a wave of anger that anyone could leave a house in such a mess. Hopefully, Matt would have it cleaned as soon as possible.

She wondered about Kayley. Daisy didn't know a lot about being a recovered alcoholic, but she was sure that avoiding situations where everyone was getting drunk or high was how-to-stay-sober-one-oh-one.

Daisy sighed. Technically, Kayley Lynch and her entourage was Matt's problem. But if there were going to be any more nights like this, Kayley and her band would fast become *her* problem too.

CHAPTER 37

@Deuxmoi Kayley Lynch spotted at vegetarian restaurant, 'The Ripe Tomato' in County Wicklow, Ireland, last night. While it's no mystery that the singer has abandoned her strict vegan lifestyle, what *is* a mystery is her dining companion, who managed to avoid the camera lens.

Daisy frowned at the photo of Kayley emerging from the well-known restaurant in Arklow. If that had been last night, she wondered if the band had come over when she'd got back to Granary House, or whether they'd already kicked off the party earlier in the evening.

Maybe she'd show it to Laura, just to give them both something to talk about. Laura seemed tense these days for some reason.

She waited until Fionn had left to get some lunch. "Laura, is everything okay?"

Laura glanced up. "Why wouldn't it be?"

"You've been kind of quiet. You're not worried about the marathon, are you? Because you don't have to –"

"I'm not worried." Laura flashed her a tight smile. "How about you, babes? How are things in Daisyland?"

Daisy felt herself weaken. She needed to confide in someone, and Laura had always been her person. Plus, she was nowhere near figuring things out by herself.

"Promise you won't say I told you so."

"*You didn't!*" Laura stared at her.

Daisy felt her face heat. "No! Matt and I just sort of, *um*, kissed."

"*I bloody knew it!*" Laura threw a manicured hand in the air. "I knew something like this was going to happen. What did I say?"

"You promised not to say I told you so.'

"I never promised anything!"

Daisy rubbed the tops of her arms. "It happened that night I had to stay at his place. But we didn't sleep together."

"Did you want to?"

Daisy tried to read Laura's expression. For the first time in ages, she saw a flash of her old friend. The one that she could talk to about anything, who wouldn't judge her no matter what.

"I think I might still have feelings for him."

Laura gave her a long look. "What sort of feelings? Because I have a very hot doctor who I'm totally in lust with but, apart from the fact that he's seen all my bits for all the wrong reasons, I wouldn't have sex with him. So do I need to worry here? Because I don't know if my acting skills can stretch to pretending to like him again!"

"Feck sake, Laura!" She shouldn't have said anything.

"Shit!" Laura huffed a sigh. "What were you thinking? Never mind the James factor, we have a strict agency ethics policy."

"Yes, I know." Talking about it actually made it seem worse. Daisy expelled a short breath. "It was a mistake, okay? I'm just … confused! I mean, I'd shoved all these feelings for Matt into a little box and closed the lid, so I wouldn't have to deal with them. And then he came back …"

"So, do you know how he feels? Do you think he wants to forget about it? Or do you think he wants you back?" She gave a hollow laugh. "I mean, I could be tempted to leave Brian if Granary House was part of the package."

Despite Laura's jokey tone, Daisy experienced an uneasy jolt of recognition. She'd spent so much time with Matt in Granary House that she'd unconsciously fantasised about living there. With Matt. She'd allowed her own tastes to influence her design decisions. In a way that she'd never allowed that to happen before. And Matt had let her. In fact, he'd literally let her design the house she'd have designed for herself! It wasn't so much a sign, as a giant-sized billboard.

She flung down her pencil, and pushed her chair away from the desk.

"He said he originally wanted closure but now he's not sure what he wants."

Laura snorted loudly. "Sorry, I just can't take that seriously, babes. He fucks off on you after five years. And now, he slides back into your life and starts messing you about? What about James? Does he think you're just going to leave James for *him*? Fucker!"

Why did Laura always view the world in black and white? She definitely shouldn't have said a word.

Laura's eyes narrowed as the silence lengthened.

"*Are* you thinking of leaving James? Daisy?"

"No, I'm not, okay? *I don't think so.* I'm just telling you what happened." She tried to calm her breathing "But I found out why he left."

An expression Daisy couldn't read flitted across Laura's face.

"He thought I'd cheated on him with James."

"*Fuck!*" Laura turned pale.

"He heard about some party we were at the summer he was in New York." She hesitated. "Brian told him I'd slept with James at it."

Laura was silent for a few moments. "Do you believe him?" she said, finally. "I don't believe that Brian would have tried to hurt you like that. Think about it – we were all friends. And why didn't Matt just ask you? I mean, it doesn't matter what happened or what he thought. He could have just asked!"

"Yeah, I don't know." Daisy bit her lip hard. "Pride, maybe? He was very hurt." Had Brian deliberately lied? She understood why Laura didn't want to believe he'd lie about something like that. But Matt had been adamant.

"You were hurt too, Daisy." Laura's phone buzzed, but she ignored it. "Do you want to check that?"

Laura shook her head. "It's just a reminder. So what are you going to do now? Because if it was me –"

"I don't know. To be honest, I'm not sure how I feel."

Laura looked thoughtful. "Why don't you let Fionn finish the project? You've done the designs, he'd just be overseeing the rest of it. And you could walk him through it."

"No, no!" Daisy was firm. "Matt is still my client, and Granary House is the best chance I've had in years of winning this award. I can't just hand it over to Fionn, you know that. Anyway, I have to make sure that everything's finished on time for the concerts."

"For the record, I think you're making a mistake." Laura frowned. "So, have you seen much of what's her name – Kayley?"

"She's moved into the guest wing, so I assume Matt's in the main part of the house now. But Matt and Kenny aren't getting on. And Kayley and her band turned the house into party central at the weekend." Daisy sighed. "They ended up breaking part of the old conservatory roof that we're incorporating into the new kitchen."

"I'm sorry, but how the hell did they break the roof?"

"Somebody climbed the scaffolding, and then grabbed on to the ceiling fan!"

"That'll do it." Laura rolled her eyes. "Bit strange that Kayley's staying there, isn't it?"

"Matt says she's hiding from the press. But as soon as she steps outside the door, somebody seems to get a photo." She took out her phone, looked up the Deuxmoi post, and passed it to Laura.

Laura studied it closely. "You know anyone can just submit to Deuxmoi, don't you? You don't have to be official press, or anything."

"I know, yeah. I just hope Matt says something to her people, so they stay out of Kenny's way. We're on a much tighter deadline, thanks to her concert. But my focus is the same as before – finish the house and submit it for the award."

Laura shot her a sceptical look. "You quite sure about that? Don't forget that if you win this award, James will find out about Matt. He'll find out about everything."

"The house is the most important thing, Laura!" Daisy hesitated. "Like I said – I'd cross that bridge if I came to it – if, by some miracle, I won that award."

Laura shook her head despairingly, and turned back to her computer.

Daisy sighed. Laura knew her too well. But Daisy didn't believe things happened by accident. Matt was back in her life for a reason. She just had to figure out what it was.

CHAPTER 38

Controversial American country singer Kayley Lynch and her new band have damaged part of Granary House in County Wicklow, the private Georgian home Kayley is currently renting. A source close to the band told the *Irish Daily News* that Kayley and her band were partying at the historic house, which is currently under renovation, when bass guitarist Greg Fields 'climbed some scaffolding in the conservatory'. He fell, breaking part of a glass roof, but didn't sustain any serious injuries.

Kayley is in Ireland to begin the final leg of her month-long, European tour on June 1 at the grounds of Granary House. She was forced to cancel all her planned American concerts after being admitted to rehab for alcohol abuse.

Daisy was sitting in her car in Matt's driveway, and had just finished reading her emails when she saw the story. She scrolled through the accompanying photos of the kitchen with the hole in the roof, the chandelier on the floor surrounded by broken glass, and reception room littered with glasses and bottles. She looked closer, and noticed what looked like traces of white powder on a corner of the dark coffee table.

Her phone rang, and Freya's name flashed up. Daisy swiped to answer.

"Hi, Freya, how are things?"

"Daisy, is this a good time?"

Daisy was wondering who the source close to the band was. Maybe Kayley had been rude to one of the camera crew making the documentary.

"*Uh*, fine – go ahead, Freya."

"It's about the occupational therapist. Will you tell your sister it's for Holly?" Freya hurried on. "It might be nothing at all, but she's not settling at school and, if she wasn't pretty bright, I don't think she'd be learning anything. Thing is, the school wants her assessed, and I trust them – they've been very good to my other kids. I just don't want to wait months to have her see someone."

"I see. Okay – I'll talk to Rosie and tell her it's for your daughter."

"Is your sister practising at the moment?" Freya asked.

"No, she's still on a career break."

There was a brief silence. "I'll leave it with you," Freya said. "Thanks, Daisy."

Daisy put a quick note in her phone to call Rosie, and went into the house. She found Matt, Kayley and Todd in the newly finished study.

"Oh, hi." Daisy flashed them a quick smile, but she had the feeling she'd walked in on something important. "I didn't mean to disturb you."

"It's fine." Matt glanced at the others. "We're finished here – let's go down to the kitchen."

The sun was streaming in through the patio doors, and Daisy was relieved to see the scaffolding was gone and the new design was quickly taking shape. She ran a hand over the smooth, pale countertops.

"Kenny's a talented craftsman."

Matt gave a short laugh. "He's just working to your designs." Turning, he closed the door behind him. "So, this is a bit awkward; I'll just get straight to the point. Did you see the story in the *Irish Daily News* today?"

Daisy nodded. "About half an hour ago, yeah."

Matt sighed. "The thing is, Kayley and Todd think one of your crew leaked it."

"What?" Daisy stared at him. "That's a very big leap, isn't it? I mean, why would they bother?"

"I don't know." Matt folded his arms. "Money, maybe? Or just to piss Kayley off. I know she can be a bit –"

Of a cow, Daisy thought.

"Highly strung," Matt said, after a beat.

"Matt, it's way more likely that someone from her own crew went to the press. Like maybe …" Daisy tried to think, "the guy who fell off the scaffolding. I mean, let's face it, he can't be very happy about that."

"Except that if it was someone in the band, there'd be photos from the night itself," Matt said.

Daisy shook her head. "Unless they were too clever to take photos because they'd know it'd be traced back to them!"

Matt raised an eyebrow.

"Look, Matt," Daisy persisted, "they can't just start accusing people!"

"Not everyone, no. We could narrow it down to whoever was here that morning." He folded his arms.

Clearly, Matt was determined to play Sherlock Holmes! "I'll ask Kenny, but I don't think it'll prove anything."

When Matt said nothing, Daisy realised that he was seriously annoyed. She suppressed a sigh. He was probably under huge pressure from Kayley's agent and publicity manager. Better to change the subject.

"So, *um*, I was wondering if you've thought about what you're putting on your walls?"

He frowned. "Haven't we already decided all that?"

Yep, definitely annoyed! "I'm talking about art. Original paintings, prints, wall hangings, mirrors – everything." Daisy smiled. "Some clients like me to pick out a few pieces, others prefer to do all that themselves. It's pretty personal."

"Oh, okay, actually, I'm way ahead of you." Matt powered on his laptop, typed something into the search bar, and turned the screen so she could get a better look. "It's a website for new Irish art, with links to all the artists' individual websites."

"*Wow*, I didn't know this existed." Daisy peered over Matt's shoulder as he scrolled down the pages. Up close, she could smell his familiar aftershave and an apple-scented shampoo. She jerked her head back. "I should tell Mum about this. She's an artist too."

Matt turned. "I'd forgotten you'd told me that."

Why had she reminded him? It didn't matter: the chances of her mother being organised enough to have her own website were extremely slim. "It's all pretty reasonable," Matt was saying. "And it's good to support Irish artists."

She and James had two of her mother's paintings, both of which Miriam had painted and given them. Daisy felt a stab of guilt that she'd never offered to buy any more.

Todd came into the room. "We're gonna head off. Daisy, we're gonna have to ask you and the rest of the crew to leave your phones in a box when Kayley is here." He gave a hard smile. "Thank you for your understanding." Before Daisy had a chance to reply, he added, "Matt, can you get heating in the guest wing sorted? Kayley says it's not working."

After he left, Daisy turned to Matt. "I'm not leaving my phone in a box, Matt. I need it when I'm working. And it's not like Kayley is some sort of recluse. The woman's on social media the whole time!"

He sighed. "I'll talk to her, but she deserves her privacy."

Daisy resisted the urge to laugh. "Matt, if I ever want a photo of her, I'll just ask."

Matt's lips thinned. "I'd better take a look at the boiler."

"Or you could wait until Niamh is out again," Daisy suggested. "If it's an electrical thing, she'll sort it quickly."

"Yeah, I also have the name of that other guy Kenny called out when we lost our power." Matt ran a hand across the back of his neck. "He said Niamh might have overloaded the fuse boards."

"Kenny said that?" Daisy frowned.

"Nope, the other electrician did."

"Did you tell him a woman did the electrics?"

"What?" He rolled his eyes. "I probably mentioned it."

"Ah, big mistake." Daisy tried not to react to Matt's expression. "Let me have a quick look at the boiler. In case it's something small that Kayley might have missed."

"Thanks." Matt briefly squeezed her hand, and she smiled, waiting for the little tingle she usually got when he touched her. Nothing. Clearly, the collective stress was rubbing off on her!

She let herself into the guest wing, remembering the last time she'd been here with Matt. Now it looked like all of Kayley's belongings had simply exploded all over the place.

Stepping carefully across the room, Daisy opened the small cupboard that housed the boiler, before going into the kitchen to try the heating clock. Nothing.

It couldn't be something big, she reasoned – the heating system was pretty new. She took another look around the boiler, hunkering down to check the meter, when something caught her eye: the master switch on the wall was turned off. She flicked it back on, and immediately the boiler started to fire up.

As Daisy turned to leave, she noticed a glass dish on the coffee table, filled with crystals. Picking up the large white stone on top, she turned it over in her hand to admire it.

The door banged, and Kayley came into the room.

"Hello?" She stopped at the door. "Can I help you?"

"Actually, I just helped you!" When Kayley continued to stare stonily at her, Daisy forced herself to smile. "I figured out the boiler – the master switch was turned off." She half-turned to point it out. "It's the low switch on the wall, it must have been –"

"Must have been what?" Kayley's eyes narrowed. "You think I turned it off? That's what you're implying, right? Because how would

I understand your strange little Irish heating systems, like it's not like we have switches in the States!"

Okaaay. She wouldn't react; she was a professional! "Well, it's sorted now."

"Don't let me delay you." As Kayley stepped aside, a movement behind her caught Daisy's eye, and her heart sank as she spotted a mouse flash by the skirting board. She'd already put down a few traps in the main part of the house, but she really should have put some down here too.

She wondered if Kayley's reaction was down to stress, or if she'd done anything to make the other woman dislike her. Kayley Lynch might be a talented singer, but she was a total pain!

CHAPTER 39

Daisy and Matt had almost finished the upstairs snag list when Matt's phone rang.

"I have to take this, it's work." He shot her a look of apology.

"It's fine, I've to make a quick call anyway." Daisy headed down to the kitchen, and made the phone call she'd been dreading.

"Howya, Daisy," Kenny said when he answered.

"Hi, Kenny." Daisy took a deep breath, and filled him in on Todd's suspicions.

"Jesus Christ!" Kenny said, when she'd finished.

Daisy braced herself for more, but Kenny just sighed heavily.

"It's not your fault, Daisy, but it's total bullshit."

Daisy glanced over her shoulder to make sure she was still on her own. "Yeah, I know, Kenny. But I promised Matt I'd ask who was around the morning after the house party."

"We had the whole crew there," Kenny said shortly. "Your decorators only came later."

Daisy hesitated. "When you say the whole crew, does that include Alec?"

"It does." Kenny sounded disappointed. "Now lookit, I don't want to rush you but –"

"No, it's fine," Daisy said, hurriedly. "Sorry I had to ask, Kenny."

He muttered something Daisy couldn't hear, and hung up.

She slipped outside, grateful to get some air, and furious with Kayley and Todd for throwing around groundless accusations. Pushing her hands deep into her pockets, she took a deep breath, and wandered down the central path that divided the kitchen garden into two halves.

Looking around, it was easy to imagine a time when the neat rows of growing plots had been full of herbs and vegetables, and fruit bushes had scrambled over the back wall that separated the garden from the orchard beyond.

She walked down to examine the tangle of branches and vines that wound around each other, trying to figure out what was there. As she got near the gate, she recognised Kayley and Todd's raised voices on the far side of the wall.

Determined to avoid Kayley, Daisy turned to leave, but stopped as something caught her attention.

"I don't blame you, Kayley," Todd was saying. "This is his fault!"

Daisy couldn't hear Kayley's reply, and she wondered if they were talking about Tim. Daisy didn't envy him. For a guy who was meant to be working on her image, Tim didn't seem to be having much luck. She glanced towards the gate again. If she left now, she'd be gone before they could walk around and find her.

As she turned, her heel caught on some broken pavement, and she tripped, falling awkwardly onto her knee and elbow.

"*Shit!*" Daisy froze, clamping one hand over her mouth as she struggled to her feet.

Her ankle felt a bit tender, so she hobbled over to the stone bench near the wall, and sat down. She was massaging her ankle when she heard Todd's voice again.

"Move back to the hotel, Kayley – you'd have your people looking out for you there!"

"You can look out for me here, Todd," Kayley snapped. "I *need* you to trust me."

"Goddammit, Kayley, we work together! How can I do my job when I have to drive to this godforsaken museum every time I want to see you?"

"You know why I'm here!" Kayley's voice rose.

"Are you trying to completely fuck everything up again? You know we need to get your career back on track."

"What don't you understand, Todd? This is bonus material – the streamers are gonna eat it up!"

"Trashing somebody's house?" Todd sounded exasperated. "Having all that stuff appear in the media?"

"Screw that!" Kayley swore loudly, and Daisy wondered if Matt had been taking drugs the day he'd agreed to let the singer and her entourage use his house.

What was the bonus material? God, what did it matter? She couldn't hang out here forever! Daisy rubbed her shoulder, wincing as pain shot through her arm. She stood, putting her sore foot to the ground, gingerly testing her ankle. It hurt.

She hobbled carefully back through the garden.

Matt was in the kitchen. "Finished my call, sorry about that."

"No, it's grand. I, *um*, was just getting some fresh air."

He frowned. "What's wrong with your ankle?"

"Oh, just twisted it slightly. It's grand." She debated whether to mention the conversation she'd overheard. Probably better not!

"So, where were we?" Matt said.

As the conversation turned back to work, Daisy wondered if Matt would raise the topic of them again. He'd thrown the ball neatly into her court. It had been the same when they'd been together: he'd let her know what he wanted but he'd leave the final decision to her. *Only remember how he used to sulk when he didn't like that decision?*

The thought gnawed at the edges of her mind. It was the reason he hadn't got to know her family better. Whenever she'd invited him down to Oranmore, Matt would suddenly produce tickets for the cinema or tell her he'd planned to see a band they liked in Whelans. If she went home without him, he'd sulk for days.

She had to admit, James had always been good about coming down to Oranmore – until this last year or two when work had become his default excuse!

Part of her wished that Matt had never come back, that she'd never let him get close again. But actions spoke louder than words, and she couldn't ignore what had happened between them the night of the storm. It was pretty clear that Matt wanted a second chance. She just needed the courage to talk to James.

CHAPTER 40

By the time Daisy got home on Friday evening, she felt like she'd come through the longest week ever. Hanging her jacket and bike helmet in the hall, she slipped off her runners, already fantasising about takeout pizza and a cold beer.

As she got to the kitchen door she stopped at the sound of Alma's voice.

"... really love it, honestly."

She heard James murmur something and, ignoring the warning voice in her head, she opened the door.

James and Alma were standing close together near the window and, as they spun to look at her, Alma hurriedly slipped something into her pocket.

Daisy stared at James. "Sorry for interrupting." She was amazed at how steady her voice sounded.

"You're not – don't be silly," James said quickly.

Daisy didn't miss the brief look he gave Alma.

"I was just on my way out, excuse me." Alma stepped neatly past her.

A moment later, the front door closed, and Daisy spun back to James. "What's going on?"

He pushed his hand through his hair. "Nothing! Why would you think there's something going on?"

Daisy sucked in a breath. Was she overreacting? She didn't think so. "Don't gaslight me, James. I just walked in on you and Alma –"

"Doing what?" James shoved his hands into his pockets. "Jesus, Daisy, if anything was going on, do you think we'd be doing it in the kitchen where you could walk in? Like you just did?" His jaw tightened. "Why would you even assume something like that?"

Because you're ridiculously close to Alma. Because I'm projecting. Because I'm just not sure about us anymore.

She folded her arms. "So what were you doing?"

James went over to the fridge and took out a beer. "Want one?"

"Maybe you shouldn't be drinking while you're on an antibiotic."

He sighed. "I'm celebrating."

"What?"

Instead of answering her, he opened the beer and necked some back.

Daisy took a steadying breath. "What did Alma put in her pocket?"

"What?"

Let it go, Daisy, ignore it. But it was a scab she couldn't stop picking.

"When I came in, Alma had something in her hand. A box."

He hesitated. "Oh, that. It was one of those Funko Pops she collects. I'd had it for ages and I'd forgotten to give it to her."

He was lying, she thought, feeling sick. But how could she challenge him when she was lying too? This was her moment: she just needed the courage to say something.

"James?"

"Aren't you going to ask me why I'm celebrating?"

"What are you celebrating?"

"We're making an offer for a new app." James sounded relieved. "It's exactly what the company has been looking for."

Daisy nodded. "Great."

"Yeah." James rubbed a hand over his face. "We're buying from a couple of college graduates. But I won't relax until it's a done deal."

Daisy forced herself to focus on what James was saying. "You'd think they'd want to develop it themselves, wouldn't you?"

His eyes narrowed. "What are you talking about?"

She shrugged. "I mean, if I'd come up with a cool idea, I think I'd want to get funding for it myself."

"Fuck sake, Daisy, whose side are you on? We're making them an offer they can't refuse. We need this!" He pushed a hand through his hair. "This is more than us just having a bad year. Ethical travel is the next big thing, and we'll be expanding it to include hotels, restaurants, shops, holiday experiences. It's next level stuff!"

"Why are you shouting at me, James?"

"I'm not shouting!" James took a deep breath. "I'm not shouting," he said more quietly.

"Fine." Daisy folded her arms. "Maybe you'll make so much money, we won't need to rent out our spare room anymore."

It was meant flippantly but, judging by James' expression, she'd made things worse.

He gave a tiny shake of his head. "Look, do you want me to order a pizza or something?"

This is important for him, Daisy, don't ruin it. "Sure. Why don't I message Alma? Ask if she wants some too."

"Probably be better if I message her." He didn't meet her eye as he took out his phone.

Of course it would be, Daisy thought. *Silly me.* To her relief, her phone rang, and she fished it out of her pocket. "It's Rosie. I'll leave Alma to you."

CHAPTER 41

Daisy spent most of Saturday morning trawling through Dublin's antique shops to find some authentic pieces for Granary House. Even though Alma had mentioned that she'd be spending the day in the college library, Daisy was relieved to get out of the house.

The previous evening, Alma had agreed to pizza, and James had managed to get her talking about her childhood in Sweden. As Daisy had listened to them chat, it struck her that James and Alma were kindred spirits.

There had been one brief, awful moment where Alma had asked her where she was working in Wicklow. Thanks to Kayley, she was pretty sure Matt was publicly linked to the place now, and it definitely hadn't been the right time for *that* conversation with James.

"*Er*, Glaston House." She'd glanced over at James, but he'd only seemed politely interested. She'd hated that she was lying to him – but they were lying to each other.

Now, she photographed a few items of furniture and sent the pictures to Matt. Almost immediately, he replied with a thumbs-up, and she paid and arranged to have them delivered.

By lunch, she'd found herself in a newly opened furniture shop off the Portobello Road, which sold a mix of genuine antiques and good second-hand pieces. She'd look through everything, she thought, grab some lunch and then head over to Ballsbridge, where she'd managed to persuade James to view a luxury new showhouse with her.

After the previous night, she'd hesitated about asking him. It was normally the sort of thing she did with Laura, or sometimes with a client looking for ideas. But she'd told him that she wanted them to spend more time together and, to her surprise, he had agreed.

Daisy wandered through the shop, inspecting occasional tables, dressers, and chairs. Every surface was covered with rattan baskets, old pottery, silver services, old costume jewellery, gilt-edged mirrors, fun, cheap prints and ornately framed paintings.

She ran her hand lightly over a mother-of-pearl hair set, before reaching for a beautifully strung locket at the same time as a heavily pregnant woman.

"Sorry, go ahead," Daisy urged.

"No, it'd look much better on you!" The woman gestured to Daisy's flared skirt and short, knit top. "You've got amazing style."

Daisy started to reply when Laura appeared from the back of the shop. "Daisy!"

"Laura!" This was perfect! They could go for lunch! "I discovered this place today! Are you shopping for a client or …" Daisy stopped, noticing that the other woman was regarding them both with interest.

"No, just browsing. *Em*, this is a friend of mine, Stephanie Ryan. Stephanie, this is Daisy Devlin, my business partner."

"Friend and business partner!" Daisy beamed and stuck out her hand. "Lovely to meet you, Stephanie. I heard Laura's redesigning your place to make it ready for a family! Congratulations, by the way. My sister has twins, but triplets is wild! At least you'll be fit – I've heard that helps."

Stephanie shook her hand. "Lovely to meet you too." She gave a nervous laugh. "I'm not sure how fit I am, but my mother's going to be staying for the first six weeks to help us out. After that, I guess we'll muddle through."

"Oh, I just meant all that running will help. My sister played tennis before she had her twins, but she doesn't get as much time now."

Stephanie frowned. "Well, I don't – "

"– really have time to chat because we're meeting that photographer in half an hour across town," Laura said firmly. "For the baby photos, remember?"

"Right." Stephanie looked a bit flustered. "Baby brain, sorry. Great to meet you, Daisy."

"See you on Monday." Laura shot Daisy a brief smile, before turning and manoeuvring Stephanie towards the door.

What had that been about? Daisy mentally flicked back over the short conversation, trying to pinpoint anything she'd said or done that could have made Laura close that conversation down so rudely. Suddenly, she wasn't in the mood for shopping anymore. She should just leave.

A well-dressed, elderly man appeared from the back of the shop. "Can I help you with anything?"

"Uh, no, thanks." Daisy managed a tiny smile.

"I'll be here if you want anything." He retreated to the back of the shop.

Daisy found herself looking at the necklace she'd picked up. She definitely didn't want it anymore.

First James. Now Laura. She wasn't stupid. There *was* no appointment with a photographer across town. The truth was, Laura couldn't wait to get away from her.

~~~~~ ~~~~~

"How much did you say these are going for?" James said as he and Daisy trooped around one of the luxurious new showhouses in Dublin's wealthy Ballsbridge.

"Two million." Daisy grinned

In stark contrast to the grand, Victorian houses with their big gardens that stood facing each other on the tree-lined road, the newly created Dodder Court was a development of just seven high-spec three-bedroom homes, built on what had until recently been a field.

"Say if we won the Lotto," Daisy mused, "would we buy one of these?"

"I thought you liked falling-down old houses." James ran his hand over a marble table in the hall. "This house looks like a giant Lego build."

Daisy thought about Granary House, and she flashed James a guilty smile. "*Ha*, hard agree." She stopped and pulled him aside. "Never mind about what sort of houses I like for a moment. What about you? Would you live here?"

"Probably not." He laughed. "It's way too big."

Daisy squeezed his hand. "I know. But we should pretend we're interested buyers." Just like all the times she and Matt had done. *Stop thinking about Matt.* "So, either we're both on huge salaries, or we've come into a massive inheritance." She beamed up at him, starting to enjoy the game she'd played so often in the past.

"Or one of us takes a hand-out from rich parents?" James said.

Daisy suppressed a sigh, wishing he wasn't always so hung up on his parents' generous offers of money, and his refusal to depend on them in any way. "Come on, James, lighten up!"

He released a tense laugh. "Sorry! Lead on!"

"There's a little garden." Daisy walked across the kitchen and stepped through the open sliding door. The tiny outside area was paved, with raised flower beds and large potted plants, and featured a garden dining set and built-in barbeque.

"Imagine sitting somewhere like this on summer evenings! I'll bet it's a suntrap." Daisy ran her hand over the hardened, glass-top table.

"Yeah, I could work here on my laptop, keeping an eye on my offshore accounts."

"You reckon if we lived here you'd have offshore accounts?"

He grinned. "I reckon if we lived here, I'd definitely need some!"

Daisy turned and looked back through the glass doors. A couple just a few years older than them, with a young child in tow, were inspecting the kitchen.

"Okay, what's your favourite room so far?"

James shook his head. "I don't have one. The best thing about this place is you, Daisy."

She stared at him, trying to remember when he'd last said anything like that to her.

"Anyway, this is all fantasy stuff. I prefer to live in the real world."

She swallowed her disappointment as he brought her back to reality. She knew he didn't mean to, but in the real world he spent most of his time hunched over a laptop, and the rest of it gaming with their lodger!

"How's that working out for you?" Shit, that sounded awful! She sighed. "Sorry, that's not what I meant."

His expression closed. "It doesn't matter – I *know* what you meant. Look, this was fun." He looked like he was about to say something else, then changed his mind. "I'd better go, Daisy. I've a lot to do."

"How about I meet you at home later and we'll go out for dinner?"

"Takeout might suit me better tonight." He dragged a hand through his hair. "I'm sorry, honestly. My head's not in the right space." He kissed her quickly and left before she had a chance to say anything else.

Daisy sat down at the table and looked around the little garden. How many secrets was James keeping from her, she wondered.

But until she was ready to tell him everything, she couldn't expect him to be honest with her either.

CHAPTER 42

Daisy locked her bike in the bike park outside the office, and slipped off her helmet, running a hand back through her hair in an attempt to untangle the knots.

The cycle in had helped to clear her head a bit, but she still felt awful after the weekend. Now that James was buying a new app, his work was bound to get even busier and, although he claimed there was nothing between him and Alma, the atmosphere at home was more strained than ever.

The one bright moment had been Rosie, surprisingly, who'd phoned on Sunday evening.

"I've been thinking about Freya's daughter," Rosie had said. "Do you think Freya would agree to let me see her?"

Daisy had been momentarily speechless. "Probably. I mean, I'd say so. Would she have to go to Galway?"

"I'd come up to Dublin. I haven't visited you in a while. Could I stay the weekend?"

"Sure, what about the kids, though?"

"Séan will manage. Look, if you don't want me to stay, just say so."

"Of course you can stay!" Daisy had almost tripped over her words. "It's just, you're not practising right now, and I don't think Freya would expect you to drop everything and come to Dublin for her."

Rosie had huffed out a sigh. "The twins have been invited to their millionth birthday party of the year this weekend. And *I* have managed to be at every single one. But I'm worn out, Daisy. When they handed me those bloody invitations, I felt like tearing them up. So I told Séan he's taking them. He can drop the boys off to Mum and Dad's, and then spend a couple of hours making sure our daughters don't fall off the top of a bouncy castle or eat too many sweets, or burst into tears because they don't like how the party clown did their face-painting." She'd paused for breath. "By the way, have you talked to Mum about this Galway market nonsense?"

Daisy had felt like a child who'd forgotten to do her homework. "I was actually about to phone her," she'd lied.

Rosie had made a disbelieving sound. "Don't forget!"

Daisy had hung up and tried to think of an excuse for phoning her mother. Not that she'd needed an excuse, obviously. But it would help.

"Would you like Kayley to write a special message for Dad on the album?" she'd asked, when she rang a while later.

"Oh, just tell her what it's for," Miriam had said, "and let her write whatever she likes. But make sure our names are spelt properly – Americans spell everything so differently."

"Grand, no bother." Daisy had paused. "So, *um*, Rosie was saying that you've taken a stand in the Galway market for your art. That must be interesting."

"Ah, I love it, Daisy!" Miriam's voice had brightened. "I meet so many gorgeous people. All the stall holders are so friendly, and the public has been so supportive. Sure, didn't I sell two paintings last week?"

Daisy had murmured something vaguely encouraging.

"But it's not even about that," Miriam had continued. "We creatives spend a lot of time by ourselves, and it can get a bit lonely. The market's a great outlet."

Daisy had fallen silent. It hadn't occurred to her that her stay-at-home mother wasn't perfectly content pottering around her beautiful house and garden in Oranmore, painting and cooking and seeing friends. But her mum was an intensely sociable person, and Daisy had suddenly realised how isolated she might feel when her dad was at work.

"I'm glad, Mum. You know, maybe you should think about putting on an exhibition? You could ask other artists to collaborate."

"I've thought about it, all right." Miriam had sounded pleased. "I was half-afraid you were going to start going on about my self-portrait. Rosie is obsessed! I should have known it'd never bother you."

***

Now, as Daisy climbed the smooth, polished stairs to their office, she wondered if her mother had suspected that Rosie might ask for Daisy's help to talk her out of selling at the market – and had cleverly cut her off with some counter tactics.

Fionn was on the phone, and Laura's desk was conspicuously empty. She opened the sash window behind her chair and sat down, just as Fionn hung up.

"Morning, Daisy. That was Laura."

"Is everything okay?"

Fionn frowned. "So, that friend who's having triplets? Laura had to take her into hospital because she started to bleed, and she has to stay in for monitoring."

Daisy tried to process this. "*Wow*, I only bumped into them at the weekend. Hang on, what about Stephanie's partner?"

"He's in Dubai on a business trip." Fionn flicked his fringe. "Laura said they're not even telling him until they know more, because what can he do over there?"

"Get home, maybe!"

How had Laura suddenly become Stephanie's go-to person, when Daisy hadn't even heard of her until a couple of weeks ago?

Fionn got to his feet. "Will I get coffee?"

"Coffee sounds great, thanks, Fionn. *Um*, quick Zodiac thing. Are Leos compatible with each other, or do they clash? Two lions together, *haha*!"

"You'd think, right?" Fionn beamed. "Nah, two Leos are a perfect match."

"A perfect match." This week just kept getting better. "Do me a favour: get me a chocolate croissant with that coffee?"

"A croissant?"

Daisy nodded. "Chocolate! And please don't make me eat it by myself."

"Gotcha."

Fionn left and Daisy wished she'd never started taking an interest in horoscopes. They were just supposed to be a bit of bloody fun!

She couldn't even remember exactly how the topic had come up over their Friday-night pizza. One moment Alma had been telling them about her childhood birthday parties in Sweden, the next she and James were acting like they'd both won the Zodiac lotto when they'd discovered that their birthdays were a day apart.

It was un-bloody-believable that somebody studying nuclear physics would have any interest in their star sign. But Alma knew she was a Leo. Just like James.

⋙⋙⋙ ⋘⋘⋘

When Daisy's phone rang after lunch, her first thought was Laura. But it was Matt.

She swiped the screen. "Hi, all good?"

"Fine." Matt cleared his throat. "Look, hope you don't mind me phoning you about this, but Kayley's pendant is missing and I wondered if you'd seen it."

"Her pendant?" Daisy frowned. "Okay ..."

"The moonstone one." Matt hesitated. "She was wondering if you saw it in the guest wing last week."

"I remember."

"The pendant?" He sounded hopeful.

"No, I remember I was sorting out the boiler." Which anyone could have done if they'd bothered to look! Had any of the crystals in the bowl been on a chain? She didn't think so. "Is it very valuable?"

"There was a diamond setting around it, apparently."

"Right." Daisy waited for Matt to say he was sorry to bother her, and that Kayley was the most high-maintenance person he'd ever come across and a total pain in the arse, but he didn't.

"I'll ask Kenny and the rest of the team to keep an eye out," she said finally. "Was there anything else?"

"Not for now." Matt sounded terse.

"Great." She wasn't sure what else she was meant to say. "It'll probably turn up, Matt."

"Yeah." He sighed. "To be honest, between all the Deuxmoi stuff and now Kayley's things going missing, Todd says she's starting to feel paranoid."

Daisy wasn't sure what Matt expected her to say.

"It's not the first thing that's gone missing," Matt was saying, now. "Alec made some wisecrack about there being a poltergeist, but I wouldn't put anything past him."

Daisy wished that she could rush to Alec's defence, but the truth was she didn't quite trust him either. "Things tend to get misplaced during a renovation, Matt. I wouldn't worry."

"Yeah, maybe." Matt sounded unconvinced. "One other thing. I've asked Kenny about it, but the guy's pretty difficult."

Daisy massaged her forehead. "Go on."

"Some of Kenny's workmen must be using the guest wing, which is a no-go area right now."

"How do you mean?" Daisy frowned.

"Kayley found peanut butter on the floor, and she doesn't touch the stuff."

Daisy remembered the mouse she'd seen. Didn't they love peanut butter? She took a deep breath.

"Matt, people have been in and out of every part of the house since Kayley arrived. Just clean it up. Oh, and get a few traps down – you could have mice, which is normal during building work."

"I'll handle it." Matt sounded exasperated.

After Daisy hung up, she looked over at Fionn. "Do you believe in poltergeists?"

He flicked his hair across his forehead. "Is this about Kayley Lynch?"

"How did you know?"

"Because it's on her Instagram reel." He picked up his iPhone, selected something and handed the phone to Daisy. "Take a look."

Kayley was standing in the driveway in the front of Granary House, her long, blonde hair tied up in a high ponytail.

"*Hey, ya'll,*" she began, "*So as ya'll know, I'm here in Ireland right now, where I'll be finishing up my Europe tour. And I'm staying in this big old house in Wicklow, in the Irish countryside.*" The camera angle turned as she panned across the front of the house, before she turned it back to her. "*So, I think what I appreciate so much about this house is its energy, which has been great for me and the band as we compose some new stuff. The only negative is that some of my energy and creativity is being challenged 'cos the house is being renovated. And some of my things have even been misplaced.*" Kayley sighed and chewed a corner of her lip. "*I just have to trust that the house finds a way to return them.*"

The video ended and Daisy handed Fionn back his phone. "I can't tell if she really believes all that, or if it's her way of saying she thinks somebody is stealing from her."

Fionn shrugged. "Honestly, I don't know either. I can't really get a vibe off somebody I haven't met."

Daisy sighed, and wrote a quick WhatsApp to Kenny. **Hi Kenny, just been talking to Matt. Have you noticed a lot of things going**

missing at GH? No, that looked wrong. She deleted the message and rang him instead.

"Is he accusing you of stealing rocks?" Kenny sounded incredulous.

"No, of course not!" Daisy said hastily. "Look, Kenny, you know if a client has a problem I'll always say it. Just so we're all on the same page."

"And how is it his problem?" Kenny huffed. "I'll mention it to the lads, but Kayley Lynch is stone mad, no pun intended, and yer man's just as bad."

"*Um*, yeah." Should she mention Alec? No, Kenny knew she had her suspicions, and she knew Kenny was watching him too. It was enough.

"Anyway," Kenny added, "That one should be looking a bit closer at her own crowd. Mad feckers, the lot of them."

"You're probably right," Daisy admitted. After she hung up, she looked over at Fionn. "I'm going out, do you want anything?"

"I'm good, thanks."

He smiled, and Daisy wished for the hundredth time that they could keep him on after he finished college.

She knew it might be possible on a freelance basis, but compared with some of the bigger firms, there'd be so little work it would hardly be fair to him.

Laura seemed exhausted when she came in at lunchtime.

Daisy looked up from her screen. "Hey, how did things go? How's Stephanie?"

Laura took a chicken-fillet roll and a bottle of water from her bag. "She'll be fine. I had to stay until her mother could get down from Donegal."

"Are the babies okay?"

"Yep, all good." Laura bit into her roll. "But she was all over the place, and the hospitals are so understaffed! I was afraid ..." She paused. "I didn't want to leave her on her own."

Daisy gave Laura a long look. "You're a good friend to her."

"I didn't do anything." Laura switched on her laptop. "What about you? Any news?"

"*Um*, yeah, James' company is buying a start-up – an ethical travel app. I think things will be okay."

"It wasn't like he was ever going to lose his job, Daisy."

"I'm not so sure."

Laura poured her water into a small glass on her desk. "So, who's behind the start-up?"

"A couple of grad students. James approached them after he saw an article about their project in an online journal."

"*Hmm*." Laura's attention seemed to be wandering.

"I also had the maddest call earlier from Matt."

"Wait, don't tell me. He's decided grouse-shooting and riding to hounds isn't actually his thing, so he's going back to his New York bachelor pad and daily hotdog habit."

"No!" Daisy managed a laugh. "Kayley can't find her pendant, and he wanted to know if I'd seen it."

Laura gave her a strange look. "Sounds like he was accusing you. Or she was, anyway."

"I doubt that, Laura." Daisy folded her arms, wishing she hadn't said anything. It didn't matter what Matt did, Laura's feelings about him were never going to change.

"I think I might book Stephanie a couple of spa treatments," Laura said, abruptly changing the subject. "She'll appreciate them in a few weeks."

Daisy remembered when Rosie had her twins. Despite her military-like organisation, it had taken months before things had settled into a new-normal routine.

"Some good salon close to her," Laura was saying, looking online. "Maybe get her hair done too."

Daisy just smiled. Laura's reaction when she and Stephanie had bumped into her on Saturday still stung badly, but the last thing she wanted was for her to think she was jealous.

She wanted to ask if she'd done anything to upset her. But deep down, she was afraid that if she said anything, she might make things worse. The truth was, she'd always considered herself closer to Laura than to Rosie, or even James. And she couldn't bear the thought of losing her.

CHAPTER 43

MyStarScope Taurus: As a current project draws to a close, you have an important decision to make. Decide wisely.

Daisy arrived at Matt's house on Friday morning, her car packed with lamps, throws, cushions, candles and other small items for the house.

Adding the finishing touches was normally one of her favourite parts of a job – it was the client's chance to see the final important details fall into place. But all Daisy felt was panic that she'd have no excuse to see Matt anymore. Even though they both knew the truth, she wondered if too much had happened, if their lives had changed too much to fix things now.

She also knew that things were building to a head with James. It was clear that he'd told Alma about the App before he'd even told her! It seemed nuts to even *share* something like that with the student who rented from them, but it was another sign of how close they were. She'd hoped to find time to talk to him properly, but she'd barely seen him since Saturday afternoon, because he was trying to "iron out some problems with the deal", whatever that meant.

Daisy was lifting the first box out of the car when she heard Matt talking to someone. She glanced around, trying to locate him, before she realised he was around the side of the house. She was about to announce herself, when he mentioned her name.

She hesitated, hugging the box a bit tighter to her. She shouldn't listen – it was none of her business. Maybe just for a minute …

For a few moments she listened for another voice, but when she only heard Matt's, she realised he must be on the phone.

"I made a big mistake … totally screwed up, Charlie … see her today … I don't know if she …"

Daisy held her breath. He was talking to his brother. *About her!*

"… not that easy …"

Daisy's mind raced to catch up with her heartbeat. He'd just said he'd made a mistake breaking up with her. Hadn't he? What else could it be? He said he was going to see her today! Here she was – he was going to see her in a couple of minutes! She didn't know if she was ready. Sounded like he was going to ask for a second chance.

Matt had stopped talking. Shit, she couldn't be standing here if he walked around to the front of the house. Except if he wanted to ask her something, maybe he'd see it as a sign that she was here, on her own, standing in the driveway! Crap, maybe not, though. She heard the crunch of gravel, and sped to the open front door. Inside, she put down the box and tried to calm her breathing.

She tried to rationalise her feelings. Did she want a second chance with him? What would that even look like? The same as before? Maybe she'd move into Granary House with him. *Interior architect finds second-chance happiness with her first love and lives happily-ever-after in her award-winning dream home.* But she didn't want to hurt James! Except would she be hurting him when all the signs …

She went back out to the car.

Matt had started to unpack it for her.

"Oh, hi." She flicked her hair, hoping he'd put her flushed face down to the exertion of carrying boxes.

"Hi, yourself." He grinned. "I assume we're taking all this in?"

"Yes." *Work talk: safe.* "These are the finishing touches. I always buy them in person. It's one of my favourite parts of the job." She sounded a bit breathless, she realised. *Breathe, Daisy.*

"Because it means you're nearly finished?" He pulled a sad face but, when she laughed, said, "I should have asked you to completely redesign the guest wing."

Was this the moment? If all the signs were there, shouldn't she be sure? She lifted two more bags out of the back of the car and followed him into the house.

"I've something for you, hang on."

Oh my God, what?

He went into the study, and re-emerged with what looked like a large painting covered in brown paper. "I thought you might like it."

Daisy tore down a small corner of the paper, her heart thumping as she tore the rest away to reveal a life-size painting of her younger self, sitting curled up in an armchair. She glanced up at Matt, then back down at the painting with her mother's signature in the bottom right-hand corner. Peering closer, she recognised a small, silver star-shaped earring in her left ear. She'd made them when she'd been in college, but had only worn them for a short time before managing to lose them on a night out in Dublin.

"Mum painted this from a photo of me one Christmas when I was home."

"It's good," said Matt. "She's very talented."

Daisy nodded. "She is."

"You look like you're trying to solve the world's problems there," he teased.

Only a few, she remembered. That had been the last Christmas she and Matt had been together before he'd left. As always, she'd invited him down to Oranmore for a few days and, as always, he'd refused.

As she stared at the painting, she wished she could travel back to that moment and warn her younger self that her life was about to go spectacularly wrong unless she could prevent a simple misunderstanding.

She looked up at Matt. "How did you get this?"

"Remember the day I was looking at that website to buy some art for the house, and you mentioned that your mum painted? Well, she has her own website." He paused. "I wanted to try to make it up to you for thinking the worst of you that summer, Daisy. When I saw this, it felt like the right thing to do."

She nodded, struggling to understand her feelings. It was a thoughtful gesture. But did he really think it could go any way towards "making it up" to her for believing the worst of her? And what had that conversation with Charlie been about? She shifted her weight, starting to feel a bit awkward as the silence stretched.

"Thanks." She managed a small smile. "I'll go put it in the car."

Matt's phone rang. "I have to take this, excuse me."

He walked away, and Daisy had the uneasy feeling that she'd let an opportunity pass. If Matt wasn't going to say anything, shouldn't she have said something herself?

Only what would she say? It was pathetic, but her thoughts about Matt and James were as woolly as the cute hand-knit jumpers in her wardrobe. With a sigh, she carried the painting out to her car, sliding it in behind the two front seats, before lifting the next box out of the boot. Now she just had to figure out how to explain it to James.

⋙⋙ ⋘⋘

The painting was still in Daisy's car when she collected Rosie from Heuston Station later that evening. There was something different about her, Daisy thought, as Rosie slid into the passenger seat, leaning over to give Daisy a brief hug.

"Thanks for picking me up," Rosie said, as Daisy drove back up the quays.

Daisy glanced over. "No bother. Will you get some shopping done while you're here?"

"Ah, maybe," Rosie said. "It's just good to get away."

Daisy frowned, trying to figure out exactly what Rosie was saying. "Is everything okay at home? You and Séan all right?"

"Of course!" Rosie tutted. "And the kids are grand. I told you, I just needed a break." She looked like she was about to say something else, then shrugged. "I got my hair cut, what do you think?"

"The shoulder-length suits you," Daisy said, honestly. "It frames your face like that." When Rosie smiled, she added, "Freya really appreciates this, by the way."

Rosie's smile widened. "Would I have met her at your birthday party?"

"No – she's not a friend, just a client. But she's stuck, so …"

"Once she understands that I can't give her an official diagnosis while I'm still on a career break."

"I told her." Daisy remembered how relieved Freya had looked when she'd told her that Rosie had agreed to assess Holly.

"This isn't about labelling her," Freya had said, firmly. "It's about helping us understand if there's any issues. Just to make things easier for us and for her."

Rosie opened her window a couple of inches. "How's James?"

Daisy opened her mouth to say he was fine, but found she couldn't get the words out. She had no idea how James was anymore, or what he was thinking most of the time. She wondered if Rosie would notice anything this weekend. Maybe she'd push her to do something; something would be better than nothing. She tried to imagine what her life would be like without James. She'd be free to give Matt that second chance. Which was what she wanted, wasn't it? She gripped the wheel a bit tighter.

"Daisy?" Rosie interrupted her thoughts. "Is everything all right?"

"Absolutely." Daisy concentrated hard on the road. "I was just thinking."

"You definitely have enough space for me to stay, don't you?"

Daisy glanced over. "There's a sofa bed," she said patiently.

"A sofa bed," Rosie repeated.

Daisy stopped at red lights at O'Connell Bridge, and searched for a change of topic. "Did you know that Mum has a website?"

"*What?*" Rosie whipped around to look at her.

The light turned green and Daisy pulled off again.

"*For her art?*" Rosie asked.

"Yep." Idly, Daisy wondered if their mother's self-portrait was on it. Probably. Why wouldn't it be? It was one of the best things her mum had ever painted. She'd worn no clothes and no make-up – and she'd painted herself honestly. She realised suddenly that she didn't care who saw it – her mother should be incredibly proud.

"Did Mum tell you?" Rosie demanded.

"*Er*, no, actually." Daisy gestured vaguely in the direction of the back seat. "Matt discovered it."

Rosie peered around her seat. "Christ, that's not it, is it?"

Daisy spluttered with laughter. "Ah come on, that'd be too weird. No, it's one of me that Mum painted from a photo she took some years ago."

"And he just happened to discover Mum's website and decided he'd buy this for you?" Rosie sounded incredulous.

"Well, yeah." Daisy shrugged. "It's kind of a long story, to be honest."

"Good thing we have the weekend, isn't it?" Rosie paused. "Have you seen the website? Is the self-portrait there?"

"No idea," Daisy said.

"Because if it is," Rosie sounded grim, "I know exactly what we're going to do."

CHAPTER 44

MyStarScope Taurus: Your trust is tested when someone you work with lets you down.

Fionn had barely said two words the whole morning, Daisy realised the following Monday. Usually, when it was just the two of them, he was happy to chat away. But this morning he seemed subdued. She wondered if anything had happened over the weekend.

Her own weekend had been good. She'd barely seen James, and Alma had tactfully kept out of the way too, giving Daisy and Rosie a bit of space and privacy to catch up.

Daisy had dropped Rosie to Freya's house on Saturday morning. Afterwards, Rosie hadn't mentioned Holly or Freya, and Daisy had known better than to ask. Her sister took patient confidentiality seriously, and it made no difference to her that she wasn't being paid.

She had, however, been highly complimentary about her house redesign, which Daisy was taking as a major win. The two days, in fact, had been the most relaxed she'd spent with Rosie in ages.

They'd also gone onto Miriam's website. Sure enough, there was the self-portrait, with a price tag of €800.

"I think the fumes from the white spirit have finally got to her," Rosie had muttered. "Who does she think is going to pay that for a painting of herself in the nip?"

"It's probably very reasonable for what it is," Daisy had said. "It's a big painting," she'd added lamely, when Rosie had glared at her.

"We're buying it!" Rosie had said.

Daisy had stared at her. "Why would we do that?"

Rosie had looked at Daisy as if she were a bit slow.

"We'll buy it anonymously obviously. I'll transfer the money to one of my girlfriends, and then I'll arrange to pick it up from her house. We're going to give it to Mum and Dad for their anniversary, Daisy! That way, it'll have to stay with them, and she can't sell it again!"

"Right." Daisy wondered if Rosie could see the small problem with this plan. If their mother saw that her self-portrait had sold for a high price, it might encourage her to begin another one. But for the sake of peace, she'd said nothing.

Now she glanced over her schedule for the day, and then looked over at Fionn. "Everything okay?"

He pulled a face. "The landlord found out about our house guests."

"The people on the air mattress?" Daisy winced.

"I think Crona told him. You know, the one who gave me the Bible?" He sighed. "Anyway, I hope she's happy now – we've all been given a month's notice."

"Shit, Fionn, I'm sorry." Daisy tried to think of something reassuring to say. "You'll get somewhere else."

They exchanged a look, and Daisy knew they were both thinking the same thing. Rental properties in Dublin were scarce and overpriced – he'd be lucky to get anywhere. "It's grand, I'll figure it out." He shrugged. "*Um*, about our social media."

"What about it?"

"Granary House and Kayley Lynch are both trending on X."

Daisy blinked. "We're not mentioned, are we?"

Fionn bit his lip. "There's a short piece in Spilt Tea. Should I read it?"

"Go ahead."

"*'American country singer Kayley Lynch claims a poltergeist is behind the disappearance of some of her possessions at the two-hundred-year old country house where she's staying in Ireland. Kayley says she consulted with Irish supernatural expert, Sylvia Boylan, who believes that the poltergeist is responsible for loud banging, flickering lights and even unexplained smells in the house. Cork-based Boylan, who authored the book 'Supernatural Phenomena in the Islands of Ireland and Great Britain', says that 'Poltergeists are generally peaceful, benign entities, and can be spurred into action by creative energies like Kayley's.' The singer, whose hits include 'From My Heart' – moved from Dublin's five-star Shelbourne Hotel to the Georgian house in Wicklow a few weeks ago, to 'escape the media'. Granary House was recently bought, having lain empty for two years. Its new owner is having the house upgraded by Dublin interior architect's firm Discerning Designs'.*" Fionn looked up. "The rest of it is just about her tour."

"Why didn't she just say that there's fairies at the bottom of the garden?" Daisy stuck a pencil into her hair. "I wish they'd leave our name out of it."

Fionn flicked his fringe and looked a bit bemused. "Why? Any publicity is good, I think. A plug like that could be worth its weight in gold."

Better not explain that she didn't want the publicity because of the risk that James might see it. Fionn already knew far too much about her private life.

"Did Laura call?"

Fionn shook his head.

Laura's behaviour was getting stranger by the day, Daisy thought. "How's your final college project going?"

"Excellent." Fionn beamed. "I'm redesigning an old shopping centre as a remote work hub. I've open-plan work spaces and quiet rooms, and communal leisure areas. There's even a crèche."

"Class! What's the unifying theme?"

"The natural world. I've plants and trees growing everywhere inside the building, and an old delivery yard redesigned as a wildflower area."

"Sounds amazing, Fionn."

"Yeah." He nodded. "Pity I'll never get to deliver it for real. I'd love to actually make the place useful again. It's such an eyesore."

Daisy smiled. "You'll get your chance, just hang in there." Her mobile rang. "Hi, Kenny."

"Daisy? I wanted to give you the heads-up." Kenny sounded grim. "Todd found a bracelet belonging to Kayley in Alec's stuff, and I've had to fire him."

"*Shit.*" Daisy wondered quickly what the ramifications would be for the company. "What did Alec say?"

"He swore he didn't touch it." Kenny paused. "I don't know what to believe now, Daisy. I was prepared to give him a chance, but the guy has form. I didn't have a choice."

"Unless Todd put it there himself," Daisy said, remembering the conversation she'd overheard between Kayley and her manager. "I don't think Todd likes Kayley staying in Granary House."

"Even if he did, there's nothing I can do. I can't risk yer man looking too closely at Alec. Todd says Alec probably took those photos of the house after their party, and made it look like Kayley's drinking again. Luckily, they've no evidence, so they can't push that one any further." He sighed heavily. "Anyway, he's off my crew."

After Kenny hung up, Daisy briefly buried her head in her hands. Shit, could things get any worse? Maybe she could talk to Tim and ask him to advise Kayley not to talk to the press at all! The last thing they needed was for Discerning Designs to be linked to something like this.

She jumped when her mobile rang again, willing it not to be Matt or Kenny with more bad news. But it was an unknown number.

"Hello?"

"Daisy? It's Brian."

She felt herself go cold. "What happened?"

"Laura had to go to the doctor this morning, and she was sent straight to the hospital." Brian's voice was tight. "They've kept her in."

"What's wrong? What hospital is she in?"

"I'm sure she'll be in touch in the next couple of days, Daisy. I have to go."

"But, Bri – "

He had hung up.

Quickly, Daisy dialled Laura's number, but the call went straight to voicemail.

❧❧❧ ❦❦❦

Daisy could barely concentrate on anything for the rest of the day. She tried phoning Laura a few more times, and when she couldn't reach her left a message to say she hoped she was all right, and asked her to message her as soon as she knew anything.

She also tried phoning Brian back. The first time his phone rang out, the second time it went straight to voicemail. Finally, she gave up pretending to work, and told Fionn to take the rest of the afternoon off, before closing early to go home.

She figured it might help to talk things over with James. No matter what was going on between them, he knew her well enough to understand how she'd feel about Laura.

She let herself in, slipped off her shoes, and walked into the kitchen, stopping dead at the scene in front of her. Alma was in James' arms. Again! Only this time, she seemed to have buried her head under his arm. For a brief moment Daisy wondered whether she was actually sniffing his armpit.

"*Don't tell me, you're buying another app!*" The words tumbled out and Daisy realised how angry she sounded. Not angry enough, though. "*You know what, sorry to burst in! In fact, sorry I'm home early. If I'd known, I would have stayed away and let you get on with – whatever this is!*"

She was turning to go when Alma pulled out of James' embrace.

"*I will go! I cannot take all this!*" She pushed past Daisy, grabbed her coat from the hall and left, banging the front door behind her.

Daisy watched her go, then turned back to glare at James. "*She* can't take it – the nerve of her! And the nerve of you! I don't care what you said before! I don't believe a word, James! There's something going on and you haven't been honest with me." *And I haven't been honest with you, either.*

"Let it go, Daisy!" James shook his head. "I have to go after her, excuse me."

"*What?*" Daisy stared at him. "What are you talking about?"

His jaw tightened. "We'll talk when I get back, okay?" Without another word, he stepped past her.

"*Maybe I won't be here when you get back!*" Daisy yelled.

Moments later, she heard the front door slam again.

Daisy collapsed into the nearest chair and burst into tears. It struck her that all this time she'd only half-believed that there was something more between James and Alma, that if she and James really worked to make things better, they'd be okay.

But none of that seemed likely anymore.

CHAPTER 45

Daisy was in bed by the time James got back. She'd been half-tempted to book into a hotel for the night, but had decided she wasn't going to let Alma push her out of her own home.

James sneaked into the room, and Daisy felt his side of the bed sag as he sat down.

"Are you awake?" he said quietly.

For a moment, Daisy wondered whether she should pretend to be asleep, but she knew she was putting off the inevitable. She switched on her light, and wriggled into a sitting position, pulling the duvet tightly over her.

"I tried calling you." He scrubbed a hand across his face. "Did you even have your phone on?"

Daisy's heart seemed to have jumped to the back of her throat. This was it: they were breaking up.

"Were you just going to tell me over the phone?"

"Look, Daisy –"

"It's fine." She tried to wet her lips. "I know what you're going to say."

"I doubt it."

"I'm not stupid." She looked at him bleakly. "I can read the signs. Actually, I've been able to read them for ages, I've just been ignoring them."

"The signs?" He frowned.

Anger surged through her.

"*You and Alma,*" she whispered furiously. "Where is she, anyway?"

"In her room," he said patiently. "Probably in bed, it's late."

Daisy edged away from him. "So you were out together all evening?"

"Yes! We had dinner."

Daisy blinked rapidly, determined not to cry. She'd been right: the signs *had* been there all along. Now it was too late to do anything. It was karma! She should never have even contacted Matt – she could easily have gone through her life without closure. Lots of people did!

"Her mother had a heart attack so she's booked a flight home tomorrow. I wanted to take her mind off things for a while tonight. She's worried sick."

"What?" Daisy's mind raced to catch up.

"She'd just found out." James leaned back against the headboard, and tucked one leg up under him.

"So when I came home earlier …"

"She was in a total state, and I was trying to comfort her. I got her to call her brother once she'd calmed down a bit. He said their mother's in hospital, but she's stable."

"Oh, that's good," Daisy said, faintly. "Why didn't you just tell me what had happened?"

"Because you immediately jumped to the wrong conclusion, and I was worried I wouldn't be able to catch Alma if I didn't go. Her dad died of a heart attack when she was fifteen, and I didn't want her to be on her own."

"I didn't know about her dad." Daisy shifted uncomfortably in the bed. She was starting to realise how little she actually knew about Alma. "So she didn't want to come back, then?"

"What do you think?" James yawned. "We just went for an Italian, and I asked them to make spaghetti and meatballs for her."

She was the most awful, judgemental hypocrite in the whole world!

"I still wish you'd said something before you took off after her," Daisy whispered. "Why didn't you?"

James looked at her. "I was pissed off, Daisy. It's the second time you've thought the worst of me. And the worst of Alma!"

"I'm sorry." The words were a whisper. "I feel horrible. I just thought … you and Alma, you're always together, and you're close. I mean, even *you* have to admit that!"

"She's a nice person, Daisy."

And I'm not. He didn't have to say it. He looked so disappointed. But it was more than that. Even if there was nothing between him and Alma, it was pretty clear there was nothing left between the two of them either.

"It's late, Daisy, maybe we should just talk tomorrow."

Daisy took a breath. "Or we could talk now."

"Fine." James' face looked waxy in the light from the bedside lamp. "But first … remember the app I was telling you about?" Daisy nodded. "It was bought over the weekend."

"But you didn't buy it?" She already knew the answer.

"Someone did a lock-out deal." James dug his hands into his hair, so bits of it stuck up all over his head. "The students rang me this morning and told me they'd been approached on Friday evening. They were offered twice as much as we'd offered, but they weren't allowed to say anything, and they had to sign everything over before Sunday."

"Oh God." She wanted to touch him, but he seemed too far away. "So, what happens now?"

James met her eyes. "It's already happened. I got fired." The words echoed quietly in the small room.

Daisy's mouth dried up. "But it's not like you lost the company money." She stumbled over the words. "It's not your fault that someone else got in there first."

"That's not how the board sees it. I should have moved quicker, I shouldn't have let anyone get in and offer a better deal." He shook his head. "We found out who bought it. Matt Deveraux. That has to be your ex, right? Did you know he was back in the country?"

James said something else, but Daisy didn't hear him. She suddenly felt dizzy and there was a strange ringing in her ears. Could Matt have known that James had planned to buy it? It wasn't possible – she hadn't told Matt anything!

It had to be a coincidence! If Matt was keeping up with the latest in the tech industry, he'd probably come across the same thing James had. She tried to calm her breathing.

"James? There's something I need to tell you."

He flicked her a wary look. "What?"

Her heart was beating so fast, she wasn't sure she'd be able to get the words out. "You know the big job I took on in Wicklow recently? It was in Granary House. Matt bought it."

James turned to look at her properly. "When did you start?"

"In March." Daisy's voice wobbled.

"And you didn't bother to mention that you'd taken on a job for the guy who treated you like a piece of dirt?" He stared at her.

"He's just another client, James." Daisy knew how weak it sounded. "And you and I don't talk about our work to each other. Let's face it, we barely talk about anything at all."

"We're talking now, aren't we?" His voice was dangerously quiet. "So, is he with someone?"

Daisy spoke quickly. "No. But the house has been busy with workmen and decorators, and Kayley Lynch and her team. They've been filming and rehearsing there. Kayley's even staying in –"

"I read that." His jaw tightened. "That was after the flood, though, wasn't it? Or maybe the place didn't flood. Maybe it was just the perfect excuse for you and your ex to …"

"Hook up?" She swallowed hard. "That's what you were going to say, wasn't it? Why would you think that?"

"Because he was the one that got away, Daisy. And you never got over him!" James' eyes glittered. "So you took up where he left off, and threw me under the bus for good measure."

"That's not fair! I would never deliberately hurt you." She pressed her hands into her stomach, wishing she could deny everything. "I never told him anything about the app!"

"Screw the app!" James was shaking now. "Tell me nothing happened between you!"

She opened her mouth to reassure him, to draw a line under all the doubt and uncertainty she felt with James. It had been nothing – a couple of kisses. Only it *had* nearly led to something more. She met his eyes and realised that he'd already guessed.

"*James!*"

"*Don't!*" He stumbled off the bed, grabbing the pillow.

"*What are you doing?*"

Their voices had got louder, she realised. They couldn't wake Alma, she didn't want her to know that they were fighting.

She dropped her voice to a loud whisper. "What are you doing?" Why had she said a thing? Now there was no going back.

James yanked open the blanket box at the end of their bed and pulled out a spare duvet.

"What does it look like?" He didn't look at her. "I'll sleep on the sofa tonight, and tomorrow I'm taking a break. I'll go to London, see my family."

"James, please – " The rest of the words withered as she caught his expression.

After a few moments, she heard him going downstairs, moving around the sitting room, then the house fell silent. She switched off her lamp and lay back down, knowing she wouldn't sleep.

She doubted James would either.

Briefly, she wondered if he'd find it easy to get another job. The tech industry in Dublin was small enough; word was bound to get around about what had happened. She tried to imagine what it would be like to lose Discerning Designs, and be forced to start all over again.

But what about them? She remembered the overheard snatches of conversation of Matt on the phone to Charlie. Right now she couldn't think about that. No matter what was going to happen with Matt, James deserved to hear about it from her first.

He just needed a bit of time to calm down. She'd talk to him in the morning.

CHAPTER 46

By the following morning, Daisy had decided that if James been looking for an excuse to break up with her, she'd handed him one in the shape of Matt. She should have been honest from the start, but right now she doubted it would have made much of a difference.

Alma had left early to catch her flight back to Sweden, but Daisy had slipped out of bed to say goodbye.

"I'm sorry, I didn't mean to wake you," Alma had whispered.

Daisy had given her a hug. "I'm the one who should be sorry." She'd pulled back, feeling ashamed when she saw the astonished look on Alma's face. "This is for you." She'd handed her a soft package, wrapped in white paper.

Alma had opened it, pulling out a long, fine-knit cream scarf. "It's beautiful."

"I made it recently. I thought you'd like it."

"Thank you," Alma had said solemnly.

"Let us know how your mother is," Daisy had urged. "And you're always welcome back."

***

Two hours later, Daisy stood in the same spot with James, before she left for work.

"It might be good to spend some time with Fiona and Daniel," she said, wondering if she should pass on her best wishes to them. Although she didn't actually know either of his siblings, and she'd no idea where she and James stood now.

He gave her a withering look. "I'm glad you think so."

"So why are you going?" she challenged. "If it's Matt, you've got the wrong idea."

"Really? Tell me how, Daisy."

"Nothing happened!" She glanced away. "Not what you think, anyway. We didn't –"

"I don't care anymore." His voice was flat. "If you'd nothing to hide, you would have told me about Matt when you took that job. And, to be honest, I don't know how much to believe."

She met his eyes again, hoping to see a fragment of the person who'd always trusted her. But his expression had hardened. She forced herself not to stop.

"What about you and Alma? Do you even realise how close you two were? Admit it, since she came to live here, you've spent at least as much time with her as you have with me!"

James gave her a long look. "You're right. At least she was easy to be around. We could just game together, and talk about normal stuff. There was zero pressure." He shook his head. "You've got this sort of ... one-track mind, Daisy. Like, everything is so intense."

So she'd been right, she thought miserably. James obviously hugely regretted that they'd ever moved in together. Or that they'd got together at all. That was why he'd been pulling away, not wanting to spend any time with her. With Alma, on the other hand, there had been no expectations, no pressure to move forward in a relationship he had no interest in.

"Yeah, well, sorry things have been so shitty." Zero points for an articulate defence, she thought, miserably.

He gave her one last look. "I'll be in touch."

After he left, Daisy burst into tears. She'd lost him, just like she'd lost Matt five years ago. Only this time, it was her own fault. If she'd been truthful with James from the start, maybe they could have talked about it. Maybe she wouldn't have been so tempted to let Matt overturn everything. But would it really have made that much of a difference? He'd still have spent all his time working – or gaming with Alma. Things hadn't started to go wrong with James after Matt's return: they'd been going wrong long before.

She tried to pinpoint exactly when. After they'd bought a house together? Or had the cracks begun to show before that? If so, they'd just papered over them when they'd rented the spare room to Alma.

Daisy blew her nose and washed her face, trying to minimise the puffy-eye look.

As she cycled to work, she realised that they'd eventually have to sell their house too. Her vision blurred, and she stopped at traffic lights, hastily pulling her bike off the road, and pressing the heels of her hands under her eyes in an attempt to stop the tears from coming again.

Reaching their building, she locked her bike, but knew she wasn't ready to face Fionn. Instead, she walked up a couple of streets and found a café, where she slipped into a window table and ordered a flat white and a large slice of lemon drizzle cake.

For a few moments, she simply allowed the background chatter of the café drift over her, before tuning into the weather report on one of the radio stations being played over the sound system. She sighed. Two more storms, Henry and Iris, were due in swift succession over the next couple of days but, by the sound of it, Storm Henry would be gone by Friday morning and Storm Iris wouldn't appear until Sunday morning. Kayley's concert would escape unscathed.

If only she could talk to someone. Not Laura. She'd warned her to come clean about Matt from the start, and she felt like a complete failure now James had walked out. It was probably a sign to change her life – it just wasn't the one she'd been expecting.

She could phone her mother, but Miriam would just tell her not to worry because it was all part of the cosmic plan.

She could phone Rosie. She'd never confided in her about James, and there was a strong possibility that Rosie would lecture her. But they'd got on better than usual the weekend Rosie had stayed. Before she could talk herself out of it, she scrolled through her contacts and hit the dial button.

"Daisy, is something wrong?"

Sometimes she wished her sister wasn't so good at reading her from the other side of the country.

"If it isn't a good time ..."

"I always have time."

Rosie sounded so sincere that Daisy felt tears threaten again. Jesus, she'd been so judgy.

"Is this about Matt?"

"Not directly." Daisy stared out the window, which had started to mist over.

She filled her in, keeping things as vague as possible, aware of other people around. After she'd finished, she braced herself for Rosie to tell her that she shouldn't have kept secrets from James, and that it was basically her own fault.

"Both of you are at fault," Rosie said finally.

Daisy sighed. "Yeah, maybe. Oh, there's one more thing. I overheard Matt talking to Charlie on the phone. I only heard bits of the conversation from Matt's end, obviously, but it sounded like he wants me back in his life."

"Forget about Matt for a minute," Rosie said. "Try to put yourself in James' shoes."

"I know he's hurt, Rosie, but I've told him that nothing really happened between Matt and me. I don't think he believes me. He even thinks I told Matt about the app."

Rosie was silent for a moment. "And there's nothing you're leaving out?"

"I don't even know anymore," Daisy admitted. "Everything's such a mess. My feelings for James, my feelings for Matt." How did she explain that she'd never fully got over Matt? That she'd managed to justify her feelings for him, even after he'd told her why he'd left. "Things just got in the way after that night I stayed over, I guess. Kayley Lynch moved into the guest wing, and every time I was there in the house, it was always full of people. We just hadn't got around to talking anymore about us." *Or doing anything about it.*

Rosie sighed. "Well, do you want my opinion?"

Ah, no, I just rang for the craic. "Please!"

"If Matt wanted you back, he'd have found time to talk to you. And you'd have found time too, Daisy."

It wasn't that simple, Daisy thought. Rosie had no idea what her job was like – what her life was like.

"Look, flirting with Matt wasn't the smartest move," Rosie was saying now. "But you've got to put him out of your mind and out of your life. You have James to think about!"

"He walked out!"

"Daisy, I know James isn't perfect, and I really wish he'd been there for you a bit more lately, but by the sound of it he was trying to hold his company together. And he obviously left because he was upset!"

Daisy pushed the rest of her coffee away. "So should I phone him and just ..." She stopped. Even if they made up now, would anything really change, or would their relationship continue to drift?

"Listen, now," Rosie said, "forget about Matt, he's in your past. Where he deserves to be, after believing those rumours. Who does that after five years with someone? *Gobshite!*"

"He was twenty-five! Guys are still immature at that age."

"Well, that was then. What about now? He bought that software James' company wanted, didn't he?"

"Rosie, Matt works in the same industry, it was just a coincidence." Was it, she thought? Of course it was, she couldn't start going down that rabbit hole.

"Well, it sounds like he moved pretty quickly." Rosie sniffed loudly. "Walk away from him! James has been a bit of a fecker lately but, lookit, he's basically a good guy. He'll get over himself and he'll get another job, and you've got your own career."

Rosie fell silent, and Daisy knew she was giving her a chance to let this sink in.

A waitress came over to clear Daisy's plate, leaving the half cup of cold coffee in front of her.

"You're right, thanks," Daisy said slowly.

Rosie tutted. "Why do I get the feeling you're not really listening to me?"

"Ah no, I appreciate it. I just need to figure it out now." She felt a rush of emotion for her sister. "Thanks."

"Anytime. Love you."

"Love you too." Daisy hung up, promising herself that she'd pick up the phone to her sister more often, rather than leave all the running to her. But it was the only promise she could keep for now. She and Matt had unfinished business and it had nothing to do with the app.

Maybe they *were* supposed to be together. They'd been together once, and there was no rule to say that happily-ever-after couldn't take a break. It didn't matter that they hadn't talked. Matt had never been the type to push. He'd never had to, though, had he? She'd always felt like the most important person in Matt's life, as long as she was falling in with Matt's plans. But he was a different person now. Once and for all, she needed to find out if they had a future.

CHAPTER 47

MyStarScope Taurus: Your dynamic quarter moon means it's time to confront an issue head on. Shoot straight, and people will respect your honesty.

Daisy tried to reassure herself that she was doing the right thing when she drove to Granary House the following day. She'd messaged James a few times, but he hadn't replied. For the first time since they'd moved in together, she'd been on her own in the house. It had given her time to think. Now she was determined to sort things out properly with Matt.

She'd rung Fionn as she left Dublin. "I'm on my way to Wicklow. Do me a favour: don't transfer calls today? Just take messages."

"Sure. *Uh*, is everything okay, Daisy?" He'd sounded really concerned.

She looked up at the sky ahead. There were dark clouds as far as the eye could see.

"Everything's fine, Fionn, thanks."

She heard Matt on the phone to someone as she let herself in, and she hovered for a few moments in the hallway, wishing she'd let him know she was coming.

She walked down to the kitchen and opened the patio doors to let in some air. The weather had been humid in the last few days, as Storm Henry approached.

"Hi." Matt came into the room. "I wasn't expecting you today."

"*Uh*, surprise!" Was she imagining it, or did he seem a bit put out that she was there? "*Um*, I was just thinking, it's going to be strange when we finish up here. I'll miss it."

Matt gave a brief smile. "I can imagine."

She was just going to say it. "I'll miss you."

In the silence that followed, Daisy wished she could take it back. He'd obviously changed his mind. And she'd just made a complete fool of herself.

Then he sighed. "I missed you too, Daisy. I was pissed off and hurt, but I missed you like hell."

But he hadn't trusted her. And he hadn't said he'd miss her now! She tried to push it out of her mind, as she forced herself to broach the subject she'd been dreading.

"*Um*, so, James got a bit of bad news. He'd been trying to buy a new travel app for the company, but somebody else got in first, and he lost the deal." She watched him carefully, but Matt's expression was shuttered. "The board fired him."

"Tough. Are you okay?"

She gave a small shake of her head, waiting for him to say something about the app. He had to know what she was talking about!

Matt nodded. "I'm sorry to hear that, but it's the nature of the business. I wouldn't worry about James – he was the Boy Wonder in college."

For a few moments, Daisy felt totally on the back foot.

They both turned as Kayley called from the hall. It was a pity the poltergeist hadn't made Kayley disappear, Daisy thought grimly. The woman's timing was awful.

Kayley glanced coolly at Daisy as she came into the kitchen.

"Hi, Kayley." Daisy smiled as brightly as she could.

"Daisy just dropped by for a few minutes," Matt said.

Daisy felt her colour rise. Why did Matt feel the need to explain her presence?

"How about I make us all some coffee?" Matt said.

She should say no. But feck it, she had as much right to be here as Kayley!

Kayley pulled up a barstool and swung herself gracefully up onto it.

"Are you looking forward to your first gig?" Daisy asked politely.

Kayley gave her an appraising look. "I suppose it might be better, now that Todd is gone."

"Oh." Daisy wasn't sure what to say. "Where's he gone?"

Kayley yawned. "The guy wanted me to postpone my concert this weekend because there's gonna be a little rain. I fired him."

"I'm sorry." Daisy remembered the row she'd overheard, and figured Todd's departure had nothing to do with the weather. When Kayley didn't reply, she turned to Matt. "I've a few last things to do, and then I'll go. I'll email you the design awards form to sign – just scan it and send it back?"

"Yeah, no problem."

Matt glanced at Kayley, and Daisy suddenly felt in the way.

"Actually, I might skip the coffee. I should really go." She slid to her feet.

She shouldn't have come, she couldn't even talk to Matt with Kayley here. And, after everything, Matt would simply exit her life again. He'd definitely changed his mind about their second chance! And if there was a piece of the jigsaw still missing, it would have to stay missing.

"Oh, Daisy, before I forget … " Matt followed her out to the hall and closed the kitchen door behind him. "Sorry about that," he said quietly. "I wasn't expecting Kayley, and I wanted to talk to you. Do me a favour and come over on Friday night? Have dinner with me, please? You can bring the form along and I'll sign it then."

Daisy hesitated. "Yeah, if you like."

Matt squeezed her hand. "Come around six. Bring Fionn! Didn't you say he was a big fan? He'll be able to see the stage, and meet Kayley. She'll be relaxing that night before the concert on Saturday."

Maybe she'd finally have that last piece of the jigsaw after all. They wouldn't see each other again after Saturday, unless Matt wanted to remain friends. Friends would be enough, wouldn't it?

Matt opened the front door. The wind had picked up and it had started to rain. With a bit of luck, the storm wouldn't be too bad, Daisy thought.

She nodded. "I'll see you then."

CHAPTER 48

Daisy knew something was wrong the moment Matt's name flashed up on her phone early Friday morning. Storm Henry had raged all night, and even though the rain had subsided to a persistent drizzle, and the high winds had died down, it had wreaked havoc.

"Hi, Matt." Daisy walked over to her bedroom window, leaning her hip against the edge, as she looked out at her driveway. "All good?"

"Actually, we're in a bit of trouble. The storm took down half the rigging and damaged part of the stage."

"Oh." Daisy noticed that one of her neighbour's trees had split down the middle, and was hanging dangerously over the footpath. "Won't Kayley's people take care of it?"

Matt sighed. "They can, but it's a big job and they don't have much time. They could do with a bit of help."

Daisy frowned. "I suppose you could ask Kenny. You have his number, right?"

"I do, yeah, but Kenny's not my biggest fan. Can you ask him for me?"

It was strange that Kenny seemed to dislike Matt so intensely, she thought. She'd never seen him clash with a client before.

"I'll ask him."

"I knew I could depend on you, Daisy." Matt's voice was warmer now. "I'll see you later?"

Daisy tried to shake off the feeling that she was being manipulated again.

"Fionn and I will be there. I'll call Kenny now."

✳✳✳✳✳ ✳✳✳✳✳

Daisy tried to shake off a growing tension as she worked on Friday morning. The previous day, she'd messaged Laura to ask how she was, and to her relief she'd replied to say she was out of hospital, but on an antibiotic, and was taking a few days off to rest. She still didn't explain why she had needed to be hospitalised and so Daisy didn't ask any questions.

I feel bad putting off Stephanie like this, Laura had added. **I'll probably do a video call from home.**

Daisy had messaged back to tell her to stop thinking about work. At the same time, she knew that Stephanie needed to get everything done before the triplets were born.

Now, she caught Fionn's eye.

"How would you feel about going out on site? By yourself?"

"Say that to me again. *Slowly.*" A broad smile crept across his face.

"It's Stephanie's place, one of those converted mews off Herbert Park. Look, I know Laura had suggested keeping the downstairs open plan, but apparently Stephanie's not sure. Maybe you could have a fresh look? Give her a ring and see if you can head out now."

"So do I get to make some actual decisions?" When Daisy nodded, he lit up. "An actual project during my final year!"

"We'll have to get everything done before her babies arrive," Daisy warned.

"Right." Fionn flicked his fringe across his forehead. "Can you manage here without me?"

"Yeah, I'll be fine." Daisy paused. "If you're not sure about anything, run it by me, okay?"

He beamed again. "Real site work and a personal meeting with Kayley Lynch! Plus, Mercury is rising for the Gemini moon signs right now!"

"Which reminds me, I should check MyStarScope for today." When Fionn shot her a horrified look, she grinned. "I know, the app's total rubbish. It's also totally fun. So what's the real deal for Taurus?"

"You want the short or long version?"

"Give me the soundbite."

"*Uh*, your close relationships are rocky at the moment, so proceed with caution!"

"*Riiiight ...*" Daisy sighed. "Any clue as to when they might sort themselves out?"

Fionn looked solemn. "Sorry, Daisy."

"It's fine." She shrugged. "Depressingly accurate, as it happens."

"Except for you and me." He looked at her. "We're sound, right?"

"Sound." She smiled. "Cheers, Fionn."

<hr />

By Friday lunchtime, Daisy had still heard nothing from James. Alma had messaged to say that her mother was making a good recovery, but she'd be completing her postgrad in Sweden. Daisy felt relieved that everything was okay, but even guiltier that she'd blamed her for James' behaviour.

Fionn arrived back Friday afternoon, and handed Daisy a coffee and a pink-and-white paper bag. "I don't know if it's too late in the day for a coffee, but I took a chance."

She brightened. "Never too late for a coffee, Fionn." She took a sip. "It tastes different."

"Yeah, our usual place is closed for staff training, so I had to go around the corner to that new bakery. Look in the bag."

She peeked inside. "Doughnuts? You got us jam doughnuts?"

"Just please don't tell Laura. She'll hate me even more."

Daisy coughed as she swallowed too quickly and burnt the back of her throat.

"Why would she hate you? Did things go really badly at Stephanie's place?"

"No. From a design point of view, it went really well."

"As opposed to what point of view?" When Fionn said nothing, Daisy said, "So, Stephanie was definitely happy?"

"Yeah, she'd changed her mind about the open-plan thing, but didn't want to upset Laura. She's just totally freaked out at the amount of stuff they'll have with three babies!" Fionn nibbled a doughnut. "She's agreed to a partial partition wall that hides a lot of the living area from the kitchen. It's my own design – a completely hollow wall that opens out with tons of storage for all their baby stuff."

"Well done." Daisy paused. "So, no problems?"

"All good." Colour crept up his neck.

"Fionn, you'd tell me if something happened, wouldn't you?" When he looked even more flustered, she persisted gently. "This business is all about building trust with our clients."

"Everything went super-well, Daisy!"

She'd better drop it, whatever it was. Presumably he'd tell her eventually. "So, are you still on to meet Kayley later this evening?"

His eyes lit up. "Totally. I can't believe I'm getting to meet her in person! *And* see her concert tomorrow night!" He chewed on his lip. "Once it's not cancelled, like. There's another storm coming."

"Not until Sunday morning."

"Yeah, hope you're right." His expression changed as something new seemed to occur to him. "So, you don't mind me crashing in on your dinner with Matt, do you?"

"No, not at all!" She managed a little laugh as anticipation shivered through her. "We've just some business to finish up."

CHAPTER 49

Fionn was quiet during the drive down to Granary House that evening, but Daisy put it down to nerves about his imminent meeting with Kayley.

"She's actually pretty nice, Fionn." Daisy was certain Kayley would be charming to her fans. She glanced over. "You're not still worried about that storm? It's over a day away!"

Fionn peered out the window. "The experts don't always get it right, Daisy. Sometimes it's about looking and reading the sky."

Daisy turned off the main road into the side road that skirted the Hevren, and led to the Granary House drive. She could understand Fionn's concerns: the sky was dark and the air was starting to feel heavy. Still, all the storms this year had been accurately predicted.

She swung carefully off the road, through the gates and down the drive, pulling the car to a stop at the house and changing quickly out of her runners into the shoes she'd brought.

"Stop stressing, Fionn, it'll be fine."

Fionn started to say something but at that moment Matt opened the front door.

"Welcome to my humble abode!" He raised the glass of wine he was holding as they got out of the car. "Fionn? I think we've spoken a couple of times on the phone."

"Yeah. Thanks for inviting me."

Matt stepped back to let Daisy and Fionn into the hall, where a delicious aroma of food drifted up from the kitchen.

"Come on down," he said, slapping Fionn on the back. "Beer or wine?"

How long would they be here, Daisy wondered. Better not to chance drinking when she had to drive a bit later. "Water or juice for me, thanks, Matt," she said.

"I'd love a glass of wine," Fionn said. He turned to Daisy. "I adore the house." He stepped down into the kitchen. "Oh my actual God!"

Daisy gave herself a moment to enjoy Fionn's reaction, as he walked around the newly extended room, inspecting everything. She was incredibly proud of Granary House's redesign, and a little sad that after tonight she'd have no reason to see it again. Unless she and Matt stayed in touch. But how likely was that? Did she even want that? Did Matt?

Still, it was obvious that Matt had been holding back. Rosie was wrong – it was becoming clear that he'd been waiting until the job was finished, to sort things out between them.

"So, is Kayley joining us for dinner, Matt?" Daisy asked. At this rate, she wouldn't be surprised if Matt had invited the whole of her band to eat with them. Still, he definitely had the room!

"Nope. She'll be along later. She's been in Dublin with Tim doing interviews so as far as I know she's on her way back now."

Daisy had opened her mouth to ask what interviews she'd done when the patio door slid open. It took her a moment to recognise Niamh as she stepped inside, shrugging out of a short raincoat.

"Niamh?"

It wasn't just the clothes that made her look completely different. Her make-up was different – less goth and more subtle. And she'd straightened her hair!

Niamh crossed her arms. "I didn't know you'd be here, Daisy."

"I've a last bit of business with Matt," Daisy said pleasantly. "I assume you were helping the crew with the repairs."

"Niamh agreed to help the crew repair all the electrics for the concert," Matt said. "I insisted she stay for dinner. Kenny's not long gone. He and Kayley's crew worked all day fixing the stage."

"Are you going to the concert tomorrow night, Niamh?" Daisy asked.

"I wasn't able to get tickets," Niamh deadpanned.

"Come, anyway!" Matt waved an airy hand. "I'll let you in from this side."

Niamh smiled at Matt and shot Fionn a pointed look.

"I'm Fionn, I work for Daisy."

"Cool." Niamh turned to Matt. "Can I help you serve up?"

***

"So, like I know all redesigns are pretty exciting and, hey, no job too big or too small," Fionn said a while later, as they sat around the table, "but this place must stand out, right? I mean, look at it!"

Daisy started to say something, but Niamh cut across her. "Totally, yeah. It's been a real labour of love for me." She flicked back her hair and smiled warmly at Matt.

Daisy coughed as some rice caught in her throat and she reached for her glass of water. She'd have taken bets that Niamh would never want to see the house again. Maybe she was just good at separating her personal feelings from the job.

Matt returned Niamh's smile. "It was a real pleasure to have you here. Could I take your number?"

Colour flashed to Niamh's face, but before she could reply, there was a drumming sound above their heads and they looked up to see large, heavy raindrops falling on the old conservatory roof.

Matt turned to peer out the door. "When did it start to rain?"

"Just now, I think," Daisy said. "It wasn't raining when we arrived." She glanced over at Fionn. "Probably just a shower."

Niamh looked at Matt. "If those winds pick up again, all the electrics will be destroyed."

"I'm sure it'll be fine," Daisy said, noticing Matt's expression.

Matt turned to Fionn. "So, tell us about your internship? Have you been able to get out on site a lot?"

The conversation drifted to more general topics, and Daisy let her attention wander back to Niamh. How had she not noticed that she'd developed a crush on Matt? Judging by her reaction a few minutes ago, she'd misunderstood him – she hadn't realised that he'd just wanted to have the number of an electrician.

She wondered if Matt knew. But, watching him as he chatted to Fionn, she was willing to bet he hadn't a clue. For Niamh's sake, she hoped she'd forget about him now the job was over.

As they lingered over tea and coffee, Daisy met Matt's eyes across the table, and knew he was thinking the same thing as her: It was time they talked.

"*Um*, Niamh, Matt and I have a few things to discuss, so I was hoping you could show Fionn around?"

Niamh frowned. "The house?"

"And the gardens, if it's not too wet. I'm sure you'd love to see the stage design, Fionn?"

Fionn's eyes lit up. "Do you think we could knock at the guest wing? Kayley should be back now, right?"

Niamh looked at Fionn as if he was an annoying little brother, before sighing and pushing her chair back from the table. "We won't be long."

Matt shot her a bemused look. "Take your time."

Daisy waited until they'd left.

"So." She looked at Matt.

He poured some more wine. "You sure you won't have one glass?"

"No, thanks. *Um*, I have the form here." She took it out of her bag and slid it across the table with a pen.

As Matt scrawled his signature across the bottom of the page, she waited for the rush of euphoria she normally felt. But there was nothing.

"I'm glad this has worked out for you," he said.

"Yeah." She nodded. "I think we've got a fighting chance at the award."

Matt paused. "I'll be honest … I had a pretty good idea you'd pitch for this job."

"You did?" Daisy buttoned up the short cardigan she'd worn with her dress.

"When I told Brian I was buying this place, he mentioned the annual award. I knew this kind of project would be perfect for it."

"Right." A thought struck her. Something she somehow hadn't considered before. "Matt … if I hadn't pitched for the job, would you have got in touch at all?" She found herself holding her breath.

"Yes," he said, after a moment. "I would have contacted you – asked you to do it. I knew you'd do a good job. And I *did* want to see you, Daisy."

So what had priority? Getting his house expertly fixed up or seeing her? She suddenly had a slightly sick feeling in her stomach.

There was a distant rumble which Daisy hoped wasn't thunder, and she forced herself to focus on Matt. She needed closure on all this.

"I know you thought I'd cheated on you that summer." She kept her voice even. "If you hadn't been so stupid, Matt, you'd never have believed that." Hadn't she believed the same of James and Alma?

"I've already apologised, Daisy." There was an edge to Matt's voice now.

"Yeah, I know." It didn't matter – she didn't want him back. All this time it seemed she'd been misreading the signs, but none of it mattered now. She had to figure things out, and Matt wasn't the answer. She took a deep breath. "What did you want to talk about tonight?"

"Firstly, I wanted to thank you for all this." Matt gestured around the room. "You should be very proud."

Daisy smiled politely. She couldn't pinpoint why, but the compliment sounded intensely patronising. "It was a group effort: it always is."

Granary House had been the Holy Grail, and she'd had carte blanche for its redesign. But she hadn't got the expected dopamine hit. And something else was scratching at the edges of her mind.

"Do you remember the other day when I told you James had been fired over a deal he'd lost?" Daisy looked closely for a reaction, but Matt's face was blank. "You asked me was I okay. You didn't ask me anything about James, though." For a moment, she thought Matt would pretend not to remember.

Then he smirked. "Why would I be interested in James?"

She allowed herself a brief, painful moment to think about James. He probably hated her. He'd definitely never trust her again. She wouldn't blame him.

"What exactly have you got against him? I know you bought that new travel app. Did you *know* that James was trying to buy it?"

Matt shot her a hard look, but Daisy dug her fingernails into the soft flesh around her thumb, and forced herself to wait.

"Brian told me that James wanted it."

He could have been talking about the weather, Daisy thought, as she stared at him in horror. But the worst part was that *she'd* told Laura, who must have mentioned it to Brian. This was all her fault.

"I just offered them a better deal." Matt shrugged. "It wasn't difficult, given your boyfriend's moral compass when it comes to business."

Daisy folded her arms tightly across her chest, trying to steady herself. "What are you talking about?"

"Come on, Daisy, don't pretend."

Her mind raced. This was crazy! Matt knew nothing about James – they'd never even met!

He sighed heavily. "Do you remember what Charlie and I were working on before I did my internship?"

"Sort of."

"Of course you do." His voice hardened. "It was an idea: a well-developed one for new airline software. The problem was we didn't have the investors, but we'd have got them. We'd planned to start pitching it when I got home."

Daisy had a sudden, awful feeling she knew where this was going.

"Only when I was away, James approached Charlie and persuaded him to sell it for a fucking pittance." Matt's expression matched his voice. "I assumed you'd told him about our idea, and about us having no money."

Her mouth dried. "I didn't tell James a thing. *I didn't even know him then, remember?* By the time you were doing post-grad, he was working and looking for opportunities to start up by himself. So he had his ear to the ground, just as he does now."

Vaguely, she was aware that the rain seemed to be getting heavier. It didn't seem important anymore.

"I suppose it doesn't matter how he found out," Matt was saying. "He robbed us: he and his investors got to develop our idea, and made millions from it, while we got nothing.'

Daisy knew for a fact that James hadn't made millions, but now didn't seem the right time to argue on that point. She glanced at the signed form in front of her.

She should just put it in her bag and go find Fionn. She needed to leave. She wouldn't have to see Matt again unless Granary House was placed in the competition. It might even win.

The irony was, she couldn't do it anymore. Not after what Matt had done. He hadn't just hurt her – he'd hurt James. She had no idea if her relationship with James was over, but she knew he'd never betray her the way Matt had. He'd never deliberately hurt the people closest to her. Before she was tempted to change her mind, she ripped up the form.

"What are you doing?" Matt stared at her.

"Coming to my senses," Daisy said, grimly. "You should sell this place, you know. It's really beautiful, but it's way too big for one person."

Matt rubbed his hand across the back of his neck. "There's no need to do this, Daisy." His phone rang and he checked the caller ID. "It's Kayley. Let me take this and then we can talk, okay?"

She wouldn't change her mind. Not now. "Go ahead. Answer it."

CHAPTER 50

Matt stood and jabbed his finger across the screen. "Kayley? Hang on, I can't hear you." He strode out to the hall.

Alone in the kitchen, Daisy slumped slightly as she looked around. She'd poured so much time and love into this house ... maybe she shouldn't have torn up the form. Only she wanted nothing more to do with Matt.

She'd been an idiot. About everything, if she were being honest. Mainly because she hadn't seen Matt for what he really was: arrogant and insecure. And, worst of all, capable of holding a grudge against her and James all these years.

"*Christ!*" He came back into the kitchen.

Daisy got to her feet. "What's wrong?"

"It's Kayley – she's stuck on the road beyond the driveway. The river's burst its banks again and the road's flooded. She tried to drive through – I think she said they couldn't get out of the car ... I couldn't hear her that well and then I got cut off – fucking signal!"

Daisy looked out through the patio doors. The rain was getting heavier by the minute, it seemed. "She and Tim will probably just have to get out of the car and walk the rest of the way. I mean, how far away from the house are they?"

"Tim got delayed so he's not with her!" Matt scowled. "So she insisted on driving back by herself. Well, I'm assuming Drew is with her." He pushed a hand through his hair. "But I think I caught the word 'injured'."

"Who's Drew?"

"Her bodyguard." He turned to go.

"Hang on!" Daisy said.

Then the patio door opened and Fionn and Niamh burst into the kitchen, sliding the door quickly shut behind them.

"It's crap out there," Fionn declared, flicking wet hair out of his eyes. "And Kayley doesn't seem to be here yet. What's the story?"

"The river's burst its banks again," Daisy said, "and Kayley just phoned to say her car is stuck on the road beyond the driveway. Tim isn't with her but her bodyguard must be. She might have said something about being injured – Matt couldn't hear properly and then got cut off." She turned to Matt. "Have you a rain jacket I can borrow? I'll come with you. And do you have some torches? Just in case?"

He nodded to one of the kitchen drawers and went out to the cloakroom. Daisy opened the drawer to find a collection of random items, from DIY bits to first aid supplies. She grabbed a couple of small torches and as an afterthought, a roll of bandage, still in its plastic packaging, and shoved them into her jacket pocket.

Matt returned with a few brightly coloured rain jackets and handed one to Daisy. "It should fit."

"I'm coming too," Niamh said, taking another jacket from him.

"Stay here, Fionn," Daisy said. "Have your phone on in case we need you. And get in touch with Tim and let him know what's happening. Oh, Matt – can you send Tim's number to Fionn right now?"

He did so.

The rain was hitting the ground hard as Matt, Daisy and Niamh stepped outside and immediately Daisy could feel it starting to soak through her tights. She glanced down at her shoes. "Go ahead! I'll catch up," she said. "I must change my shoes."

She opened her car, grateful there was no need to lock it out here, and kicked off her shoes, throwing them into the back, before sitting briefly in to pull her runners back on.

She just hoped the flooding wasn't as bad as last time. If she couldn't drive, she'd rather swim home than be stuck here another minute. Briefly, she wondered how long it would be her home. Maybe she and James would be one of those couples who couldn't afford to sell and would be forced to live separate lives under the same roof. It was a depressing thought.

She hurried to catch up with the others at the gate and, as they stepped out onto the road, the water rushed up around their legs.

Matt waded ahead.

"*Fuck*," Niamh muttered. "We're lucky there's no electricity wires along this road. If a wire came down in this!"

Crap! Daisy hadn't even thought of that. "You're sure there aren't?" She looked up nervously.

Niamh shook her head. "Nah, they're on the other side of the house." She raised her voice to be heard above a loud rumble of thunder. "I noticed the first day I arrived out."

"*I can't see the car!*" Matt shouted back to them.

Daisy squinted along the road. No car yet visible. She waded on. Was it her imagination or was the water getting deeper? It certainly seemed to be getting faster.

"This is pretty scary shit," muttered Niamh.

Matt stumbled over something and almost fell into the water. As he righted himself, Daisy and Niamh caught up with him and they waded on.

"Where the fuck's the car?" Matt muttered. "If anything's happened to Kayley ..."

"Sucks for her!" Niamh said. "You can't control the weather."

Matt glared at her. "*Kayley could be injured! In any case, she's panicking!*"

Niamh stopped for a moment to find her footing. "Yeah, but you're not responsible for her. Like, you barely know her!"

Matt halted. "Actually, I do." He was breathing heavily, from anger and effort. "Look, you both might as well know. Kayley and me – we're together."

Niamh stopped walking. "What the *fuck* are you on about?"

What did he say? Daisy halted. *Together?*

And suddenly she realised the truth. She just hadn't registered the clues. She was the woman in the photo in Matt's bedroom. And he was the reason she was starting her Irish tour in the grounds of an old house that until a few months ago only a small number of people even knew about!

She stared at Matt but he didn't meet her eyes.

"Kayley and I dated for nearly a year. We've been on a break."

"But you're back together now?" Daisy almost laughed.

Matt started to speak, but Niamh yelled over him. "*How come nobody knew? I mean, she's this big country singer, and somehow nobody knew she was dating you?*"

"Of course people knew." Matt spoke with savage civility. "The public didn't know, that's all. We kept it private, because that's what we wanted. Look, we're wasting time." He waded on.

Niamh waded after him.

"*That's such horse shit!*"

Daisy followed. "Niamh! It's actually none of our business!" She did her best to inject a note of warning into her voice.

Niamh didn't reply, and Daisy wasn't sure if she could hear her. The rain seemed to have got heavier. Now it was hitting them sideways, the strong winds and the water rushing around their legs threatening to unbalance them with every step.

It *was* her business, though, she thought, suddenly. Matt had *made* it her business!

"*Why didn't you tell me, Matt?*" Daisy shouted to be heard. "*You could have just said something!*"

Daisy saw a flash of understanding in Niamh's expression, but forced herself to focus on Matt.

He swung around. "We only got back together this week. That's what I wanted to tell you earlier tonight."

Daisy stared at him for a moment. How could she have misread so many signs?

"And that I'm her new manager."

"*What?*" Daisy laughed now. "That's a bit outside your expertise, isn't it?"

He shook his head. "Whatever. We're wasting time."

He turned and waded further down the road, the water hitting his knees.

Resisting the sudden urge to leave, Daisy waded after him, mentally relaying every conversation they'd had since he'd come back, every stupid coffee and pancake he'd made her. The night she'd stayed at the house could have gone so differently if she'd allowed it. Would Matt and Kayley still have got back together if it had? It didn't matter anymore – she had to stop wondering about 'what ifs'.

"*I knew there was something going on!*" Niamh shouted. "*She was always hanging around, flirting with you. That's why she moved in. I didn't think she'd stick it out when things started going wrong! She's such a spoiled cow!*"

Matt either hadn't heard or was ignoring her.

Niamh was right, thought Daisy. Kayley's move from a five-star hotel in Dublin to an old house in the countryside, in the middle of a major redesign, had nothing to do with the paparazzi!

And despite everything that had gone wrong after she'd moved in ... after she'd moved in ... Daisy turned to look at Niamh. Through the dark and the rain, she could just make out the expression on her face, as Niamh met her eyes.

It had been Niamh who'd decided to overhaul all the electrics. And Daisy had trusted her, or at least she'd trusted Kenny. She remembered the day the house lost power. None of Kenny's team had been able to figure it. Could Niamh have done something? And then all that stuff about Kayley – including the photos – had been leaked online. She'd blamed Alec, but Alec had no reason to mess things up. Maybe Niamh had hoped that if she made things uncomfortable, Kayley would move back to her luxurious hotel suite?

She had no evidence. But if Niamh *had* been behind even some of what had happened ... she needed to steer the conversation in a safer direction ...

"When did you become Kayley's manager?" she asked Matt.

"What?" He glared at her. "Why does it matter?"

It didn't matter – she already knew.

"*Why did you lead me on like that?*" Niamh yelled.

Daisy and Matt both turned to look at her.

Tears seemed to be streaming down her face, although it was hard to tell with the rain. Things had officially reached peak weirdness, Daisy thought.

"What are you talking about?" Matt glared at her.

"Niamh, I don't think this is the time." Daisy wished she'd just stayed at home and emailed Matt the stupid form.

Niamh waded up to Matt and poked him in the chest. "I'm talking about you dicking around. Tonight, you even asked for my number!"

"Because you're an electrician!" Matt sounded exasperated. "And you and I were just having a bit of craic. I doubt the rest of the crew could even have an intelligent conversation. And that boss of yours is a grumpy prick."

Had Matt always been such a snob, Daisy wondered. How had she not seen that?

"*You leave my dad out of it!*" Niamh shoved Matt so hard he almost lost his balance.

What? Shit, thought Daisy, *I can't afford to lose Kenny!*

"Niamh, forget it – he's not worth it!"

"You're Kenny's daughter?" Matt rolled his eyes. "Figures."

He turned and waded on, then halted abruptly. "There's the car!"

The SUV was tipped on its side in the ditch close to the riverbank, water flowing all around it. As Matt headed for it, Daisy dialled 999, shouting into the phone to be heard. As she hung up, she noticed Niamh was heading back towards the house. She cupped her hands around her mouth. "*Niamh, where are you going?*"

"*Leaving!*" Niamh didn't bother to turn around.

"*We might need you!*" Daisy yelled back.

When Niamh ignored her, she rang Fionn.

"*Fionn, can you hear me?*" She heard a faint reply. "*Message me when Niamh gets back to the house.*" Zipping her phone away, Daisy waded on, her eyes starting to hurt as she squinted into the rain and wind.

As they got to the car, another part of the riverbank burst, sending more water rushing onto the road. Daisy tried not to panic as she battled to stay standing. The water was now well over her knees. It was then she noticed that one of the old trees that lined the riverbank had fallen across the road, completely blocking it.

"*Oh shit, Matt!*"

"It must have come down just after Kayley got through," Matt shouted. "It could have hit her car!"

He waded the final few steps and, after a few attempts, heaved himself onto the side of the car.

"Give me a torch, Daisy."

She handed him one. He wiped his sleeve across the window to try to clear it, before shining the torch into the car.

"I can see Kayley! She's lying down. *Kayley? Can you open the door?* Shit, she's not moving! *Kayley!*" He pulled hard at the handle. "*It won't budge!*"

"What about Drew?" Daisy called.

"He's in the passenger seat. He seems to be out cold! Or worse. He probably banged his head when the car overturned."

"Do you think it's locked from the inside?" Daisy swayed as a wave of water hit the back of her knees.

"Hang on, it might be just stuck. I'll try to force it!"

Half-standing now, his legs braced either side of the door, Matt gave a loud grunt as he tugged on the door.

It came suddenly away, and Daisy watched, as if in slow motion, as the momentum threw him back off the car onto the flooded road.

He fell backwards, plunging under the water.

CHAPTER 51

"*Matt!*" Daisy waded forward to help him.

His face had emerged from the water, his eyes closed, his head back, and he seemed to be unconscious. Hunkering down, she tried to slide an arm around his shoulders but her hand snagged on something hard and rough and she realised there was a large jagged rock under the surface. He must have hit his head on it. *Shit!* She managed to get her arm around his neck and pulled him upwards.

"*Matt! Matt, wake up!*"

She put a hand on his chest and was relieved to find he was breathing. Then he moaned, but didn't open his eyes.

Crap! What was all that dark stuff on her sleeve? *Oh God, blood!* The back of his head had been cut badly. *Fuckity-fuck!* This was really serious. He could die! *Could* he die?

Now what? If only she'd done that first-aid course in college. It had clashed with the upcycling clothes module. And lovely as it was to give charity castoffs a new life, it was feck all use right now.

Should she try slapping his face? Maybe not! If she started she mightn't be able to stop. Instead, she leaned close to his ear. "*Matt? Can you hear me? Wake up!*"

She could cheerfully strangle Niamh right now. If she hadn't flounced off like that, at least she'd have some bloody help. Right, there was nothing for it!

Half-standing, she dragged Matt closer to the car and, with a lot of swearing, managed to prop him against the side. Then she tugged at the end of her skirt, hoping to tear off a strip of it. Shit, they always made this look so easy in films! The bandage! She'd nearly forgotten. She took it out and tore open the wrapping. Fumbling, she tied it as tightly as she could around Matt's head, trying to ensure that the knot was over the wound in the hope that the extra pressure would lessen the blood flow.

She'd done as much as she could. Bracing herself, she tucked her skirt into her knickers and managed to scramble awkwardly onto the side of the car.

Crouching close so she wouldn't fall off, she shone the torch in through the open door. Kayley was lying wedged between the two front seats, her eyes closed. Drew was slumped in his seat belt. Daisy couldn't tell if he was breathing.

She clung on to the top of the car as tightly as she could as she reached in, grasped Kayley's thigh and shook it. "*Kayley? Wake up!*"

Kayley gave a soft moan and Daisy sagged in relief.

Slowly, Kayley's eyes opened. "Daisy!" she gasped.

"You're okay, Kayley. Help is coming." She hoped to Christ it was, and quickly.

"Is Drew okay, Kayley?"

"I can hear him breathing," she said.

"Okay, good."

"What about my concert tomorrow?"

As if that mattered! "Least of our worries! Can you get out if I pull you up?"

"I can't." Kayley winced. "I think I've dislocated my shoulder. The car tipped over and I got out of my seatbelt, but I slid down here and now I'm stuck. I think I passed out for a while after I called Matty." She moaned in pain. "Where *is* Matty?"

Thunder rumbled again in the distance, and Daisy sent up a quick prayer that it wouldn't move across to them before the rescue services arrived.

"Matt's right here. He's actually sitting on the ground, because he fell as he was getting the door open." She saw Kayley's expression, and added hurriedly, "He'll be fine, honestly."

God, she really hoped he'd be fine! It'd be nice to have some help, but she didn't think she'd be getting any from Matt. Which seemed strangely fitting.

"There's help on the way," she said. "Just try to hang in there! And don't move! Being stuck between the seats is keeping you safe."

Kayley gave a faint smile. "You're sweet. I can see why Matty was with you for such a long time." She winced, briefly closing her eyes. "I'm sorry we didn't get to know each other better."

Or at all! Daisy was pretty sure Kayley hated her.

"He told me about you, you know." Kayley's voice was a bit weaker now, and Daisy hoped she didn't lose consciousness. "I was kinda afraid you'd want him back."

"Ah no, definitely not. We've both, *uh*, moved on." Nope, *this* was peak weirdness.

"You know, it meant a lot to Matty ..." Her eyes fluttered closed again.

"*What meant a lot? Kayley? Kayley?*" Daisy no longer cared what Matt thought or felt, but she was fairly sure she had to keep Kayley awake. "*Kayley? About Matt!*"

With an obvious effort, Kayley opened her eyes again.

"He told me you guys are back together," Daisy said. "I'm glad."

"Yeah." Kayley sounded exhausted. "I don't want to keep it quiet this time. I don't care what Matty says. Things are different now – I'm in a good space. Rehab was the best thing I ever did. For me and Matty."

Daisy wondered why Matt would have wanted to keep his relationship with Kayley a secret. Maybe for the sake of her career? Fans preferred their idols to be single and notionally "available".

Kayley moaned again, and Daisy silently willed the emergency services to arrive. They'd probably have a boat, although she'd no idea how they were going to get Kayley out of the car. *Shit*, the tree! How would they lift her over the tree into a boat? Maybe she should phone them back – although they were probably already on their way!

Kayley's face spasmed in pain. "Where are they?"

"They'll be here soon." Glancing down, Daisy could see the top of Matt's head. At least he was still upright, she thought grimly.

She froze, as what sounded like thunder threatened to deafen her. As the noise grew louder, she strained her head back to look up. To her relief, she saw it was a rescue helicopter.

CHAPTER 52

As the blades spun overhead, Daisy slid back down off the car and crouched beside Matt. His eyes were open but glazed, and she wondered if he remembered what had happened.

"Kayley?" he mouthed.

"She's fine."

The helicopter hatch opened and two of the first responders lowered slowly to the ground. Daisy's body was flooded with relief as she relinquished the responsibility to them.

After Matt was winched up to the helicopter in a simple harness, Kayley was airlifted in a stretcher. Finally, Drew was pulled out and after a quick assessment, airlifted in another stretcher.

One of the first responders, who introduced himself as Conn, insisted Daisy come with them.

"I don't want to leave you. It's a short flight, and we have to get the other three to hospital while it's still safe to fly."

She sat opposite Matt in the back of the helicopter, as Kayley lay on the ground between them, her stretcher locked securely in. Conn had wrapped thermal blankets around her and Matt, and secured Kayley's upper arm to minimise movement, before giving her an injection for the pain. He'd also cleaned Matt's head, and covered it with a temporary bandage.

Meanwhile, the other medic attended to Drew, checking for breathing and elevating his legs. Daisy released a small sigh of relief as Drew opened his eyes.

"Kayley?" he said.

"She's here, she's fine!" the medic said, slipping some earbuds into Drew's ears so he could talk to him as he continued to run checks.

Daisy put her hands over her own ears in an attempt to block out the noise of the blades, as the chopper turned and headed back towards Dublin.

Conn slipped on a headset, then produced three packs of earbuds, handing a pack each to Daisy and Matt.

"Can she use them?" Matt gestured to Kayley as he put in his own buds.

"Sure." Conn leaned down and carefully popped them in Kayley's ears.

As he tuned them all into the same channel, the background noise faded, and Daisy became aware of how loud her heartbeat sounded in her ears, how cold and numb every inch of her body was.

She took a deep breath, holding it as long as possible, before slowly releasing it.

"Do you remember what happened?" Conn asked Matt.

"I remember leaving the house." Matt shook his head. "Kayley was … I remember the car."

Conn nodded. "You probably have a concussion. We've an ambulance waiting for us at the heli-pad on a GAA pitch near Sandymount in Dublin. It's the safest place to land." He looked at Daisy. "You should consider going with them to get checked out."

Daisy clutched the blanket tighter around her. "I wasn't hurt, I just want to get home." As she met Matt's eyes, he glanced away. She realised she didn't care what he thought anymore.

While Matt and Kayley were being airlifted, she'd sent a quick message to Fionn, updating him on what had happened, and he'd messaged back to say that he, Niamh, and the band were staying overnight and, judging by the smell, some of the drains around the house seemed to be overflowing. Daisy decided not to tell Matt. He'd find out soon enough.

"Jeez, those painkillers are strong! I can't feel anything anymore," Kayley said. "Can I sit up?"

"Sorry." Conn was firm. "You have to keep that shoulder immobile."

Kayley sighed heavily. "So, when will I be able to gig?"

"Gig?" Conn frowned.

"I'm Kayley Lynch – the singer? I'm meant to be starting my Irish tour tomorrow night at Granary House."

"The doctors will be able to give you a better idea." Conn caught Daisy's eye.

Daisy knew what he was thinking. If her shoulder was dislocated, Kayley's tour would probably be cancelled. She glanced over at Matt, and knew he'd guessed it too.

Matt looked down at Kayley. "No matter what happens, Kayley, I promise you'll be okay."

Kayley seemed to brighten. "Thank you for rescuing me, Matty."

Daisy wondered if Kayley would thank her too, but Matt and Kayley were now looking deeply into each other's eyes.

Or as deeply as possible, she supposed, given that one of them was lying down.

"I wanna do a live-stream to my followers," Kayley said. "Matty, can you get my phone from my bag?"

Daisy eyed Kayley's tiny, designer bag on the ground beside her, marvelling that it had survived the evening.

"Daisy, would you do us a favour?" Matt said.

Daisy was fairly certain she never wanted to do anything for Matt again. It was an incredibly freeing thought.

Matt handed her Kayley's phone. "Can you live-record Kayley?"

One last thing wouldn't matter, Daisy thought. She glanced at Conn, who gave a brief shrug. "Once she doesn't overdo it," he said.

"You ready, Kayley?" Matt gave Daisy a quick nod.

"Hi, y'all!" Kayley waved up at the camera. "So, quick update. I was supposed to start my Irish tour tomorrow evening, but the car I was driving overturned in a bad storm, so right now I'm being flown to hospital." She paused. "But I want ya'll to meet my Irish boyfriend, Matt Deveraux, who I've been staying with at his ancestral home in County Wicklow!"

Daisy gave a snort of laughter, which she managed to turn into a cough, as she panned the phone briefly to Matt.

"We've kept our relationship out of the public eye," Kayley continued, "but I wouldn't be here tonight if he hadn't rescued me."

Nothing like a nice, neat spin on the truth, Daisy thought.

"I just wanna say I've no idea what's gonna happen now," Kayley blinked away some tears, "but thank ya'll for showing me so much kindness and love. As ya'll know, my daddy's family are Irish, so I've always felt drawn to this little country."

Daisy caught Conn's expression, and had to bite the inside of her cheek hard.

"Since you came into my life, you've changed me for the better, Kayley," Matt said.

Daisy quickly panned the camera towards him, hoping they'd finish soon.

Matt reached into his pocket and took out a small black box. It was identical to the one in which he'd presented her spare key for Granary House, Daisy realised, swallowing nervous laughter.

Trying to ignore sudden turbulence, she kept the phone as steady as possible, as Matt opened the box to reveal a large, square diamond ring. Idly, Daisy wondered whether Kayley would have preferred a moonstone but, judging by her expression, she couldn't have cared less.

"*Oh! My! God! I can't believe this is happening!*" Kayley's voice broke.

Which made two of them, Daisy thought.

"Kayley Lynch, will you marry me?" Matt said.

"Yes, of course!" Kayley had started to cry now

Idly, Daisy wondered if the painkillers were starting to wear off.

Matt slipped the ring on Kayley's finger and they kissed.

Daisy recorded three more seconds before hitting the stop button. She caught Conn's eye. "Nope, no idea!" she said.

Conn exchanged a glance with his colleague, who looked like he was trying not to laugh. "Congratulations, guys. Okay, we'll be landing in a few moments."

Daisy leaned back in her seat and closed her eyes. Today had been the longest day of her life.

All she wanted was to go home.

CHAPTER 53

As the helicopter landed, Daisy felt a fresh wave of adrenalin rush through her as she noticed TV cameras, reporters and photographers waiting outside. She braced herself as Conn helped her down.

"*Daisy!*"

She shielded her eyes as she peered into the crowd, and spotted Tim battling his way through. "How's Kayley?" he asked.

"*Um,* she's over there." Daisy turned in time to see Kayley being stretchered into the ambulance. "She hurt her shoulder when the car flipped over. It might be dislocated."

"Bollicks to that!"

Daisy folded her arms tightly across her, shivering under the emergency blanket still wrapped around her. "How did you know where we'd be?"

"One of the band members let me know Kayley had been airlifted. I think they must have let the press know too. Anyway, after that, it was pretty easy to find out where they'd be landing." He peered at her. "You're frozen. Probably suffering from shock too. Do you want to go to hospital?"

She shook her head. "I'll be fine." As she looked over, she caught Matt's eye as he was helped into the back of the ambulance with Kayley, before the doors closed and the ambulance pulled away.

Somebody thrust a microphone in her face. "Tara White from Channel Five news. Are you part of Kayley Lynch's entourage? Can you tell us exactly what happened?"

"I'm ... I'm not part of her entourage." She wished she could stop shivering.

"I'm Tim Meaney, Ms Lynch's publicist."

The reporter flicked the microphone to him.

"Kayley's performance at Granary House in Wicklow this evening has been cancelled because of the flooding." Tim spoke clearly. "Kayley got into difficulties on a flooded road, and she's on her way to hospital to be checked out. That's all for now. Thank you."

"*What can you tell us about Kayley's fiancé?*" someone shouted.

"*How did the couple meet?*"

"Kayley will release a personal statement when she's ready." Tim was firmer now. "Thank you, again."

The flashes of a dozen cameras blinded Daisy's vision, as reporters continued to shout at them, but Tim turned Daisy away.

"My hire car is parked just over here. Come on, I'll give you a lift."

Daisy yawned, grateful to let someone else make the decisions. "That would be great."

She relinquished the emergency blanket to a paramedic and followed Tim.

As they drove away, she wriggled down into the passenger seat, already regretting having left the emergency blanket behind as she tried to stop herself shivering – what was she thinking?

Tim turned up the heater. "That's partly adrenalin, you'll be exhausted later."

She was exhausted now! "You know this seat is going to be soaked."

He shrugged. "It's a hire car, and it'll dry out. Sorry you had to sit through that nauseating spectacle, by the way."

Daisy frowned. "You mean the proposal?"

Tim nodded. "I was keeping an eye on Kayley's social media. So were those reporters, obviously. Her fans will love it, which is the main thing. Because we'll have to cancel or reschedule her tour."

"She'll just have to listen to the doctors, I guess." Daisy tried to sound upbeat.

Tim smiled grimly. "I was thinking about her new manager."

Daisy looked at him. In spite of everything, she was reluctant to speak badly of Matt.

Tim seemed to read her mind. "Kayley told us you and Matt used to be together."

"Yeah, it ended five years ago."

"Can I be brutally honest?"

"Said no PR person ever," Daisy joked.

Tim shrugged. "I've decided to trust you. Kayley met Matt at a big charity event in New York. When they started dating, I advised her to keep it quiet. Matt wasn't involved in the industry, and to be honest, Todd and I didn't really trust him. I don't know why – just a feeling. The thing was, he wanted to keep it quiet too. Maybe he understood more than we gave him credit for. Then he just broke it off. But, to be honest, Kayley was a real mess by that stage. It was around the time that first video of her went viral, and she went into rehab."

"Okay." Daisy could feel the heater in the car blowing warm air around her feet.

"When she got dry, she decided she'd do a European tour. A few weeks later, Matt contacted her and offered her Granary House. Kayley thought he was trying to help." Tim pulled a face. "Maybe he was. Anyway, he sent her a video of the house and grounds and really bigged it up as the perfect venue for her first Irish concert. And once she agreed to move in, Todd and I guessed they'd be back together."

Matt had told her that the promoter had contacted *him*. Why hadn't he just told her the truth?

It seemed he'd had his eye on the bigger picture all along. Granary House to lure Kayley back to him, and make it easy to persuade her to fire Todd and let him step in instead.

"Still, the streamers will lap up that helicopter proposal." Tim increased the wipers' speed on the window. "Financially, Kayley is starting to look very strong again."

"Right." Daisy yawned. "I wasn't expecting that proposal thing. I didn't even know they were in a relationship."

"The proposal was meant to happen at the concert tomorrow night." Tim flicked her a look. "Remember that scene at the end of *Notting Hill*, where Hugh Grant turns up at Julia Roberts' press conference, and asks for a second chance? Kayley was going to be on stage, and Matt was to be miked up in the centre of the crowd. He was going to walk up onto the stage and get down on one knee!"

Daisy giggled tiredly. "Did you plan that?"

"Nope! They planned it together," Tim said. "But if you tell anyone, I'll deny it."

God, she'd been so naive. How had she ever thought that Matt had been pining for her, or that they had some sort of future together? The only second chance he'd wanted had been with Kayley.

"If Kayley has any sense, she'll make him sign a prenup." Tim sped up the windscreen wipers.

Daisy rested her head back. "It'd suit both of them. Matt's quite well-off too."

"He's not in her league, Daisy."

She glanced over. "Maybe not, but he's done really well for himself." When Tim said nothing, she added, "Why do I get the feeling there's something you're not saying?"

Tim pursed his lips.

"It's just, Matt beat my boyfriend to a business deal recently," Daisy persisted. "And he'd have needed a lot of money to do that."

Tim looked a bit uncomfortable. "Kayley *did* mention that Matt needed money for some work project, so she loaned it to him." He indicated and changed lanes. "I suppose the guy had enough to buy that big house, but nobody has bottomless pockets."

Matt had needed the money to buy the app, she realised. She shouldn't be surprised: he'd always managed to get exactly what he wanted.

At some stage in their relationship, she'd started to see that. But, by then, admitting that her relationship with Matt was anything less than perfect would have felt like a failure. Plus, most of the time, it had felt pretty good.

"I've worked with a lot of artists and their managers down the years," Tim said. "Todd was doing a good job. But after that video was leaked, he had a tough time handling the fallout. We released statements to the press, but any time some reporter managed to put a direct question to Kayley, she'd do more damage. The best Todd could do was to make sure her former employees got what they were owed."

"Kayley told me Todd didn't have her best interests at heart."

"You think Matt does?" Tim grimaced.

Daisy was quiet for a few moments. "What will you do now?"

"Wait and see." He shrugged. "At least she's done the documentary. And we'll use the accident and the proposal to counter some of the negative stuff that's been released recently." He glanced over. "I'll get some photos of Matt and Kayley to Deuxmoi, along with a few lines about how he wouldn't leave her side in hospital."

Daisy just nodded. She was dreading the conversation she'd have to have with Kenny about Niamh. "You'll still work for her, then?"

He chuckled. "Don't worry about me, Daisy. If that doesn't go to plan, something else will turn up."

She wished James had a bit more of that attitude. For a brief moment, she even wished that Alma was still there – at least she wouldn't be going home to an empty house. Maybe after a hot shower and some tea, she'd phone Rosie. Or her mother. Or even both. She needed to hear the soothing, comforting voices of her family.

They were driving through Rathmines now, she noticed, and still heading in the right direction. Tim pointed to her address in the GPS.

"I'm going to drop you right to your door."

"I really appreciate it." Daisy yawned.

He gave her a shrewd look. "You've had a rough time of it. Not just tonight either."

Daisy said nothing, as another wave of exhaustion hit her. Maybe she wouldn't bother phoning anyone tonight; she'd just go straight to bed. Right now, she could sleep for a week.

CHAPTER 54

James was sitting at the end of the stairs when Daisy got in, the only light in the house coming from the slightly open kitchen door.

"You're home," she said.

He scrubbed a hand tiredly over his face. "Yeah, I think my flight was one of the last to take off from London before this storm." He looked at her. "You're soaked."

Daisy said nothing as she stripped off her raincoat and toed off her soggy runners, before peeling off her torn, wet tights, every inch of her numb with cold.

"I'm going to shower."

James looked like he was about to say something, but instead he simply nodded and got up to let her pass by him.

Upstairs, Daisy turned the shower dial to the hottest setting she could manage and stepped under it, the hot spray stinging her clammy skin. She braced herself against the tiled wall, and closed her eyes, as the water poured over her head.

Mentally, she wandered through Granary House. She'd been so excited to redesign the Georgian home. Every part of it, from its beautiful hallway, grand reception rooms and extended, light-filled kitchen, to the understated elegance of its ensuite bedrooms were perfect, she knew. Yet all she felt was mild satisfaction at another job well done.

Gradually, the tension drained out of her body. She turned off the tap and wrapped herself in towels. By the time she came down in pyjamas and dressing gown, James had turned on the heat in the sitting room.

"There's wine." He gestured to the bottle and empty glass on the coffee table. "Did you eat?"

"Yes, I had dinner." Daisy poured herself some wine and took a large gulp.

"I messaged you. And called you. When you didn't answer, I was worried you might be driving to Galway in this. So I called Rosie."

"What? Oh God, she'll be phoning every hospital in Dublin!"

"It's okay, I let her know." He leaned forward. "I called Laura earlier too."

"Was there anyone you didn't call?" Daisy sighed. "I didn't even know you were back in the country, James."

"I know. I'm sorry. Laura didn't know where you were but she gave me Fionn's number. He told me the fucking rescue services were being ..." James clenched his jaw.

Daisy realised he wasn't angry – he was upset. He knew about the rescue.

"He said a few of you went out to Granary House tonight."

Daisy looked at him. "Matt invited us out. He thought Fionn could meet Kayley. And I had some business to finish up with him."

"Right." James' voice was flat. "Are you hurt?"

Not physically, she thought, shaking her head. "I should go to bed. We can talk in the morning."

"I'd prefer to talk now. Please?"

Oh God, this was it. Daisy folded her arms. "Are we over?"

"I don't know, Daisy. You tell me."

She curled her fingers hard into her sides. "You left, James. In a bloody sulk."

His jaw tightened. "You lied to me! How do you think that made me feel?"

"How would I know how you feel anymore, James? All you do is work. We don't talk, we don't hang out – we *barely* have sex. You seem to hate visiting my family. We never see yours!"

"You can go and see Mum and Dad whenever you want. I'm not stopping you."

Daisy opened her mouth to say she wasn't comfortable visiting James' parents on her own, when she was so unsure about her and James as a couple. Especially as the last time they'd been there, his dad had asked if they were ever going to have "a day out".

At the time, James had seemed annoyed by the question, so she'd laughed it off. Privately, she'd wished they'd at least talked about it.

"Do you blame me for working the way I've had to?" James demanded. "TakeOff was struggling, it's still struggling!" He dug a hand through his hair. "I was talking to Mike and Ciara today. They're sorry about what happened, but they're worried about their own jobs."

"I didn't know things were that bad," Daisy admitted. "You should have said something."

"What could you have done?" James raised his voice. "Anyway, you're so competitive, I didn't want you to think ..."

Daisy folded her arms. "You didn't want me to think what?"

James' eyes slid away, and when he spoke again, he sounded utterly defeated.

"I didn't want you to think that I was a loser."

"I don't think you're a loser." Daisy struggled to take everything in. "And I'm not *that* competitive!"

He looked at her. "Yes, you are! You never seem to want to talk about normal stuff: you just quiz me about work. Or you go on about that award you want to win. Which you probably will, one of these days. But if you don't, will your life actually fall apart?" He pushed a hand roughly through his hair, causing bits of it to stand up. "Wouldn't it be a lot worse if your company had to shut down? Or if you'd messed up so badly, that Laura said she didn't want to be your partner anymore?"

That wasn't fair! She didn't talk about work all the time. Maybe a lot of the time, though ...

"James, the reason I ask about work, is because you're always working." Daisy tried not to sound defensive. "And any time we're supposed to be doing stuff together, you use work as an excuse to escape." Damn him, anyway, he didn't get a free pass! "How do you think I felt at my birthday party? You pissed off home with Alma!"

"That's *not* what happened, Daisy! *And I didn't fancy Alma!*" James spoke through gritted teeth. "I'm pretty sure she didn't fancy me either. I just liked hanging out with someone who saw me as a person."

"*I* see you as a person!"

James slumped back in the chair. "Are you having an affair with Matt? Just tell me."

"Of course I'm not!" Daisy's face burned, as she remembered all the times in the last two months when she'd fantasised about Matt and her together again.

In her fantasies, James had happily slipped out of the picture, and Matt had stepped back into the frame as if the past five years had never happened. Rosie was right: she was a flake. Matt's ego was as fragile now as it had been when they'd been together. But the truth was, she'd been nursing her own ego too.

"We're not back together, James. He's with Kayley."

"So why didn't you just tell me that the last time I asked?"

"I didn't know about Kayley. But would it have made any difference? I tried to tell you nothing had happened between us, but you didn't believe me."

When James said nothing, Daisy tried to organise her thoughts.

"Remember when you said before that it was my fault that Matt bought that app? The thing is, I didn't tell him, but I *did* tell Laura and she mentioned it to Brian. Matt told me earlier this evening."

She met James' eyes, and half-wished she hadn't said anything. Too late now. She might as well go on.

"Matt said he bought the app as payback for you buying his and Charlie's airline software five years ago. He said you'd ripped them off by giving them a fraction of what it was worth."

James' face had lost all its colour, and Daisy felt her heart break a little.

"I told him you wouldn't have done anything like that."

"So, let me get this straight." James' voice sounded strange. "Your ex-boyfriend is taking revenge on me because of something that happened five years ago?"

"Something he thinks happened, obviously."

He shook his head. "Maybe if he'd tried harder to get some seed money for his idea, instead of just blabbing to everyone about it."

"Well, yeah." Daisy frowned. "But that's nothing to do with you. I mean, you gave Matt and Charlie a decent price, didn't you?"

He sighed. "It was early days for me and the others, Daisy. I had to get the company up and running, and I gave them what I thought I'd get away with. Charlie signed a contract. What else do you want me to say?"

"That you didn't stiff them?"

"*For fuck sake, Daisy!*" He gave an angry laugh. "It was business! Matt was shooting his mouth off – all I did was go to his brother with an offer."

Daisy felt a bit sick. "Do you know that he and Charlie fell out over that? Matt didn't want to sell – he said you screwed them over."

"Charlie wanted out!" James said tightly.

"*What?*"

"Charlie only helped Matt develop that software because Matt asked him to."

Daisy stared at James, wondering what else she didn't know about him.

"How come you never told me you bought that software from them?" she said finally.

"Because I barely knew you at the time, *remember*?" James sounded exasperated. "I mean, I knew you'd dated Matt, but it didn't seem that important that I'd had some business dealings with his brother!"

Daisy felt her eyes closing, as a fresh wave of tiredness hit her. "Well, I guess he never forgave you. For what it's worth, I'm sorry about the app."

"Is that it?" James said.

Was that what? Her brain seemed to have shut down. She just wanted to sleep, and wake up tomorrow morning with this whole evening behind her.

She'd had no idea what closure looked like, but she could never have foreseen what had happened tonight. If there were any loose ends on Granary House, she'd get Fionn to look after them. She'd send Matt the final bill. She and James had already paid heavily for everything else.

CHAPTER 55

A total of seven people have died as a result of Storm Iris, including an elderly driver and two passengers, who were killed when a tree fell on their car in Galway city.

Meanwhile, American country singer, Kayley Lynch, was forced to cancel her first Irish gig at Granary House, County Wicklow, when the car she was driving overturned in heavy flooding. Ms Lynch dislocated her shoulder, but in a dramatic rescue was airlifted to hospital in Dublin by the emergency services, along with her Irish fiancé, Matt Deveraux, and two other people.

The worst of the flooding has been in the West, Midlands, and South East, with counties Wicklow, Wexford, Waterford and Cork badly affected. A number of rivers and canals burst their banks, causing dangerous flash floods in many towns and rural areas, and Gardaí and army-led teams worked through the night to evacuate people to safety.

Roads across the affected counties are mainly 'bad but passable' this morning, with the exception of some minor roads, mainly in Wexford and Waterford.

Daisy had organised to get her car collected the following morning from Granary House. She'd wondered briefly whether to message Matt first, but decided against it. The less contact she had with him now, the better.

James had been gone by the time she'd got up that morning. Daisy had no idea where he was, given that he didn't have a job anymore, but after everything that had happened the night before, she guessed that he needed some space.

It was very likely that he was planning to end things between them, she knew.

And while part of her wanted to curl up in a corner and pretend it wasn't happening, she knew deep down that everything that had happened in the past couple of years had led them to this point.

Halfway through the morning, Freya rang to ask if she could drop by that evening, to discuss some last-minute details. Given how well Freya's job had gone, Daisy just hoped she wasn't questioning the bill. The way her week was going, she wouldn't be too surprised.

She arrived at Freya's house shortly after five.

"Daisy, good timing."

Freya let her in, and Daisy followed her down to the kitchen, where Freya indicated a barstool at the island unit.

"Sit down. I love these, by the way – where did you get them?"

"Oh, Ikea." Daisy flashed her a quick smile.

"Good old Ikea." Freya dropped two espresso pods in the machine and pressed a button.

Daisy wished she'd just skip the coffee and get straight to the bad news. She sat up on the stool and waited for the machine to do its thing. Matt had always made such a big deal about his coffee beans and espressos. Had that been real, or just part of his elaborate ploy to soften her up? Make her feel like there was a point to it all? What had he wanted? Closure? Revenge? Even now she wasn't sure.

He'd messaged her just after lunch, to say that the doctors had rotated Kayley's shoulder back into place, but that she'd need time to recover, and they'd cancelled her Irish tour.

Daisy had simply wished her a speedy recovery, congratulated Matt on his engagement, and told him she'd email her invoice.

Now Freya handed her a mug of coffee.

"Thanks. I see you've made a start on the garden." Daisy gestured outside, where the whole lawn had been rotavated.

Freya waved a hand airily. "Polish landscaper. His team only started today, but they work fast."

Daisy nodded, wishing she could shake off her edginess.

Freya took the stool opposite her.

"So, how can I help?" Daisy said.

"We'll get to that, I promise." Freya gave her an appraising look. "Tell me what happened at Granary House?"

Daisy hesitated. "What have you heard?"

"Niamh called by to put some more sockets into my office yesterday." Freya's mouth twitched. "She told me about the other night."

Daisy tried not to react. "How much did she say?"

"Not much, don't worry. But I saw the stories about Kayley Lynch and Matt Deveraux all over the news today."

"Right. So, uh, Granary House was quite a big job." Daisy sipped her coffee, playing for time. "There was a tight deadline and we'd a few hiccups along the way. But we managed it, we always do." *Not bad, Daisy.* If she ever wanted a career change, she could go into politics!

"Niamh also said that Matt Deveraux had agreed to enter his house for the award."

Daisy couldn't tell Freya the truth! Apart from the fact that she wouldn't care about her love life, it would be totally unprofessional to divulge what she'd done.

"Yes, but we decided in the end that it wouldn't suit."

"I like your discretion, Daisy." Freya gave a wry smile. "Actually, there's a lot about you that I admire."

Daisy wondered where the conversation was going.

After all this time, it appeared Freya was gearing up for a heart-to-heart.

"You know the thing about being a solicitor?" Freya crossed her ankles carefully on the rung of the stool.

It pays well, Daisy thought.

"You have to be discreet. I am! I don't gossip at the school gates or in the supermarket." Freya shrugged. "Actually, I'm rarely at the damned supermarket. There's nothing as satisfying as having a week's worth of shopping delivered to your door." She looked at Daisy expectantly.

Feck it, Daisy thought. "Matt Deveraux's my ex. We were together for five years. Things just got a bit … complicated. And it didn't feel right to use Granary House."

Freya nodded. "I caught you on the nine o'clock news last night, getting out of that helicopter."

"My fifteen seconds of fame." Daisy grimaced. "Matt and Kayley and her bodyguard were all hurt, but they'll be fine."

Frey looked thoughtful. "I saw that place in the property pages when it was up for sale. I'd say you did an amazing job."

"Yeah, it's a special house."

"So is this one," Freya said.

"This is a real home." Daisy smiled. "I loved working on it."

"I know." Freya clasped her hands around her knees. "And I wanted to thank you properly for asking your sister to see Holly. We're following her advice, and it's already started to make a difference."

"Oh, I'm glad." Daisy spoke quickly. "Actually, Rosie volunteered to do it. I didn't ask her because of her career break. And, I have no idea what she said, Freya. Rosie is completely professional."

"I know." Freya waved her hand dismissively. "But if it hadn't been for you, it would have been months before Holly was assessed. So if you'd still like to use our home as an award entry, you'd be more than welcome."

Daisy blinked. "Seriously?"

"Just one thing." Freya gestured around at the walls, one of which she'd turned into a family photo gallery. "No photos, nothing that would identify us. Feel free to replace them with whatever you want. You know, do your magic!"

"It'll be my pleasure." Daisy felt a rush of elation. "Thank you." She slipped down off the stool. "I have a permission form in my bag. Give me a few minutes to fill it out, and you can sign it now." She owed Rosie a huge thanks.

"Sure. Oh, while I think of it, Niamh must have dropped this yesterday when she was here. I was hoping you could give it back to her." Freya opened a small drawer in the island unit, and placed a piece of jewellery on the countertop.

Daisy recognised it immediately: it was the moonstone pendant Kayley had been wearing the first time she'd met her. The one that had gone missing from Granary House.

CHAPTER 56

Fionn was playing Matt's proposal video on his phone when Daisy arrived in the following day. He jumped when she came in, stabbing frantically at the screen as he tried to stop it.

"*Shit, crap, sorry!*"

Daisy sighed. "It's fine. No feelings were hurt in the making of that video!"

"Right." Fionn looked a bit doubtful. "Can I just say that the guy's a total tosser and you're way too cool for him?"

"*Ha*, hard agree. Thanks, Fionn." Her mobile buzzed, and she quickly checked the caller ID before answering. "Hi, Kenny, did you get my message?" She walked over to the window.

"I did, yeah." Kenny cleared his throat. "I'm sorry, Daisy, I really am. I spoke to Niamh and she confessed to taking those pictures of Kayley, and talking to the papers. She took that stuff that went missing, too. She was going to give it all back, you know – she doesn't want Kayley's bloody jewellery, but the woman treated her so badly." He paused. "She had a bit of a crush on that bastard! And he was messing with her head, Daisy – even *I* could see it!"

No wonder Kenny hadn't liked Matt – he'd probably guessed that Niamh would get hurt.

"What about the other stuff, Kenny? The electrics? The peanut butter that Kayley found in the guest wing? Was that Niamh?"

"I don't know." Kenny sounded gruff. "Look, I'm sorry I didn't tell you who Niamh was, but none of the lads knew either. She didn't want everyone thinking she was only there because of me. In her defence, she's still grieving for her mam."

His voice cracked, and Daisy felt a pang of pity for both of them.

"Don't worry about it, Kenny, honestly. People can do strange things when they're grieving." *Or hurt.*

Kenny cleared his throat, louder this time. "I'll make sure whatever she took gets back to Kayley. I can just hide them around the house, and Kayley can blame the feckin' poltergeist."

"I'll leave it with you, Kenny. Look, I'm going to courier Kayley's moonstone pendent to you. I don't care what you have to do. Just make sure that she finds it at Granary House!"

"Gotcha. And obviously I'll hire back Alec for the next job." He paused. "I'll understand if you don't want Niamh working for you, though."

Daisy thought quickly. "I'll give her one more chance, Kenny. Have a chat with her and sort it out. I don't want her not to work. *Um*, do you mind me asking you something, though?"

"Go on, yeah."

"Did Niamh know about Alec?"

"Yeah, she did." Kenny sighed. "I thought I was protecting her. Look, she's not proud of what she did, Daisy, she's really sorry."

She'd half suspected that Niamh had found some way of blaming Alec. Kenny had unknowingly given Niamh a scapegoat, and she'd used it! There was a beeping noise on her phone.

"Kenny, I have to go, but tell Niamh she's on a warning. If she ever pulls a stunt like that again, I won't let her work on any of my projects."

"I hear you, Daisy. She won't."

Kenny hung up, and Daisy swiped to answer the next call.

"Daisy Devlin, hello?"

"Hello?"

She almost dropped the phone. "Kayley?" She'd found out, she thought. Matt had obviously told her! He'd had time since the other night to think about everything Niamh had said, and he'd joined the dots. Oh God, now Kayley could sue the company into the ground and there'd be nothing she could do!

"… figured I never gotta chance to thank you properly," Kayley was saying.

Daisy snapped to attention. She was *thanking* her? Maybe she wasn't about to sue her.

"You still there?" Kayley sounded a bit impatient.

"Sorry, still here," Daisy said. "You were thanking me?"

"For rescuing me." Kayley spoke firmly. "I figured I had to thank Matty for the live-stream. You did a great job on that, by the way. I mean, it was a bit shaky but that wasn't your fault, with the storm and all."

"Right, no, you're welcome."

"Anyways," Kayley continued, "I wanna repay you."

"Repay me?" Daisy echoed.

Kayley sighed. "I'm not crass enough to offer you money, obviously."

"Obviously. And, *um*, I'd never accept money, Kayley," Daisy said smoothly.

"That's what I thought." Kayley sounded like she was getting into her stride. "But, as you know, I've a huge social-media following, and I'd be more than happy to endorse your little company!"

Daisy was flummoxed for a moment. "Oh, right."

"Unless you don't want my help!" Kayley huffed.

"No, it's not that, not at all." Daisy's mind raced. "*Um*, how's your shoulder, by the way?"

Kayley sighed. "Healing. I'm in a sling but as long as I don't go making any big, sudden movements, the doctor says it'll be good as new."

Daisy took a deep breath. "In that case, there *is* something else you could do."

CHAPTER 57

As Daisy put down the phone to Kayley, Laura swept into the room.

"You're back!" Daisy went to hug her, but something stopped her. There was an energy about her she couldn't quite put her finger on. "How are you feeling?"

"I'm great." Laura gave her a concerned look. "What about you?"

For a brief moment, Daisy wasn't sure what she meant. "Oh, the mile-high proposal?" She laughed. "I'm so over it!"

"*Hmm*." Laura turned to Fionn. "How did you get on at Stephanie's place?"

"Excellent." He gave a nervous flick of his fringe. "I'll just, *um*, let you two catch up, while I ..." He stood, but Laura stopped him.

"I was talking to Stephanie, and I know she told you."

"What happened?" Daisy glanced from one to the other. "Told him what?"

Laura kept her eyes on Fionn. "Would you have told Daisy?"

"Hello?" Fionn's eyes widened comically. "I value my life too much!"

There was a moment's silence, then Laura burst out laughing. "You're not the worst, Fionn. I'm going to miss you."

Fionn beamed. "Does this mean I've grown on you?"

"Oh, let's not get carried away!"

Daisy cleared her throat loudly. "Anyone want to tell me what's going on?"

Laura waved a hand in her direction. "Sit down."

Daisy glanced at Fionn, who was still smiling widely. She's *known* he was hiding something from her! She walked back over and perched on her desk. "I'm sitting. Now, talk."

"First, I'm sorry about all the bloody drama. I know you were worried when you heard I was in hospital. The thing is, I couldn't face talking to anyone." Laura smoothed a hand over her sleeked-back hair. "Not even you, babes."

But she'd confided in Stephanie. Daisy hated how jealous she'd become.

"Now, don't scream, but I'm twelve weeks pregnant, and I thought I might be losing the baby. But everything's fine! They checked me out and it was only a slight bleed, which is okay, apparently, so ..." Laura trailed away, colour rushing to her cheeks.

Daisy stared at her for a long moment. "You're pregnant?" She clamped her hands to her mouth as a gasp escaped her. "Oh my God ..." she stopped. "Hang on, you're happy, right?"

"I'm happy." Laura's eyes glittered brightly.

Daisy pushed herself off the desk and then she was hugging her and Laura was hugging her back.

"Don't squash me." Laura laughed as Daisy pulled quickly away.

"Sorry, sorry." Daisy took Laura's hands in hers. "I just wish you'd told me."

Laura swiped a finger under her eye. "I couldn't, Daisy. This was our fifth round of IVF, and we wouldn't have even *tried* again if I hadn't met Stephanie. She invited me to her support group, for couples with fertility issues." She paused. "When we saw Stephanie and Peter finally get there, we decided to give it one final try." Laura was smiling now. "The doctor says once I don't overdo things, I should have a healthy pregnancy."

Daisy squealed and threw her arms around her again.

"Group hug?" Fionn looked hopeful.

Laura glanced over and extended one arm. "Come on, then. But this will *not* be a regular thing!"

As Fionn wrapped his arms around the two of them, Daisy felt a rush of pure happiness for her friend.

Laura was the first to pull away. "Stephanie didn't mean to put you in that position, Fionn," she said. "She thought you knew. And I had no idea Daisy would send you, or I'd have warned Stephanie not to say a word."

"Hey, don't even mention it." Fionn flicked away his fringe.

"I can't believe I didn't guess," Daisy admitted. "I kind of thought you were just putting on a tiny bit of weight, but I figured it was either a side-effect of your new contraception, or that you were bulking up for your training."

Laura burst out laughing. "You know I've no intention of running a marathon, don't you? Not at the moment, anyway. I just needed an excuse for eating more, and not drinking, without you getting suspicious."

Daisy remembered something else. "That needle I saw …"

"I had to self-inject coming up to the procedure." Laura sighed. "I had that excuse ready in case you ever spotted one of them."

Daisy caught Fionn's expression. "Are you feeling okay? You look a bit …"

"Sorry, I should have just left when you started talking about …" He swallowed. "I'm a bit squeamish."

"We won't talk any more about it, I promise." Laura winked at Daisy. "Not in front of you!"

Fionn looked relieved as he picked up the box of doughnuts. "So, can I get you a coffee?"

"Not for the moment." Laura shook her head. "But you can get me a green tea. I'll have it with my avocado toast."

"One green tea coming up!" Fionn turned to go.

"Oh, and Fionn?" Laura said.

He turned back.

"Stephanie told me she was really pleased with how things went yesterday. Well done."

Fionn's ears turned pink. "Thanks."

After he left, Daisy looked at Laura for a long moment. "I'm a complete dope for not guessing. You were pregnant at my birthday: that's why you weren't drinking."

"Yeah, I'd just found out." Laura shrugged slightly. "My periods have always been fairly irregular, which didn't help when we were doing IVF."

"You know you could have told me what you were doing, Laura? I'd have understood."

"Ah babes, I know. But I didn't want you wondering if I was okay all the time. Not when we work together – it would have been intense!" Laura stretched, and for the first time Daisy could almost make out a tiny rounding under her clothes. "I'll want to take time off after the baby is born, maybe even a year."

Daisy glanced towards the door. "I'll have to get maternity cover for you."

"*Hmm.*" Laura's eyes twinkled. "Can I suggest someone?"

"Fionn?"

"He'll have graduated, Daisy. We could give him a trial period? Just don't throw him in at the deep end."

"Yeah, I won't tell him yet. He needs to concentrate on his final project for college."

Laura sat down. "Good. By the way, don't you dare tell him I suggested it."

Daisy grinned. "I won't say a word."

CHAPTER 58

"Daisy, you look stunning!" Miriam crossed her large, old-fashioned kitchen that Saturday evening and took one of Daisy's hands in hers. "Twirl!"

Daisy twirled, the deep blue of her full, knee-skimming dress catching the light. When she came to a stop, she hugged her mother.

"You look amazing, too, Mum."

Miriam, who was wearing a long, sage-green dress with sequins around the hem and sleeves, gave a half-bow, her lavender perfume filling the warm air.

"Thank you. Now." She clapped her hands. "Our guests aren't due for another hour, but knowing your sister she can't wait to get here to boss around the catering staff. They'll be setting up in the marquee."

"*Ooh*, I'm dying to see it!" Daisy smiled brightly, determined that neither of her parents would worry about her this weekend.

It wasn't the first time that she'd come down to Galway without James, so when he'd told her that he was meeting someone on Saturday morning about a job, and could do with a couple of days by himself, she'd pretended to understand. Although all the signs pointed in one direction, Daisy had decided to give things one last try. But right now, she owed it to her parents to enjoy their anniversary party and not think about James until she got back home.

When she'd arrived earlier in the day, she and Rosie had taken their parents aside and presented them with Miriam's self-portrait. Daisy had been a bit nervous that their mother might be a bit offended by what they'd done. But Miriam had burst out laughing, and hugged them both hard.

"Wasn't that fierce thoughtful of you both," she'd said. "I'd no idea it was the two of you who bought it!"

Eric had draped his arm across his wife's shoulder. "Great idea altogether, girls." He'd winked at them both. "How about we put it in our bedroom, Mim?"

Daisy and Rosie had both held their breath.

"Whatever you like!" Miriam had said, beaming.

Relieved that their gift had gone down so well, Daisy had allowed herself to get excited at the surprise she'd arranged for them. After she'd told Kayley about her parents' anniversary party, she'd asked if she would record herself wishing her parents a happy anniversary, and singing her dad's favourite song. To her astonishment, Kayley had offered to come in person instead.

"I thought the doctor said total rest and no performances until your shoulder heals," Daisy had said. "Also, they're in Galway – it's the other side of the country!"

Kayley had burst out laughing. "Ya'll are so cute! You know that Texas is ten times bigger than the whole of Ireland?"

Daisy *had* heard that before, but she'd pretended complete ignorance. In her experience, anyone she'd ever met from Texas loved telling people just how vast it was!

"It'll be just fine, Daisy," Kayley had said. "I'll fly down, and you just book me a good hotel nearby. Two rooms. I'll pay!"

"Two rooms?" Daisy had said, worried that Matt would be coming too, and wondering about the separate room.

"I'm bringing Tim," Kayley had assured her. "So?"

Did stuff like this actually happen in real life, Daisy had wondered happily.

"Thank you, Kayley. I'll give you my sister's number; she's organising everything."

Rosie had messaged Daisy after lunch, to say that Kayley and Tim had checked into Oranmore House, and Séan would slip out from the party at around nine to collect them.

Now Miriam adjusted one of the sparkly, jewel-green clips that held her hair back from her face. "Has Rosie told you about her plans for September?"

"No?"

"She's going back to work part-time." Miriam beamed. "I'm delighted. It's the first time that girl has listened to me since she was ten!"

Daisy knew it was more likely that helping Holly had been the catalyst for Rosie's about-face, but she just murmured her agreement.

Miriam gave her an appraising look. "Everything all right, loveen?"

"Absolutely, Mum. *Er*, how many people did you invite tonight, by the way?"

"Ah, sure, what's the point in leaving anyone out?" Miriam slipped her hands into her pockets, and seemed to think for a few moments. "Did I ever tell you how much I missed you when you went off to college at seventeen? Rosie was here, of course. She's such a home bird, really. But I feel I got to know the adult Rosie, and I'm not sure I ever really got to know the adult you."

Daisy wondered about the abrupt change of topic. "You were the one who encouraged me to go to Dublin, Mum!"

"Of course!" Miriam looked surprised. "It was what you wanted. But I missed you like mad."

"Right." Daisy felt a fresh onslaught of guilt. All those times she'd promised she'd come home for the weekend, only to cancel at the last moment because of Matt. "Dublin was just where I wanted to stay, I suppose." She knew it wasn't what her mother meant.

"We never got to know Matt either, did we?"

Miriam Devlin: mind-reader. "He was always a bit weird about meeting you guys." Daisy flushed. "I should have seen it as a major red flag. To be honest, Mum, there's been red flags with James too." Shit, she couldn't believe she'd let that slip! "Well, not really red flags, not at all, in fact," she added hurriedly. "And it's not the right time."

Miriam arched her eyebrows. "Actually, it's the perfect time, Daisy. Now, I'm glad you've managed to put Matt behind you. When someone hurts you like that, it leaves its mark. But I don't think James is like him at all. You need to stop letting your experiences with Matt colour your decisions."

Oh God, why had her mother picked tonight to start psychoanalysing her?

"Matt's definitely in the past, Mum. I've finished his job and I've finished with him. Forever! I'm not even using his house as my award entry."

Miriam nodded approvingly. "He's not important! You and he were never meant to be together."

Despite everything, Daisy started to laugh. "You obviously saw the signs before I did."

Miriam shrugged. "He left you – that was the only sign I needed. Anyway, I wonder if you take those signs a bit too literally. They're meant as a guide, not a rule book. At the end of the day, Daisy flower, your life is how you design it."

Her mother was right. She'd wasted so much time wondering what she'd done wrong, and tried to find so many excuses for Matt when he'd deserved none.

"Now, I have a few of my own touches for this evening." Miriam went over to the kitchen table and lifted two large, carved wooden bowls, filled with sweets. "Put these on the side tables, will you? I've told everyone that children are very welcome, not that you have to be a child to enjoy a few sweets." She smiled. "Go on. Have a good look at the marquee before everyone arrives."

Daisy took the sweets from her mother, grateful to have something to do, and relieved that Miram hadn't pushed too hard to get her to talk about James. There'd be plenty of time to figure things out later.

CHAPTER 59

Daisy stepped into the marquee and took a moment to admire her surroundings. The tented room seemed deceptively larger than her parents' garden, its high ceiling strung with hundreds of tiny, coloured fairy lights that threw rainbow colours onto the pale wooden floor.

Narrow tables, covered with bright, old-fashioned cotton cloths in florals and stripes, and dotted with jam-jars containing wildflowers and tealights, ran the length of the room. It was the perfect backdrop for their celebrations.

She was walking over to the trestle counters along the far wall to deposit the sweets, when the opening bars of Ed Sheeran's 'Lego House', strummed on a guitar, filtered through the silence. As Daisy glanced around to locate the speakers, somebody started to sing, and it took Daisy a few moments to realise it was James. She spun, searching for him, and spotted someone in the far corner of the marquee. Was she hallucinating? Why was he here? *How* was he here?

He finished the first verse and stopped singing, but continued to strum through the chords.

"Hey." He tipped his head to one side.

She swallowed hard, remembering the first time she'd heard him play the song.

"Hey, yourself." Had Rosie asked him to come? Or her mother, maybe? Daisy had told him about Kayley but he hadn't said very much. Alma had been the real fan, she supposed. "I haven't heard you play that in years."

"I know, yeah." He shrugged. "I'm a bit rusty."

"No, it sounded lovely. I don't understand, though – I thought you had meetings about a new job?"

James' mouth tightened. "There weren't any meetings. Look, if you prefer, I can go."

"No! You just got here."

"Do you want me here?"

She was starting to feel exasperated. "Of course! I'm just confused: you said you weren't coming."

"Yeah, I know." He put down the guitar. "I wanted to surprise you."

"You did." She gave a hesitant smile.

"I'm sorry I've let you down, Daisy."

She closed the gap between them, and took his hands. "You haven't let me down. You're here, aren't you?"

"Yes, but my job ..."

"I don't care about that. You'll get another one when you're ready." She looked at him. "What you said before about me always going on about work – "

"I'm sorry – "

"No, you were right." Daisy scrambled for the perfect words. "I know I'm a bit intense. I think it's because it's just me and Laura, and I need to make things work. But I never meant you to feel that was all I cared about."

He nodded. "I know I locked you out, Daisy. I didn't want you to know how bad things were. There was no point in both of us worrying." He shoved a hand through his hair. "Maybe I should have asked my parents for help – they've been offering for long enough."

"We'd have managed, James." He seemed to have aged these past few months. How had she not noticed? "I'm not telling you what to do, but I think we'll be grand."

He glanced down at their hands. "Actually, I think I might have been a bit harsh on my folks."

Daisy waited as James met her eyes again.

"I saw Daniel and Fiona when I went to London. Apparently, Mum and Dad are always going on about how well I'm doing!"

Daisy looked at him. "Did you tell them that – ?"

"It's all I hear about them? That I'm such a complete twat, I thought our parents were comparing us?"

"Why don't you have a family WhatsApp group?" Daisy said.

"Fiona just set one up." He frowned. "I'm not sure why we didn't have one. Not that it'll make any difference to my folks – they'll still phone us all regularly. But I might phone them a bit more too. And go see them."

Daisy nodded, and they stood in silence for a moment.

Finally, James said, "Tell me about Matt."

Time to tell the truth, she thought. "I thought it was some sort of sign that he was back in my life. Which sounds really arrogant, but things had been so crap between the two of us ..."

"So you thought that was a sign as well." A flicker of hurt crossed his face.

"I'm really sorry."

"Yeah, so am I."

Neither of them said anything for a few moments, and Daisy realised she wouldn't blame him if he just left.

"For what it's worth, James, I've been an idiot about Matt. But I'm completely over him. I'm just sorry he ever came between us." She took a breath. "Not just in the last couple of months – in the whole time we've been together."

He nodded. "I guessed."

"You couldn't have." Daisy swallowed. "I never talked about him."

"I know." His voice was dry. "You remember, when we first met, I didn't want to rush things between us?"

Daisy rolled her eyes. "You kept me in the friend zone for so long, I didn't think you were interested."

"I was, Daisy! I knew you were special. And I didn't want us to be a rebound relationship, so I waited. But that whole time, you didn't once mention Matt!"

"Wait, you *wanted* me to talk about Matt?"

"It would have been normal! We were friends, remember?" A muscle twitched in his jaw. "I always got the feeling he was still there, between us."

He was right! Matt had taken up enough room in her head – and her heart – to keep James at a distance all these years. And while she'd been hurting after the break-up, James had been wondering all this time if he'd ever live up to him. She'd been so stupid, wasting so much time and energy on the memory of someone who wasn't half the person James was!

"Now what?" she said, quietly.

"That depends, Daisy."

She sighed. "All I know is that I don't want things to go on like before. You know, us living together but not really – " She stopped and pulled away from him. "Sorry, I've no right to pressure you, especially right now."

"You're not pressuring me, Daisy." He slipped his hand into his jacket pocket and took out a small, green-velvet box, identical to the one her vintage earrings had come in for her birthday. "I wanted to give you this."

More earrings, she thought. A noise behind her startled her, and Daisy spun to see Rosie pass by the door of the tent.

When she turned back she saw that James had dropped to one knee, the now-open box held up. Nestled inside was an emerald ring, set in tiny diamonds.

"It's vintage," he said.

For a moment, she couldn't speak. "Are you ...?"

He nodded. "Marry me, Daisy. I love you, and I don't think you really knew that. I want to try to make things right."

Her eyes travelled back to the ring. "It's beautiful!"

James got to his feet. "Do you not want to marry me?"

She blinked hard, determined to hold it together. "I'm just worried that it's not what you really want. I don't want you to think that this is a quick fix."

"You're right, it won't be." He hesitated. "I bought this the same day I heard the news about the app. But I wanted to wait until the deal was done before asking. And now ... look, maybe the timing is crap because I've just lost my job but – "

"Yes. Yes, I'll marry you." Daisy swiped away the tears that had started to roll down her cheeks.

"Yes? Are you sure? I mean, I'd understand if you wanted to –"

"I'm sure, James."

He slipped the ring out of its box and slid it on to her finger.

It was a perfect fit, she thought, smiling as she carefully dabbed at her wet cheeks.

"Full disclosure?" James said. "Alma saw it too."

"Alma?"

"I wanted another woman's opinion." He looked a bit sheepish. "She thought you'd love it."

A fragment of a conversation drifted back. "That day I got in from work, when you and Alma were hugging, was that ...?"

"Yeah."

Daisy stared at him. "You hadn't told her about the app."

"Of course not. I'd just showed her the ring, and she was really happy for us. I think she would have liked if I'd proposed while she was still renting from us."

"Right." The pieces were rapidly dropping into place. "So when I saw her put something in her pocket –"

"It was this." James shrugged. "She couldn't give it back to me in front of you, so she put it in my coat pocket on her way out."

"Oh God." She'd thought the worst!

"I'm sorry about me and Alma," James said.

"I thought –"

"There was nothing between us, that's the truth. But I was wrong to game with her the whole time and ignore you like I did. Give me another chance, Daisy?"

"I don't expect you to stop gaming," she said.

"Maybe we should take up something together," James whispered.

Daisy wrapped her arms around his neck, and he tugged her closer. "Can I ask you something?"

He smiled. "Anything."

"Do you think you might like to be a fireman sometime?"

James' smile widened. "I assume you're not suggesting a career change?"

Daisy shook her head. "I was really thinking how clothes might maketh the man!"

James leaned his forehead against hers. "I think I could arrange that."

"Excellent." She beamed. "I've got something a bit more PG in mind, too. It involves socialising with other people."

"So it doesn't involve this?" He leaned closer and kissed her.

When he released her, Daisy giggled. "Pretty sure it doesn't."

"Will I like it?"

"I'll be doing it!" she said.

"I'll like it then."

She gave him a serious look. "Does this mean that you'll finally feel like part of my family?"

James nodded. "I'll be there at every kids' birthday party." He tucked a finger under her chin and met her eyes, his gaze as serious as hers. "And I'll never make you feel like you don't matter to me, Daisy. Speaking of families, Miriam and Eric invited my folks to this thing. Rosie insisted they stay with her."

Rosie was endlessly surprising, Daisy thought, snuggling as closely as she could to him. "Promise you'll dance with me tonight, James?"

"All night, Daisy."

She smiled against his chest. "I love you so much."

His voice rumbled over the top of her head. "I know this isn't very romantic, but thank fuck for that."

She looked up at him, feeling a rush of pure happiness. "Actually, that's the most romantic thing I've ever heard."

CHAPTER 60

Laura was standing at the window, looking out at the street, when Daisy got to work that Monday. She was turned, half in profile, her tiny bump just about visible. Daisy stopped for a moment, wondering if it would ever be her.

She cleared her throat and Laura turned. "Hey."

"Hey, yourself." Daisy smiled. "You have that pregnancy glow."

Laura folded her arms. "Are you going to start getting mushy, babes? Not sure I'm up for it. Stephanie is already threatening to throw me a baby shower. The woman's living in a Hallmark movie."

Daisy walked across the room, and took hold of Laura's hands.

"Listen to me, Laura Nealon. You are about to have a baby. And it will be the most special baby in the whole world, because you will be its mother! So if Stephanie, or anyone else wants to throw you a baby shower, you're going to embrace it. Do all the good stuff and treasure all the memories!"

Laura blinked hard. "How long have you been saving up that speech?"

"I never thought I'd be saying it to you."

"Fine, I'll have the shower. But only if you come."

"Nothing would keep me away."

"And you have to be godmother. And promise that you'll never buy a single sensible present."

Daisy started to laugh. "It'll make a change from buying for Rosie's kids."

"So, how are you? And how did your mum and dad's anniversary party go? I would have loved to be there. " Laura had been too sick to travel. "Did Kayley come through?"

"She performed two songs," Daisy said proudly. "We recorded the whole thing, so Dad can look back at it anytime he wants! I swear, Mum and Dad's reaction when she appeared on that stage was even better than the performance. Apart from the song James accompanied her on, which was pretty amazing!"

Laura's eyes widened. "*Wow*, I'm sorry I missed that.

"I'll show you the video," Daisy said. "She even hung around for a while afterwards. Stuck to Cokes all night, by the way."

Laura grinned. "That should help squash a few rumours! So, was she the highlight of the evening?"

"Not quite." Daisy stuck out her hand to show off the emerald ring. "It's official: we're joining each other's family WhatsApp groups."

"*Oh my God!*" Laura inspected the ring. "Vintage?"

Daisy nodded. "He proposed before the party!"

"And this is what you want? You're sure? I mean, that night the four of us went out, the tension between you two was insane!"

Daisy flushed, remembering how angry she'd been with James that night, how secretly thrilled she'd been when she'd bumped into Matt. She'd seen it as another sign. It had been: a sign to sort things out with James, rather than expect Matt to be the solution to her problems!

"I didn't realise how much I loved him until I said yes, Laura. And how much he loves me too! But the best thing is, he's not one *bit* like Matt!"

Laura flashed her a stern look. "So that demon is completely exorcised?"

"Banished forever!" Daisy sighed. "I think things were supposed to work out like this. I mean, I'm sickened for James that he lost his job. And I hate what Matt did. But at least now I know what happened five years ago. I always felt ..." she swallowed hard. "I always doubted myself, wondering what I'd done to make Matt leave like that."

"Well, now you know: it was all James' fault."

"Laura!"

"Joking!"

"But that's why Brian has always been a bit weird around James, isn't it?" Daisy met Laura's eyes. "Hey, it doesn't matter, they don't have to be best of friends just because we are."

"No." Laura spoke slowly. "Daisy, there's something I never told you, and I think I should have ..." She stopped, her eyes sliding away.

Daisy frowned. "What?"

"Daisy, promise me you'll keep in mind that I never, ever meant to hurt you?"

"Okay." Daisy's stomach cramped nervously.

Laura wrapped her arms around her slender frame. "That party, the summer Matt was away? I stayed that night. And the following morning, I bumped into Brian as I was coming out of the house." She looked up. "It was just bad timing. He was passing the house on his way to that little pharmacy on the corner, remember it?"

"I remember it." Daisy could hear her heart thumping.

Laura took an audible breath. "Brian asked me why I was there, and I should have just said I'd stayed over and crashed on the sofa, but I panicked and said that you'd stayed over, and I was bringing you some clothes so you could change."

"Oh my God!" Daisy stared at her. "But ..."

"I didn't say you'd been with anyone." Laura looked anguished. "You have to believe me! But I guess Brian told Matt."

"But that's what I don't understand! Why did Brian assume I'd slept with James?" What was she missing? "Wait, you told me you didn't believe that Brian told Matt."

"I know, I'm sorry. But Brian only told Matt what he assumed." Laura spoke quietly. "One of James' housemates told someone that James had a girl in his room all night; they just didn't know who it was. And James never said."

"Right." It took Daisy a moment to understand. "That was you?" She choked out the words. "You slept with James?"

"I'm so sorry, Daisy, I feel awful." The words came out in a rush. "I promise you it only happened that one night. And you and James weren't even friends at the time, remember?" Laura looked at her anxiously. "Maybe you should sit down."

Daisy did as she was told, and Laura pulled her own chair over and sat. "Do you hate me?"

"I don't know how I feel." Daisy took a breath, then noticed Laura's expression. "No, of course I don't hate you. I just don't understand why you never told me. Or why James didn't either." It hurt, she realised, that the two people she'd trusted the most had kept that from her all these years.

"Did you ever plan on telling me?" she managed.

"Daisy ..." Laura's face had drained of colour. "We both had way too much to drink that night, and we never spoke about it afterwards." She swallowed visibly. "I know I should have told you, but I felt shit that I'd cheated on Brian, especially when I knew you'd never cheat on Matt. And when Matt broke up with you, I didn't think ... I didn't put it together, babes, you have to believe me!"

Daisy pressed the heels of her hands against her temples, and tried to think. "I still don't get it. If Brian told Matt that, then Brian *knew* why Matt broke up with me. Did he not tell you?"

"Not for ages. And by that stage you'd met James, and I – "

"You knew that if you said anything to Brian, he might start asking questions," Daisy said. "And he might have found out that it was you who'd slept with James."

Briefly, Laura closed her eyes. "It felt too late. I thought I'd cause more damage."

Daisy struggled to take it all in. "Was that why you told me I shouldn't get together with James?"

"No!" Laura shook her head. "I mean, when you guys started hanging out, I was afraid it was too soon after Matt had left, but you and James were a slow burn."

"The opposite to me and Matt."

"Right." Laura picked at a thread on her skirt. "By then I was afraid to admit that I'd slept with him in case things got weird between us. And, yeah, I kind of thought James might even tell you when the time was right. I'm so sorry."

Daisy stood and walked over to the window to stare into the street. Finally, she turned back to look at Laura.

"All these years! You knew why Matt left and you never said a word!"

"Daisy, I swear, by the time I found out, you and James were a couple – a proper couple. And Brian and I were *married!*" Laura's voice wobbled. "I know it was cowardly, but I couldn't risk it."

This was one of those sliding-doors moments, Daisy realised. She could be angry at Laura for keeping that night a secret. Or she could accept that she'd been in an impossible situation.

She looked at the vintage ring on her finger, its green stone bright in the sunlit room. Suddenly, she didn't care that James had never told her, either. It had happened before they'd got together, and he'd chosen to protect Laura by saying nothing. In fact, things had worked out exactly as they were supposed to.

"It doesn't matter, Laura, none of it's your fault, it's Matt's. He just assumed the worst."

"And then he broke your heart." Laura's eyes glittered.

"Yup." Daisy managed a shaky laugh. "And five years later, I got to record him asking his famous American girlfriend to marry him."

"I never really liked him." Laura met Daisy's eyes and they exchanged a quiet smile.

"I'm guessing Brian still doesn't know?" Daisy said.

"That I slept with James that night? Jesus, no."

"He never has to, not now."

Laura sighed. "I told him about Matt, though. That it was his fault that things ended between you back then."

Daisy wondered how to ask the next question. Better to be straight.

"Is that why Brian doesn't like me? Because he thinks I cheated on his best friend?"

"Maybe." Laura shrugged. "I never talked about that party because, well, now you know why. Anyway," she looked a bit uncomfortable, "I kind of thought that you guys didn't like Brian and he was just picking up on that. And I know Brian isn't perfect. I mean, I told him that he was a dick to James that night in Pink Gin."

Daisy gave a small smile. She doubted Brian would ever be her favourite person, but it was a lot of time wasted over misunderstandings. Judging by Laura's expression, she was thinking the same thing.

"How's James?" Laura said, finally. "Has he been looking for something else?"

"He's looking. There's nothing yet, but he'll get something."

"Any word from Alma?"

"Yeah, she's not coming back. Her mother's still quite weak so Alma's organised to finish her college year online."

They turned as Fionn arrived in, carrying a tray of takeout drinks in one hand, and a cake box in the other. He beamed, carefully placing the items on his desk, before flicking away his fringe.

"I hope you don't mind, but I bought a cake: chocolate. Because we're celebrating." He blushed. "Well, I'm celebrating."

"If you are, so are we." Laura stood and walked over to peek inside the box. "Fancy! So, what are we celebrating?"

"Me submitting my final project. My tutor thinks I'll get a First."

"*Aw*, that's fabulous.' Daisy stood up and gave him a side hug. "We're so proud of you, Fionn." "Thank you." Fionn swiped his little fingers under both eyes. "I'm pretty psyched! *Aaaand*, I have more news."

"Did you get another job?" Daisy managed to keep smiling. "If you did, we're delighted for you." Now she'd have to advertise maternity cover for Laura. It'd be weird to be working with a complete stranger, though. And Fionn had fit in so well, it was hard to imagine he'd been part of the team for such a short time.

"No, nothing like that. I mean, your offer still stands, yeah?"

"Of course." Daisy and Laura spoke in unison.

"*Whew!*" He grinned. "No, it's just, I've made plans to travel for the summer with friends, but I'll be back at the end of August. Unless you need me before that."

Laura glanced at Daisy. "I'm not planning to stop working until the end of October, so that's fine by me."

"Go, have a great time, do everything you want." Daisy smiled. "But I'm glad you're coming back to us."

"Me too." He flicked his fringe again. "Now I just have to sort out somewhere to live."

If there was ever a sign! "We'll have a spare room going in our place now that Alma's gone," Daisy said. "If you want it, and if you wouldn't mind renting from me and James."

"No way, I'd love it! Can I afford it?" Fionn gave a cheeky grin.

"You can afford it!" Daisy said firmly.

"*Um*, do you not have to run it past your boyfriend? I don't want him to think –"

"James will be chill, Fionn. I know you – that's a good start."

"Are we cutting that cake?" Laura said.

Fionn blinked. "Absolutely, yeah, I'll take it out to the kitchen and get some plates."

"Come on." Laura flicked her hands towards him. "I'll help. I need a bit of a treat, now that I'm not drinking coffee."

Daisy sat down and opened up her emails, scrolling down until she came to the one she'd been waiting for.

Dear Ms Devlin, thank you for your submission to this year's Interior Architect of the Year Award. The long list will be announced on July 15th. We will be in touch if your submission is successful. Good luck, The Association of Interior Architects Ireland.

Freya's house was a strong contender. And she'd done her best: the rest was out of her hands. Her phone buzzed, and she hesitated when she saw Matt's name flash up. Taking a deep breath, she swiped her finger across the screen.

"Hello, Matt." She glanced towards the door.

"Hi, Daisy." There was a pause. "This a good time?"

"I'm in the office. If it's something to do with the house, I'll ask Fionn to phone you."

She could hear him sigh.

"It's not the house. Look, I'm sorry for how things ended between us last time you were here. The whole thing with James wasn't all your fault."

Daisy almost laughed. "I didn't think it was." She didn't bother to speak quietly now. "Anyway, you got what you wanted. There's just something I don't understand, Matt. Was it all just a game to you? The house, coming to my birthday party, that gimmick with the keyring – the night I stayed over! Be honest, because I really don't care. I'm just curious."

"It wasn't a game, Daisy." Matt paused. "It's complicated. The truth is, I still had feelings for you even though I was angry when I believed you cheated on me. And then, when you told me you hadn't ... look, I shouldn't have let things go as far as they did. I never wanted to hurt you."

And what about Kayley? If anything had happened between us – if I hadn't called 'stop' that night – did you even consider that you could have hurt her too?

When Daisy said nothing, Matt's voice hardened. "Did James deny what he did that summer? I'll bet he did."

Daisy made herself count to five. "If you mean the deal he made with Charlie, he didn't, because there was nothing to deny. The three of you did well at the time. Now you've bought out a start-up that James' company was trying to get. There's nothing else to say."

Matt gave a harsh laugh. "We both know there's more to it than that, Daisy. But life's too short, and I wanted you to know I've forgiven you."

There was a weird buzzing in Daisy's ears. "You've forgiven me?"

"I'd like us to be friends. I made that final payment, by the way – I wanted to clear all my debts. Look, I'm staying on for the summer, until the concerts are over. But I'm starting to miss my life back in New York, so Kayley and I will divide our time between here and the States."

Daisy slid in behind her desk and opened the banking app on her screen, quickly tapping in the personal access code for the company's bank accounts. Matt's payment had cleared that morning. She released a quiet breath and focussed her thoughts.

"Here's the thing, Matt. Friends don't treat each other the way you treated me. They don't assume the worst or go out of their way to hurt other people in that person's life."

"You mean James? That was just business, Daisy."

"Which is exactly what you and I are, Matt: just business."

"Ah, Daisy, don't be – "

"I take it you're happy with the work on Granary House?"

There was a pause. "You know I am."

"Good. You have the office number if you need to reach us again."

"Don't do this, Daisy!" Matt said. "You're the one who always believed in signs. We're back in each other's lives for a reason. It'll hurt both of us if cut me out."

She hesitated. What if he was right? Maybe it would be better to at least be on speaking terms with him. *Do you want to have anything to do with the person who deliberately hurt James?*

"You know, Matt, that's just a risk I'll have to take." She hung up as Laura came back, carrying slices of cake on two plates. Daisy looked at her. "How much did you hear?"

"Enough to be so fucking proud of you."

Daisy turned the phone over in her hands, before putting it down on her desk. "It felt like the best decision I've ever made. Apart from saying yes to James, obviously."

Fionn came in with the last slice of cake. "*Uh*, if this is private, I can just – "

"This is the office, Fionn," Laura handed Daisy a plate, "and you're part of the team. So, stop apologising. Excellent cake, by the way." She turned back to Daisy. "Matt is a delusional narcissist, and you had a lucky escape."

Daisy laughed. "I did, didn't I? I actually feel a bit sorry for Kayley. She's okay when you get to know her. Mind you, after Saturday night, the whole of Oranmore think they know her!"

"Hey, speaking of Kayley." Fionn found his phone, and scrolled quickly to something. "She posted this on TikTok earlier today." He handed it to Daisy, who turned up the volume and she and Laura watched a short video, starting with Kayley standing in front of Granary House.

"*Hi guys! So today, I just wanted to show you where Matty and I will base ourselves when we're here in Ireland. This is Granary House. It's a two-hundred-year-old Irish house that's had an awesome makeover by an Irish firm called Discerning Designs.*"

"Fuck me." Laura turned to Daisy. "You know if this goes viral here, it could bring serious business our way."

Kayley flipped the camera around and began a full tour of the house, chatting about her favourite rooms and pointing out various details.

Daisy stared, mesmerised. She'd walked through the house so many times, but watching it like this through somebody else's eyes was like seeing it for the first time.

Kayley finished the tour in the walled garden. "*So, just past that wall are the awesome grounds where I was supposed to play before I got hurt the night of the storm. But I can't wait to gig here as soon as my shoulder has healed. That's it for now, guys. Love you all.*" She blew some kisses and the video ended.

Fionn took his phone back. "Sick, right?"

"Totally sick." Daisy grinned.

"I mean, do we even need an award if we're getting this sort of publicity?" Fionn said.

Laura glared at him. "*Oy!* Watch it."

Daisy rooted around her bag, and took out the key Matt had given her for Granary House. Popping it and a company card into a small, padded envelope, she wrote Matt's address on the front and put it in the out tray. Then she grabbed her phone and headed downstairs.

Standing on the top step outside the front door, she rang Rosie. Her sister picked up on the second ring.

"Daisy, hi, is everything okay?"

"Everything's grand." Daisy felt a rush of affection for her. "I'm sorry to just call you out of the blue. I just ...' She stopped. 'I just wanted to say thanks for everything."

There was a moment's silence on the phone.

"Okay, now you're really worrying me," Rosie said. "Did you get some bad news? Hang on, have you changed your mind about James? I'm here for you, no judgment."

Daisy leaned back against the wall. "Nothing bad, I swear. But I know you'd be there. I guess I just wanted to say I'd like to keep in touch a bit more."

"Oh, class." Rosie seemed stunned into silence again.

Daisy hurried on.

"I'd better go, I'm in work, talk to you soon." She hung up, and immediately called James.

"Hey, you," he said.

"Hey, yourself." A warm breeze whipped her hair across her face, and she tucked it behind her ears. "I just rang to say I love you."

"I love you too." She could hear the smile in James' voice. "Oh, that board games café you suggested? I've booked us a table for Sunday afternoon."

Daisy smiled back. "It'll be cool!"

"Daisy, don't worry about anything, promise? We'll be all right."

"I know, I'll see you this evening."

Daisy hung up and scrolled through her phone, reading back through all the messages she and Matt had sent each other since his return. She selected them all and hit delete. Then she opened her contacts, searched for his name and hit the delete button again.

She stood for a moment, eyes closed and face tilted up to the sun. As an afterthought, she opened the MyStarScope App on her phone. Her horoscope for the day read: "**A fresh breeze is coming your way: go explore. You never know what exciting things await.**"

"Which is as good a sign as any, Daisy!"

She beamed at the two men who shot her bemused glances as they passed by the door.

Then she tucked her phone into the pocket of her dress and went back inside.

THE END